THEY SHALL *NOT* BE ASHAMED

A Spiritual Biography

*"Thou shalt know that I am the LORD:
for they shall not be ashamed that wait for me."*
—The Holy Bible, Isaiah 49:23

Ellen Myers

TATE PUBLISHING, LLC

They Shall Not Be Ashamed by Ellen Myers
Copyright © 2005 by Ellen Myers. All rights reserved.

Published in the United States of America
by Tate Publishing, LLC
127 East Trade Center Terrace
Mustang, OK 73064
(888) 361–9473

Book design copyright © 2005 by Tate Publishing, LLC. All rights reserved.
No part of this publication may be reproduced, stored in a retrieval system or transmitted in any way by any means, electronic, mechanical, photocopy, recording or otherwise without the prior permission of the author except as provided by USA copyright law

All Scripture quotations marked "NASB," are from the *New American Standard Bible—Updated Edition* ®,

Copyright © 1960, 1962, 1963, 1968, 1971, 1972, 1973, 1975, 1977, 1995 by The Lockman Foundation. Used by permission. All rights reserved.

All other Scripture quotations marked "KJV" or unmarked are taken from the *Holy Bible, King James Version,* Cambridge, 1769.

This novel is a work of fiction. Names, descriptions, entities and incidents included in the story are products of the author's imagination. Any resemblance to actual persons, events and entities is entirely coincidental.

ISBN: 1-59886-13-3-6

Acknowledgments

In November 2003 I reread a paper I had written in 1978 about the philosopher John Dewey (1859–1952), the father of American public education, Humanist Manifesto I, and the American Civil Liberties Union (ACLU). Could I write the story of a rebellious young man today who becomes the second John Dewey? I remembered a story idea I originally had in 1946 and which intermittently recurred from time to time. I had sometimes prayed that I might yet develop it to our Lord's glory. Instantly the whole outline for Part 1 of this book and the vivid picture of "James Barron" shot into my mind. For his anti-Christian worldview, I could draw on my many years of studying philosophy.

Today our entire culture shares James Barron's philosophy of flagrant self-idolatry. We who call ourselves Christians also largely practice this philosophy, even in our own families. We have now almost completely discarded our former "traditional values" or "Judeo-Christian morality," already disregarded in earlier generations and themselves merely the outer heritage of true Christian faith in genuinely converted hearts.

Originally I had intended Part 1 to be the entire story with an entirely different ending. But a man's real life begins only after his conversion! The virtual killing James Barron endures in Part 2 at the behest of the anti-Christian powers now ruling society is commonly meted out in the West today to atheist opinion leaders who turn to Christ. They are among the nearest we have here comparable to the millions of severely persecuted Christians around the world, of whom we worldly, lukewarm "Christians" are not worthy (Hebrews 11:38), and for whom the Church should (but does not) pray daily. 'The passages describing James Barron's personal participation in pro-life activities at the Hellmann Abortion Clinic in Part 3 are based on stark reality. There actually were real "escorts from hell" here in Wichita, Kansas! They wore specially made T-shirts which said, "Taking patients to the gates," and below this message in big letters: "ESCORTS FROM HELL."

The account of the assault of such escorts upon James Barron, his subsequent arrest and his lockup at Battle Hill's police headquarters is based on what really happened to my granddaughter Karen Myers. She was peacefully and legally demonstrating with a group of pro-lifers at a concert by pro-abortion singer Cher on March 14, 2003, when they were approached by two Sedgwick County sheriff's deputies at the entrance of the Kansas Coliseum (near Wichita, Kansas). Deputy Edwin Simpson issued an unlawful order to Karen and others to move back from the Coliseum driveway 100 feet. Simpson, a tall, heavy man, grabbed Karen, a small, slender 20-year old girl, twisted her arms and slammed her to the ground. He then put his full weight on her back with his knee and handcuffed her as she screamed in pain and begged him to stop hurting her. So severe were her injuries that she was rushed to the hospital via ambulance from the scene that evening.

Some pain remains, and physical therapy was needed immediately and is still required from time to time as I write.

An arrest was issued for Karen, and when she found out about it, she voluntarily reported to police and spent part of a day in a holding cell in the Sedgwick County jail in January 2004. The description of James Barron's holding cell in this book exactly repeats Karen's description of her cell to me. Karen's case finally came to trial before a jury on Tuesday, August 25, 2004, and Karen was found "not guilty."

All persons and organizations not listed separately as real are entirely fictional and not intended to resemble any real, living person, except the following. James Barron before his conversion is partly modeled after John Dewey, and Lucinda Barron after Dewey's mother (see Postscript to Part 1).

My model for Sylvia was my dear daughter Becky, who once cried out aloud so everyone heard her at our church's Sunday morning service, praying that a friend of the family might come forward at the altar call (a Sunday later he did!).

"Little Karen" Margrave is lovingly modeled after my dear granddaughter Karen Myers. Thank you, Karen, for letting me name her after you, for patiently listening to me tell you the story as it was being written, and for giving me the idea for the anniversary day breakup between James and Karen.

Swenson Books is partly modeled after my favorite bookstore, Eighth Day Books in Wichita, Kansas, where the Wichita C. S. Lewis Club met for many years. Imagine Lonely Prairie, Battle Hill, Battle Hill University and Fairfield University anywhere in the Midwest—perhaps except Kansas, my beloved home state. Fairfield University is lovingly modeled in part after Oklahoma Wesleyan University.

The deathbed conversion of Tom Barron in Part 1 is almost exactly like my own dear mother's conversion in 1964.

My beloved father's deep joy and steadfast trust in our Lord under Nazi persecution (he was anti-Nazi and remained married to my Jewish mother and hence without any paid employment throughout Hitler's twelve-year rule) was the most important witness bringing me to Christ. The exemplary Christian patriarch Dr. Van Houten in Parts 2 and 3 is partly modeled after him. Would that all of us combined strong theological convictions with strong biblical 1 Corinthians 13 love as did he!

The end of Part 1 is due to my son Mark's dear wife Debra, who did not like my earlier ending. Therefore James finally walks the road to God all the way, and in God to certitude, peace and joy, and therefore Parts 2 and 3 could be written. Thank you, Debra!

In the late 1970s I took a few college philosophy courses. Some of James' evasive answers to Karen in Part 1 were given to me by philosophy professors I knew, especially his final dodge of the Pascal Memorial. The courses I took convinced me that philosophy without God can never be certain of anything. In my discussion of the problem of knowledge in Part 1 I am especially indebted to J. Budziszewski's superb book *What You Can't Not Know* (Dallas: Spence Publishing Company, 2003).

I thank all my dear family, especially Becky; Sandy Earle; Gloria Follett; Ann, Charla, Dagni and Linda, my friends in our "Potluck/Bible study"; and Al, Pam and David, my friends in our church's Christian Education Committee for your patient listening and especially your prayers while this work was in progress. Most of all I thank our wonderful Lord, Who brought it to fruition almost sixty years after its first spark sprang up in my mind.

Ellen Myers

THEY SHALL *NOT* BE ASHAMED

Part 1

"The Road to Certitude"

The one principle of hell is "I am my own!"

—George MacDonald

God of Abraham God of Isaac God of Jacob
Not the God of philosophers and learned men
Certitude Certitude Feeling joy peace
God of Jesus Christ
Forgetfulness of the world and of all save God . . .
I have separated from Him
My God wilt Thou leave me
Let me not be separated from Him eternally.

—From the "Pascal Memorial"

The foolishness of God is wiser than men;
and the weakness of God is stronger than men.
Not many wise men after the flesh, not many mighty, not many
noble, are called: But God hath chosen the foolish things of the
world to confound the wise; and God hath chosen the weak things
of the world to confound the things which are mighty;
And base things of the world, and things, which are despised, hath
God chosen, yea, and things which are not, to bring to naught
things that are: That no flesh should glory in his presence.

—The Holy Bible: First Corinthians 1:25–29

To the Reader

Every philosopher and writer mentioned by James Barron, Dr. Freeman and Dr. Nancy Berger in Part 1 is a real, historical person, as are Bob Dylan and of course Blaise Pascal.

The following persons, events, movements, and writings are real:
- The Scopes Trial of 1925, where evolution teaching in public schools won the war against creation teaching
- The Roe v. Wade U. S. Supreme Court decision of January 22, 1973, which legalized abortion from conception till birth
- The Nazi song "Today we own Germany/Tomorrow the whole world"
- The Free Speech Movement
- Cubism and Pablo Picasso
- The novels of Albert Camus, Victor Hugo and Alexandre Dumas
- Dr. Benjamin Spock (*Common Sense Book of Baby and Child Care*)
- The Zero Population Growth group
- Francis Schaeffer (*How Shall We Then Live?)*
- Dr. David Noebel (Summit Ministries, P. O. Box 207, Manitou Springs, CO 80829);
- Dr. Henry Morris (*The Genesis Flood;* Institute for Creation Research, P. O. Box 2667, El Cajon, CA 92021);
- The Missouri Synod Lutheran Church
- Dr. Alfred Rehwinkel (*The Flood)*
- Rev. Walter Lang (Bible-Science Association, now Creation Moments)
- William Ernest Henley (*"Invictus"*)

All other persons and organizations are entirely fictitious and not intended to resemble any real, living persons.

Alphabetical lists of real persons and organizations in Parts 2 and 3 are appended to these parts in their own places.

Table of Contents

1. James Barron; His Family and Background 12
2. Lucinda Barron's Conversion; the Dorrie Fisher Scandal; Fern Lowrie. 13
3. James and Evolution 16
4. Nagging or Prayer? 20
5. Our First Real Meeting; the "Atheist Syndrome". 23
6. "The Times They Are A-Changin'"; I Study Philosophy 26
7. A Quarrel about "Saint Francis" 29
8. A Good Philosophy Course; Utilitarianism; "Question Authority" .32
9. I Can't Trust Him! Why Go On? 36
10. My Parents' Counsel 39
11. Peace and Joy in the Lord 42
12. Dinner at the Barrons; Tired of Uncertainty? 45
13. Swenson Books; George MacPherson; The Pascal Memorial 48
14. A Conditional Marriage Proposal 52
15. "Either God or a Bad Man" 55
16. The Ayn Rand Lecture and Dr. Berger 58
17. Studying with George; Agonizing Over James; the Problem of Knowledge Solved 61
18. The Problem of Pain; First Anniversary; The Voice 64
19. Recovery; Robert's Prophecy; George and I 67
20. Family Reunion; A Very Happy Ending; James, Dr. Berger and Feminism 70
21. Home and Family; Dinner with the Freemans 73
22. The C. S. Lewis Club; A Double Wedding; James and the "Reality Principle" 77
23. James' Doctoral Thesis; Sylvia; James' Marriage; "His Service is Perfect Freedom" 80
24. Good Death 83
25. Dylan and Ecstasy; James' Successful Career 87
26. Catastrophe: The Rousseau Academy Massacre. 90
27. The Deaths of Lucinda and Ecstasy "Stacie" Barron 93
28. James' Divorce; The Consolation of Philosophy 96
29. Swenson Books; The Family Reunion; Sylvia Draws James In. . . .99
30. The Weakness of God 102
Postscript. 105

1
James Barron; His Family and Background

Until recently James Barron was often in the news as one of the leading philosophers of our time. Much of his private life has also made media headlines. However, the news media never unearthed the story of his relationship with me, Karen Margrave, while we were both students at Battle Hill University, nor have they paid attention to his rebellion, beginning early in his youth and indelibly marking most of his life, against the Christian faith of his mother Lucinda Barron.

Our family became acquainted with the Barrons in 1958 when my father joined the music department of the public school system of Lonely Prairie. The Barrons attended First United Christian Church, whose teachings had a decisive influence on James. It was Lonely Prairie's oldest and most prominent church, part of a denomination which had once firmly stood on the Bible as God's own inerrant Word and the final authority for Christian faith and practice. However, it had already begun to depart from these "fundamentalist" doctrinal precepts before the turn of the twentieth century. By the time we came to Lonely Prairie, First United Church had become a stronghold of theological liberalism. Its senior minister, Rev. Dr. Clyde Brassfield, eagerly took it upon himself to teach the confirmation classes for young teenagers and new inquirers. These classes furnished James with many intellectual arguments against his mother and later against me when we tried to win him to Christ.

The foundation of Tom Barron's wealth was the prosperous construction firm started by his father. Tom was said to have a finger in every money-making enterprise in our community, some fifty miles from Battle Hill, which then as now boasted one of the major universities in the Midwest. Gossip had it that on out of town business trips Tom would occasionally spend a night with some young waitress or typist casually picked up along the way. Tongues also wagged about his relationship with Fern Lowrie, a secretary in his company's main office, but as his marriage to Lucinda seemed to endure unaffected, the rumors gradually died down.

Once in a while there were suspicions of Barron Construction's undue influence, gifts, shady financial dealings, or campaign contributions looking like rewards to political candidates for services rendered. None of these suspicions were ever confirmed by the local media. But then Tom was known to have invested money in the leading newspapers and TV stations of our region as well. For a time he served as mayor of Lonely Prairie, but when he retired, the candidate he had hand-picked to succeed him was resoundingly defeated at the polls. Tom had not expected this public rebuff, was surprisingly and vocally bitter about it, and never ran for public office again.

I liked big, friendly Mr. Barron when we met for the first time at a school party hosted by the Parent-Teachers Association of our elementary school in the late fall of 1958. I was twelve years old and in grade six. My new friend and classmate Neva, the little sister of James and his younger brother Robert and the last of the Barron children, was with me and wanted me to meet her parents. After easily finding her jovial father in the midst of a bustling crowd, we finally discovered her mother in the school kitchen where she was loading a tray with dainty sandwiches to be served the guests.

Lucinda Barron was a tall, graceful lady with lovely dark hair and brown eyes, dressed in the quietly elegant style of the fifties. I had liked Mr. Barron; I instantly loved Lucinda. For Tom making friends with people was his natural stock in trade, a tool serving him well in this world. For Lucinda it was a unique, completely unselfish openness to everyone she met, a deep longing to give them real, lasting joy. In retrospect I am sure, and Neva agrees with me, that this was one of the deep changes in Lucinda Barron produced by her conversion to Christ.

2

Lucinda Barron's Conversion; The Dorrie Fisher Scandal; Fern Lowrie

The first time we heard details about Lucinda Barron's conversion was soon after moving to Lonely Prairie at a dinner with Bill and Jean Holcomb, our next door neighbors and fellow members of Grace Baptist Church. Lucinda's conversion had happened at the church's annual week-long fall revival in October 1956. Jean Holcomb, a good friend of Lucinda, had invited her to it, and she attended every evening with her two younger children. At the last service Lucinda came forward and softly but firmly declared her faith in Jesus Christ as the Son of God and her personal Lord and Savior.

"I was very pleased but also surprised to see her do this," said Jean. "After all, she was a well-known member of First United Church, where they look down on us Baptists as stupid 'holy rollers'. But I had thought there was a chance that she might."

"We had heard a little about Mrs. Barron's 'getting religion'," said my mother. "The people who told us said it was because of her husband's affair with one of his secretaries."

"Yes, that was the reason," said Jean slowly. "You see, Tom was Lucinda's first and only love. She took his unfaithfulness very hard."

We were all silent for a while. Finally my mother asked: "How did Mrs. Barron's life change after that revival?"

"It was chiefly an inner change," answered Jean Holcomb, "and at first only her closest friends—and I suppose, her two younger children who came to the revival with her—could notice it. Outwardly Lucinda's life went on almost exactly as before. She has stayed married to Tom and remained a member of First United Church. However, a few months after the revival Lucinda began to speak up against some of the teachings and projects of First United Church, and she still does."

"And she tries to attend the special services at our church," added Bill Holcomb. "Most importantly, after the revival she regularly keeps bringing Robert and little Neva—she's about as old as you, Karen—to the meetings of our children's and young people's groups. They attend First United only on Sunday mornings with all their family."

"Yes, that's true," said Jean happily. Then her face clouded over as she mused, "So what's really happened is that when Lucinda came to Christ, Robert and Neva came with her, but Tom and James, the oldest boy, did not. We must hope and pray they will come in, too. What a joy it would be for Lucinda!"

"Yes," said her husband slowly, "but I think it is very unlikely that Tom Barron will ever take that step. It would take a miracle! Tom is a worldly man who loves his wealth above all else. And most of his cronies and business friends attend First United."

"How about James?" asked Jean. Her husband shook his head sadly.

"If anything," he answered, "from all I know about him, James is even less likely to side with Lucinda about Christ than is his father."

A few months later my parents discussed the latest Lonely Prairie scandal: Dorrie Fisher, a young student in my father's classes, had suddenly left town because she was pregnant. As was still common in such crisis situations at that time, young unwed mothers-to-be would be sent out of town by their families to give birth far away from home and then to give up their babies for adoption. Pregnancy outside marriage was considered deeply shameful and concealed from neighbors and acquaintances as much as possible. Certainly no pregnant unmarried girl would think of continuing her studies in the public high schools until or after the baby's birth, as is so common now. That practice was accepted only gradually after the Supreme Court legalized abortion till birth in 1973.

What made the scandal a favorite subject of gossip was the widespread speculation that the father of Dorrie's child was James Barron. He had been her steady boyfriend for some time before her departure from Lonely Prairie. My parents reported some of the comments they had overheard.

"Young Jim is taking after his grandpa Durant," knowingly chuckled some of the older folks, "Frenchy was quite a skirt chaser in his younger years."

"Just as Tom Barron is now," chimed in others.

There were also comments from more serious-minded people. "Financial help is all the Fishers should expect from the Barrons," they said. "They ought to have raised their daughter more strictly—no dates during the week, strict curfew in the evening, chaperone-supervised teenage functions."

Still others pointed out, "After all, nothing serious ever comes from such affairs. Of course the Barron boy wouldn't marry the girl. There used to be shotgun weddings in the old days, back in the 1870s and the Wild West, but not any more."

Most people condemned Dorrie alone, or at least more than James. "It's up to the girl to set the boundaries," they said. "Boys will be boys and go as far as the girls let them." Then more knowing chuckles and smirks from many upstanding, church-going opinion-setters of the community. No one my parents knew felt sorry for Lucinda Barron except Jean Holcomb, who now shared more details about her and James with my mother.

"Yes, it was James who got Dorrie pregnant," she confirmed. "It gave Lucinda great grief. She was deeply unhappy not just because James had done this, but that he had no love for Dorrie at all. He told Lucinda that he had never been serious about her. 'No fear,' he said, 'I never had any intention of marrying her.' For him she had been a sort of experiment, a guinea pig. What would it take to seduce a shy, mousy young girl like Dorrie? All he wanted was to see how far he could get her to go, and by what means. He had not the slightest pity for her when she got pregnant. He cared nothing at all for the baby, even suggesting that someone else might be the father. 'She let me sleep with her,' he said, 'why not someone else, too? Why should I be responsible?' Lucinda was stunned by his total lack of concern for anyone but himself. 'It isn't right,' she kept repeating, 'how can he be so completely selfish even though he is still so young? He is only seventeen! What kind of man will he be when he is all grown up? How many other people will he hurt, and not care?'"

Lucinda was also unhappy that Tom did not take the matter seriously. "Let James sow his wild oats now," he had said complacently, even with a tinge of approval. His attitude made Lucinda reflect with grief on the examples her husband and her own father had set for James. Neither Tom Barron nor Grandpa Durant had taken their marriage vows very seriously. Both had expected their wives to have an indulgent, tolerant, almost amused reaction to their frequent infidelities. The community actually expected this seemingly inborn and incorrigible behavior from "Frenchy" Durant because he was of French extraction. This reaction was impossible for Lucinda's mother, the strait-laced daughter of stern, hard-working German immigrants. The adulteries of her husband made her very unhappy as well as permanently unforgiving, vindictive and quarrelsome, which in turn served as Grandpa Durant's excuse to go on as he was. Divorce was not an option for Bertha Durant. It was almost unheard of in that generation, and a divorced woman's lot was hard and despised.

Lucinda understood and pitied her wronged, embittered mother but also loved and secretly preferred her philandering but cheerful, likeable father. Thus it is not surprising that she was attracted to and married Tom Barron, who was in many respects just like him. What made her husband different from her father was Tom's long, serious affair with Fern Lowrie, which also had important meaning for James. For Fern Lowrie was in many ways like Dr. Berger, the woman who had so much influence on him later.

Fern was as unlike Lucinda as possible. Lucinda was a tall, slender, handsome woman with wavy dark hair and dark brown eyes. Fern was pleasant-looking but not beautiful, of medium height, a little stocky, with light brown hair kept cut short, and light blue eyes. Lucinda was gentle and sympathetic while Fern was assertive and matter-of-fact in dealing with others. Lucinda's greatest concern was the care of her children. Fern was dedicated to her career and never married. She certainly never depended on any man, including Tom Barron, materially or emotionally; in that respect, too, she was much like Dr. Berger.

Lucinda, the daughter of a wealthy, respected family and had never needed to work to support herself. Fern, who grew up in a chaotic, poverty-stricken home, had always had to earn her own living. Lucinda loved to wear softly feminine clothing, according to the prevailing fashions; Fern always dressed somewhat mannishly in severely tailored business suits accented by crisply ironed, snowy white blouses. She obviously wanted to impress other people as a serious, no-nonsense, business-oriented person with professional goals and abilities and little need for private relations.

From all accounts I heard she was always extremely efficient in her office work at Barron Construction. In addition, she became so knowledgeable about private investment opportunities that she moved to Chicago and worked up to vice-president of a major stock brokerage firm after she and Tom Barron broke up. This was the formidable career woman who had become Tom Barron's mistress about two years before Lucinda's conversion.

James, who had often met Fern, told me later that his father was drawn to her at least as seriously as to Lucinda, or perhaps even more so. "I wish I had known Fern before I married your mother," he once confided to James, "we could have conquered the world together. She was so ambitious, so focused on her work, such a wonderful planner! She had the mind and the drive of a man." It was the highest praise for a woman Tom could think of, and James never forgot it. The way he saw it, his father esteemed Fern as an ally in his endeavor to amass wealth and worldly influence, rather than for sensual satisfaction or romance. James, I believe, felt exactly the same way about Dr. Berger.

3

James and Evolution

After the Dorrie Fisher scandal, Neva told me about an event in James' life which had taken place about a year earlier. She recalled that this event was James' sudden, eager and complete acceptance of the teaching of evolution. Though he had doubtless heard of it earlier, he was not seriously taught it as proven scientific fact until his high school biology and earth science classes. What had puzzled her mother greatly, Neva said, was that after James immersed himself in evolutionist science teaching, "a very surprising thing happened with him. His whole attitude changed toward school work. He also became much more openly rebellious against my mother." Neva had been present when Lucinda had discussed the matter with James.

"What's your problem, Mother?" James had asked, smiling, "I thought you should have been happy about my enthusiasm for evolution. It certainly improved my attitude toward school." He went on in a tone which was both conciliatory and challenging: "The surprise was that I suddenly became the top student in my class. And weren't you happy about that?"

"That's true," said Lucinda slowly, "you used to just get by in elementary and junior high school. Your grades were average or less in every subject."

"And how many times you used to nag me about that after you became so serious about your religion," James chuckled, half teasing, half resentful. "I can still hear you tell me again and again: 'Do the very best you can with the talents God has given you, James! Do not let them go to waste!' Remember? Well, what you and your God couldn't do, evolution did. After it really got hold of me, I began to work hard in school. It was because I suddenly understood that the teaching of evolution could not give any certainty about anything."

"I still don't see why that would change your mind about school work," said Lucinda.

James laughed contemptuously and snapped back, "I didn't think you would. You don't ever think things through to their logical end! If you did, you would see that there is no certainty in evolution, yes, but that's only the first step."

Lucinda hesitated. Then she attempted to explain what disturbed her, groping for the right words: "I guess what attracted you so much about evolution, James, was not exactly its lack of certainty. It was the absence of any rules, any order, anything fixed, wasn't it? Didn't you say that with evolution anything and everything was possible? That with evolution there were no boundaries, no limits to anything?"

"And you didn't like that," James shot back, "of course not! You Christians are scared of uncertainty. You want to be safe—'saved' as you call it. You want rules, order, everything fixed by your almighty God once and forever. You want boundaries and limits to everything. But if evolution is true—and modern science has proved that it is—then God isn't needed as our creator and master. The world came into being—or rather, always existed—and simply developed, evolved, all by itself over millions and millions of years, without beginning, without end, without direction. Anything could happen."

Neva remembered that at this point James sat up straight in his chair, his dark eyes shining, passionately confronting both his mother and her. "He looked different," she said slowly and softly, picturing the scene in her mind, "he looked as though he wasn't himself. Even his voice was different somehow, almost as though someone else was speaking through him. I felt scared of him!"

She recovered herself and told me what James had said to Lucinda and her next: "You are scared of evolution because you Christians want a *static* world. I want a *dynamic* world. And that's what evolution gave me last year, and it changed my life! From then on I could live in total freedom. I didn't have to obey any authority. I could question every tradition or rule. I could set my own goals. I wouldn't need to do something because 'everybody is doing it' but could 'do my own thing' as they say. I would never need to stop." As Neva was telling me this, I suddenly suspected with horror that one of the first of "his own things" James had felt free to do might have been to seduce poor Dorrie Fisher and then to abandon her and their child.

Neva continued sharing what she remembered of James' passionate speech. "It wasn't worth getting good grades," James had sneered, "when the only goal I could ever work for all my life according to your rules was to grow up to get a decent job or run a good business to make money so I could raise kids to grow up to make money so they could raise kids to grow up—you get the idea. I wanted to break out of that cycle—and I did. I wanted to teach as many others as I could, especially my friends—my classmates—young people, my own generation and the next—to break out of that cycle, too. That became my goal in life! So I set out to become the valedictorian of my high school graduating class, and I will. I intend to win the scholarships and to do whatever it takes that will enable me to go to Battle Hill University and major in philosophy, no matter what you and Dad might think about that. That is what evolution will get me, and much more beyond that. I want to be ahead of the pack when it comes to get rid of the old morality and bring in the new, for all that is part and parcel of replacing God and the Bible with evolution. Becoming a leader of that movement will get me a top job at a top university with influence on all our society in the end. Just you wait and see!"

Neva said that after James stopped, Lucinda only shook her head sadly and silently. I knew enough about the subject of evolution to understand that as a Christian she could never compromise with her son's acceptance of evolution and rejection of God, nor, therefore, could she be happy about his life's goal.

Neva told me that afterwards her mother tried many times with her usual gentle but unflagging persistence to convince him that evolution was by no means a scientifically proven fact. James was as persistent as she and much more hostile with the rashness of youth. He rejected her efforts with his newly acquired high school arguments. He also tried on his mother the glib conciliatory reassurance Rev. Dr. Brassfield preached from First United Church's pulpit and taught in its youth confirmation classes, which was one of the many "liberal" teachings Lucinda was opposing. Dr. Brassfield's argument went like this: "The Genesis story of how the world began is a beautiful, poetic myth. God simply used evolution to make the world. Most likely the 'days' of Genesis are not literal days but millions or billions of years." I had learned at Grace Baptist Church that this compromise abandoned the biblical foundation of the Christian faith.

Neva said that after a little pause James went on the attack again. "As I said, I plan to major in philosophy in college," he said, "of course Dad won't be too happy about that. He wants me to get a degree in business administration so I can eventually take over Barron Construction. His advice to me is to 'run a good business to make money so you can raise kids to make money, etcetera, etcetera', just as I said before. Dad has his rules and order, too, Mother—not so different from your own." Neva noticed that he paused to observe how that arrow hit her, for he knew very well that Tom Barron's worldly rules and order were utterly different from Lucinda's deep desire to lead her life according to the Bible. Then he resumed in a bantering tone: "Well, Dad has got Robert to step into his shoes, so all is well. Robert will see to it that the labor of Grandpa Barron and Dad will not have been in vain: Barron Construction will provide prestige and wealth for the third generation of Barrons."

When I remembered Neva's story after truly meeting James a few years later, a Bible verse, Exodus 20:5, came to my mind, "I the LORD thy God am a jealous God, visiting the iniquity of the fathers upon the children unto the third and fourth generation of them who hate Me." The "first generation" had been his grandparents, those stern, hardworking, homesteading, church-building pioneers or children of pioneers. Like everyone I knew, I had always looked up to them with respect. But had their goal to acquire prestige and wealth become their idol, their god?

The answer to this question was almost certainly yes for Lucinda's parents. What about Tom's? Here is what I knew about them.

Marvin Barron was the son of pioneer parents who had homesteaded near Lonely Prairie. Their farm prospered under their hard work, and they were able to help Marvin financially when he started Barron Construction after World War I. The business did well in the "roaring twenties" and survived the Great Depression of the 1930s. Its greatest expansion came after World War II in the booming economy of the 1950s when Tom Barron took over its management. Grandfather Marvin and Grandmother Thelma retired, bought a luxurious traveling camper and visited all resorts and vacation spots their friends and travel agencies recommended.

"We didn't see much of them," Neva had told me. "They were almost always gone. They would travel north in the summer and south in the winter. They would send us picture postcards from all the places they visited and bring us children gifts when they stopped here between trips, but they never stayed long. They didn't miss us, it seems, and so we didn't really miss them."

Neva told me that her mother felt they could have done something better with their time. She was comparing them to retired friends who traveled around the country too, but to bring food and clothes to orphanages and to help build or repair church buildings. Once she spoke of this to James, who angrily told her to stop talking about service and usefulness to other people and especially not about religion—Grandpa and Grandma Barron and everyone had every right to do whatever they wanted. Lucinda had objected. She thought that people should act like Christ, who never stopped being there for others. James had replied that Christ was her God but not his, and that one's own wishes must come first.

4
Nagging or Prayer?

When I visited the Barrons as James' girlfriend in the summer of 1965, Neva told me that her normally easy-going, tolerant father had been furious about her mother's becoming "a religious maniac." He often vented his anger before James, then 15 years old, whom he found conveniently open to his complaints and who always remembered his father's reaction.

"When Mother became a Christian," Neva explained sadly, "our family was split: Mother, Robert and I were on one side, Dad and James on the other." This division reduced what the Barrons did together as a family. Previously they had often gone together to social functions, sports events and movies. Lucinda replaced many of these outings with religious activities, especially on Wednesday and Sunday evenings when she, Robert and Neva would attend our church's prayer meetings and Sunday evening services, both long abandoned at First United Church.

"The most serious and permanent change in our daily lives," Neva said, "was Mother's insistence that we had Bible study and prayer together almost every evening. She hoped that Dad would lead it. That was unrealistic—Dad hated the whole idea! Mother was very disappointed. She kept nagging him about it. Of course that didn't do any good."

It was hard for Neva to speak of this shortcoming in her mother. However, she believed it was the main reason why Lucinda had failed to win James to Christ and wanted to warn me against the same error. So she went on, "If Mother has one fault, it is her habit of telling people gently but stubbornly over and over again what she thinks is right or wrong, and what they should do about it. It just makes people more determined not to do it. Now she did it with Dad. 'You need to do what's right for your family and be our spiritual leader,' she would say. He would cringe and roll his eyes to the ceiling when he thought she didn't notice."

Neva sighed helplessly and continued, "In the end Dad got totally fed up with it. He changed his working hours so he had to be gone on business almost every night. And he was very angry with her," she added, "because she wanted us all to leave First United Church and join Grace Baptist. Dad and Mother had head to head quarrels about it. He would shout at her so the whole house could hear him. She would speak softly and gently so we couldn't understand. They had never quarreled like this before her conversion, not even over his affair with Fern Lowrie."

Unexpectedly Neva chuckled. "It was clever Grandpa Durant who found the solution to both problems! Mother later told Robert and me the story. Grandpa first talked to Mother and suggested that she ask Dad to end his affair with Fern if he expected Mother to remain at First United Church. Then he took Dad aside and counseled him to promise Mother that he would stop seeing Fern if Mother would stay at First United Church. Dad and Mother thought it over and finally followed Grandpa Durant's advice. Dad must have kept his side of the bargain because Fern left Barron Construction shortly afterwards and moved to Chicago. Mother kept her side of it, hard as it was for her, because she had promised. She has remained at First United Church to this day."

"Did James ever come to your mother's Bible studies?" I asked.

Neva shook her head, but reconsidered. "He did come once in a while," she mused. "I think he was mostly just curious, though from time to time he would say something which showed he had taken a real interest in what the Bible said."

"Like what?" I wondered, hoping to hear something about James that might help me draw him to Christ.

"It was whenever we spoke about prayer," Neva answered slowly. "James listened very carefully and asked many questions. He was really interested in prayer. I think he still is, deep down in his mind."

"Prayer?" I repeated, taken aback. Was it possible that the cynical James Barron I thought I knew who called any belief in communication with God "illusion" or "mysticism," had once wanted to learn more about prayer, and perhaps still did?

Neva nodded. "Oh yes," she said, "he argued with Mother over many other parts of her beliefs. But when she spoke about prayer, or when she prayed aloud, he did not interrupt or contradict her. He would be quiet and thoughtful. He wouldn't even smile when she prayed, as he did sometimes when she spoke of other things—you know, his special smile, arrogant, contemptuous."

I knew all too well what she meant. That special smile was one of his favorite weapons to silence people who disagreed with him. Neva continued, "Yes, Karen, I am pretty sure that even now he is still uneasy about prayer. I wouldn't be surprised if he actually did pray sometimes by himself, in secret." After a moment of thought she added earnestly, "You see, when it came to prayer, Mother simply did it after her conversion. She didn't preach about it. She didn't nag and prod other people to do it. She just trusted in God, praying to Him out of her need for Him. She said that little children can't help wanting to talk to their father, and she was now God's child. That was her heart's desire, her joy, and James understood. He was drawn to her childlike love and joy. He saw the difference in her about prayer, and he was touched by it."

My heart skipped a beat. How I was longing for James to share the faith, love and joy his mother and I had! "Oh Neva," I exclaimed, "if James can pray, there is hope for him!"

Neva sighed deeply. "I agree with you," she said. "I wish Mother could have stopped nagging and prodding him about 'being right with Jesus'! But she couldn't. She wanted so much to bring him around, to make sure he was on the right path, just like she had done in earlier years about his school work. She thought the way to accomplish this was by constantly laying down the law to him. She was brought up that way herself by her mother."

"How do you mean?" I asked.

"Grandma Durant came from an old-fashioned German background. She worked very hard to keep a totally neat and spotless home; 'cleanliness is godliness,' she often said. She had hard and fast rules about everything. She believed that it was her job to be free with her criticism or advice about whatever she felt was amiss in our home or with us children. And just like Mother she would 'remind us' about such things again and again. The difference was that Grandma Durant scolded outright while Mother only nagged gently and softly."

"Grandma Durant's generation had more authority," I reminded her.

"Yes," Neva agreed, "but the foundation must have been missing, or it would not have broken down so quickly in our generation. All their hard work and strict living was not enough. The foundation is faith in God and His Word. Mother found it, and so did Robert and I. Mother ought to have stopped fretting over James but simply have trusted God for him. She didn't fret like this over Robert or me!"

"Remember," I said gently, desiring to defend Lucinda, "you two were younger than James, and you were not as strong-willed."

Here I might add a few words about Robert and Neva. Like James, Robert grew up to be tall, slender and handsome. Like James, he had a good mind and did well in school though never with his older brother's sudden driven ambition after his encounter with evolution. He had come to share his mother's biblical Christian convictions almost immediately after her conversion, as had Neva. Much like Lucinda he tried to win James to Christ, but without success. Eventually they went their separate ways with minimal contact between them.

After Tom became seriously ill and retired in the late 1960s, Robert took full charge of Barron Construction. He manages the company honestly and is content with a much more modest income than his father's. Neva told me that he always wanted to live according to the biblical prayer of Proverbs 30:8–9: *"Remove far from me vanity and lies; give me neither poverty nor riches; feed me with food convenient for me, lest I be full, and deny thee, and say, 'Who is the LORD?' Or lest I be poor and steal, and take the name of my God in vain."* That is exactly like Robert! He is given to cite appropriate Bible verses at every opportunity. One of his favorite passages, which he uses often with business friends, is Psalm 62:10: *"If riches increase, set not your heart upon them."*

Robert and his wife have two sons and two daughters, all grown up now and all faithful Christians. Neva is happily married to a Christian family lawyer. They also raised several children whom they schooled at home.

What a wonderful harvest Lucinda reaped from her conversion in Robert and Neva and their families! True, unlike her eldest son, they never became famous by the world's standards; they only quietly and faithfully love, trust and obey her God and theirs day by day. Lucinda welcomed all her grandchildren by Robert and Neva with great love and joy, including Neva's sweet little Sylvia, born in 1970 with what is now called Down Syndrome, but was then known as "mongolism" (an evolutionist name—the slanted eyes of "mongoloid" people supposedly reflected their racial rank below "Caucasian" white people). Sylvia was a sunny, affectionate child who loved everyone and whom everyone loved in turn—everyone except

James, who told Neva that Sylvia should have been aborted, and later that, thank goodness, such people did not have long lives.

5

Our First Real Meeting; the "Atheist Syndrome"

I met James for the first time when Neva invited me to the Barron home for a sleep-over. The Barrons lived in Forest Ridge, Lonely Prairie's most exclusive neighborhood. I could not help comparing Neva's luxurious home with my own family's much more modest dwelling. This awkward feeling surfaced again in the early evening when I sat beside Neva at the Barrons' family dining table. Robert and Mrs. Barron were there too, but Mr. Barron was away on business. Everything around me was much more elegant than I was used to. I hoped that the way I was dressed and my table manners would measure up to the Barrons' standards.

This was the moment James strode in with an indifferent, "Sorry I am late." He was tall, very slender, his dark hair tousled, his face full of lively energy, his mouth with the hint of a smile. He looked very much like his mother. How handsome he is, I thought, and then, I can see why Dorrie Fisher fell in love with him! I quickly dismissed my next thought that this handsome boy was not innocent any more—he knew what it was to go all the way with a girl.

"What's for dinner?" he asked.

"Just a moment," Mrs. Barron said. "We have a house guest tonight—Neva's friend Karen Margrave. Karen, this is our son James. James, meet Karen."

He smiled politely. "Glad to meet you, Karen," he said.

"Glad to meet you, too," I murmured back. That was all. Why should he pay much attention to a friend of his little sister?

After that evening James and I ran into each other fairly often until he left home for Battle Hill University, and then only once in a while during vacations till 1964 when I graduated from high school and he received his undergraduate degree in philosophy *summa cum laude* and a distinguished graduate teaching assistantship at Battle Hill University. Neva told me that he had had one or two passing relationships with girls; "He loved them and left them, as usual," she giggled. I giggled with her; the love life of my friend's older brother was a subject for gossip, no more. That fall I too went to Battle Hill University with a special grant to major in music education.

And that was when James Barron and I truly met.

On the morning of September 16, 1964, I was on my way to the cafeteria for an early lunch. And there striding towards me came James Barron, tall and slender, wearing dark slacks and a white shirt open at the neck, strikingly handsome as ever. He saw me, recognized me and stopped.

"Little Karen Margrave!" he exclaimed, looking me over with sudden interest, "all grown up and so attractive! So you are studying here too now?"

I confirmed I was. He asked where I was going now, and then turned around, saying he would have lunch with me so we could visit a bit. After all, we hadn't seen each other in a while! Soon we walked through the cafeteria serving line and carried our lunch trays to a secluded little table near a window offering a scenic view of the sunny lawn outside. James had steered us here with the ease of total familiarity. Of course he had been on this huge campus among its tens of thousands of students for years.

For a while we talked about the university, some professors, and the courses we were taking. James obviously felt very much in his own element here. To me it was all strange and vaguely intimidating, just as the Barron home had been at first.

"Don't worry, Karen," he said, "the campus is overwhelming at first, but you'll soon get used to it. And as it happens," he added with unexpected eagerness, "I have some free time this afternoon. I could show you around if you like."

He really meant it! He was becoming interested in me! Flattered but uncertain, I stammered a little as I said that I didn't want to impose on him; after all, we didn't know each other all that well.

"That's all right," he said, "we can get to know each other better as I give you a tour of the campus—or at least part of it. One afternoon isn't really enough time to see it all, but it's a start."

"But you hadn't planned on it," I objected.

"No, I hadn't," James said, "but that's okay. I like the unexpected. Also, I would really like to have someone with whom I could share something that happened this morning. We could trade—I would show you the campus and you could listen to my story. Is it a deal?"

I looked at his eager face and half laughingly agreed that it was a deal. And so that afternoon I strolled at James' side across the central campus of Battle Hill University, listening to his tour guide remarks about the college buildings but also to the description of his victory in a classroom debate that morning.

It seemed James had been the discussion leader in an upper division philosophy course on epistemology, "the study of how we can know what we claim to know," James explained. I had never heard the word before in my life and was intrigued. How do we really know anything? I wondered. How, for example, can I know God? The words of Jesus Christ in the Gospel of John came into my mind: *"This is eternal life, that they may know You the only true God, and Jesus Christ whom You have sent."* Our eternal lives depend on whether we know God! I thought. But He has made provision for that. We can know God because He made Himself known to us through Jesus Christ. That is the only way.

While I was still reflecting on this, James was explaining that a "syndrome" was a group of signs or symptoms together indicating a disease or abnormal condition. A student in his class had claimed that there was an "atheist syndrome" consisting of an atheist person's childhood fear and rage against a bad or absent father, and various psychologically caused ailments in later life such as recurrent stomach trouble and migraines. Charles Darwin was a famous example. People with the atheist syndrome did not become atheists on the basis of sound reasoning but due to their flawed backgrounds.

"Of course it was all nonsense, really," James said with happy condescension. "My class didn't see that right away, so I had to take the lead in shooting it down. A, it is a form of an elementary fallacy, the *ad hominem* argument," he stopped, realizing that I did not understand, and explained, "meaning an argument against a speaker personally, not against what he is saying. You see, even if all atheists suffered from an 'atheist syndrome,' it would not show that atheism itself is false. B, there are famous atheists who got along just fine with their fathers and were in good health all their lives. That shows that there is no such thing as a general 'atheist syndrome.' End of discussion."

"There is one thing I don't understand," I mused after a few moments of reflection, "how did the 'atheist syndrome' ever come up in the first place? What was the connection between it and how we can know things?"

"Oh, that," James said reluctantly, "let me think. Oh yes, this same student said that sometimes people may not know something because they do not *want* to know. The 'atheist syndrome' means that some people do not want to know God because they think God is like their bad father."

We walked along in silence as I digested this information. Why had James hesitated to share it? The answer came quickly: the student had raised a relevant, even very important point, namely, that people's willingness to receive knowledge may well be the decisive factor in receiving it. But James had not dealt with that point! Instead he had misled the class into concentrating on the flaws in the "atheist syndrome." I stopped walking.

"It was a trick," I almost whispered.

"What was a trick?" James asked sharply, also stopping.

"You avoided the real question: whether people can *willfully suppress* knowledge." Before I could stop myself, the next words burst from me: "That's exactly what the Bible says in Romans 1:18–20: *'For the wrath of God is revealed from heaven against all ungodliness and unrighteousness of men who suppress the truth in unrighteousness, because that which may be known of God is manifest in them; for God hath shewed it unto them. For the invisible things of him from the creation of the world are clearly seen, being understood by the things that are made, even His eternal power and Godhead, so that they are without excuse.'"*

Now, too late, I remembered again what I had repeatedly heard at home and from Neva about James' rejection of the Christian faith of his mother. Would he now reject me and my faith too? I must tell him the truth while I still could.

"You have to be honest with God," I pleaded. "You cannot just play mind games about him. You can pray to Him, and if you do that honestly, He will answer you."

James said shortly, "I'll think about it." With a rueful laugh he added, "It serves me right. I should have remembered that you are Neva's bosom friend from Grace Baptist Church." He started walking on, and I followed. After a brief pause he halted again and confronted me.

"Karen," he said earnestly, "I take it we both want to start seeing each other. At least I do. But if we do that, you'll want to win me over to Christianity. Neva may have told you that my mother tried that unsuccessfully for years. I will try to make you see that your faith is an illusion. After all, you are intelligent! So what'll it be? Shall we go on seeing each other?"

For a fleeting moment I considered saying no and ending our relationship then and there. But I said yes because I wanted to win James to the faith, just as he said. I also said yes because I was already falling in love with him and thought that he felt the same way about me.

6
"The Times They Are A-Changin'"; I Study Philosophy

Our relationship began well, I believe, because we became more closely acquainted only gradually. Both of us already had full class schedules. Thus we could see each other only once or twice during the week for quick lunches or strolls across the campus, and for longer meetings only on those weekends when we were both in Battle Hill. This was relatively rare, for I sometimes visited my family at home and James, young as he was, had already begun his lifelong round of presenting lectures on contemporary philosophy and education on college campuses around the country and preparing articles on these subjects for publication. "In the academic world you must publish or perish," he kept saying when explaining why he had so little free time.

He was almost always preoccupied with some pressing writing project or threatening deadline. I realized that when he had offered his supposedly "free time" to show me the campus the day we first met, he had made a real sacrifice to get to know me better. He had also been a little less than truthful, but of course I took this as a sign of his attraction to me.

There were more such signs as time went on. First and foremost, James showed unfeigned interest in my piano playing. All the Barron children had taken piano lessons, and though James no longer practiced, he shared my love of classical music and usually listened to it on the radio of his car. Despite his tight schedule, he would occasionally slip into the university music department's student practice rooms to listen when I practiced, and later he attended my piano recitals. This spurred me on to do my very best work; I practiced longer and harder, and there was much more passion and engagement in my performances. James noticed this and commented on it with praise. I began to look forward to and later to expect his presence at my practices and recitals.

When I asked him why he liked classical music, his answer astonished me.

"It gives me rest and peace," he answered, sighing, "especially the older classical music with its beautiful harmony and resolution of any discords at the end of each composition. Older classical music compositions tell complete stories with beginning, middle, and end. Contemporary music comes to us in bits and pieces. It mirrors or rather it preaches human action in bits and pieces in the world today."

"What do you mean?" I asked.

"Look at our century," James said, "World War I. The Great Depression. The Nazis. The Communists. The Holocaust. World War II. The Cold War. Vietnam. Here we are in 1964, with the Free Speech Movement against university regulations, hippies and 'flower children' against law and order, the Civil Rights Movement against segregation, more and more mind-altering drugs. And then, of course, we have the new music and the new prophets by music. You must have heard it. You must have listened to them."

I nodded. Yes, I had heard the new hip-swinging, guitar-strumming, mop-headed musicians all right, for they were heard and seen everywhere including on television, the new exploding mass communications medium. But due to the influence of my parents and my church, I had not listened to them often, much less idolized them as had so many of my fellow students in high school. James chuckled.

"It's a social revolution all right, Karen," he said, "and the new music is its assault weapon among us young people. Bob Dylan wrote a song about it, 'The Times They Are A-Changin'. It's a big hit, and rightly so! The man is a true prophet of what is right ahead of us. I haven't heard it described better anywhere! First he speaks to today's cultural leaders, the writers and critics—and I am about to be one of them, or already one of the youngest in their ranks—and tells us to keep our eyes open for what is happening right now. We haven't won the battle quite yet between the old and the new way of life, but we are well on the way to victory. He tells the older generation that they can't understand us young people and therefore should not criticize us. He tells them that they can't tell us what to do any longer because we are beyond their rules and orders. He tells them that if they aren't willing to be on our side to get out of our way. Bob Dylan is absolutely right! It'll be a whole different world within the next twenty years, and I am helping to make it so!"

He took a deep breath and continued excitedly: "You see, my life work is to connect the dots from the past to the present—to make clear that the new world is just the result of streams of thought that have been with us since the beginning of mankind. I'll tell it to you in your own words. What we see today is just the present outworking of what the serpent told Eve in the Garden of Eden: there are no trees from which we may not eat. As a matter of fact, we must eat of them all to test their effects and so become wise. It is exactly as John Dewey," he saw I did not recognize the name and explained with his habitual patience towards my ignorance, "the father of modern education, one of America's greatest philosophers, taught: we must abandon the old 'spectator theory' of analyzing the world as though we were outside observers. To advance the social sciences, he said, we must 'learn by doing,' that is, by imitating the modern laboratory method of hands-on experimentation which has advanced the natural sciences so much. I am working on an article about this right now. My grad school faculty advisor thinks it will be accepted by a philosophy journal she helps edit."

James was about to stop at this point, but was so wound up that he could not help going on "And from John Dewey there is a direct link to the philosophy of our day, existentialism. Existentialism justifies total individualism and tells us with Jean-Paul Sartre to 'authenticate ourselves' by our actions moment by moment. There is enough material here for more than one article or seminar. I generally like Sartre's existentialism—it's very dynamic and action-packed—but sometimes I long for rest and peace."

Instantly I remembered and said aloud these words: "'Thou hast made us for Thyself, and our heart is restless till it rests in Thee.' That's from the *Confessions* of St. Augustine. He is speaking to God. I have heard it somewhere long ago—probably in a sermon at our church."

James looked at me in surprise. For a moment neither of us spoke. Then he said slowly:

"'Our heart is restless till it rests in Thee.' It's amazing to me how you can come up with the right quote at the right moment! You make me think of something else St. Augustine said. Here it is, as best I can quote it: 'I have read in Plato and Cicero sayings that are very wise and very beautiful; but I never read in either of them: 'Come to me, all you who are weary and burdened, and I will give you rest.'"

Neither of us spoke again right away. That was an unforgettable moment of mutual peace and good will, one of the best ever between us.

Next James urged me to learn more about philosophy so I could understand him and his work better. "I can't go on trying to share things with you properly when I have to wonder all the time whether you can follow me all right," he said. "You really should take an introductory philosophy course next semester." He went on to recommend a couple of professors, he said, who taught the regular freshman introductory philosophy class as he himself would teach it.

For a while I demurred. If I did what James wanted me to do, my parents, who always took total interest in my study plans, were sure to find out and ask me why I, a music education major, wanted to study philosophy of all possible subjects. In my mind I heard them quote the relevant Bible passages: *"Beware lest any man spoil you through philosophy and vain deceit, after the tradition of men, after the rudiments of the world, and not after Christ."* Colossians 2: 8. Or 2 Corinthians 11:3: *"But I fear, lest by any means, as the serpent beguiled Eve through his subtlety, so your minds should be corrupted from the simplicity that is in Christ."*

As the serpent beguiled Eve through his subtlety! I remembered how James had spoken approvingly of "the streams of thought which began with the serpent in the Garden of Eden: there are no trees from which we may not eat," and how he had seen himself as the heir and interpreter of the serpent's message in our time. Now he wanted me to study philosophy so I could "follow him all right." If I did that, I would have to tell my parents that since I first came to Battle Hill University I had been dating James Barron, the James Barron who had fathered

Dorrie Fisher's child and was not a Christian. How could I explain to them that this relationship now demanded my study of philosophy taught as James would like it? How could I defend it even to myself?

There was only one explanation or defense: I would do it for James' sake, to have answers for him that would disentangle him from his errors. I told myself I was like a missionary traveling to a foreign country to evangelize the lost. I wanted so much to win the lost one I loved to Christ! If I took the course as James wanted me to, it would show first and foremost that I loved him. I shrank from admitting this to my parents.

I wrestled with the decision for weeks, right up to the deadline for spring enrollment. James kept prodding me, first gently, then more and more firmly. In the end I said yes. But by that time the freshman introductory philosophy courses taught by the professors James had recommended were filled up. I made a last minute decision: I signed up for a course open to freshmen named "Historical Survey of Western Philosophy" taught by a Dr. Francis S. Freeman. I hoped that it might give me ammunition for doing battle with James, indispensable information I had not received at home or at church.

7
A Quarrel about "Saint Francis"

James was angry when I told him that instead of enrolling in a freshman philosophy class with one of the professors he had recommended to me I had signed up for Dr. Freeman's "Historical Survey of Western Philosophy" class. It was a raw December day, and we sat at our usual little table in the cafeteria about to have our first serious disagreement.

"So you will be brainwashed by old Saint Francis!" he exclaimed, fighting to keep his voice down. "Why in the world didn't you ask me about him before taking his course?"

I explained that when I enrolled, this had been the only philosophy course open to freshmen which was still accepting students. It had been too late to ask anyone's opinion about it, and it sounded like it would give me the background information I needed to understand James better. Inevitably James was hurt and offended when I blurted out my relief that by taking this general course, I would not have to tell my parents about my real reason for taking it—namely, my relationship with him.

"We have dated every two or three days for almost a whole semester now," he said. "You mean you haven't told them about us yet?"

I admitted it.

"And why is that?"

"You want to become a professional philosopher. I wanted to find out what my folks might think about that, so I talked with them recently about philosophy in general. They mistrust it, especially modern philosophy. So I didn't tell them about you."

"What else might they not like about me if they knew about me?" James asked angrily. I felt it was no use hiding the truth.

"They have heard about you for years from Neva and their own friends," I answered, "They don't like it that you don't get along with your mother because she is a Christian. They—we all—everyone in Lonely Prairie knows about you and a girl you got pregnant when you were both still in high school."

James laughed, half in anger, half with contempt.

"That's Lonely Prairie for you," he said. "Everyone knows everything about everybody! All right, so you are still keeping me a deep dark secret from your family. You won't be able to do that much longer! I'll soon have you come with me to visit my own folks. If you haven't told yours about us by then, the Lonely Prairie grapevine will take care of it." He laughed again, this time with amusement and even some tenderness. "Yes, I want to take you home soon to reintroduce you to them," he repeated. "It's time the Barron family found out that now you are more than Neva's friend. And I have a good suggestion for you, little Karen. You could tell your folks that we ran into each other early in the semester and that you keep meeting with me because you want to convert me to Christianity. That's what I will tell my parents, Neva and my pious brother Robert. My father will laugh and make crude jokes about it, but the others will say God put you in my way and welcome you as their ally with open arms." He tried to put his hand on mine, but I pulled it away.

"What you say may be true," I said miserably, "but it wouldn't be the whole truth. My parents would know right away that there is more to my meeting you than my desire to convert you. They were already suspicious when I brought up the subject of philosophy because I have never been interested in it before. My dad even asked outright whether there was a young man involved. I said no. I lied. I think he knew but he didn't pursue it. My mother didn't say anything, but I think she knew, too. I could tell they were becoming concerned."

"Smart people, your parents," James said with a laugh. "You can't hide much from them, can you?"

"I never really wanted to," I said. "We are very close. I am afraid to hurt them, and telling them that you and I might be getting serious about each other would hurt them, at least now. I am sorry." I looked at James pleadingly, but a dark frown appeared and deepened on his face.

"You are an adult now, Karen," he answered. "You have to make up your own mind on what to do or what friends you have. You can't always bow down to the authority of your parents or your church."

"All I can think of right now," I said, "is that I don't want to hurt my parents. They have been hurt so badly in their lives already! You see, I had a brother who drowned in a neighbor's swimming pool when he was only three years old. I was just a baby then and don't remember it, but we still have pictures of him in the house. Such a beautiful, happy little boy! I am the only child they have left, and they love me so much. They are the best parents and friends anyone could have."

"I can't say that about me and my parents," James said slowly, "my father is away from home most of the time, and my mother—as you said, we don't get along because she is a Christian. I know she means well and that she loves me. Believe it or not, I love her too! She tries so hard to be close to me, but she always brings up Christ and I hate that. It's a little like that for you and me, Karen. In fact you remind me very much of my mother."

"I don't look much like her," I said, attempting to smile. He smiled back.

"No," he agreed, "you are not as tall as she is and less queenly, little Karen, with your long, shiny honey blonde hair, beautiful blue eyes and sunny smile. But inside you are a lot like her. You care deeply about everything, just like she does. You don't 'like' thoughts, or actions—you love them or hate them. You don't 'like' people, you love them. I wonder whether you could ever hate anyone." He put his hand on mine, and this time I did not stop him. For a moment we sat silent and content.

Then James returned to the matter at hand, meeting his family and mine. Blithely, as though everything was and would be just fine, he said, "I still want you to come home with me soon. We'll just have to be up front about us with everybody. Your parents and the Christians in my family would probably guess that while you want to convert me, I want to convert you too—away from God. But except for my father they would all root for you, especially my mother. Her greatest desire in life is for me to get right with Jesus!"

Then suddenly he pulled his hand away from mine. "But when it comes to that course with Dr. Freeman," he said sternly, "withdraw from it."

"Why?"

"Because—because," James thought hard to formulate his answer, "because Dr. Freeman is about to retire. This is the last course he will teach at Battle Hill U." Then he burst out in unconcealed fury: "And good riddance, too! He is just an old fossil. My faculty advisor told me he fits into the Philosophy Department like a square peg into a round hole. All the other professors disagree with his views, especially the younger up-to-date ones. If he didn't have tenure, he would have been let go years ago."

James stopped briefly, then added hotly: "And he has no flexibility, no give-and-take in discussions! Dr. Berger—my faculty advisor—says that what bothers her most about him is that he is outwardly always very courteous and kind, but underneath it all he doesn't give an inch. Stubborn as a mule! Hard as a rock! Behind the times—as I said, an old fossil. A dinosaur." He took a deep breath, then said with finality: "So you must withdraw from his course right away."

His unsubstantiated attack upon Dr. Freeman and his ordering me to drop the course made me angry in turn.

"One thing you haven't done, James," I said sharply, "is explain to me what exactly Dr. Freeman believes and teaches that you want me so much not to hear. You called him 'Saint Francis' a moment ago. By any chance do you and your

Dr. Berger and the other philosophy professors dislike him so much because he is a Christian? A serious, informed, effective Christian with real answers? Are you afraid he might convert a skeptical student to Christ, or that he might help a student like me who already is a Christian to defend my faith?"

James did not reply. I could see I had hit the mark.

"And another thing," I said, determinedly standing my ground against James for the first time, "you have no right to order me to withdraw from his course! You cannot order me to listen to no one but yourself or to teachers who agree with you. You always tell me to make up my own mind and not give in to the authority of my parents or my church. Well, that applies to your authority too, or to the authority of the philosophy department." After a moment of thought I added this final thrust, "You said I would be brainwashed by 'old Saint Francis'. I think you don't like me to take his course because you wanted to brainwash me yourself, or have me brainwashed by those other professors."

After a tense pause James spread his hands and shrugged. "Okay, okay," he said, "I am sorry I seemed like I ordered you to drop Freeman's course. It's just a great disappointment to me that you might take it. Couldn't you just drop it to please me and take the Introduction to Philosophy course when I teach it next fall?"

But my spine had stiffened. "I will do no such thing," I said. "I will take Dr. Freeman's course and learn all I can from his teaching. Then we will see if I find it necessary—or want to please you enough—to take your course next fall, too. I make no promises about that. And you had better wait a while before taking me to your family."

"All right," James said resignedly in a more conciliatory tone, "I guess I can do nothing about it if I want to go on seeing you."

8

A Good Philosophy Course; Utilitarianism; "Question Authority"

I actually began to look forward to study the history of Western philosophy and came to Dr. Freeman's first class with eager expectancy. I was not disappointed.

Dr. Freeman was a scholarly man in his late sixties. "I will begin the course," he said, "with a statement by Rene Descartes, one of the most important and famous philosophers in history. Here it is: 'There is nothing so absurd or incredible that it has not been asserted by one philosopher or another.'" We looked at him in amused surprise.

Dr. Freeman asked us whether we had already heard of any Western philosophers, when they lived, and what details of their thought we might remember. He wrote the correct answers on the blackboard and made additions here and there.

The combined knowledge of the class, especially the older auditing students, was not inconsiderable, and thanks to what I had picked up from James I could make a few contributions about modern philosophers myself. Toward the end of the class period a skeleton list of Western philosophers from Greek antiquity to our own generation covered the blackboard for us to copy in our notebooks.

During that spring semester of 1965 Dr. Freeman helped us integrate the bits and pieces of knowledge we already had. We learned where the most influential philosophers followed one another on the historical time line and on the more subtle lines of ideological kinship. Of these, Dr. Freeman said, there were essentially two, the more "naturalistic" or "materialistic" line represented by modern thinkers like Nietzsche and Sartre, and the more "spiritual" or even "theistic" line represented by St. Augustine, Thomas Aquinas and Jonathan Edwards in America. Of course not every philosopher fitted this rough classification exactly, and in a way philosophers were like boys forever drawing circles in the sand at the seashore, each drawing his own circle so it would intersect but not coincide with the earlier ones, each insisting his circle was the best. Once Dr. Freeman told us of the Russian philosopher Vladimir Solovyov who made his name by a pantheistic philosophy he called "panentheism" but rejected it publicly at the end of his life to return to orthodox Christianity, and of the Jewish Frenchman Henri Bergson, author of the famous pantheistic treatise *Creative Evolution,* who converted to Catholic Christianity in his old age while the Nazis occupied France in the early 1940s. "Don't ever classify anyone's faith unless you know how he died," Dr. Freeman concluded.

Dr. Freeman helped us see how we might recognize and reject plausible but false philosophical premises, analogies or arguments, for example, the argument from consent ("fifty million Frenchmen can't be wrong"—oh yes, they can!). He taught us certain timeless rules of reasoning, such as Aristotle's identity principle "A = A" which declares that a thing cannot be itself and also something else at the same time, or the truth that an "ought" cannot be deduced from an "is," with its enormous implications for the teaching of ethics.

Finally Dr. Freeman explained the implications for philosophy, especially ethics, of accepting evolution and denying biblical creation. I saw that the very foundation of a Christian worldview lay precisely here. I also saw later that James, along with many clear-thinking atheists, had understood this far earlier and better than most Christians today.

James, of course, did what damage control he could. He got together with me after almost every class session to ask me probing questions about it, at first with no comment. But when we came to Rene Descartes and his famous starting point "I think, therefore I am," I couldn't help laughing a little about this pronouncement. "After all, there are many things in the world which do not think, yet are!" I said.

James smiled condescendingly. "Yes, there are other evidences besides thought that might show something exists," he said coldly, "but you are missing the main point. For Descartes the first problem in philosophy was to make sure that we truly know what we think we know. The new method he introduced was that he explicitly started with himself as the one thing whose existence he could not possibly doubt. His principle of doubting everything before accepting anything led to modern thought today." I remembered that this problem of how we can know had come up at our very first meeting and wondered whether it would ever stop hounding us.

A few days later James had me go with him to a public lecture he himself was to give at the student union over the lunch hour. It was one in a series usually delivered by full members of the philosophy faculty, and he was proud that he, a graduate teaching assistant, had been asked to take part in it. His topic would be "Utilitarianism for our Generation." Since I had never heard him speak in public, I readily agreed.

Soon we were in the large central court of the student union among hundreds of informally dressed students. There was also a sprinkling of faculty, including a youngish woman with short cropped hair wearing a severely cut black pant suit, then still a rarity for women. She saw us from afar, waved to James, who waved back, and came toward him. It was Dr. Berger, and James left me to meet and follow her through the crowd to the speaker's podium. She was there to introduce him to the audience, which she did with lavish praise for "our most promising graduate teaching assistant." James took his place behind the microphone, very handsome as he stood there straight and tall, silent till the crowd became still and ready to listen. Here are the essential points of his lecture.

"Utilitarianism? What's that?" James began. "It's a philosophy which says that utility, usefulness, is the standard by which action is to be judged, and that that which is useful is that which is good or worthwhile. Utilitarianism also teaches that all moral, social or political action should be directed toward achieving the greatest good for the greatest number. In the form of modern existentialism, which calls us all to authenticate our lives by the choices we make, it is the philosophy we need for our generation to overcome the present establishment, which keeps imposing the outdated values of an older generation upon us." He spoke much like the student leaders of the revolutionary Free Speech Movement, which had shaken up the University of California at Berkeley in the fall of 1964 and was now producing aftershocks at other colleges across the country. There was scattered applause among the student listeners.

James went on: "The roots of utilitarianism can already be detected in the hedonism of Democritus, 460–370 B.C., and Epicurus, 340–270 B.C. I will not bore you with many historical details but skip on to Jeremy Bentham, 1748–1832. He founded utilitarianism by that name and taught, rightly I believe, that pleasure is the chief end of life, as did his chief disciple, John Stuart Mill, 1806–1893. By the way, the older generations, much as they paid lip service to religion, law and order, also sought pleasures wherever they could find them. Why else is prostitution the oldest profession?" The audience chuckled approvingly. "The motto of most people has always been, 'Eat, drink and be merry, for tomorrow you die.'

"Another defender of utilitarianism, Herbert Spencer, 1820–1903, who believed in evolution along with the great Charles Darwin, was optimistic about evolution creating better conditions of life, so that people would adapt their individual conduct to what was most useful to society at large and take pleasure in altruistic actions. Of course this meant that Spencer attached a greater value to altruism than egoism. Bentham had already tried to measure and rank pleasures by their respective values. Mill did the same in principle when he stated that it was better to be Socrates dissatisfied than a pig satisfied. His opponents seized upon this remark to call utilitarianism a 'pig philosophy.'"

There was scattered laughter among the audience as James went on: "Bentham, Spencer and Mill were wrong on that point. We want a completely non-judgmental, pure utilitarianism permitting us to pursue our individual pleasures with no moral strings attached. As soon as you introduce any values besides your own pleasure, you also reintroduce authority which would replace your ranking of your own pleasures by its own. To this I say, question authority!" Here James unbuttoned his outer shirt and showed the crowd the black T-shirt underneath, on which the words QUESTION AUTHORITY were stenciled in red. A roar of applause went up.

This slogan was challenged a moment later when James opened the meeting for questions. Immediately a tall young man sitting not far from me raised his hand and was recognized. "It was Hitler's pleasure to exterminate the Jews," he said. "How would your non-judgmental, pure utilitarianism deal with that pleasure?"

"With education," James answered. It was a wrong move.

The questioner instantly objected: "But education teaches value judgments, in this case, that Nazism and anti-Semitism are wrong. Your non-judgmental, pure utilitarianism would break down right there."

A handful of people in the audience applauded, myself included. James glared at me but also rallied to a counterattack. "The full answer to your question," he shot back, "is what is happening all around us right now. All value judgments and truths are becoming relative. Education no longer imposes absolute values but clarifies them. That change began with John Dewey and is transforming education as we speak." He took a deep breath and added: "Our society is already immoral now by the old standards, but you have seen nothing yet. Abortion will be legalized as a woman's choice and backup to birth control. All forms of making love, no matter how perverse they may be called today, will be legal. Traditional marriage and family will end. Parents will leave their children so both can do their own thing. Drugs will be freely available. Finally the very voice of the old morality will be silenced."

Applause and more questions followed until Dr. Berger ended the meeting. I hurriedly made my way to the first questioner to thank him for his stand. His name was George MacPherson. He told me that his family owned Swenson Books, located not far from the campus, and suggested that I visit it some time. "We carry all the works by C. S. Lewis," he said, "they are very helpful if you want to deal with talks like the horrible one we just heard." Our eyes met in total agreement.

Then James caught up with me and hustled me away.

9
I Can't Trust Him! Why Go On?

"We have to talk," I told James as we left the student union central court. He looked down at me with a smile, which faded quickly as he scanned my face. I must have looked as I felt, bursting with total indignation and determined to express it.

"All right," he said and added after a quick look at his watch, "I have about half an hour till my next class. Let's find a quiet place." Sure in his knowledge of the location as he always was, he led our way up some stairs to the first floor where there were empty lounges and conference rooms. He entered one of them, comfortably furnished with overstuffed sofas and armchairs around gleaming tables, closed the door behind us and chose a seat near the huge window from which we could see nearby buildings, students swarming to and fro between them, bare trees swaying in the early April wind, and bits of sky laden with swiftly passing heavy gray clouds. An intercom system was piping in soft, soothing music, making an incongruous accompaniment to our dispute.

"I could tell you didn't like my lecture," he said, "I didn't expect you to agree with it when I took you there, but I am surprised you are so angry about it."

"It was your old trick again," I fumed, "evading a relevant point by substituting something else, just as you did with the 'atheist syndrome' when we first met. This time you substituted modern education and your prophecy about our supposed valueless future for the real point of the first question, which was that some pleasures, like Hitler's pleasure in killing millions of innocent Jews, are absolutely wrong and can't be tolerated. How could you have stood there and taught that there are no absolute truths and values?"

"I didn't," James said, looking straight at me. I half rose from my seat.

"If you lie to me like this again," I exploded, determined and despairing at once, "we are through! Perhaps we are through right now! I mean it." I could feel my eyes burn with barely restrained tears. How could I bear to look at James, now so much part of my life and constantly in my thoughts, and consider that he and I might break up that very day?

"No, I didn't," James repeated, "I didn't teach that there are no absolutes. I only said that modern education will lead society there. And I didn't use any trick when I spoke about education. That student said education teaches value judgments. In answer I pointed out, truthfully, that education has been changing and no longer teaches but clarifies value judgments. I pointed out, truthfully, that all value judgments and truths are becoming relative."

"And what about that theatrical business with your QUESTION AUTHORITY T-shirt? That was teaching, teaching at its best—with a wonderful visual aid!

You must have had that shirt especially prepared for your lecture."

"What if I did?" said James, "I didn't think of it as teaching. I thought of it as a show of solidarity with the Berkeley Free Speech Movement. I thought it would go over well with that crowd, and with Dr. Berger and the rest of the faculty people there. And I was right. They all loved it." With a smile he added, "You see, I must think of my future career."

This answer silenced me for a moment. A horrible suspicion arose in my mind. Had the entire lecture been only his means to ingratiate himself with the professors who could help him advance in his profession? How much of it did he really believe? Perhaps nothing but worldly ambition ultimately motivated him. This meant that the way to turn him to God was to show him the futility and emptiness of worldly success. My anger with him receded.

"Oh James," I said half apologetically, "when I heard you speak, it didn't sound to me like you were only stating facts about modern education. I thought you were in favor of what it does and wanted to teach the students to think like you did. Now I am not so sure. Maybe you did it all just for your career. But if that's true, it's not so good either. For even if you reached the top with all the fame, influence and wealth you could wish for, it would not last forever. Besides, what if you lost much more than you gained with your success? 'What shall it profit a man, if he shall gain the whole world, and lose his own soul?'"

James stood up and stepped to the window, looking out for a little while with his back turned to me. He seemed to be pondering a decision. Then he returned to his seat, his mind made up.

"I'll be completely truthful with you, Karen," he said. "Understand that I do believe everything I said at the lecture. I do not believe in absolute rights and wrongs. I believe with utilitarianism or existentialism that to fulfill our own desires and pleasures is our only purpose in life. Of course we can oppose other people who want to interfere with our pleasures, peacefully if possible, by force if necessary. The reason for doing so can only be the utility, usefulness, to ourselves, never some higher moral law from beyond this present world."

"But—but," I stammered, aghast, "wouldn't that mean that the strongest and most ruthless would rule the whole world in the end? And that gets us back to Hitler and the Holocaust! The Nazis wanted to rule the whole world! They had a song about it which went like this: 'We will keep marching on/Though everything collapsed in shards;/For today we own Germany,/Tomorrow the whole world!' It was wrong, I tell you—absolutely wrong! Other things are absolutely wrong too—like abortion, killing your own baby—how can that be right? There might be a better world if only we lived up to what we really know is good and right . . . ," my voice died away.

James answered slowly and gently: "You must face up to the fact that there is only one world, this world, here and now. All else is wishful thinking. That which *is,* reality here and now, must and will overcome the false idea that something different or better *ought to be.* That was the essence of my answer to the question that student asked. It is my answer to your question now."

After a brief silence he added still more gently, "I sincerely mean that answer. I don't believe in any other reality than the here and now. That's why I am concerned about my career, too, but my career is not my first concern. My first concern is to be answerable to no one but myself—to be 'the master of my fate, the captain of my soul,' as William Ernest Henley says so well in his poem 'Invictus.' That's why I reject the Creator God of Christianity above and outside this world. I don't believe that this world is fallen from its originally created, perfect condition due to Adam's or our sin. No. What is, is right, as Hegel said. And evolution, a scientific fact, bears it out."

I shook my head. I could feel tears trickling down my cheeks as I said: "You will never get me to believe any of that."

"You will come to see," James said, "that your faith is nothing but an illusion due to the indoctrination of your folks and your church. Even many professing Christians and churches no longer believe it—my parents' church in Lonely Prairie is a good example."

"Numbers of supporters can't establish whether something is true," I countered, remembering Dr. Freeman's rejection of the argument from consent. James chuckled.

"You got me there," he acknowledged. He looked at his watch. "I have to run," he said. "Let's call it a draw for today. I'll see you soon."

We got up. James walked a few steps to the door, then suddenly turned back and put his arms around me. I felt an instant urge to repel him but stood still and let him hug and kiss me.

"I do love you, sweetheart," he said. "Don't give up on me. You have more effect on me than you may think." With these words he left.

When I was sure he was really gone, I rushed from the room, downstairs and out across the campus to the fine arts building, found a free piano practice room and hammered the most passionate, fury-filled pieces I could remember over and over again on the keyboard till the storm in my heart gave way to calm reflection. I sat there on the piano bench and did some hard thinking. I decided, first, that I had been right: James had indeed tricked his lecture audience by discussing modern education instead of the validity of moral values. Second, James had knowingly lied to me when he denied having taught his audience, for what else but teaching goes on in a lecture?

Lastly, he had told me the truth about his own worldview and the place of his career within it, but had he told me the truth about loving me? In view of his fundamental, long standing self-centeredness, how could he really love me or anyone? This is why I had endured but not responded to his hug and kiss. Perhaps he had just been manipulating me as he had been manipulating those students. Perhaps he had been doing this so long that it had become part of his character. He had been doing it already years ago, with Dorrie Fisher. Was I merely another Dorrie Fisher to him, to be seduced not physically (and perhaps that, too!) but spiritually, only to be thrown away when he could get no more pleasure out of me? I remembered Neva's remark about her brother's girl friends, "He loved them and left them, as usual." Why should I be different? I started crying again, remembering the good moments of growing closeness between us, my joy of seeing him, of dreaming of a future with him after his conversion, and yes, of marriage.

"But I can't trust him," I murmured sadly to myself. "After all the times we have seen each other, I still don't really know him. Is there any good reason to go on?"

Yes, there was. James had told me not to give up on him, and that I had more effect on him than I might think. I prayed that this, at least, was true, and for God's protection, leading and wisdom as I decided to follow up on it despite the odds.

10

My Parents' Counsel

A couple of weeks afterwards we had our week-long spring break, and both of us were planning to spend it in Lonely Prairie with our families. This would be the time, James said, that he wanted to have me visit his family. He proposed that we drive to Lonely Prairie together in his car after he had taught his last class Friday evening, but I refused. I would leave in the early afternoon in my own car. I explained that I wanted to have my own transportation during the vacation. My main and unspoken reason, however, was that I wanted to see my parents and tell them about James before he took me to the Barrons; I certainly did not want to arrive at my home in his company. James instantly guessed what I was thinking and acquiesced with a touch of irony, "Nipping the Lonely Prairie grapevine in the bud, eh? You're wise."

And so that sunny Friday afternoon I traveled alone along the superhighway from Battle Hill to Lonely Prairie and enjoyed the stark beauty of the familiar mid-western plain in its endless expanse beneath the white-blue sun-lit sky. How much I loved to see it again! How much I had needed to leave Battle Hill, that large bustling city, and especially Battle Hill University, the self-contained ivory tower within it, for a few blessed days of respite from classes, tests, piano practice and recitals, and from the now almost daily meetings with James which were my joy and my torment. Reluctantly, I began to think about how to speak of him to my parents.

The hour-long drive ended all too quickly. I parked in the driveway of our home and walked up the stairs to the front porch. There stood my mother in a pretty flowered dress, smiling happily, arms open wide to hug me in welcome. I hugged her back, resting my head on her shoulder with a slump of my body and a sigh of relief. When we pulled apart again, her smile had vanished and her eyes were fixed on me with concern.

"Is anything wrong, Karen?" she asked.

"No, Mom," I answered hesitantly, "not really. Not wrong exactly. But there is something I need to tell you and Dad—something important."

After a moment of silence she said with forced cheerfulness, "You can tell us both after supper, then. Let's get your things inside now, and you can freshen up a bit. Dad will be home soon and we'll eat. I fixed your favorite supper."

Supper came and went, my mother and I did the dishes, and we joined my father in our living room. My parents settled back on the old, saggy sofa. I sat across from them on the beloved rocking chair, a family heirloom on which Mother had rocked my late little brother and me. It still creaked a little at each swing just as it always had. Everything here, including the signs of age and decay, spoke comfortingly of the older days with their long established, sure and cherished ways of simple, ordered living in duty, love, and mutual trust.

"Karen has something she wants to tell us, Dad," my mother said. My father nodded. I looked at them silently, noticing that they were just a bit older, my mother a little grayer, my father a little more bald, their faces more patient than four months ago.

I told them about James and me as briefly and clearly as I could. I described our deep differences about Christianity and philosophy. In answer to my mother's anxious question, I reassured my parents that James and I had never been intimate. I ended with the news that James was planning to tell the Barrons about us and to have me meet them with him right away.

My parents looked at each other. They did not seem as surprised by my report as I had expected. I instantly learned the reason why.

"So you are the girl," my mother said.

"What do you mean?" I asked.

"Jean Holcomb talked to me a little while after Christmas," she explained, "you probably remember that she is also a very good friend of Lucinda Barron's. She heard from Lucinda that James had told her he had met a girl early in the fall semester at Battle Hill University whom he had dated steadily since then. 'You'll be happy to know that she is a good Christian girl,' he had told Lucinda, 'the only hitch is the difference in our worldviews. She wants me to become a Christian, but I will not knuckle under to your God, and if I did, it would pretty well destroy my career. So I hope to convince her to give up her faith or at least to tolerate my unbelief, just as you tolerate Dad's.' And now we know—you are the girl."

"We are very worried about you," said my father, "James Barron is not the sort of young man we had hoped you would fall in love with. In a way he is the exact opposite. Surely you remember about him and Dorrie Fisher whom he got pregnant when they were both still in high school." I nodded.

My father went on, "Next, and most importantly, you know from your friend Neva about his fighting with Mrs. Barron over Christianity. Karen, this is deadly serious! The Bible tells us not to be 'unequally yoked together with unbelievers.' There can be no permanent bond between you and James Barron unless he becomes a Christian."

"And if you tolerate his unbelief, as he might want you to," said my mother, "you would be very unhappy. Mrs. Barron tolerates her husband's unbelief, but with great sadness. Besides, they were already married when she became a Christian. That's a different situation entirely, in which the believing wife should stay with the unbelieving husband as long as he is willing to stay with her—and of course, there is hope that he may yet come to the Lord. We are all praying for that."

"What about before marriage?" I asked faintly. "Is it all right for a girl to stay with an unbeliever as long as he is willing to stay with her if there is hope that she may convert him?"

My parents looked at each other in deep perplexity, pondering their answer to this crucial question. Finally my mother said heavily, "Is there really hope of that for you? From all we know about James Barron, he is a hardened, self-centered enemy of Christianity. I am afraid you will lose precious time in your life by trying in vain to convert him, and maybe the chance to meet a much more acceptable young man. Oh how I wish you had never become involved with him!"

"He does seem to really be in love with me," I countered. "Won't that help me to win him over?"

My father looked at me fondly. "He may well be in love with you," he said with a smile. "You are very lovable, inside and outside—though I may be prejudiced saying so." He became serious again: "But I am afraid that the price he would have to pay to stay with you for good will seem too high to him. He is probably right, you know, about destroying his career by becoming a Christian. It is already more difficult to be a Christian as a high school teacher today than it was ten years ago, as I know from experience. James is preparing to teach at an elite university, where hostility toward Christianity is doubtless much stronger and more influential than at Lonely Prairie Central High."

My father took a deep breath and continued: "I must also warn you that he may try to deceive you by a false profession of faith. You said yourself that according to his utilitarianism or existentialism or whatever, he wants all the pleasure he can get with no moral strings attached. Why would he not lie to you to win you over?"

I sat silent, stunned. I had never thought of this possibility, but I had to admit to myself that it was real. How could I guard against it? How could I ever trust James?

My mother broke in passionately: "And that is not love! He may *want* you, but does he really love you? Real love is to want and do what is truly good for the other person. He had no real love for poor Dorrie Fisher or their child. Why would he have real love for you?"

"And have you considered," added my father, "that his social background is very different from yours? You must have felt that already all the times when your friend Neva invited you to the Barrons. It's not a sin to be rich, but it can easily spoil children growing up in wealthy homes. A lot of those student leaders of the Free Speech Movement and war protesters come from well-to-do families. They are self-centered and don't know what it means to earn one's own living. They never had any real duties. No wonder they don't see how unrealistic it is to think and teach others that you should live only for yourself! If they come to power, they will destroy our society. And James is one of them! He is not right for you, Karen. Let him go, the sooner the better."

"If real love is to want and do what is truly good for the other person," I said, "and if I have real love for James, can I let him go unless I am sure that he will never come to Christ? I am not sure of that now. I believe I must keep trying to help him come to the Lord, at least for a while."

"Karen," my father said, sternly for the first time, "our Lord can bring James to Himself without you in His own time by other means. Don't fool yourself, thinking that your being in love with him means God commands you to stay with him against your parents' counsel."

"That's right," agreed my mother, "we both believe it would be best if you broke off with him now. Actually, if he really loves you, your very decision to do this might prompt him to be in earnest about seeking the Lord."

"I'll think about it," I said, and added, "Pray for me, whatever I decide. It will hurt me either way."

11

"Peace and Joy in the Lord"

Saturday morning came and with it a phone call. My mother answered; it was for me. I could tell she was upset and guessed that it was James. He wanted to arrange the time at which he could pick me up and take me home to meet his family.

"I'll have to talk to my folks about it," I said. "They may have plans for the weekend for all of us."

There was a brief silence before he answered, "Well, talk to them as soon as you can and call me back. I have already talked to my folks about bringing you. They thought lunch today might be nice."

"Okay," I said, "I'll call you back later, bye," and hung up. It was all I could bring myself to say to him. I found my mother in the kitchen cleaning the top of the stove; she always tackled some hard or messy job when she was agitated. I told her why James had called.

"You'll have to get out of it," she said anxiously. "It would make it harder to break off the relationship with James. In fact, meeting his parents and family this way would mean you two are thinking of marriage. You can't go along with that! You can't!" Her voice trembled. She scrubbed harder at a stubborn grease spot.

My father joined us and found out what we were talking about. He completely agreed with my mother and told me to call James back and tell him we had already made other plans for the entire weekend. "And don't let him talk you into visiting his family next week," he admonished. "Tell him you can't make any arrangements now. It would be even better if you could tell him to forget entirely about bringing you to meet his family because you believe you shouldn't see each other any more."

I called James back and told him only that we couldn't meet over the weekend. He made no effort to set a date for the following week but merely said he was sorry, wished me a good weekend and hung up.

As they say, "Absence makes the heart grow fonder." That Saturday was one of the longest, dreariest days I had ever known. I spent it helping my father put our garden in order, a job I usually enjoyed, but not this time. I thought longingly of James, whom I would certainly have seen today had we been in Battle Hill. I suspected he had understood that our entire relationship was in jeopardy. How would he react? I half anticipated that he might show up unannounced at our house in person and anxiously looked at any passing car or approaching pedestrian, but James never came.

On Sunday morning we went to Grace Baptist Church as usual. James was still uppermost in my mind, but meeting old friends and neighbors and listening to choir and sermon helped distract me. I thought I might meet Neva and Robert, but they were not there. The pastor announced that Dr. Martin Johnson, a professor at Fairfield University, would speak to us tonight on the topic "Joy and Peace in the Lord."

After the service we went home to the excellent lunch my mother had prepared ahead of time, followed by her home-made apple pie. We talked about my father's teaching work, more difficult now due to students' declining discipline, and my mother's working part time away from home since I left for college. We also talked about television's growing influence, the growing number of divorces, rising crime, and other signs of social deterioration.

We rested in the afternoon, had a light supper and drove to church for the evening service. We entered the sanctuary, and there in a pew sat Mrs. Barron, Robert, Neva—and James! Neva joyfully rushed forward to hug and kiss me while Mrs. Barron, Robert and my parents exchanged more formal greetings. Then Mrs. Barron introduced James to my parents, "his first time here," she said with quiet joy. He courteously rose and bowed to them as they stared back at him blankly, unsure how to receive him. I was standing with Neva, my eyes fixed on him, my heart pounding. He turned to me with a smile, his face very joyful and very beautiful in his joy. I remembered the place in the Book of Acts where Stephen stood before the Jewish Council, which looked at him and "saw his face as it had been the face of an angel." So James' face appeared to me at that moment.

"Hello, James," I said, mindless of everyone else. "How are you? I am glad to see you."

"I am glad to see you too," he said. "I hoped I might, here, tonight." He stepped over to Neva and me and told her: "How do you like it, Sis? Your best friend is my friend too now." Neva said, "That's great" and smiled. It was obvious that all the Barrons knew about James and me. They all seemed happy about it, unlike my parents who still stood rooted to the spot, visibly perturbed and at a loss for words. Then Mrs. Barron invited us to share the pew with her family, and soon we all sat there together, with Neva by my side and James next to her. Other church members furtively looked at us, and here and there we could see women whispering to each other. Tomorrow all Lonely Prairie will know about us, I thought, but what did it matter? I was happy.

Then the organ began to play, the song leader stepped forward, and we stood and sang several of the beautiful old hymns I loved. James sang with us; he had a fine baritone voice and used it well. I stole a look at him across Neva's head; he quickly looked back, our eyes met and we were glad. Oh yes, it was a blessed evening! And the best was yet to come.

Our pastor made some announcements and then introduced Dr. Johnson, who propelled himself to the front of the sanctuary in a wheelchair. He had the muscular arms, strong upper body and withered legs of the long-time paraplegic, and the serene face of one who has overcome much pain. He told us about his family and children, the eldest with muscular dystrophy, who had needed constant care and died a year ago. "Sixteen years ago, when our handicapped boy was almost four years old," Dr. Johnson said, "I went on a mountain-climbing excursion with a group of friends. I attempted to climb a steep rock, lost my foothold and fell about fifty feet to the bottom. My spinal chord was severed in my lower back. I have been in a wheelchair ever since."

He stopped for a moment and then continued calmly: "There are many pleasures I can no longer enjoy, many bodily functions I have lost, many duties of a husband and father I can no longer fulfill. I am heavily dependent for my care on my dear wife and children, my friends and fellow Christians in my church. It has lasted for sixteen years now and will last for the rest of my life."

He pushed himself up a little straighter in his wheelchair, cleared his throat and spoke a little louder: "But that is not the whole story. I could have been killed, brain-damaged, or left a quadriplegic, but I thank God that did not happen. I thank God I am alive and have the use of my head, arms and hands. I thank God I can continue to teach and support my family. I thank God we had our handicapped son with us to love for nineteen years before he died. I thank God his suffering is over, for I know he is now with our Lord, 'at whose right hand are pleasures for evermore.' Earthly pleasures are so small and short compared to our Lord's!

"I thank God for the peace and joy in my heart. It is not earthly peace and joy; my earthly life is hard. It is and can only come from beyond this world. It is His peace and joy which He in His love for me has shared with me and even increased through my trials. My faith in Him has not only endured but become infinitely stronger.

"There are many Bible verses about the peace and joy of our Lord. My heart rejoices every time I read them, often with tears of joy. Here are a few: *'The joy of the Lord is your strength'*, Nehemiah 8:10b. *'Weeping may endure for a night, but joy cometh in the morning,'* Psalm 30:5. *'The meek also shall increase their joy in the LORD, and the poor among men shall rejoice in the Holy One of Israel,'* Isaiah 29:19.

"It is wonderful to think that our Lord is joyful over us! *'The LORD thy God in the midst of thee is mighty; he will save, he will rejoice over thee with joy; he will rest in his love, he will joy over thee with singing,'* Zephaniah 3:17. *'If we have been his good and faithful servants, He will praise us and tell us to enter into His joy,'* Matthew 25:20, 22.

"The peace in our hearts, which we want and need so badly, comes only from Him! Jesus Christ told His disciples, *'Peace I leave with you, my peace I give unto you, not as the world giveth, give I unto you,'* John 14:27. He prayed that his people might have his joy fulfilled in themselves, John 17:13. *'He prayed that the love wherewith his Father had loved him might be in his people, and he himself in them,'* John 17:26. *'I am one of his people and I testify that his prayer for me has been fulfilled abundantly.'"*

I looked at James. He did not notice me at all. His eyes were riveted on Dr. Johnson, his face dead serious.

"But you have to draw near to him," Dr. Johnson ended, "Christ did not pray for the world at large. You have to be one of his people to receive his peace and joy. Do not be among those to whom he will say in the end, *'Depart from me. You are not of my sheep; my sheep follow me, but you did not. You would not know me, and I never knew you.'* Come to him now while you still can."

12

Dinner at the Barrons; Tired of Uncertainty?

Our pastor gave the altar call. Two people responded. The service ended.

"What did you think of Dr. Johnson, James?" Mrs. Barron asked. We all listened intently as James answered, "What he was and everything he said really spoke to me."

His mother said joyfully, "I am so glad!" Then she turned to my parents and me. "I was sorry Karen couldn't visit us yesterday," she said, "but how about dinner tomorrow evening, Karen? Please let her come," she added entreatingly to my parents. They looked anxiously at each other and reluctantly consented. A time was set for Neva to come and pick me up, and our families separated with friendly parting words between me and the Barrons and brief good-byes to them from my parents.

At first my parents kept a stony silence on our way home. Finally my father grumbled: "That was some comment your James made when his mother asked him what he thought of Dr. Johnson's testimony. 'Everything he said really spoke to me.' Now we really know what he thought about it!" He ended with an ironic chuckle.

"To me it meant he was very impressed by it," I replied, and added, "and Mrs. Barron understood it that way too. That's why she was glad about his answer."

"Hmm. Poor Mrs. Barron—she has learned to be satisfied with very little," my father said, shaking his head. After a little while he mused aloud, "Maybe that's how you answer questions about your opinions when you have studied philosophy. No simple yes, what I heard was good, or no, it wasn't. Always leave yourself a way to swing one way or the other after you have thought it out, or worse, depending on who you are talking to." After another little pause he added, "Or else they don't waffle around like this on purpose. Maybe they can't ever be certain about anything if they leave God out of their thinking, as James does. They can't help it."

We reached home soon afterwards and stopped talking about James and philosophy.

The next day I visited with several old girl friends from high school and church. In the late afternoon Neva picked me up in the nearly brand new car her parents had given her for her high school graduation. I mentally compared my modest second hand car paid for by my parents and myself just before I set out for Battle Hill University to it, and of course to James' dashing sports car acquired when he entered graduate school. Yes, as my father had pointed out, the Barrons were very wealthy, and we Margraves were not.

Soon we sat around the table in the Barrons' dining room, just as we had many times while Neva and I went to school together. However, it was different for two reasons. First, I was there no longer merely there as Neva's friend but as James' girl friend as well; and second, Tom Barron was present with us tonight and greeted me jovially. Lucinda did her best to make me feel accepted and comfortable, warmly assisted by Neva and Robert, but James was saying little and seemed prepared for some sort of unpleasantness. I remembered his prediction that his father would laugh and make crude jokes about my trying to win him, James, to Christianity. He wants to be ready to defend me, I thought and was pleased. However, nothing disturbing happened except a prolonged coughing spell wracking Tom toward the end of the meal. It was my first intimation of the lethal illness which was beginning to ravage him. I noticed Lucinda's look of deep concern and felt sorry for them both. All the wealth and luxury they possessed paled before the trial ahead.

After dinner we moved to the Barrons' living room. James suggested that I play a piece or two on their grand piano. "Play that lovely one by Schumann you played at your last recital," he asked. To his family he added, "She is a wonderful pianist. I have listened to her play many times. It's been one of the good things in my life this past school year." So I took my place at the piano and played Schumann's famous "Traeumerei," and afterwards the beautiful first movement of Beethoven's "Moonlight Sonata." The family applauded after each piece. I returned to my seat at James' side.

"You are good enough to become a concert pianist!" said Neva admiringly, "Have you thought of that?"

"No," I answered, "I am majoring in music education. I'll teach music in high school like my father does. It will be much easier on me than practicing the piano day and night as a concert pianist must."

"And it'll leave you time to get married and raise a family, huh?" said Tom. He said it good-naturedly, but I felt my face get red and was at a loss for an answer. After all, Tom knew that the man I might marry was his eldest son!

James came to my rescue quickly. "And a very good reason, too, for not becoming a concert pianist," he said, putting his hand on mine. Tom said under his breath, and not good-naturedly this time, "He's got it badly, hasn't he!" There was an uncomfortable silence. Finally Lucinda began to speak of something else.

After a little more conversation with the family, James said he would take me on a little drive and then home. "And don't get lost on the way," his father said jokingly and winked at me while James frowned and hurried me away. He drove off with me, in charge as usual, and headed for Lonely Prairie's beautiful Riverside Park. He parked close to a bench near the river. We walked to it hand in hand and sat down. Tall city lamps were spreading a golden light which sent sparkles across the rippling water. The sunset was still glowing red on the western horizon, and the first stars twinkled in the dark sky. James put his arm around me and I leaned my head against his shoulder. This is so good, I thought, and then, if only it could last! If only James could become a Christian!

"Your visit went quite well," James said. "You mustn't mind my father. He wanted me to marry the rich daughter of one of his rich friends, and now it looks like that won't happen. On the other hand, my mother couldn't be happier about us."

"My own father and mother would side with your father," I said. "You are not a Christian, and you are becoming a professional philosopher." A memory struck me, and I chuckled. "My father said a funny thing last night on the way home from church. He didn't like your answer to your mother about what you thought about Dr. Johnson's talk. 'He really spoke to me' wasn't good enough for him. He said that perhaps philosophers waffle as they do because they leave God out of their thinking and must therefore always be uncertain about everything."

After a moment James asked, "Did your father ever study philosophy?"

"No," I answered, "but there is a verse in the Bible he has been thinking about a lot lately, Colossians 2:8: *'Beware lest any man spoil you through philosophy and vain deceit, after the tradition of men, after the rudiments of the world, and not after Christ.'* He has heard or read enough about philosophy to know that not all philosophers teach the same principles, while the Bible teaches the same from start to finish."

"It's amazing to me," James said thoughtfully, "that he could know about the uncertainty of philosophers. I thought only people who have studied philosophy would understand that. Your father is quite right. We modern would-be philosophers can never state anything with absolute certainty! Did you know that John Dewey said that every statement of truth, to be really true, must contain a reference to its own opposite?"

"No, I didn't know that," I said, "and I am sure neither did my father. It seems completely absurd to me. How in the world can anyone believe that?"

"You not only can but must," James answered wearily, "if you believe this is the only world there is, that it arose by evolution, and that all things are always in continuous flux or change. It's not really new, you know. It goes back to ancient Greece, even before Socrates. Heraclitus put it this way, 'You can't bathe in the same river twice.' Nothing remains the same. Therefore there is no such thing as absolute truth in this world. Therefore we must always be tentative in what we say." He added with a sigh, "At times I get very tired of it all."

We sat in silence again for a while. The remnants of the sunset had vanished from the western sky. Then James hugged me more closely and said: "I was very impressed by Dr. Johnson's talk last night."

"I knew it!" I exclaimed joyfully.

James went on, "It was the best witness to Christianity I have ever heard. No one can gainsay such a testimony of joy and peace from someone who has been through so much."

"That's right," I agreed happily, "and he isn't the only one. There are many more testimonies like Dr. Johnson's. Think of Fanny Crosby, blind since childhood, who wrote many songs of great joy...."

I could feel James shaking his head. He interrupted, "There is just one problem. How do we know Dr. Johnson and all these others got their joy and peace from God? They say so. They believe it, but that doesn't confirm it's true. Isn't there a famous scientist or philosopher who actually met God and wrote it down right when it happened?"

"There is the Apostle Paul on the road to Damascus," I suggested.

But again James shook his head. "That experience can be accounted for without bringing in God. Paul, or rather Saul, felt guilty after having helped stone Stephen to death," he said. "He needed to feel forgiven. That's how Rev. Brassfield used to explain away the 'Damascus experience' in my confirmation class. 'Conversion is only a psychological event,' he said. That may have been reductionist thinking. It could be refuted by the testimony of an experience with God no one could explain away."

"So you want a testimony of a scientist or philosopher's actual meeting with God which nobody could explain away," I repeated slowly. "I'll try to find it for you."

"If you find it," he said, "it might bring me to the place where you want me to be."

13

Swenson Books; George MacPherson; The Pascal Memorial

The remainder of spring break passed uneventfully, in part because James was diligently working on a term paper about the English philosopher Thomas Hobbes.

From what little he told me about him, and from other information I had already learned in my class with Dr. Freeman, I knew that this man's work was one more link in the ideological chain leading from "the serpent at Eden" to the existentialism of the 1960s. I began to see that my mission to convert James to Christ was not merely confronting James' own unbelief but the influence of many other past and present godless thinkers. My heart sank at the thought that I might have to study them one at a time and come up with weighty arguments against them. I was not up to such a task! What weariness, what revulsion to even contemplate it! James himself had said that at times he himself got very tired of it all.

But what he actually got tired of was not so much the work itself, the endless reading, digesting, summarizing and abstracting the important points for himself and his teaching, remembering and reformulating them in term papers, lectures, seminars, conferences, one on one tutoring and articles for philosophical journals. What he got tired of at times was the uncertainty of all he read and wrote. I suddenly felt great pity for him. "What a torture," I whispered to myself, "never to be certain about anything!"

But also, what an imposture it was to attack certainty in God on the basis of total uncertainty, doubt and speculation! But the imposture might work if one let himself get entangled in it! It had worked with James all too well. It hadn't worked with me yet, but if I got involved in it much more deeply, it very likely would.

It all went back to the serpent at Eden and his doubting question, "Yea, hath God said?" For James in particular, this imposture had begun with questioning biblical creation as the origin of the world and replacing it with evolution. My church and my parents had assured me that evolution was false but had not provided me with evidences against it from science. I thought that such evidences must exist and that someone must have found and described them. I needed to get hold of the descriptions and share them with James.

I also decided that my way of dealing with the philosophical influences on James could not be to study philosophers like Hobbes or Sartre themselves in order to refute them. Doubtless Christians much wiser than I and already familiar with such influences were engaged in the forefront of that battle. For me, thank God, it was easier. I only needed to learn from someone like Dr. Freeman where to draw the line between "godly" or "ungodly" philosophies. There might also be Christian writers whose books I could read to help me. I remembered that George MacPherson had mentioned the works of C. S. Lewis, available at Swenson Books, his family's bookstore. Perhaps I could read one or two of these and pass them on to James.

Of course I would also do the best I could to find the testimony whose parameters James had laid down for me, a record written down by a scientist or philosopher of his encounter with God right while it was happening. Upon sober thought I felt I would never find such a testimony. Weren't all testimonies written down after the events, not in the midst of them? How rash I had been to tell James I would try! I prayed God would help me succeed in this quest.

When classes began again after spring break I approached Dr. Freeman and asked him whether he knew of such a testimony, and if not, where I might look for it. He asked me whether I was looking for it for myself or a friend. I said it was for a friend whom I hoped to help believe in God, who had said such a testimony might bring him there.

Dr. Freeman did not know of any such testimony but was less pessimistic than I about the possibility that it might exist. "That is the beauty about our Lord's providence," he said. "He gives us what we truly need at the right time. If your friend truly needs it, God will provide the testimony he asks for." After a moment of thought he added compassionately, "Of course your friend may refuse to believe in God even if such a testimony should turn up. He seems to be of a very philosophical turn of mind. If you will forgive me, he may find a way to reason himself out of obeying the terms he himself has set for coming to the faith."

Then Dr. Freeman suggested I visit Swenson Books and ask about the possibility of finding the testimony I was looking for, and also about literature on worldviews by Christian authors. "All too few Christians are in the market for such books nowadays," he said. "How thankful I am for these few, and so, I am sure, are the good people at Swenson Books. I wish you success with your search, and if by good providence you should find the testimony you are looking for, let me know." I thanked him and promised I would.

The next afternoon I made my way to Swenson Books, located close to the campus in a majestic, rambling house of Victorian vintage. I walked through the door with its glass panel bearing an old-fashioned etching of a stylized rose and came into a large, somewhat shadowy room with high ceilings, dark wood floors, densely crowded with tall, full book shelves. There was a cozy section with upholstered benches and a large table beneath a wide bay window in the far corner; a middle-aged man in jeans and flannel shirt and a well-dressed lady sat there reading. Between several book cases were narrow hallways leading to other parts of the ground floor. A staircase, its wall decorated with pleasing old-fashioned engravings, led to the second floor. A sign pointing upstairs read "Fiction and Used Books." Lovely classical radio music played very softly in the background. I loved it all at first sight.

A tall young man came to meet me and asked if he could help me find something. We instantly recognized each other. "George MacPherson!" and "We met after that lecture on utilitarianism!" we exclaimed at the same time. We shook hands like long-lost friends and smiled at each other. He was very different from James, not quite as tall but broader, sturdier, his hair dark blond, his eyes light blue. I introduced myself and explained what I was looking for.

And wonder of wonders, George knew right away how to help me! "What you need," he said immediately, "is the 'Pascal Memorial.' It is exactly what your friend asked for."

"What is the 'Pascal Memorial'?" I asked, hardly daring to believe my search had been so short and easy.

"It is the record Blaise Pascal, a great French scientist of the seventeenth century, wrote of his meeting with the Lord," George answered. "Come with me, and you can read it for yourself." He led the way through one of the narrow hallways to a different part of the store. There he went to a tall bookshelf labeled "Philosophy and Religion: France," pulled down a certain book and opened it to a page in the middle.

"Here we are," he said. "Read this page. This is the 'Pascal Memorial'." I took the book from him, and this is what I read:

The Year of Grace 1654
Monday, November 23
From about half past ten in the evening
till about half past midnight
FIRE
God of Abraham God of Isaac God of Jacob
Not the God of philosophers and learned men
Certitude Certitude Feeling joy peace
God of Jesus Christ
Forgetfulness of the world and of all save God
He is only to be found through the Gospel
Greatness of the human soul
Joy Joy Joy Tears of Joy
I have separated from Him
My God wilt Thou leave me
Let me not be separated from Him eternally
This is eternal life knowing Thee the only true God
And Him Whom Thou hast sent Jesus Christ John 17:3
Jesus Christ
Jesus Christ
I have separated from Him I have run away from Him
I have denied Him crucified Him
May I never be separated from Him
He is only to be kept through the Gospel
Total and sweet renunciation
Total surrender to Jesus Christ and to my director
Eternally joyful
for one single day of renunciation on earth!

When I had finished reading, George explained: "The original copy of the 'Pascal Memorial' was a single sheet of paper. It was found sewn in a seam of Pascal's coat after he died in 1662. The words are jotted down unevenly, without further clarification or elaboration, just as they would be if they are notes he tried to make of the experience in the midst of the experience itself.

"Pascal was a great French mathematician, physicist, inventor and writer. His major work, besides scientific treatises, was the *Pensees,* a defense of the Christian faith, published after his death and still prized today."

I thanked him and asked him to make me three photocopies of the Pascal Memorial. I could not resist asking him, "How did you know so quickly it was what I needed?"

"I found it about a year ago and have read it many times since then," George answered, "because I saw that when Pascal confessed he had separated from Christ, run away from Him, denied and crucified him, God came to him and gave him so much joy. It was the same with me when I became a Christian."

14

A Conditional Marriage Proposal

I could not wait to see James and give him a copy of the Pascal Memorial the next day after my class with Dr. Freeman. Of course before leaving the classroom I took the time to give a copy of the Memorial to Dr. Freeman as well. He was surprised and pleased that I had found it so quickly, read it then and there with evident joy and heartily thanked me for it. "I will share it with our class, too," he said. "It may help other students besides your friend. It does indeed seem to be exactly what your friend wanted."

We walked together to the classroom exit, where "my friend" was already waiting for me. I was about to introduce him to Dr. Freeman but remembered in time that they must already know each other, and how intensely James disliked "Saint Francis." Dr. Freeman, of course, immediately understood the situation. He said, "Oh hello, James," to me, "So James is your friend? I hope he realizes how fortunate he is to know you," and quickly walked away.

As soon as I was alone with James, I excitedly told him I had found the testimony about meeting God he had wanted. We walked to a bench by the sidewalk near the building and sat down together. I quickly opened my knapsack, pulled out the second copy of the Pascal Memorial and held it out to James. He was visibly taken aback and hesitated to take it from my hand, but finally did grasp and read it. Then he stared straight ahead into the distance without a word, his face somber.

It was certainly not the reaction I had hoped for. I was painfully disappointed. But what reaction could I reasonably have expected? Doubtless I had indulged in wishful thinking and foolishly looked forward to his instant surrender to God upon receiving so quickly the testimony of a famous scientist's meeting with God, which he himself had asked for. Memories of movies made for the Christian market I had watched and Christian romance novels I had avidly read in my teens flashed through my mind. In those stories the unbeliever was always converted to Christ in the end thanks to the faithful witness of his beloved. That was the standard plot of Christian fiction, and I had fondly imagined it was God's plot for James and me in real life. But was it? My father had rightly told me that God did not need me to bring James to Himself; He could do that by other means and in His own perfect timing. It need not be right now; it might well be later, even much later, and was possible as long as James lived.

However, all that was an overall principle, but James and I sat here right now and I must do something! "Well, James?" I prodded, "what's your answer to the Pascal Memorial? It's exactly what you wanted to have, isn't it?"

"I didn't think you could put your hands on something like this so quickly," James said dully, still not looking at me.

"I didn't think so either," I agreed excitedly, "at first I thought it would be impossible to find a testimony according to your specifications! I was sorry I had promised you to look for it! But actually it turned out to be easy. Can you believe it? It was at the second place where I asked." I babbled on happily as I recalled my visit to Swenson Books and with George MacPherson, "It was at Swenson Books. Dr. Freeman recommended it to me. The clerk—or rather, a member of the family which owns Swenson Books—immediately knew what I needed and got it for me. I was so glad! And here it is. And you had better tell me what you think of it right now!"

James finally turned his head and looked at me. "I think it is very impressive," he said slowly, "very impressive. It does seem to be exactly the kind of record I wanted to see."

Suddenly there was a torment in his face and eyes I had never seen there before. He spoke in a low voice: "I love you so much it hurts. I think of you all the time. You are before me while I teach, write, speak, do research, and seeing you makes it all seem false and useless. I embraced evolution and the uncertainty it brought to my worldview because it freed me from all moral rules and concerns, and especially from my mother's Jesus. Then you came into my life. I fell in love with you at first sight on that sidewalk near the cafeteria on September 16, 1964, and in you my mother's Jesus confronts me more strongly than ever and makes that uncertainty, which I loved and prized so much, unbearable. What do you think it does to me to read Pascal's jubilant 'certitude, certitude, feeling joy peace'? Don't you understand how it draws me away from all my present life to that joy he had—that you have?" He broke off and abruptly turned his face away; I thought he was near tears.

"Oh James," I said, near tears myself, "I love you, too! Surely you know that. It's just that—just that—your philosophy. . ." My voice trailed away. He knew all too well what was on my mind.

He turned around to me, took both my hands in his and said, "I have thought many times of asking you to marry me. But I knew you would say no because of my philosophy. Suppose I asked you whether you would marry me if I gave up my philosophy and either exchanged it for a Christian philosophy like that of Saint Francis—I mean Dr. Freeman," he smiled apologetically, "or some other profession altogether. Would you say yes then?"

My whole heart was longing for him as I answered: "Not 'if' but 'when,' James. *When* you have done this—*when* you have given up your philosophy and turned to God and Christ as Pascal did, *then* if you asked me whether I would marry you, I would say yes. But not before."

I was determined to step up my unremitting efforts to help James become a believer, now that he seemed more open than ever before. True, he never came to deal properly with the Pascal Memorial, which was intensely disappointing and discouraging for me. I asked him again once or twice what he thought of it. Finally he said, not looking at me, "Philosophy has a very hard time dealing with experience." I thought then, and still think so now, that this statement was a declaration of the fundamental bankruptcy of every philosophy whose starting point is man, not God, for man's whole life is experience. For James this statement was also the ultimate cop-out to extricate himself from the implications of a testimony he himself had asked for.

It dawned on me only now, blinded as I had been by being in love with him, that he had probably specified the parameters of that testimony *on purpose* in such a way that no such testimony could ever be found. Yes, it must be so! That is why he had been so baffled and reluctant to take the copy of the Pascal Memorial from my hand when I gave it to him.

But there were other ways to witness to him of the God whom he tried so hard to keep at arm's length even while tempted to accept Him for my sake. During the remaining weeks of the semester, I often visited Swenson Books and spent hours reading books by C. S. Lewis in that comfortable little nook by the bay window. I discussed them with George MacPherson, who went out of his way to be available for me. I could tell he was becoming interested in me, and I sometimes caught myself thinking how much easier and better it would be for me if he were the man I loved and might marry rather than James. We were both Christians, close in age, background and interests, and the longer we knew each other, the more we saw how much we had in common. The dark, awful obstacle of James' hostile, active unbelief and self-absorption which weighed so heavily on me in our relationship was totally absent in George. George was *reliable,* to me the character trait indispensable in a man. And he was handsome too in his own way, with his honest, open face, his broad shoulders, the guileless simplicity, strength and trustworthiness written all over him.

I thought that from the beginning I had been attracted by James' looks, his tall, slender body, his dark hair and eyes, his well-shaped, intelligent face. A Bible verse struck me, *"The LORD seeth not as man seeth; for man looketh on the outward appearance, but the LORD looketh on the heart."* 1 Samuel 16:7. Now I saw that I still did not really know his heart, the real innermost man. Why had he said that loving me so much hurt him? Now I understood: it hurt him because his love for me warred against and wounded his self-love.

I began to use more Bible verses in our conversations. I told James many stories I had heard or read of men who turned from atheism to Christ. C. S. Lewis, whom I now knew as the twentieth century "apostle to the skeptics," had been a philosophically minded atheist before he turned to Christ in his early thirties. He described his conversion in his autobiography *Surprised by Joy.* John Newton, who wrote the well-known hymn "Amazing Grace, how sweet the sound/that saved a wretch like me," had been a godless slave dealer who came to Christ, abandoned his trade, and served Him faithfully the rest of his life. General Lew Wallace, an atheist who studied the evidences for Christ's life and death in order to reject Him, accepted Him instead and wrote the world-famous novel *Ben Hur* to honor Him. I told James of Vladimir Solovyov and Henri Bergson whom Dr. Freeman had mentioned in his class. There were many more.

James heard me out patiently but often absent-mindedly. I could tell that something else increasingly preoccupied him. When the semester ended, he still had not come to the faith.

15
"Either God or a Bad Man"

Toward the end of the spring semester James told me excitedly and with unconcealed pride that thanks to his faculty advisor's recommendation he had been chosen to teach a short summer course on "objectivism," the brand-new atheist-individualist philosophy of a popular writer named Ayn Rand. "I'll have plenty of preparation to do," he said, "the woman propagates her thought system chiefly by thick novels, none of which I have ever read. They have become bestsellers, especially among very intelligent young students. Dr. Berger wants me to find out and teach why. She says that if I do a good job this summer, I may well be asked to teach this course and others like it at other top universities later on."

He looked away from me into the distance when he resumed slowly: "What I will concentrate on in my academic work from now on is to study the very latest trends in philosophy, evaluate them, and present them with the right slant to students and opinion leaders in America and perhaps the whole world. I will be on the cutting edge of my profession. This summer course is preparing me for my future place of leadership just as I imagined it when I first understood the full meaning of evolution years ago in high school."

I was very disturbed by James' vision of his future. "It all sounds very exciting and ambitious, James," I pleaded, "but it would be completely opposed to what you need to do if you are serious about," I plunged bravely ahead, "us getting married. And even if I were not in the picture, please remember one thing before you go ahead with your plan to become a world leader."

"What's that?" James asked with an edge of anger.

"Without God in your heart, all your worldly fame and prestige would amount to nothing in the end. In Jesus Christ's words, what shall it profit a man if he shall gain the whole world, and lose his own soul? Or what shall a man give in exchange for his soul?"

"That's what my mother used to say to me repeatedly," James said icily, "she majored in trying to frighten me with the eternal damnation of my soul." He saw the sadness in my face and added more gently, but also with a touch of weariness and annoyance, "If you want to win me to your God, little Karen, stick with telling me of the peace and joy you think he gives. And quit throwing all those failed atheists at me as you have done these last few weeks! It's just another form of the false argument from consent."

"No, it is not," I answered, "it is a collection of the records of many individual experiences like Pascal's, all leading to God and Christ. Maybe not all of them speak to you, but some should. For example, couldn't you follow General Lew Wallace's example and study the evidences for Christ's life and death with an open mind."

"I was already doing that at First United Church," James interrupted me with sudden eagerness, "and especially in Rev. Brassfield's confirmation class. I came away from there believing Christ was a great human teacher, but not God. I could still go along with that view today if necessary. I wish you could, too! How about it? It would solve our whole problem!"

For a brief moment his suggestion tempted me. Why not go along with it? Why persist in this everlasting controversy about Jesus Christ with the man I loved and who loved me? Could I not give a little ground over a point of human theology to bring us together?

I wonder what might have happened if by then I had not yet read C. S. Lewis's *Mere Christianity* and discussed it with George. "C. S. Lewis says," I countered, "that what you just said about Jesus is the one thing we must not say." I summed up Lewis's argument from memory as best I could: "He says that a man who was only a man and said what Jesus said about himself would be either a lunatic or the Devil of Hell. Either Jesus was and is the Son of God, or else crazy, or a demon. You can shut him up in an insane asylum, or kill him, or worship him as your Lord and your God, but don't ever call him a great human teacher. He has not left that open to us. He did not intend to."

James looked disappointed. Only after a minute or two did he comment soberly, "It's a form of the old argument for Christ's deity first used by St. Augustine: *Ut Deus ut malus homo*—either God or a bad man. How interesting that it can still serve a modern defender of Christianity! I'll think about it." One of his typical noncommittal put-offs, I thought sadly. However, I knew I had answered him rightly, and my plan to continue weekly readings at Swenson Books was reinforced by this interchange.

Because of our full schedules both of us decided to remain on campus all summer, except for the weekends which we would usually spend visiting our families. My visits with my parents were somewhat strained but easier than when I had first told them about James and myself, because I had kept them fully informed about our continuing relationship. They made no secret of the fact that they kept opposing it and worried about me deeply and constantly. My father was especially upset about James' first demanding a testimony like the Pascal Memorial and then rejecting it when confronted with it. "That shows you can't trust him, Karen," he kept repeating.

Both my parents were aghast about our agreement about James' marriage proposal and my acceptance of it "not if but when" he became a Christian. "And when will that be?" my father demanded glumly. My mother told me she was praying for James to become a Christian and for me to marry a good Christian man, "not necessarily James but someone else," she emphasized. On the other hand, Lucinda Barron, Robert and Neva did all they could to bring our relationship to a happy fruition. During the weekends I always had at least one and usually two meals with the Barrons. By the end of the summer even Tom had come to accept my presence there as more or less normal.

Several times Mrs. Barron and Neva met with me alone to counsel with me about how to win James to the faith. Mrs. Barron pointed out that the issue of evolution versus biblical creation lay at the root of James' unbelief and needed to be addressed. "There must be more scientific information against evolution now than I had when James was still in high school," she said, "I have checked with Grace Baptist Church, but their library is small and had nothing on that topic. Of course everything in the public library supports evolution." I promised to look for helpful information the next time I visited Swenson Books.

On another occasion Neva once again urged me to talk to James about prayer. I had naturally shared much more about him with her, my best friend and his sister, than with Mrs. Barron. She listened to me with complete sympathy, grieved with me over her brother's atheistic philosophy and rejoiced over his love for me. She believed it was genuine because "you are the first girl friend he has kept bringing home with him regularly," because "he is still with you after almost a year," and because of "the way he looks at you—just like David looks at me." Neva glowed as she spoke of her own young man, David Ploughman from our church, her future husband.

Finally and, she felt, most importantly, James had never tried to be intimate with me. "I am sure that's a first for him," she said, "and I am sure that's why he broke up quickly with all his other girls. He got all he wanted—a one-night stand—and they were stupid enough to let him charm them into it. It's different with you. He wants to be with you all his life."

"He'll have to become a Christian to make that happen," I said, "I mean a Christian like your mother, Robert, you and I, not like at First United Church." I told Neva what James had said to me about the teaching about Christ he had received from Rev. Brassfield, that he thought he could live with it and wondered whether I might accept it too in order to eliminate the problem between us.

"And you can't do that," Neva agreed. She broke out passionately: "Who would know that better than Mother, Robert and I? We can't communicate with our dad or James. They think our faith is just an illusion, an emotional binge, or an opinion we could take or leave, when it is our life, our foundation, our guide for living our lives step by step, day by day."

Robert had come in and overheard his sister's last words. He added sadly, "It's true, Karen. My father and my brother dislike my mother, Neva and me as legalistic, judgmental kill-joys. We pray for them and pity them as lost and blind, living only for what will perish in the end—like treasure hunters out for glass beads instead of diamonds. We are all unhappy with each other. You know how it is between James and Mother! And it would be the same for James and you if you married him as he now is. That's why the Scripture tells us, 'Be not unequally yoked together with unbelievers.' It's forbidden not only because God wants to keep His people uncontaminated, but because He wants us to share in His joy and peace. His law and His love are one and the same thing."

16

The Ayn Rand Lecture and Dr. Berger

It turned out that I had free time on the morning James was to begin teaching his short course on Ayn Rand, and he invited me to sit in on the introductory session. He had not been joking earlier when speaking of Rand's "thick novels"! He had shown them to me before, and I had both admired and felt sorry for him for having to read and analyze them all at relatively short notice. As we walked to the classroom together, I saw that he was confident, even exhilarated about his imminent task, like a student about to take an important test for which he is well prepared and knows he will ace. He told me Dr. Berger might be there to observe how he taught the class. "She will not be disappointed," he said nonchalantly, taking it for granted.

There were some forty students in the classroom, mostly clean-shaven young men dressed conventionally, but also a sprinkling of bearded hippies, a few plain, studious-looking young women, and two or three girls with no makeup, long unkempt hair and wearing the popular embroidered bell-bottom jeans of the sixties. Dr. Berger was there, wearing one of her black pantsuits, sitting in the back with an open notebook on the student desk in front of her. I sat down somewhere in the center with a good view of James, who strode toward the platform with its teacher's lectern and a table. A huge blackboard was on the wall behind it. James laid out the books on the table and spread out some notes on the lectern. My heart skipped a beat, for he looked exactly as he had when we first met, very handsome in his long-sleeved white shirt open at the neck and black slacks.

The bell rang, the students sat up, and James introduced himself and began his lecture. From the beginning he had his audience with him, speaking with obvious inward engagement but also clearly and slowly so no one had trouble following him. When not occasionally refreshing his memory from his lecture notes he looked all over the room to make eye contact with the students. He often left the lectern to walk back and forth or to come closer to his audience. From time to time he wrote notes on the blackboard in print easy to read. Clearly the students loved him! I thought his presentation method was masterful, stole a quick look at Dr. Berger in the back and saw from her smiling face that she thought so too. I remember the lecture well, and here are its main points.

James began with a biographical sketch of Ayn Rand, born Alice Rosenbaum in St. Petersburg, Russia in 1905, immigrant to America in 1925, married to Frank O'Connor and childless. He listed her best-selling novels *We the Living, Anthem, The Fountainhead* and *Atlas Shrugged,* all written to preach her philosophy known as "Objectivism." James made clear that he would discuss Rand's philosophy behind her novels rather than their literary merits.

He stated next that Rand's novels appealed chiefly to very intelligent young people because such people were often harassed in school by their inferiors due to their superior performance. There were many nods of agreement among the audience; James was evidently on the right track. An additional factor for Rand's popularity among this group was that Rand's heroes were people of genius and she condemned less gifted people who did not willingly accept the leadership of their intellectual betters.

"Perhaps the most important reason for Rand's appeal to very intelligent people," he continued, "is her basic belief that human reason should be man's," he smiled at the girls in the class, "or woman's only basis for making decisions. Rand's 'objectivism' is indeed 'for the new intellectual,' the title of one of her non-fiction books."

As James listed the books, he lifted them up and wrote their titles on the board. "As some of you already know," he continued, "*We the Living* is set in Soviet Russia after 1917. *Anthem* is a utopia where individuals exist wholly for the collective, bear numbers rather than names, and have even lost the knowledge of the word 'I' until one heroic young rebel rediscovers it. *The Fountainhead* pits individualism against collectivism in America through the struggle of Howard Roark, a brilliant architect, against the forces of evil personified in the journalist Ellsworth Toohey and the parasitic 'second-hander' Peter Keating. Its totally unconventional heroine, Dominique Francon, seeks to destroy both her lover Roark and herself because she cannot bear the thought that they must live in a world ignoring their worth." James smiled at his audience as he added, "You might be interested in watching the movie made from *The Fountainhead,* featuring famous actor Gary Cooper, the heroic sheriff of 'High Noon,' in the role of Howard Roark."

He then described the plot of *Atlas Shrugged,* Rand's latest, most important novel, with its hero John Galt, an inventor leading a strike against collectivism by brilliant, noble industrialists practicing a morality of rational self-interest. "In a way, all you need to read of *Atlas Shrugged,"* James hefted up the heavy volume in his left hand, "is John Galt's long speech about his philosophy, or rather Ayn Rand's, toward the end of the book. Come to think of it," he added, "that's true of other Ayn Rand novels, too. Howard Roark makes a long speech in his defense toward the end of *The Fountainhead* which tells you the book's ideological basis and purpose. Kira Argounova and Andrei Taganov in *We the Living* do the same. Forgive me a bit of literary critique: in *We the Living* the characters are still real people, while those of the later novels seem mere artificial constructs to personify Rand's ideas."

James went on to give capsule descriptions of Rand's major ideas. He reported that Rand championed untrammeled laissez-faire economics with due esteem and material rewards for men of creative genius, for her the fountainhead of man's progress and prosperity. A passionate atheist, she believed that the concept of God was degrading to man because a perfect God would be above man and a reproach to him. "Rand thinks each man is his own god," James ended, "she makes this quite clear already in her early novel *Anthem,* whose hero proclaims at the end that he sees the face of god, which is 'this one word: I.'"

Finally he turned to some problems with Rand's philosophy as he saw them. One was her starting point, Aristotle's A=A, the law of identity. "I believe she does not go back far enough to the matter of origins," he said, "according to evolution, all things are in a process of change. This may require additional discussion." A second problem was Rand's hero John Galt's consideration of suicide as escape from an intolerable quandary in *Atlas Shrugged.* Was that really rational? Could suicide ever be considered a victory?

A third problem was Rand's approval of rape in a major scene between Howard Roark and Dominique Francon in *The Fountainhead.* "Can or should Rand's 'morality of rational self-interest' sanction rape?" James asked. "This, too, may be a subject we will discuss in our course. I myself, like Rand, do not believe in God and reject the entire 'old morality' of rules and regulations. But I admit I draw the line at rape," he smiled, "perhaps because I haven't ever found it necessary when making love." The audience chuckled, and the girls among them looked with pleasure at their handsome young instructor. James ended his lecture, "As the Haight-Ashbury flower children have been telling us: 'Let's make love, not war,' and I say, let's begin with our love-making itself!"

The whole audience spontaneously applauded. James gave the class homework for the next day, a short paper on one of the possible problems with Rand's philosophy, and gathered up his notes and the Rand books as he visited with several students who stopped by the table and enthusiastically praised him. I felt sure all his listeners would be back the next day and every day of the course's ten. His introductory lecture had been a complete success.

By now Dr. Berger had made her way to us. This was the first time I saw her up close. She seemed about thirty years old and was, I thought with a touch of pity, rather unattractive and unfeminine. Her washed-out dark blonde hair was cropped short and somewhat untidy; her sharp blue eyes scrutinized me through rimless glasses and her thin lips were pressed together in cold, unfriendly appraisal. Except for the soft pale skin of her round face and the bulge of her breast beneath her severe black suit jacket she might have been a short, somewhat stocky man. As James introduced us to each other, I sensed a wave of hostility from her hit me, and I shuddered. He must have felt it, too, for his mood, still exultant after his successful lecture, became sober, even subdued.

"I hope you were satisfied with my presentation, Dr. Berger," he said respectfully, every inch the dutiful student to his powerful professor.

"It was outstanding, James," she replied without hesitation. She spoke matter-of-factly and firmly, leaving no doubt that this was indeed her judgment and that it was as it were carved in stone. James took a deep breath of relief. Dr. Berger went on in the same tone: "I had no doubt you would do well—you are by far the best graduate student our philosophy department has had in years, maybe ever."

She started walking toward the exit, beckoning James to follow her, with me trailing behind them, and said, "I have already contacted colleagues I know in the philosophy departments of Harvard, Yale, Columbia and of course Herbert Spencer University, my alma mater. An invitation to teach this Ayn Rand course for them is bound to come from one or several of them soon. Another contemporary philosopher you might look at for future teaching projects is Herbert Marcuse, or perhaps that unorthodox Freudian professor at Nebraska Wesleyan University, Norman O. Brown."

By now we were leaving the classroom and walking along the hallway. James looked back quickly, almost furtively, to see where I was. I accelerated my steps to catch up with him. Dr. Berger stopped walking and looked at us. Again I felt her hostility, cold and malevolent, toward me.

"You have the chance of a lifetime, James," she said to James. "Don't blow it. I'll see you in my office after lunch." She nodded to us dismissively and walked quickly away.

17

Studying with George; Agonizing over James; The Problem of Knowledge Solved

James and I met for lunch as we now did every day. I praised the way he had delivered his Ayn Rand lecture but had reservations about some of his comments afterwards, especially about Rand's approval of rape. James became thoughtful.

"Perhaps technically it wasn't rape," he mused, "because Dominique Francon *wanted* to be forcefully taken and shamed. What I said about it was cute but superficial. There is something deeper about that scene which nags at me. That's one of the troubles with philosophical analysis—you always worry that you haven't gone deep enough." He sighed tiredly. "It's one of the things that bothers me about doing philosophy all my life."

"Dr. Berger expects you to," I said. He sighed again.

"I know," he answered, "she has invested a great deal of time and effort in grooming me for future leadership. It means a lot to her personally to see me succeed. That makes me uncomfortable sometimes, especially when thinking of, well, leaving it all."

"She must suspect somehow that you are thinking of that," I said. "That's why she told you this morning not to blow your chance of a lifetime."

James nodded. In sudden recognition I exclaimed, "And that's why she didn't like me! She understood that I might come between you and a career in philosophy."

James pushed away his half-eaten lunch. "I noticed that she didn't like you," he said, "and I think you are right about the reason. She has warned me that I shouldn't think of dating seriously as it would distract me from my work. She has a point," he grinned. "You may draw me away from it entirely!"

He became serious again. "In fact," he said softly, "I am torn day and night between you and going on doing philosophy. Why give it up? Take my lecture this morning. I loved everything about it, the rush of adrenaline, contact with the students, being in charge and in the limelight, even the pressure on me to do well! I wouldn't mind doing this again and again all my life and influencing all society besides. On the other hand, how can I stop seeing you? I can't even think of it."

We turned to some lighter talk and left, James for his meeting with Dr. Berger, I to visit Swenson Books to go over C. S. Lewis's daunting *The Abolition of Man* with George MacPherson. I also wanted to talk with him about James' problems with Rand's philosophy. I had no doubt that George would have good answers for me from the Christian perspective and hastened to meet him.

The rambling old building of Swenson Books had become a sort of second home to me by now. George was waiting for me inside. "Let's go to our special coffee-and-snack room for our customers today instead of the bay window," he said and led the way to a cozy back room filled with the lovely light of the afternoon sunshine streaming through the stained glass windows. There was a big table covered with an embroidered cloth, surrounded by several thickly upholstered old-fashioned chairs. On a sideboard, a large coffee maker was brewing fresh coffee next to a big platter with various kinds of fresh home-made cookies. Pretty little napkins and paper cups were stacked nearby. "My mom made the cookies," George invited, "have some for desert. You must have had lunch already." The aroma of the coffee and the delicious smell of the cookies made my mouth water and I helped myself to both, as did George.

We sat down across from each other at the table, sipped coffee and slowly munched our cookies, without need for words. George looked at me with a smile on his face. I understood that he loved me and wanted to do me only good. Being here with him in this beautiful old place made me feel carefree and relaxed, as when I was a little child visiting my grandparents and eating cookies in their old home in the country.

I could never be that carefree little child again! Instead I was beholden to James Barron and had been agonizing over him for nearly a year. How could he actually feel tortured by having to choose between his philosophy of uncertainty and lawlessness, and me whom he said he loved—or rather, between himself as god, and my God, the God of his good mother, the God giving crippled Dr. Johnson peace and joy, the God of Pascal? How long would he halt between these two choices? How long would I have to wrestle with the tortuous thoughts of John Dewey, utilitarians, existentialists, or Ayn Rand?

And suddenly I burst into tears and wept aloud, shaking with my sobs. George got up, walked around the table and silently put his hands gently around my shoulders from behind till the onslaught of my grief ebbed away. When I was quiet again, he returned to his seat, smiled at me and said calmly, "Let's study C. S. Lewis's *Abolition of Man* now, okay?"

That afternoon I came to understand that what C. S. Lewis called the *Tao* in *The Abolition of Man* was the same as what he called the natural law in *Mere Christianity*. God imprinted this natural law, which reflected His own character, on man's heart when He created him in His own image and likeness. Therefore, we cannot "not know" God's law for us, but rather since listening to "the serpent in Eden" we are "suppressing it in unrighteousness" and *then* do not know it, but not innocently.

My whole confusion about "the problem of knowledge," which had plagued me ever since my very first meeting with James, suddenly dissolved. I could have wept again, but this time with sheer joy, when I finally saw the glorious meaning of biblical creation for human knowledge. Not Descartes' principle that to know anything we must start with doubting everything and with our own thought, not Dewey's and James' uncertainty principle based on evolution, but God Himself and His creation of man in His own image and likeness is the only correct beginning of knowledge and wisdom. *"Of course! 'The fear of the LORD is the beginning of knowledge,'"* I exclaimed.

George smiled and added, "Proverbs 1:7."

Further, there are no other moral laws besides God's own. *The Abolition of Man* taught me that the innovators who would abolish God's laws must use parts of these very laws to establish their various "new moralities," while rejecting other parts. Thus Ayn Rand chose reason over compassion for the poor, the Nazis chose love of one's own race over love of neighbor, and the Communists chose equality of possessions over equality of justice, and so on.

C. S. Lewis also spoke of the future "conditioners," who would be able to abolish man's present nature and to impose a new one on him by eugenics and psychological conditioning. They would completely reject God and His natural law so that only their own will or whim might be done. The thought struck me that James was well fitted by his ambition for leadership and his self-absorbed, lawless philosophy to be one of them. Perhaps Dr. Berger had already recognized this and hence invested her time and efforts "in grooming him for future leadership." C. S. Lewis also cast doubt on evolutionist assumptions in anthropology by saying that all civilizations might well have ultimately come "from a single centre." This last point reminded me of asking George about materials on the scientific problems with evolution, about a possible conflict between the law of identity and evolution, and finally, about how Ayn Rand's approval of suicide and rape fit in with her "morality of rational self-interest."

"Whoa!" George exclaimed, "let's tackle these one at a time. As to scientific materials against evolution, we carry a fairly new book, *The Genesis Flood* by Dr. Henry M. Morris, published in 1961. It is excellent and respected even by evolutionist scientists. I think it will begin a growing movement among Christians with scientific credentials who believe in biblical creation to show how scientifically bankrupt evolution really is. We have other materials as well in the store, a book on the lack of transitional fossils in the fossil record, and a booklet on the fraud of 'Piltdown Man' discovered in 1953." I looked the materials over and bought them for Mrs. Barron.

"As to the law of identity and evolution," George said when this transaction was concluded, "you can see for yourself that there is a problem. Evolution can be defined as continual change of all things, so for a consistent evolutionist nothing can always remain the same. His definition of identity ought to be 'A is not A', which is self-contradictory and therefore logically false. However, a godless person correctly believing in A=A needs to ask where the law of identity comes from since it cannot come from evolution. Only the Creator can design permanent identity for His creatures."

Then we discussed Ayn Rand's "morality of rational self-interest," suicide and rape. "I haven't read any of her books," said George, "can you tell me a little more about the suicide and rape passages in them?" I told him what I had heard from James in his lecture and at lunch. George reflected for a little while. Finally he said, "I have two comments. One, of course neither suicide nor rape have a place in a morality of rational self-interest. How can either of them rationally benefit you? This is all the more true for a woman perverse enough to *want* to be raped! Two, Rand's violation of her own philosophy shows that people cannot even keep the laws they make themselves. Human reason is a very fallible guide! Everybody really knows that. How many people can keep their New Year's resolutions? Even for unbelievers it is true that 'all have sinned and come short of the glory of God.' Only the 'god' they sin against is their own self."

18

"The Problem of Pain"; First Anniversary; The Voice

I shared George's comments about Ayn Rand with James the next day. He was most impressed with what George had said about everyone's breaking the law, including his own law for himself. "It's also very true that human reason is fallible," James agreed, "and that means that if this world is all there is, there is no infallible guide for human action. We must just put up with our errors and their consequences as best we can, or else abandon any laws entirely."

"Or turn to God," I countered. I followed up joyfully with my new understanding of the natural law as imprinted on our hearts at our creation in God's own image and likeness. "We cannot 'not know' God's law," I concluded. "We just don't *want* to know it or God, and that is why we suppress it in unrighteousness."

James laughed. "That's what you told me the first time we met, little Karen," he said teasingly. "Remember? I'll hand it to you—you can defend it much better now instead of just quoting it from the Bible."

I disregarded his put-down and begged him, "Please stop resisting God,

James! Give up your belief in this world as all there is. Forget about evolution! Nothing I or others have said to you so far has convinced you. But there is one more way, and in all honesty you must try it—prayer! Pray! Go directly to God. Tell Him frankly that you don't believe He exists, but that you will if He can show you He is there, and mean it! He will answer you, and all will be well with you, and with us, too."

"I *have* thought of praying many times," James said softly, "my mother's prayers are the only part of her religion I have always respected. I even tried praying once in a while when I was younger, but I never really meant it because I was afraid He might answer me. And then I would know He was there and I would have to obey Him!"

"But He is good and He loves you," I said. "Obeying Him would never harm you."

"Oh no?" James said, suddenly viciously angry. "What about Dr. Johnson, imprisoned in his wheelchair? What about your Blaise Pascal? I found out that he died at only thirty-nine years of age, suffering all his life from excruciating headaches caused by incomplete fusion of his skull bones when he was a baby. What about C. S. Lewis? His mother died of cancer when he was a little boy. His beloved wife Joy died of cancer after only three years of marriage, and he died after years of suffering from severe kidney trouble. You only told me half their stories. You left out their suffering! But suffering—the problem of pain—is probably the most important argument against your 'good, loving' God, His existence or His goodness. What's your answer to it?"

Now this was one issue which we had addressed many times at Grace Baptist Church. We had never believed that Christian believers are exempt from pain, nor that they can simply "name and claim" God's blessings. So I felt able to answer James, and I began, "Sometimes our sufferings are caused by our own wrongdoing. We reap what we sow! Then God allows our sufferings to bring us to our senses so we stop doing wrong."

"Okay," said James disdainfully, "that's the easy part. How about innocent people? What wrong did Pascal do before he was even born?"

"None that I can see," I agreed, "I know many people suffer terribly through no fault of their own. C. S. Lewis wrote about this problem in his book *The Problem of Pain*."

I took a deep breath and went on: "The book of Job in the Bible deals with this question. Job is a good man who worships God. Satan tells God Job only worships Him because of His blessings, but will 'curse Him to His face' if the blessings stop. God allows Satan to take away all Job's children, all his fortune, and finally his health. Job's wife tells him, 'Curse God and die!' None of his friends can comfort him. Job prays that he might speak to God Himself. His prayer is answered! God Himself appears to Job and speaks to him. Job answers, *'I have heard of thee by the hearing of the ear: but now mine eye sees thee. Wherefore I abhor myself, and repent in dust and ashes.'* Job 42:6. Job's suffering was allowed," I ended. "So he could not merely 'hear of God by the hearing of the ear'—as you have,

James—but saw Him, really saw Him in the end. And that is the answer! All Job's sufferings were as nothing compared to seeing our Lord! It was the same for Dr. Johnson—you heard him. It was the same for Pascal—you read his Memorial. Oh James, do as Job did—pray! Yes, when you see Him, you will 'abhor yourself, and repent in dust and ashes,' but then you will have certainty, joy and peace, just like Dr. Johnson, just like Pascal, just like C. S. Lewis. Please, please, pray to Him! Pray to Him right now," I entreated. "If you want to, we can pray together."

"No!" James exploded, "I will not do this under pressure! If I do it, I will do it alone!" He added more calmly, "I promise you I will think about doing it." We were both silent for a little while. When we began to speak again, it was about his upcoming birthday, July 14. "That's France's national holiday," James said, "based on the taking of the Bastille prison in 1789 in the French Revolution. Enlightenment philosophers prepared the way for it, especially Voltaire and Rousseau. It shows you what philosophers can accomplish—the overthrow of a whole social system!" I sadly saw that he was back on the track of his worldly ambition.

During the remainder of the summer James was especially gentle and courteous towards me. When my own birthday arrived in August, he brought me a lovely bouquet of two dozen red roses, to which a little note, "To my little Karen, with all my love, James" was attached. I expected that he would soon choose God and me over philosophy. Only one thing made me worry—James was becoming visibly thinner. His clothes began to hang loosely on his body. His face became gaunt, his cheeks hollow, his eyes seemed sunk in their sockets. When we had meals together, he would push most of his food away unconsumed. His family noticed this too and asked him what was wrong. He said he just didn't have much appetite in the heat of the summer.

But I was sure there was a deeper reason. I dimly sensed that it might be connected with his choice about us. Or perhaps he was concerned about his study plans for the fall and beyond? The next school year would be his last before receiving his master's degree. I dared not ask him for answers because otherwise everything between us seemed to be going so well.

When enrollment began for the fall semester, James informed me that he would spend most of it away from Battle Hill University. "Dr. Berger has arranged for me to teach my Ayn Rand course at Columbia, Yale, Cornell and Herbert Spencer University," he said, "all expenses paid, good honoraria, and excellent publicity in the circles that matter! It counts towards my master's degree and opens my way to my doctorate and then a top teaching position."

"So we won't see much of each other," I said regretfully.

"Yes, that's the only drawback," James nodded, "but I will be here in Battle Hill in mid-September. Let's have an extra-special celebration of our first anniversary, September 16." He said he was making reservations for us now for dinner at Battle Hill's most prestigious restaurant. He seemed preoccupied and less happy about it all than I would have expected, but I gave it little attention. Despite the news about his new intensive teaching schedule I thought that he would tell me at this special celebration that he had prayed, met the Lord, and chosen me over his career.

The evening of September 16, 1965 arrived. James, dressed to the teeth, arrived punctually to pick me up in his elegant sports car. Soon we sat at a lovely table by the window of the luxurious penthouse restaurant with a splendid view of Battle Hill. We had a wonderful meal, but James ate almost none of it. I could not help asking with concern, "Are you not feeling well, James?"

"I am all right," he answered shortly. He sat up straight in his chair and said, "It's over between us, Karen. This is our last time together."

I stared at him, stunned. He went on without looking at me, "I did what you told me that day after the Ayn Rand lecture. I thought about praying. I was about to do it. And then a voice spoke to me in my mind."

"A voice spoke to you?" I whispered.

"A voice spoke to me," he repeated with a far away look; his voice, deeper than usual, seemed not his own. "It said, 'Why the hell are you worrying about prayer? This world is all there is, in perpetual flux, and you can just lie back on it, like a swimmer on the waves.' I was suddenly completely relieved! I didn't worry about God and prayer any more. And I decided I would break off with you."

"You mean this happened the day after the Ayn Rand lecture, weeks ago?" I asked. He nodded. I said dully, "And you hid it from me all this time. And why did you plan our break-up to be so horrible and despicable for me—like a stab in the back?"

"Dr. Berger said it would be best this way, because it would stop you from asking me to reconsider," he said. "My mind is made up! Don't hope for my conversion any time soon, if ever. So this is good-bye, little Karen! Don't take it too hard. You won't have to study philosophy any more, and you'll meet someone else in due course—a true believer, no doubt." There was a hint of pain on his face as he said this.

I suddenly smiled, thinking of George MacPherson. "I may have met him already," I said, "and while your decision hurts me, it must have hurt you at least as much. That's why you could hardly eat all these weeks. You knew deep down in your heart that you were choosing the wrong way."

19

Recovery; Robert's Prophecy; George and I

Days of dull sadness followed that fateful evening. I was in shock, not so much about the break-up itself but about the manner in which James had planned it and carried it out. He had said that Dr. Berger had advised him to act as he did so I would not try to change his mind; her involvement in ending our relationship infuriated me most about the whole event. What business was it of hers? I stormed in my heart and mind. How dare she tell him how to act towards me? Finally I came to terms with it as a sign of his extraordinary acquiescence to his masterful mentor. What he had done to me, I reflected, was in accordance with her steering, but the final responsibility had been his.

I was surprised by the relative calmness with which I bore the unanticipated final separation from James during the next few weeks. I was amazed that I had not cried at the break-up itself, nor afterwards. Where were my tears? I wondered. Had I not loved him after all? Then I remembered my sudden helpless outburst of weeping at Swenson Books in the presence of George and recognized that my almost unbearable agony of being tied to James in his self-absorption, ambition and godless thought had surfaced then ahead of the break-up and prepared me for it. For the first time after that horrible anniversary celebration I felt grateful for it, because the burden of my perilous love for James had been lifted from my heart, and my uneven, desperate struggle against his philosophy need no longer oppress me. From now on all that I could still do for him was to pray for him.

I did several other things to make my parting from James easier. I never ate in restaurants where we had eaten together. I stopped listening to pieces of classical music he had especially liked. I avoided all the places where we had been happy together, the sidewalks where we had walked hand in hand, the piano practice rooms where he had listened to me, and especially "our" little table in the student cafeteria. Eventually I could eat at "our" restaurants, listen to "our" music and approach "our" places of poignant memories again without painful emotion.

It was only after reaching this point of deliverance that I shared what had happened with my parents. They could not hide their relief. "We were against this relationship from the beginning," they said again and again. "We were so afraid for you! Thank God it is over now!" We rejoiced together about my release from what they had rightly considered a dangerous bondage all along.

It was very different for Mrs. Barron, Robert and Neva to learn that I was no longer James' girlfriend and probable future wife. All James had said to them was that we were not seeing each other any more. Neva told me that her mother had immediately asked him in a trembling voice whether there was any way we could reconcile. He merely said no and shook his head. Mrs. Barron had begun to cry. Later she told Robert and Neva of her fear that the last best chance of coming to Christ might have gone from her firstborn son's life when he broke up with me. Robert and Neva sadly agreed, but encouraged their mother. "As long as James remains alive, there is hope," Neva said. "We must just continue to pray for him harder than ever."

Robert, always the most Bible-centered of us in his thinking, cited several passages from the Book of Proverbs to the effect that people who *"set at naught all God's counsel, hated knowledge, and did not choose the fear of the Lord,"* would *"eat of the fruit of their own way, be filled with their own devices"* and be destroyed by them. He predicted that James would reach the pinnacle of fame and influence he craved, but would lose everything which could give him real joy and life by his own choice and guilt, just as he had lost me. "God's wisdom, which he has rejected," Robert ended, "says in Proverbs 8:36: *'He that sins against me wrongs his own soul: all they that hate me love death.'* God willing he will suffer enough pain to recognize that and change his course before it is too late. Sometimes unbearable pain is God's last instrument of mercy to rescue people like James from their false way."

Neva felt that this prophecy was already beginning to be fulfilled because she saw that James, too, was devastated over what had happened though he did his best to conceal it. "With his other girls," she said, "beginning with Dorrie Fisher, he just 'loved them and left them' with no regrets, and if asked about them, he would even joke about them. It's quite different with you! He won't talk about you at all. And there is no new girl in his life either. And one more thing," she continued, "you know how little James ate and how thin he got during the weeks just before he broke up with you? Mother, Robert and I, and even Dad think it was because he was already torn up inside about leaving you soon. Dad even guessed that before the rest of us did! Whenever he saw James push away his uneaten food, he would mutter, 'He's got it badly,' just as he did that very first evening when you visited us as James' girl friend. Remember?"

I nodded. Yes, I remembered. Tom's remark had embarrassed me then; now its perspicacity showed me he had known his son better than I. He had thought James' deep attraction to me a sort of severe sickness, and so had James in the end.

"Well, James has never recovered from that," Neva went on. "He is still as thin as a rake, and when Mother worries and prods him to eat right, he says being thin is healthy and to stop pestering him about it. Of course he is busier than ever, traveling all over the country to give his special lectures on campus after campus. His philosophy and his career are all he has left."

When I was sure I had reached the point of full deliverance weeks after my breakup with James, I went to Swenson Books to resume the study of C. S. Lewis books with George, whom I had not seen all this while. We were now in November 1965, with Thanksgiving ahead. My old feeling of total comfort and peace returned instantly as I entered the store. I am home again at last, I thought as I looked around for George. And there he was, helping a customer find a book, just as he had helped me find the Pascal Memorial months ago. He looked up, saw me, and a smile of joy instantly transfigured his face. I waved to him, went to our old place in the nook by the bay window and waited till he was free to join me.

"Where have you been all these weeks?" he asked after we had exchanged greetings.

"It's a long story," I answered evasively. Then I remembered how discreet he had been that afternoon when I burst out crying, asking me no questions and making no comments but simply and wordlessly comforting me by the touch of his hands on my shoulders. I decided to be completely truthful with him, regardless of the outcome.

"A close friend broke up with me in September on the anniversary of the day we first met," I said. "It took me a while to get over it. I didn't want to come here until I did. Now I have."

George looked at me silently for a few moments, his face serious, full of compassion but also of dawning joy. Finally he answered, "Are you sure you got over it?"

I nodded. "Yes," and said, "I am sure. I think I actually started getting over it right here with you in the customers' snack room when I had that crying spell, although the actual break-up came weeks after that."

"I was so sorry for you," George said, "I knew you were really hurting deep down and must have been carrying that hurt for a long time. If only I could have carried it with you—for you." He stopped. I could tell he feared he had said too much, too soon. But he hadn't! He had told me what I had sensed for some time but had secretly longed to hear only since James had left me. I felt my lips expand in a joyful smile. We looked at each other, and our eyes met in complete understanding and agreement. We both remembered the first time this had happened after James' horrible lecture on utilitarianism, and George remembered something else along with it.

"James Barron was the friend you broke up with, wasn't it?" he said, and explained, "I think I know because when you and I first met after that horrible lecture, he showed up and hurried you away from me the way a close friend would."

"So you have known all along about me and him," I murmured.

"Well, not for sure," George answered, "but yes, I wondered about it. I also wondered why you wanted to know so much about philosophy. It didn't seem to come naturally to you. But it fitted in if you were his friend and wanted to bring him to Christ."

"You are right," I agreed. "That's why I came to you to help me find a testimony like the Pascal Memorial. And you led me to it. It was exactly what he—James—said he wanted. But when I gave it to him, he dodged it." I sighed with relief; that disappointment did not matter any more.

One other thought came to me. "So you knowingly helped me in my efforts to win him to Christ," I mused. "You must have understood that if I did, he might, well, win me for himself."

"Yes," George said, "that's why I never told you before how I felt about you. I had to wait to do that till your battle ended one way or another. I thank God it ended as it did."

20

Family Reunion; A Very Happy Ending; James, Dr. Berger and Feminism

That afternoon George told me about his family and his plans for the future. As I had already surmised, he was of Scottish descent. His father had married into the Swenson family, pious Norwegian Lutheran Christians who had established the bookstore and bequeathed it to George's mother. George was the youngest of four children; his older brothers and sister were already married with families of their own.

"We all have a family reunion every five years," he said. "Last time we had over thirty people! They are all Christians, and it was like a little bit of heaven. That's how I picture heaven, Karen—a huge family reunion with all our family in Christ from all tribes and nations through history seated in rich royal wedding clothes at our Father's wedding banquet, sharing our lives forever with Him in love, peace and joy. There would be no more death, no more lying or hatred, no more crying, no more sickness or pain. And nothing and no one from outside the family would be allowed to come in and disturb our joy!"

George told me that he was pursuing a humanities degree at Battle Hill University and would graduate next spring. "And then I will work full time in the store," he said. "You see, when my parents retire, Swenson Books will come to me. Our family has talked it over and settled it some time ago. I am the only one of the children who is really interested in running it. It's part of our common inheritance, but I would gradually pay off their shares to them over several years. I would never be wealthy but earn enough income from Swenson Books for me and my family. After all, it supported my parents and us four children. I want to have a family with at least that many children, too."

I said that perhaps his future wife might work and contribute to the family income for a while if necessary, as was the rule now in so many young families. "I would not want my wife to work outside the home," George said decisively, "certainly not after we had children, or only after our children would be grown up and gone. Raising a family is full time work, especially for the mother!" I agreed and replied that this had been the way for my father and mother as well, though they had raised only me or at most my late little brother and me in the early years of their marriage. I said that I would love to have several children. I, an only child, had often felt lonely as I was growing up, and I had sometimes felt my parents were a little too wrapped up in me and my doings. With more than one child, there was no danger of that! George and I were getting along splendidly and felt more and more at home with each other.

By now it was late in the afternoon. George invited me to have dinner with his folks. I agreed, thinking how easy and natural it would be to meet them, and how hard it had been to meet the Barrons with James. George asked one of the clerks to close up the store when it was time, and we left side by side. We had not far to go; the MacPherson home was a spacious old house right next to the store. It was larger than that of my parents, but just as simple and down to earth inside, not like the Barrons' luxurious residence. There was no gap between the lifestyles of the MacPhersons and the Margraves, and we were all Christian believers. We fit well together.

George's parents received me warmly, and I felt comfortable with them right away. It seemed as though they already knew about me from George. He confirmed this to me after the dinner when walking me back to my car. He had spoken to them about me after I had studied C. S. Lewis with him for several weeks to bring a close friend to Christ. He had also told them that he was becoming interested in me, but couldn't tell me this as long as the other man was in the picture. The weeks when I had stopped coming to the store had been hard on him, but when I came back this afternoon and told him about my breakup with James, he was "the happiest man on earth" and couldn't help letting me know immediately how he felt about me, telling me of his long-range plans, and introducing me to his folks.

By the time we said goodbye that evening, we were virtually certain that we would marry and "live happily ever after," though George did not propose to me until after having asked for and received my own parents' permission to do so just before Christmas. How quickly it all happened, and how utterly different from the way it had been with James! George and I were engaged on New Year's Day 1966.

We were married in June 1966 after he graduated with honors from Battle Hill University. Since Neva Barron was my best friend, I asked her to be a bridesmaid at our wedding. My breakup with James had never affected our closeness, and naturally she kept me abreast of what was going on in his life. She had much to tell me about him during the frequent times we met before my wedding.

"He got his master's degree this spring," she said, "and he moved away to the Baltimore, Maryland area to get his doctorate at Herbert Spencer University. That's the alma mater of Dr. Nancy Berger, who was his faculty advisor at Battle Hill University all through grad school. You might have heard already of Herbert Spencer University. It is almost as well-known by now as Harvard or Yale, and one of the most liberal, radical universities in the country. It's a hotbed of student and faculty revolutionaries. Even Dad, whose health has been poor lately and who isn't too interested in public affairs any more, heard rumors about it and argued with James about getting his doctorate there. But James was bound and determined to go there. And that is not all," Neva added with the excitement of one passing on really interesting news, "Dr. Berger is going there with him. He says she has been named their dean of students."

"My goodness," I said, "that's the third year they will have been together most of the time."

"That's right," Neva said. "When Dad found out about it, he asked James outright whether they were going to bed together. James snorted and said, A, she was too old, and B, she was too ugly. Dad grinned and agreed; he and Mother had met Dr. Berger when they attended James' commencement."

Neva also told me that James had written his master of philosophy thesis on the topic "The Necessity for Feminism" and gave me a copy to read. As a direct insult James had dedicated it to his mother with the inscription, "To my mother, Lucinda Barron, who taught me what not to believe." The thesis began by tracing modern feminism to the French philosopher Simone de Beauvoir and especially to American writer Betty Friedan's book *The Feminine Mystique,* published in 1963 and a runaway bestseller. It condemned traditional homemakers as unpaid domestic slaves or idle mistresses of their husbands. It urged women not to waste their time and talents on wiping babies' noses and bottoms, on dusting furniture, trying out new recipes, or hosting unneeded parties to entertain their so-called friends. It predicted that homemaking would be more and more despised and rejected as modern women abandoned home, kitchen and kids, exercising their equal rights to work with equal pay in positions hitherto reserved for men. Sexism in all its forms, James wrote, must stop.

James predicted that complete women's liberation would follow the universal use of contraceptives backed up by legalized abortion. In the near future, James opined, very few full-time homemakers and traditional families would be left in the advanced countries of the West and eventually everywhere. While groups like Zero Population Growth were very concerned about rising population when his thesis appeared in 1966, James believed that due to sterilization, birth control and the breakup of traditional marriages, the world population would be stabilized and even decrease within a few decades. James stated that since traditional marriage was already riddled by domestic difficulties, infidelity and skyrocketing divorce, and anyway established now only for convenient sex rather than reproduction, non-traditional marriage between consenting adults of the same sex would be accepted within one generation. James also sharply condemned all traditional religions, especially Christianity, for relegating women to the status of second-class citizens and encouraged the more progressive churches to open their leadership ranks to them. Women pastors and priests, he said, should and soon would be as accepted in the ministry as men.

This thesis, Neva said, was published as an astonishing but farsighted picture of the future in a prestigious avant-garde magazine, earning James his first respect as a daring opinion leader. She also said that he was now suffering from a painful stomach ulcer, probably due to extreme stress during writing the thesis so soon after the stress of his breakup with me.

21

Home and Family; Dinner with the Freemans

The summer of 1966 was one of the happiest in our lives. It was also one of the busiest. George worked full time at Swenson Books. Since I still had two years of study left till my graduation, I took a summer course in music theory at Battle Hill University. In August I became pregnant, and we as well as our entire family looked forward to the birth of our first child.

After our wedding we moved into a little house in Battle Hill's old town, not too far from Swenson Books. We had been able to buy it at a much reduced price as a "fixer-upper" needing much repair, painting, and redecorating. We tackled and completed all the work by the end of the summer, with Dad MacPherson and George's brothers pitching in most evenings and weekends.

The yard had been neglected for years. My father, who loved to do gardening, drove in from Lonely Prairie almost every Saturday morning to stay with us all day to dig, till, weed, trim trees, bushes and hedges, mow, cart off debris, lay out and pave a footpath in the back yard, plant roses in the front, and whatever else he could think of to make our place more beautiful. My mother and I helped him, much as we had done at home with his annual garden spring chores. I also did some "step and fetch it" work for the MacPherson men; my mother laughed and said she had done the same for my dad when they were first married.

On Saturdays Mom MacPherson would prepare a hearty dinner for us all in their comfortable, shady old home. We ate it around the MacPherson's big family table, sometimes together with George's siblings and their families. After the meal the two fathers would discuss church matters, theological questions or politics, or watch sports on television, while we younger men and women would chat about the latest family and work news while we cleared the table and did the dishes and cleanup. The older children would play in the fenced yard outside or upstairs in their parents' old bedrooms with their parents' old toys, while the little ones took naps curled up on sofas or on blankets on the living room floor.

It all reminded me of that time a year ago when I sat with George in the back room of Swenson Books and ate his mother's cookies, remembered my carefree times with my grandparents and burst out crying with my agony over James. I had thought then that I could never be a carefree little child again, but I had been wrong. True, I was grown up now, a wife and soon to be a mother, and would have cares and burdens to bear throughout my days on earth. But deep in my heart I was carefree and at rest, for I was where I belonged, with my husband and my family, loving and being loved forever.

I suddenly thought of James' master's thesis on "The Necessity for Feminism." How much lasting harm it would do to the young women who followed his call to concentrate upon themselves and their worldly ambitions, and to despise and reject the humble, faithful service of a wife and mother to her husband and children! How much permanent harm it would do to their children! I also saw that his thesis was a declaration of war upon families like mine. I realized for the first time that his decision for his career and against me did not involve only him and me but everyone whom its consequences would touch. "He will infect the whole world with his lawlessness and the lack of peace in his heart," I thought in sudden fear, "if he reaches the place of leadership he wants. And he is well on his way!" I said a quick silent prayer for James' salvation, for our family and all families like us, and for the world.

One evening in September Dad and Mom MacPherson invited us over for dinner. They told us that old friends of the family would also be there who were looking forward to meeting me as the newest member of the MacPherson clan. Their friends turned out to be Dr. and Mrs. Freeman. He and I gladly renewed our acquaintance and brought each other up to date on what we had been doing since I took his course. Dr. Freeman had retired immediately afterwards and was now working on a book on the declining influence of Christianity on society in the twentieth century.

"It is a sad story," he said, "and all too little known in Christian circles. I see hardly any attempt among Christians to at least be informed about what is going on outside our church walls. Even most Christian colleges are blind to the culture war all around us or reluctant to engage in it. Swenson Books is truly an oasis in the desert of indifference, willful ignorance or deliberate compromise among us." He would have said more about this subject, which obviously troubled him deeply, but Mrs. Freeman asked him to let me tell them about my life since I had been her husband's student.

"What Edna means," Dr. Freeman said, smiling, "is that she would like to hear how you and George met and got married. And George," he told my husband, "you are welcome to add details if you like."

"We met for the first time," I said, "after a horrible lecture about utilitarianism which James Barron gave at the student union." I explained how James had made common cause with the Free Speech Movement followers on campus, how he had displayed his "Question Authority" T-shirt, and how he had sidestepped George's question about Hitler and the Holocaust. I told the Freemans how I had run to thank George for his question and comment after the lecture and learned about Swenson Books.

"And then James Barron came and hustled Karen away from me as fast as he could," George added. "I understood they were close friends then." He suddenly laughed. "Do you know," he said to no one in particular, "in a way Karen and I owe our marriage to James Barron! He was God's catalyst to bring us together. We met for a while every week to study C. S. Lewis books to help her fight James' philosophy."

"And after James and I broke up," I said, "I came back to Swenson Books and saw George again. From there on everything fell quickly into place between us—and here we are. "

Dr. Freeman nodded, quoting Romans 8:28 *"All things work together for good to them who love God,"* he said slowly, looking at George and me with fatherly approval. However, Karen," he added to me, "I am certainly glad to see that James Barron is no longer in your life. I was quite concerned about you when I saw you with him the day you brought me a copy of the Pascal Memorial. I knew you were trying to bring him to Christ and was almost certain you would be sadly disappointed. You see, being a member of the philosophy department faculty kept me well informed about him and even more about his faculty advisor, Dr. Berger. I am now retired and do not see my old colleagues every day, but current news still reaches me. All that has happened since you two parted company proves how good God was in separating you from him."

"James' younger sister is my best friend," I said, "she attends the church where George and I were married and was one of my bridesmaids at our wedding. She told us James and Dr. Berger were now both at Herbert Spencer University, and she gave me a copy of his 'Necessity for Feminism' thesis. George and I have both read it. We think it is horrible, much worse than that speech on utilitarianism, though right in line with it."

"It might as well have been Dr. Berger's thesis," Dr. Freeman said. "It was totally inspired by her. She boasted about it to the rest of the philosophy faculty. She read us parts of it and finally had copies made for every one of us. Even the most radical among us were hesitant to endorse it unreservedly, though most of us approved it in principle. The tone was hers—the clipped sentences, the elitist arrogance against lower wicked mortals in traditional families like yours, the enthusiastic praise for Simone de Beauvoir's *Second Sex* and Betty Friedan's *Feminine Mystique*—that was Dr. Berger all right! The prophetic stance, predicting what would come to pass within the next generation or two, was contributed by James. Those two make quite a team and will go far in today's intellectual climate. It remains to be seen, of course, whether all his prophecies will come true. In view of the ignorance and apathy of Christians today I am afraid they might."

We were all silent for a while. Then George mused, "I wonder how Dr. Berger became the way she is now."

Surprisingly Mrs. Freeman spoke up. "Some time ago," she said, "Francis and I attended a faculty tea in honor of the outgoing president of Battle Hill University. Somehow Dr. Berger and I found ourselves sitting alone together at a little table apart. She must not have known who I was, for she began confiding in me. She said parties like this for a domineering male were a wicked waste. She went on to tell me of her childhood and youth. She came from a wealthy family in Maryland. Her father died early, and her mother remarried a man who molested Nancy repeatedly while she was growing up. She hates men with a passion. 'All men are scum,' she said, 'I will never submit to any of them.' Nancy inherited a substantial fortune from her late father on her twenty-first birthday. She told me that her goal was to liberate women so they could get back at men who have hurt them or tried to dominate them. She chose a career in philosophy to reach her goal. 'It's not in street riots but in college classrooms,' she said, 'that social revolutions are begun.'"

"And now at thirty-three she is dean of students at Herbert Spencer University," said Dr. Freeman, "I hear she is instrumental in helping to start so-called 'Departments of Women's Studies' at all major universities, where James' thesis on feminism will be taught."

"And she has got her hooks into James Barron," said Mrs. Freeman, "I can't help feeling sorry for him."

"Don't, Edna," said Dr. Freeman, "he chose what he got—and it will hurt many others."

22

The C. S. Lewis Club; A Double Wedding; James and the "Reality Principle"

During the next two years Swenson Books thrived. Pursuant to a suggestion by Dr. Freeman we started a C. S. Lewis Club, which still exists as I write. It met in our customers' snack room every month. Dr. Freeman served as its first president. It was open to anyone interested in the work of C. S. Lewis as well as related Christian books. We soon hosted a group of well educated believers from all Christian backgrounds united on the basis of what C. S. Lewis had called "mere" Christianity and had true fellowship regardless of our church roots. I believe C. S. Lewis would have heartily approved of our club. Eventually it outgrew the snack room and moved to the elder MacPhersons' large living room.

I loved to sit in on the club's meetings and to deepen my understanding of C. S. Lewis's wonderful books. We were also endeavoring to apply his teachings to our own lives and to society, and to acquire and share his books and other materials on the topics we thought most relevant to Christians confronted with the moral decline all around us. George and Dr. Freeman lost no opportunity to emphasize the crucial importance of biblical creation, especially of man's creation in God's image and likeness, as the foundation of a truly Christian worldview able to defend the faith and overcome opposition, much as I had done in my confrontation with James.

While C. S. Lewis had not dealt much with evolution and even used it on rare occasions to illustrate points of his other teachings, he had written a funny poem against it named "Evolution," which Dr. Freeman delighted to read to us at one of our meetings. Mom MacPherson with her Lutheran background was very happy to tell the club of the monthly newsletters published by the Bible-Science Association, founded in 1963 by Missouri Synod Lutheran pastor Walter Lang. She also introduced us to Lutheran theologian Alfred Rehwinkel's excellent book *The Flood,* one of the very few major works available at that time which attacked evolution from a scientific perspective.

I well remember one meeting when George spoke about the evolutionist anti-Christian bias in almost all the liberal arts classes he had attended at Battle Hill University. At that time radical students and faculty members were mounting a campaign to end all teaching about or by "dead white males," and to do away with "Western Civilization" courses then still mandatory for all freshmen. George's introductory art history class, for example, had neglected all Christ-centered medieval art, touched relatively lightly on the magnificent art of the Renaissance and Baroque periods, but lavished much time and praise on cubism and Pablo Picasso. In his second year French course, the textbook had been Albert Camus' nihilistic novel *The Stranger* rather than one of the many beautiful classical novels by

Victor Hugo or Alexandre Dumas. In English literature Shakespeare was out, but contemporary science fiction writers with a radical bias were in. The social science courses, psychology, sociology, and anthropology were mine fields to destroy the faith of Christian students, "and most Christian students are completely unprepared for the attacks upon Christianity by atheist professors and textbooks," said George sadly. He felt that philosophy was the worst and history the best among the liberal arts classes, though much depended on the professors teaching them. "Don't be discouraged! We must remember Psalm 92:7," Dr. Freeman commented, *"God allows the worthless works of man to grow up like weeds and flourish, only to be destroyed in the end."*

Our family also thrived. George Lewis MacPherson was born to us in May 1967 and our second child was on the way when we received an invitation to attend the double wedding of Neva and Robert Barron to take place on June 15, 1968 at Grace Baptist Church in Lonely Prairie. I had already met David Ploughman, Neva's fiancé, and Robert's future wife Beth Sanders at church years ago. I knew James was bound to attend and was a little apprehensive about meeting him again. However, almost three years had now gone by since our breakup, and of course George would be with me, so what could possibly happen between us except hellos and good-byes? We went to the wedding, leaving little George in the care of my parents.

The double wedding of the two younger Barron children was magnificent. All the parents seemed content with the choices their children had made, including Tom Barron, the only merely nominal Christian among them, who beamed proudly as he led his beautiful daughter Neva down the aisle. The brides pledged to "love, honor and obey" their husbands as long as they both would live according to the traditional wedding vows.

A gorgeous reception and luncheon followed in the church basement. Here the many guests were all crowded tightly together. Neva insisted that she and I sit together and led us to the head table next to the rest of her family. To my dismay James sat directly across from us. He looked as gaunt, tired, and drained of energy as the last time we had met. He shot a brief glance at me but turned his head away immediately. The Barrons were engaged in a lively conversation about various concerns of their own. George and I could not help overhearing them, and when George was drawn into their discussion by James later he could not help responding.

After a while there was a lull in the conversation, and James asked whether he could tell us a little about his work on his doctoral thesis. He said part of it dealt with a contemporary philosopher named Norman O. Brown. "This man is the darling of the radical student movement today," James said. He told us that Brown wrote two books, *Life Against Death* and *Love's Body,* which made him famous as a revolutionary thinker in academic circles. His message was composed of Freudianism, his own unbiblical brand of "Dionysian" Christianity, and Zen Buddhism. His idea of "polymorphous perversity," an expression much heard in public at the time, meant that each and every part of the body should be used in sexual play.

Brown, James continued, approved of any and all instincts, desires and drives of man without restriction. He wanted to abolish any distinction between evil and good, filth and cleanness; the way Brown put it, James said, was that "every throne was a toilet seat and every toilet seat a throne." Brown believed in evolution and therefore saw words as merely arbitrary human sounds. He condemned all human action as nothing but "excrement." His entire work, James said, was designed to undermine reliance upon human reason.

"And now," James said, "listen carefully, for I would welcome your input here. Brown exalts outright clinical madness or schizophrenia as the right way of life. Now in schizophrenia a person's thinking process breaks down. He cannot distinguish between himself and what's not himself. It's much the same as what happens with people addicted to psychedelic drugs. We have all heard of young people high on drugs who fall to their death from a precipice or high building during their pipe dream because they do not see or comprehend what's right ahead of them. Denial of reality through drug use or in schizophrenia can lead to death. Yet Brown opposes the hospitalization of schizophrenics as a device to sustain society's prejudice in favor of the so-called 'reality principle.'"

"What's your question to us?" broke in Robert impatiently, "whether Brown is crazy himself? Can't you see that for yourself and say so?"

"I am very tempted to do just that," said James, "but they love Brown at Herbert Spencer U. They think he has a point about opposing the 'reality principle,' and I agree."

"And what might that point be?" Robert asked.

"If there is a true, hard and fast 'reality principle' which you must obey or die," said James slowly, "and the self-destructive experiences of our spaced-out hippies and schizophrenics as well as the life-sustaining experiences of you and me confirm it, then the next question is, where does it come from? It has all the marks of deliberate creation by an intelligent designer—the Creator God of the Bible. I believe what Brown calls the 'reality principle' may be God's foot in the door to the minds of people like me."

After a brief pause James added, "Of course 'reality principle' is Brown's term for people's idea that there is a real reality as distinguished from what is not real. He rejects it because it sets rules for us to live by, thus limiting our freedom to do anything we want. The Herbert Spencer faculty, or at least Nancy Berger, rightly sees God lurking behind it. She wants me to slam that entry door from God shut!" He became urgent, almost desperate as he ended, "But how can I? How can I help but know that there is a difference between what is real and what is not? How can I deny reality—deny that anything really is—do a doctoral thesis about it?"

I could hardly believe my ears. Was I about to see James' conversion? I could see Mrs. Barron move her lips as in prayer. Robert sat silent, obviously afraid to ruin what might be the salvation of his brother.

"Speechless, little brother?" sneered James, "all right then, let's hear what you others have to say. I don't suppose my own flesh and blood wants to tackle me, but how about you, Mr. MacPherson? I understand you run the Christian bookstore five blocks away from the campus of Battle Hill U. Is there anything in your books that could help me?"

George, surprised at being singled out for answering James, remained silent for a moment. He told me later he quickly prayed for God's help. Finally he replied,

"You cannot deny that the reality in which we live exists. You are right that it points to its Creator, God. As the Bible teaches in Romans 1:20: *'The invisible things of him from the creation of the world are clearly seen, being understood by the things that are made, even his eternal power and Godhead.'* Yes, reality is created, and it is His foot in His door to you. He has led you to this door by one of His enemies. How marvelous, how much like Him! In the book of Revelation 3:20 Christ says, *'Behold, I stand at the door and knock: if any man hear my voice, and open the door, I will come in to him, and sup with him, and he with me.'* Open the door, Mr. Barron, and let Him in."

23

James' Doctoral Thesis; Sylvia; James' Marriage; "His Service is Perfect Freedom"

The wedding reception ended and James had remained silent. At least, I thought, he had not tossed one of his non-committal remarks at George, like his customary "I'll think about it," "very impressive," or "you really spoke to me," which I still remembered with a wince of pain from my past efforts to win him to the faith. Perhaps his silence was promising after all. Shortly afterwards he left to catch his return plane to Baltimore, with brief impersonal good-byes to George and me.

Neva, Robert and Mrs. Barron thanked George for his witness to James. Robert was especially impressed by George's use of Romans 1:20 and creation. "I never realized before," he said thoughtfully, "how the very existence of the world can be used to turn an atheist to God. I was taught to use a step by step approach to evangelism which doesn't go into creation at all. It works with people who have had some acquaintance with Christianity and vaguely believe in God, but today we run into more and more people who are totally ignorant of both. They are like the heathen Gentiles of New Testament times. And of course James isn't alone today in his self-absorption, worldly ambition and rejection of Christ. I will talk to our pastor about it."

We later learned from Robert and Neva that within weeks James had fallen back on evolution to account for the existence of reality. After all, evolution allowed that the real world might always have existed, albeit earlier in more primitive form. Evolution also meant continuous change, so that evolutionist "reality" was not the "hard and fast" creation of God compelling men to obey its rules or die. On the contrary, men might make themselves the gods and shapers of evolution by John

Dewey's "learning by doing" experimental method!

Nancy Berger had counseled James not to deal in depth with Brown's "reality principle," but to discuss him only as a link between existentialism and emerging New Age "spirituality." In this manner, and by leaning on evolution, he could avoid entrapment by theism pursuant to questions about origins from the examiners of his doctoral thesis. "Not that I expect any such questions at Herbert Spencer U," James had said, "we have no George MacPhersons on the faculty." He sarcastically told Robert to thank George for his help, though it had not worked the way George had intended. However, he said, it had made him realize anew how indispensable evolution was to the atheist worldview.

In due course James' doctoral thesis was accepted and earned him his doctorate in philosophy in the spring of 1969. It also earned him his appointment to the faculty of Herbert Spencer University. In 1970 his thesis was published as a scholarly book with the title *The Metamorphosis of Philosophy: From Atheism to New Age*. Swenson Books received a promotional flyer about it from the publisher and George obtained a copy. Both George and I read it. It was well written, accessible to people without much philosophical knowledge like myself, and proved uncannily correct in its bold analysis and preview of the direction and effect of twentieth century philosophy. It was translated into several major world languages and used in philosophy classes across the country.

Neva had noticed one unrelated detail in James' reports on his thesis. "He used to speak of Dr. Berger as 'Dr. Berger' or 'my faculty advisor'," she told me with a frown. "Now he calls her 'Nancy Berger' or just 'Nancy.' They have definitely become much closer." She said her father had picked up on this, too, and suspected they were having an affair as he had when both first went to Herbert Spencer University. "James denied it then and still does," Tom Barron had told her, "but I don't believe it this time. The woman is older than he and plain as a pikestaff—not remotely like pretty little Karen Margrave whom he almost married in '65. I wasn't in favor of that then," Tom had sighed, "but compared to the Berger woman, I wish to God he had gone through with it!"

Before the next major news about James our own little Mary Anne MacPherson arrived in November 1968, Robert's first son Robert Jr. in April 1969, and Neva's daughter Sylvia in May 1970. Little Sylvia was born with Down Syndrome, then called "mongolism." Neva wept when she first broke the news to me over the telephone. She told me that both her doctor and a medical encyclopedia in their home had agreed that "these little idiots are best put in an institution before you get attached to them." Her husband David was furious when he read this advice and trashed the encyclopedia. "Sylvia is our little girl, and we are going to keep her," he said.

Neva fully accepted her little daughter only after a terrible inward struggle. Only a year or two later did she confide in me with tears that one night during Sylvia's second week at home, when David was away, she had considered placing the baby into her own bed beside herself and then putting a pillow over her head to smother her. She was planning to pretend later that it had happened by accident.

"And then," Neva said, "I remembered Jesus' words in Matthew 25:40: *'Inasmuch as ye have done it unto one of the least of these my brethren, ye have done it unto me.'* I couldn't do this to Jesus! And I cried out to Him, 'I can't carry this burden any more. You tell us in Psalm 55:22 that we should *'cast our burden on you, and you would sustain us.'* Now keep your promise! Carry my burden of a retarded child and sustain me. And He did! Immediately it was as though a burden was physically lifted from me till I could feel it no more. From then on I truly loved little Sylvia. She began to thrive and is now a great joy to us all."

In the early 1970s the movement to legalize abortion in America began in earnest. Of course James was one of its intellectual leaders and advisors. George and I remembered that he had already forecast this development years ago in his lecture on utilitarianism. Severely handicapped children including "mongoloids" were the first candidates for abortion; some states already had laws on the books authorizing it for them. We suggested that Neva tell James about her deliverance and the joy Sylvia gave her now. Neva had already thought of this, written out the story and mailed it to him. His answer was that Sylvia should have been aborted to spare everyone much pain and expense. Ostensibly to comfort her and David he informed them some time later that mongoloid children like Sylvia usually did not live long. It took them a great effort to forgive him.

In July 1971 George and I could share the joyful news of the birth of our third child and second son with our families and friends. Almost by return mail we received announcements from Robert and Beth Barron about the birth of their second son and from David and Neva Ploughman about the birth of their healthy first son. How blessed we all were with our new little ones!

Soon afterwards the members of the Barron family received another piece of mail. It had the effect of a bombshell on them all, but especially on Tom and Lucinda. It was an invitation to the wedding of Dr. Nancy Berger and Dr. James Barron, which would take place in a Baltimore hotel in late August 1971. Tom, Lucinda and Robert flew to Baltimore to attend, and George and I heard about it later from Robert.

There was a civil marriage ceremony, in which the couple promised to give each other comfort and assistance as long as their mutual affection should endure. They did not exchange rings. Robert told us that James looked haggard, somber, and much older than his thirty years. On the other hand, Nancy, who assumed the name "Berger-Barron," looked content and younger than her thirty-eight years. She also looked much more feminine than the elder Barrons remembered. Her hair was fashionably arranged in many short curls, and her face was beautifully made up. She walked proudly at James' side on high heeled shoes and wore a lovely lavender dress.

"What's happened to this ugly duckling?" Tom Barron had wondered. Lucinda noticed that Nancy's dress fit rather loosely at the waist. "She is expecting," she whispered to her husband. Her words were confirmed when they talked to James and Nancy at the reception. Nancy told them that they had been living together for about a year. They had agreed that they would get married if she became pregnant.

"And I wanted to," she added, "time was running out for me to have children. I needed that experience to round out my life." Their baby was due in April 1972; if a boy, they would name him Dylan after Bob Dylan, the singer. James just stood by silently. Tom Barron said later that you could tell right away who wore the pants in that marriage.

Nancy also told the Barrons that she and James had made a pre-nuptial legal agreement so that their income and property would be fairly divided, and that she would have sole custody of their children if their marriage should end. "After all," she had said, "I am independently wealthy, and who can tell if our marriage survives?" It was obvious that the thought of a possible future separation from James was already on her mind.

As I was listening to Robert's report, I remembered how James had become subdued and respectful before Nancy after the Ayn Rand lecture. She had planned his breakup with me, guided his academic career, and now made herself ruler over his private life as well. In his self-centered quest for worldly leadership he had willingly become more and more subservient, almost a slave, to this woman. I remembered a sentence from the Anglican Book of Common Prayer which someone had quoted at a meeting of the C. S. Lewis Club: "O God, who art the author of peace and lover of concord, in knowledge of whom standeth our eternal life, *whose service is perfect freedom.*" There in that one little sentence is the contrast, I thought, between service to God and "freedom" without God. If only James could see that and even yet choose rightly!

24

Good Death

Tom Barron came to share his wife's faith shortly before he died of lung cancer and emphysema. It was in February 1973, and James had an unintentional but crucial part in it.

Tom had been a heavy cigarette smoker ever since his high school years, for smoking was glamorized as a sign of maturity, elegance, manliness and social know-how ever since the 1920s. The illness took years to run its course. Tom proceeded from more and more severe and long-lasting bouts of coughing to vainly seeking the help of physicians, then dosing himself with various "alternative" medications. All this was accompanied by desperate and always failing attempts to stop smoking. Towards the end came frightening episodes of hospitalization when Tom was unable to breathe as his lungs increasingly failed to function even with the help of his oxygen tank. Through it all Lucinda was by her husband's side with gentle, patient, unfailing kindness and love.

During Tom's last hospital stay, the Supreme Court legalized abortion from conception till birth in its landmark "Roe v. Wade" decision of January 22, 1973.

Shortly afterwards James Barron's pioneering article, "Good Death," defending not only that decision but also assisted suicide and the killing of the terminally ill and the severely handicapped, was reprinted from a nationally known and very influential philosophical journal in newspapers and magazines across the country. James had recently been appointed full professor of ethics on the faculty of Herbert Spencer University. "Good Death" made him nationally and even internationally famous. It is often quoted by pro-life defenders to show where the "pro-choice" campaign must lead, and by the "pro-choice" side as a well reasoned defense of their compassionate position. It became an indispensable part of college freshman philosophy and ethics textbooks everywhere.

The Clarion, Lonely Prairie's monopoly newspaper, displayed an abbreviated version of "Good Death" on its editorial page. In a sidebar accompanying the article the Clarion honored James Barron as one of the most promising opinion leaders of the next generation. It credited his reflections on the birth and early childhood of a mongoloid niece and on his father's terminal illness for the "passionate intensity and engagement" of his article.

One of the hospital nurses brought the paper to Tom, congratulating him on his brilliant son but somewhat troubled when he asked her about her reaction to the article.

"Dr. Barron asks for legalization of 'mercy killing'," she said, "but who would give the final injection? Wouldn't it have to be a doctor or even a nurse?"

"Let me see that article," said Tom. After having received and flown over it, he shook his head.

"James doesn't say," he replied. After a moment he added in a shaking voice: "He says it's being done right now in American hospitals here and there. My God! That means people like me cannot trust their doctors any more—or their nurses. Every time we hear a doctor or a nurse coming, it might be the end of our lives."

At that moment Lucinda entered the room for her regular morning visit. She had already read James's article and overheard Tom's conversation with the nurse. After the nurse left, she went over to her husband and gently kissed him as she always did. Then she sat down by the side of his bed. She thought sadly how different he looked from the young, handsome, self-confident man with whom she had fallen in love so long ago. He was not so old, only in his early sixties, but how emaciated he had become, how grey his thinning hair was, how hollow his voice! She saw the yellowish pallor of his lined face, the deep dark rings below his sunken eyes and suppressed a shudder. He could not be far from death—and he still did not share her faith!

Tom stared at her, terror in his eyes. "Did you read James' article in the paper this morning, Lu?" he asked hoarsely. She nodded.

"Lu," he almost whispered, "will you pray for me?"

He had never asked her before in his life to pray for him! This was God's answer to her prayers for him, her desperate prayers this very morning when she was driving from their home to the hospital. Please, please, Father, for Jesus' sake please bring my dear husband to Yourself. Don't let him die apart from You.

But what shall I pray now? What words? I need to pray for myself first! Give me Your wisdom, give me the right words, Your words, Lord, now!

Instantly Lucinda remembered a Bible passage, James 1:5–8. She pulled out the little New Testament she always carried in her handbag, found the passage and read it aloud, to herself as much as to Tom: *"If any of you lack wisdom, let him ask of God, that giveth to all men liberally, and upbraideth not; and it shall be given him. But let him ask in faith, nothing wavering. For he that wavereth is like a wave of the sea driven with the wind and tossed. For let not that man think that he shall receive anything from the Lord."*

She looked up at her husband—and a miracle happened! His eyes met hers; the terror had left them and been replaced by shining joy. Tears were running down his cheeks, yet at the same time a jubilant smile transfigured his face.

"It's so simple," he said softly, and again, more loudly, "It's so simple! Why didn't I see it before? All we have to do is ask Him, and He'll give it to us! He'll even give us the faith to ask! If we just ask, He answers. He is THERE! He hears and He answers!"

And then Tom turned to the telephone by his bed and dialed Neva's number. When she answered, he told her joyfully, "Neva! I am a Christian too now!" Neva immediately shared this news with Robert, and soon afterwards with George and me. All the family greatly rejoiced together.

James' "Good Death" article had produced the terror which made Tom ask Lucinda to pray for him and thus led to his conversion.

Tom died peacefully a few weeks later. George and I went to his funeral, conducted at First United Church. It was attended by many community and state leaders. After all, Tom had been a former mayor of Lonely Prairie and one of its most well-known entrepreneurs. It was only right in the town's eyes that he should be interred with all fitting ceremonies and honors.

Rev. Dr. Brassfield had accepted First United Church's invitation to come to Lonely Prairie from his prestigious post at Harvard (or perhaps Yale, or Columbia—I never can remember which) to deliver the main obituary sermon. Lucinda had at first objected to his coming, but in the end she gave in because he was not to be the only speaker; he would preach after James and Robert, in that order, both of whom were to share memories of their father. Robert understood that the challenge and the burden of an uncompromising Christian testimony at his father's funeral lay upon him.

James spoke of his father's hard work to preserve and enlarge the business inherited from his grandparents and of his disappointment when he, James, chose a different life goal. Nevertheless his father had shown him the greatest love possible for a parent—to give his son the priceless freedom to differ from himself substantially in thought and deed. Tom Barron, James ended, had been an ideal father and friend, whose untimely and painful death had deeply grieved his family and friends. However, this death also pointed to a better future when the protracted medical efforts, which now only prolonged a terminal patient's and his family's suffering, would be made unnecessary either by early cures or by the "good death" of assisted early departure.

Robert confirmed James' praise of their father's hard work. But, he continued, a price had to be paid: Tom's frequent absence from home and family and his misunderstanding of their deepest needs, needs much deeper than material well-being. "This price," Robert said, "was exacted in two important ways. First, my father's preoccupation with and tension about the work, from which he sometimes sought release in inappropriate ways (thus gently he spoke of Tom's periodic infidelities and his long affair with Fern Lowrie); second, the deep inward, spiritual rift between my father and some members of our family which, as some of you may know, lasted for years and hurt both us and him (Lucinda's conversion, and Robert and Neva's attending Grace Baptist Church).

"But praise God, both these wounds were healed just recently. On his very death bed our dear father came to sure faith in our loving Heavenly Father Who, as Christ tells us in John 3:16, *'so loved the world, that He gave his only begotten Son, that whosoever believes in Him should not perish, but have everlasting life.'* He came to know that God is really there and hears and answers prayer. We had three more weeks together, really together, for the first time in our lives. And we can be sure, as he was sure in the end, that we will be together again with joy in heaven for ever and ever. For as Jesus Christ told Martha, grieving for the death of her brother Lazarus, in John 11:25–26: *'I am the resurrection and the life: he that believeth in me, though he were dead, yet shall he live: and whosoever liveth and believeth in me shall never die.'* And for the sure knowledge of this truth the years of pain and suffering he had to endure were a small price to pay. He understood this and said so himself in the end. Do not grieve but rejoice, for all is well now with our dear father! He is absent from the body—that old dying body and all its pain—and present with our Living Lord, with whom there are joy and pleasures forevermore."

Dr. Brassfield's concluding eulogy centered upon the living memorial of Tom Barron in his civic achievements and among his many friends. It was delivered with just the right balance of stoic resignation to his loss and admiration for his work.

Not long afterwards Lucinda transferred her membership from First United Church to Grace Baptist Church. To her surprise and joy several families made the move with her. A small trickle of people hungry for spiritual nourishment, especially families with small children, began to leave First United Church at this time and slowly grew. When First United Church celebrated its Centennial in the mid-1980s, it was dying; there were no more small children in the congregation left at all.

25
Dylan and Ecstasy; James' Successful Career

For many years after Tom Barron's death George and I had little personal news about James because the Barron family did not receive much either. Except for sending occasional announcements about academic honors they had received, James and Nancy had broken off their ties with Mrs. Barron, Robert and Neva. We learned from Mrs. Freeman that Nancy had broken off her relations with her own family years earlier when the inheritance from her late father had given her complete financial independence.

Lucinda correctly thought that James and Nancy's ostracism against the Barrons was due to their Christian faith. She offered to help take care of little Dylan and later Ecstasy during the many times when James and Nancy were away from home on their frequent trips to conferences, seminars, and other teaching or speaking engagements. They always declined, at first politely, saying they had already made other arrangements, then more and more curtly. Finally they sharply demanded that she stop offering her help because they did not welcome her influence on their children. They never acknowledged any greetings or gifts the Barrons sent them or their children for their birthdays or Christmas. Lucinda was heartbroken over their banishment from the lives of her eldest son and his family.

In the spring of 1977 James announced the birth of a daughter in September 1976 in the only lengthy, detailed and frank letter he sent the Barrons during all these years. He wrote that this would be their last child, as Nancy was now over forty years old and the birth of the baby had been difficult. They had called the little girl "Ecstasy," a fitting name for the time of boundless personal freedom in which she would grow up. He also wrote that it was much harder on him and Nancy to bring up the children than they had expected. "Perhaps there is something to be said for the use of old-fashioned authority in dealing with children and youth," he admitted. "After all, parents have a right to self-fulfillment, too." At that time he wrote an article on childhood education expressing this insight with the title "Was Dr. Spock Wrong?" (Dr. Benjamin Spock's permissive *Common Sense Book of Baby and Child Care,* called "the best-selling book in the world after the Bible," was then the unquestioned secular authority on child rearing.) James' article was widely read and applauded by the general public but must have raised eyebrows among the elite of progressive educators and philosophers on his side; we would call it "politically incorrect" today.

James had enclosed a small picture of the new baby as well as one of Dylan, now about four years old. He was a beautiful little boy with dark, curly hair and dark brown eyes. Lucinda said he looked very much like James had at that age. Little Ecstasy looked quite different. She had straight blonde hair, hazel eyes and an expression of reserve, even mistrust on her little round, serious face. Lucinda had both pictures enlarged and framed, and hung them in her bedroom with the pictures of her grandchildren by Robert and Neva, by now eight in number. I am sure she prayed for them all every day.

The dearth of direct personal news from James did not mean that we had no news at all about him. This was the period when news media reports about his meteoric rise to professional fame became more and more frequent. Every few months, it seemed, there were newspaper and television spots about Dr. James Barron addressing some influential regional or national conference about issues of the day. He was appointed or elected to many national and international government advisory councils on public affairs. By the beginning of the 1990s he had reached the zenith of his professional career.

Twice during these years friends living near Baltimore sent the Barrons newspaper clippings with photos showing James and Nancy with their children. Both Dylan and Ecstasy looked straight at the photographer with frowning, mistrustful, almost hostile faces. Dylan promised to be very handsome when grown up, like his father had been in earlier years. Ecstasy seemed awkward, a little plump, and short for her age. On both pictures James looked rigid and dissatisfied. Nancy had returned to wearing mannish dark pant suits. Of course it was impossible to guess from nothing but these two newspaper photos how the family was getting along together, but they did not look happy.

George and I also received a continuous trickle of second hand private news about James, Nancy, and even Dylan and Ecstasy from Dr. and especially Mrs. Freeman. Mrs. Freeman credited an old school friend of hers for the information she received. Her friend's daughter Vivian Sims, in her thirties, divorced and childless, worked in the administrative offices of Herbert Spencer University and had come to know "Dr. Nancy Berger-Barron" quite well. Nancy often confided her personal problems to her, which she then shared with her mother, and her mother with Edna Freeman. Some of the reports were quite alarming and bode ill for the future.

Dylan and Ecstasy spent very little time in the presence, care and nurture of their parents. James was almost constantly gone. Nancy had not breast-fed either of the children nor taken care of their other daily needs herself; her academic career was her first priority and made staying at home to take care of a baby impossible. Anyhow she shunned it because she considered it part of a woman's traditional slavery. Therefore there had been a constant change of nursemaids and nannies, employed both day and night during the years before each child was old enough to be handed over to a childcare center.

The center that James and Nancy Barron chose was among the best and most expensive ones in the area, for they could well afford it on their combined incomes and Nancy's inherited wealth. But even so there had been unanticipated problems. Dylan and Ecstasy became very aggressive toward each other and other children and increasingly rebellious against their parents. Buying them more and more toys did not help but rather made them more demanding. In addition they caught colds, diarrhea and other sicknesses much more often than what was normal when children were still raised by their mothers at home rather than by paid employees in day care centers with many other children of unknown backgrounds and health. These results really stood to reason and were borne out by reliable studies published much later when the truth could no longer be concealed by progressive opinion leaders and social reformers. But how else could wealthy parents committed to their all-important professional careers like James and Nancy Barron provide care for their children, not to speak of the rapidly growing number of divorced and single mothers forced to work away from home to earn a living?

Some time later Dr. Freeman heard that James was becoming known at Herbert Spencer University as their faculty's most successful seducer of women students. Herbert Spencer University being what it was, he was quite free to "love them and leave them" without fear of official reprimands. On the contrary, his reputation was rather enhanced by his frequent one-night stands.

Reportedly a fellow professor had asked Nancy what she thought of her husband's escapades. She had shrugged and said that her husband and she were not bound by traditional marriage vows or rules and free to do as they pleased. She only hoped he wouldn't infect her with some sexually transmitted disease caught from one of his young women! This story rang true, but we also heard from Mrs. Freeman that Nancy raged against James before her confidante Vivian Sims every time he took up with yet another woman. "All men are scum," she would hiss while Vivian nodded, thinking of her own ex-husband, "and James is scum all through! How dare he treat me like this after all I have done for him! I'll pay him back tenfold someday if it's the last thing I do!"

"James had better be careful," Dr. Freeman said when he heard this, "hell hath no fury like a woman scorned!" But James was not careful; the stories of his brief affairs multiplied as the years went by. Soon afterwards Dr. Freeman, now in his eighties, passed away peacefully. He was greatly mourned by us all. His warning about James came true a few years later.

When Dylan and Ecstasy reached school age, they were placed in the most progressive year-round boarding school their parents could find, Rousseau Academy. My father had heard much about it at Lonely Prairie public school teachers' training sessions. It was financed by generous grants from a foundation started by a multimillionaire industrialist and had won international admiration for allowing its students total freedom. In the lower grades they spent their time roaming the spacious school grounds with the newest, safest playground equipment, watching and imitating children's shows on television and learning a minimum of basic academic skills when they felt like it. In the upper grades excursions to the inner city as well as taking part in marches for peace, civil rights or the "pro-choice" movement were added to the curriculum to teach the young people social involvement. Classrooms were large living rooms where the students sat or lay on the floor around their non-directive teachers, known as "facilitators."

Sex education began in the first grade and continued through high school, emphasizing and teaching the use of condoms and other birth control devices while ridiculing virginity and traditional marriage. The school was among the very first to teach acceptance of homosexuality and lesbianism as alternative lifestyles. It also offered instruction in how to contact "spirit guides" and other occult practices of the burgeoning New Age movement. "We were told this was the wave of the future and we should use all we could of it in our own teaching," my father told us. We saw an hour-long television program on new trends in education emceed by James Barron. He described the school in detail and proudly told his audience that his children had attended it throughout all their school years.

It was at this school that Dylan Barron became close friends with Edison Aldridge, who had easy access to rifles and hand guns. It was at this school that Ecstasy Barron changed her name to "Stacie" and became pregnant at the age of thirteen.

26

Catastrophe: The Rousseau Academy Massacre

"Oh dear God, how horrible!" I exclaimed as George and I were watching the six o'clock evening news on Friday, July 13, 1990. A reporter, mike in hand, was interviewing a teenage girl standing in front of an imposing school building with a big sign, "Rousseau Academy—Summer Session 1990" above the entrance. Her breath came in uneven gulps, her hair was disheveled, her face distorted and streaked with tears. She told of her terror in her classroom early that afternoon. She had been lying on the floor, her eyes shut, when she suddenly heard a shot, looked up and saw that a bullet had struck Tony Brent, a boy in her class, in the forehead. His blood was flowing across his eye and down his cheek. He was not moving. "He was dead," she repeated, "he was dead! Then there was another shot and another shot and Nate Willis lay there dead, with blood all over his chest."

"Did you see the person who did it?" the reporter asked.

"Yes," the girl said, "it was Dylan Barron. Dylan Barron!" She shuddered. "He was standing there with Edison Aldridge. They both had big pistols in their hands. Dylan laughed, aimed his gun at us and said, 'I'm giving a birthday gift to my father. His birthday is tomorrow.' Then he pointed his gun at Mr. Blunt—that's our facilitator—who was coming towards him. 'Here's one more for you, Dad!' he shouted and fired—and Mr. Blunt cried out and fell down, with blood all over his chest and dead just like Nate Willis."

She burst out crying. "We couldn't even hide," she sobbed, "we were all lying on the floor! The room was empty of furniture today because we were having our weekly 'Sensitivity Training,' where we stretch out on the floor and touch and feel each other all over our bodies. Oh my God, I'll never do that again!" George and I looked at each other, speechless. We had never heard of such "sensitivity training" before, but found out later that it was not entirely a pioneering specialty of Rousseau Academy but also used in other schools and colleges at that time. There were several more interviews of students and teachers. Altogether five upper class students and two teachers had been killed.

Both Dylan Barron and his friend Edison Aldridge took part in the murders. When police arrived and were about to take them into custody, they turned their guns upon themselves and fired bullets through the roofs of their mouths into their heads, dropping down dead instantly, their mutilated heads in pools of blood. Over and over again that night and through the weekend the television broadcasts showed the bodies of the victims and the murderers being covered by blankets and carried away on stretchers. They also repeatedly showed photos of the victims and the killers. I felt a pang of acute grief the first time I saw Dylan Barron's picture because he looked so much like James had at that age.

Soon afterwards we caught an interview with James on television. The interviewer treated Dr. James Barron, "the most renowned and respected American philosopher of our time," with utmost sympathy. James never looked straight at the camera and spoke in a wooden voice drained of all emotion. He seemed much older than his forty-nine years and winced once or twice as though in physical pain. I remembered that he had once suffered from a stomach ulcer and thought with pity that he probably still did. He denied all knowledge of what might have motivated his son to give him his macabre birthday present. "Perhaps he was high on drugs," he said dully, "or perhaps the other boy was leading him on." We already knew from the earlier publicity, however, that according to all their classmates Dylan was the leader and Edison the follower among the two.

Nancy had refused to be interviewed about the event but released a public statement putting the blame for Dylan and Edison's deed upon the ridicule and bullying they had endured from the classmates they had killed, and which the two teacher victims had not stopped. George and my father thought she might be right because ridicule and bullying were perennial problems in all schools, and because other students told news reporters that Dylan and Edison had been teased and called names at Rousseau Academy. But that could not have been the only reason, for why had Dylan called the whole massacre a birthday gift for his father? It looked like Dylan had wanted to get back at both his school tormentors and his father at once by this one spectacular act of defiance and revenge.

Newspaper editorials and opinion columns also speculated about the reasons why Dylan and Edison, both from prominent, wealthy families and raised in one of the best progressive educational institutions of the country, might have committed their violent acts. "Rousseau Academy is on the cutting edge of bringing up young people with the utmost possible freedom," wrote one well-known pundit, "no pressure whatsoever to conform in any way to outdated traditional goals or methods of education was put on its students. The killers' parents were well educated, open-minded, progressive people who gave their children space to live as they pleased from childhood on. What motive, then, could Dylan Barron possibly have had for his outburst of violence and hatred against the school and especially against his father?" The role of Edison Aldridge, who had supplied the weapons and bullets from his father's well stocked gun cabinet, received much less news media attention. They portrayed him as an unfortunate tagalong, almost another victim of his determined and charismatic friend.

George and I, all our extended family, our friends at church and at the C. S. Lewis Club, as well as Lucinda, Robert and Neva agreed that James and Nancy had not been good parents and bore much of the responsibility for what had happened. They had distanced themselves from their children ever since their births in every way they could. They had made very clear to them early on that they did not enjoy their company but considered them a burden and a hindrance in the way of their own self-fulfillment. Even when they showered them with toys in childhood and other expensive gifts as they grew older, the children must have sensed that these gifts were not signs of love but rather blackmail their parents paid them to be left alone. Perhaps they also saw that their parents did not even love each other and wondered why they had ever married and put them into the world in the first place.

Finally, and we believed most importantly, James and Nancy had taught their children by word, attitude and example that they were "free to do their own thing" because this world was the only world there was, in perpetual evolutionist change and therefore with no absolute truth, right or wrong. Lucinda remembered James quoting the philosopher Hegel to her with approval many years ago, "What is, is right." Well, Dylan's last "own thing" had been the Rousseau Academy Massacre, and according to Hegel and James it had occurred and hence been right, no matter what it did to innocent or weaker people or even to the perpetrator himself. It was the final outworking of what had begun in the minds of men inspired, as James had told me early in our relationship, by "the serpent at Eden."

Soon after the dead were buried news coverage virtually ceased about "the Rousseau Academy Massacre." Because James Barron was Dylan's father and because the news media wholeheartedly approved of the school's educational policies, it was not publicly discussed in depth again.

We did not know until some time later that the news media had been completely silent about the most important source of information the police had found among Dylan's personal effects. It was a meticulous diary he had kept since entering the seventh grade at Rousseau Academy. That diary had been so damaging to the reputation of Dylan's parents, especially his father, that the media gatekeepers would not allow even excerpts from it to be published. Thanks to Edna Freeman and her connection to Vivian Sims, however, we heard about significant parts of Dylan's diary long before others.

We were astonished and frightened to realize how much Dylan had understood already early in his life of the relationship between his parents and how bitterly he had resented it. In a way he had been going through the same red hot stormy rage against his parents that I had felt immediately after James broke up with me. The difference was that I suffered that rage for a few weeks and only once, whereas poor Dylan suffered it over and over again all his life. With uncanny insight for one so young, he came to see that his mother was exercising command over his father in a bizarre relationship involving almost all aspects of his life. He knew that she had directed his graduate and doctoral studies. He knew that she had smoothed his professional advancement. He knew that she had chosen Herbert Spencer University, her own alma mater, as the academic institution for his home base from which to guide the world.

And not only that—Dylan had understood that his mother had manipulated his father, younger and more handsome than she, into living with her and then marrying her to give her children while her biological clock was still ticking. How weak his father must have been to consent to all this! The only way he had asserted himself had been his many extramarital affairs, of which Dylan was well aware.

All Dylan's young manhood rose up in fury against this weak, despicable father. He finally planned the Rousseau Academy Massacre to show how much he hated him.

27

The Deaths of Lucinda and Ecstasy "Stacie" Barron

Lucinda Barron, now in her early seventies, frail and suffering from high blood pressure, arthritic joints and weakening eyesight, was the only member of her family to fly east for Dylan's funeral. It was the first time since Robert and Neva's double wedding that she and James had seen each other face to face, this time in deep grief over the horrible loss of their son and grandson.

They said little to each other at first, being almost strangers after the many years of separation and with James and Nancy's cruel rejection of Lucinda's offer to help care for the children still on their minds. But after the funeral when James took his mother back to the airport, perhaps never to see her again, they sat together in the waiting room till her flight left and opened their hearts to each other. After her return to Lonely Prairie she told Robert and Neva about their bittersweet conversation.

For the first time since his teens James had seemed softer about his philosophical attitude towards his mother and her faith. "What happened with Dylan made me realize how hard it is to raise a child," he said. "I had honestly thought I did the right thing in allowing him total freedom and not spending much time with him. I admit it suited my own preferences as well, but I had rebelled so much against my own parents and you in particular that I thought it best for Dylan to spare him my interference entirely. I was wrong, both as a son and as a father. Will you forgive me?" Lucinda began to cry at these words; James, too, had tears in his eyes as they hugged each other.

"Dear son, of course I forgive you," she said as they drew apart again, "but we both know our differences go deeper than just what you did. They go down to what you believed and probably still believe," she took a deep breath and bravely added, "about God and Christ." Saying these words, she was afraid he might get up and leave. Did these words not sound like her entreaty "Be right with Jesus" he had hated so much in his youth?

James did not answer right away. Finally he answered thoughtfully, "Before July 13, I would have told you that matter was settled once and for all, and never to bring it up again. Now I can't do that. What I have been through has made me think over my whole life and worldview." Lucinda felt her heart miss a beat; would her son now reconcile himself to God? Her hope grew as he went on, "The last time I did that was before," he too had to take a breath and stop briefly before going on, "before breaking up with little Karen Margrave. That was the big turning point for me. I almost came to God and Christ that year with her, but veered away when the voice told me how easy it was just to lie back on what is." He laughed bitterly. "Oh yes! It was easy to lie back on Dylan's hateful 'birthday gift' and being buried in a closed coffin so his head couldn't be seen. The voice lied."

"What voice?" Lucinda whispered.

"A voice that spoke to me in my mind—a thought, if you will, only it seemed to come from outside myself." James looked away from her as he continued, "I used to call it the only mystical experience in my life. But lately I have wondered whether that voice wasn't also behind the picture of my future I imagined when I was still in high school—the picture of becoming a world leader by way of philosophy. That did come true, you know."

He went on with a tinge of pride, "The world today is being shaped by my words. I am to our generation what John Dewey was to his, or Voltaire and Rousseau were to theirs." He stopped himself for a moment and frowned. When he resumed, his earlier mood of sober reflection and near repentance had changed to blatant boasting, "I guess Rousseau Academy is one of my philosophical children. Dylan is gone, but Rousseau Academy will survive, flourish and set the pace for public education everywhere. Western civilization is dying and I am hastening its death. So be it."

Her flight was called and these were the last words of her eldest son Lucinda took back with her on her return. She told Robert and Neva that she was in agony about him. When I heard of it, I saw that once again he had seemed on the verge of sharing her faith and once again veered away into his self-idolatry, just like so often before with me.

About ten days later she died very suddenly from a stroke. Robert and Neva thought that her fresh agony over James might have precipitated her death. Many members of the Barron and Durant families and a huge crowd of Christian friends like George and I filled the sanctuary of Grace Baptist Church. Because we who had known her closely knew she was now with God in eternal joy, we did not grieve for her but only for our own loss.

James had flown in for the funeral. He sat apart from his family in the same pew as that Sunday evening long ago when crippled Dr. Johnson gave his message of peace and joy in the Lord. As it happened, George and I sat across the aisle from him. I looked across just as James looked my way. Our eyes met. His face lit up in a smile of welcome. I nodded briefly in acknowledgment and turned away. I never looked back. I felt a distant sadness, remembering that this man's youthful, beautiful face had once looked to me in this very place like the face of an angel. Now he was a stranger, and we might never have known each other.

The Rousseau Academy Massacre was soon followed by another no less public and no less horrible tragedy in the lives of James and Nancy Barron. It began just one month after Lucinda's burial, when James and Nancy were informed by the Rousseau Academy that their daughter Ecstasy, then thirteen years old, was two months pregnant. Ecstasy revealed that the father of the baby was Edison Aldridge, Dylan's companion in the Massacre.

James and Nancy decided right away to have the baby—they called it "the product of conception"—aborted. There was no problem about this because it was not the first time the Rousseau Academy had had to deal with a student's pregnancy. The school believed that it had done the best it could to prevent it from happening by its comprehensive sex education program from first to twelfth grade, making contraceptive devices and birth control pills freely available, and referrals to abortion clinics as backup for contraceptive failure. Abstinence from extramarital sex was never promoted because it was a severe restriction on the students' freedom to choose their own lifestyles. It would also have been an unwanted concession to biblical morality.

Ecstasy, or "Stacie" as she wished to be called because she hated the name her parents had given her, furiously resisted her parents' decision. She was a plump, ungainly girl, especially in the heavy, oversized, extra long-sleeved sweaters knit with huge stitches and reaching to the knees, worn over tight stirrup pants, which were all the rage for teenage girls that fall. She felt Edison Aldridge had been the only person in her life who had shown her any affection. "I loved Edison, and he loved me," she kept screaming at James and Nancy, "and I want to have his child. You have no right to have my baby killed!" She also screamed at them that they had always told her she was to be free to live as she liked, so why did they now impose their will on hers? "Why don't you let me have my baby?" she would sob, almost always ending furiously, "I hate you! You never loved me! I wish you were dead! I wish I had never been born!"

In September 1990 after weeks of this struggle James and Nancy exercised their legal authority over their daughter, now fourteen and still a minor. She resisted them to the very end when they had her anesthetized by force and the abortion performed at a clinic recommended by the Rousseau Academy. Her last words to them before the anesthesia took hold were, "I hate you! I wish you were dead!" The parents took these words in stride, believing Ecstasy would feel different about it all once the abortion was behind her.

The final horror followed: Ecstasy's uterus was perforated during the "procedure" and after profuse internal bleeding she fell into a coma. She was transferred to a famous Baltimore hospital where she lay unconscious and on life support for over a year. Somehow the news media got hold of the story, which was splashed over major newspapers and television shows and the sensation-peddling scandal sheets at grocery check-outs all over the country. This time the fame and reputation of James as a great philosopher and opinion leader did not protect him from unwanted notoriety; the names Dr. James Barron, Dr. Nancy Berger-Barron and Ecstasy "Stacie" Barron became household words, and their biographical details juicy material for the writers of opinion columns, psychologists and counseling services.

When the medical experts at the hospital where Ecstasy was lingering agreed in late 1991 that no improvement in her condition was likely, the question of discontinuing her life support arose. A heated public campaign between pro-life people wanting to save Ecstasy's life and "pro-choice" people wanting James and Nancy to "pull the plug" followed. James, the well-known author of the pioneering "pro-choice" article "Good Death," which had brought his dying father to Christ almost twenty years ago, could not well resist the "pro-choice" side's call for ending Ecstasy's life support, and Nancy agreed with him. This decision was implemented shortly before Christmas 1991 while pro-life demonstrators unsuccessfully picketed the hospital. Ecstasy's death was another milestone in the battle over abortion which had begun in 1973 and still rages today.

28

James' Divorce; "The Consolation of Philosophy"

In January 1992 immediately after Ecstasy's termination yet another blow fell on James, his bitter and messy divorce which dragged on for almost a year. Here was one more occasion for a prolonged news media feeding frenzy involving this famous man who had only just approved his teenage daughter's forced and botched abortion and then her death by withdrawal of her life support. At least the media silence about the Rousseau Academy Massacre was still mostly kept, probably because other influential patrons of the Academy besides James and Nancy had enough pull behind the scenes to enforce it.

We could not help but feel sorry for James as the news reports about the divorce multiplied. Nancy was totally vindictive and left no stone unturned to put all the blame for the failure of their marriage on him. Though Dylan's role in the Rousseau Academy Massacre was not explicitly brought forward before the divorce court, Nancy and her high-powered divorce attorney made extensive use of his diary to show what a despicable father and husband James had been in the eyes of his son, and how Dylan's revulsion against James had led him to commit murder ending in suicide as a "birthday gift" to his despised father.

James' many brief affairs with young women students were cited over and over again, sometimes with the assistance of some of the young women themselves who were eager to take vengeance on this older man who had used and discarded them. Nancy's attorney had made inquiries into James' early life and unearthed the Dorrie Fisher story as proof of his innately corrupt character. Nancy portrayed herself as the faithful, innocent, betrayed and longsuffering wife of a thankless scoundrel whose career she had nurtured and promoted for many years and whose children she had borne self-sacrificially.

James retaliated by arguing convincingly that Nancy had married him solely to have children while her biological clock was still ticking, and that he was the one who had sacrificed himself in accommodating this plain older woman. "If Dylan hadn't been on the way, I would never have married you!" he shouted at her across the courtroom.

"If you hadn't been able to make him, I wouldn't have married you either!" she shouted back. The scandal sheets loved it. James pointed to the couple's pre-nuptial agreement as proof that Nancy had never intended the marriage to be permanent. He had felt himself entitled to limitless extramarital affairs because the marriage was undertaken by both parties with the explicit understanding that it did not bind them to biblical faithfulness, as proven by their wedding vows. One of his witnesses was the professor from Herbert Spencer University whom Nancy had told that both she and James considered their marriage non-traditional and were both free to do what they liked.

James' marriage was dissolved in January 1993 by the now common "no-fault divorce" with no blame attached to either party. Their property was divided according to the couple's pre-nuptial agreement. The court granted Nancy's petition that her maiden name be restored. There was one additional development which now began to be reported in the sensation-hunting scandal magazines sold in supermarkets. We knew that James had moved out of the residence he had shared with Nancy when the divorce began, but we did not learn until now that Vivian Sims had moved in to replace him as soon as he left. The two women had become very close friends and were seen together everywhere. The scandal magazines did not scruple to hint that Nancy Berger and Vivian Sims might be lesbian lovers.

This allegation was confirmed a few months afterwards. For some time already more and more homosexuals and lesbians had been emboldened to "come out of the closet." Now Nancy and Vivian took this step as well with considerable public fanfare. This, of course, must have been a further painful blow to James' self-esteem. In the summer of 1993 he left Herbert Spencer University and accepted a position as "Philosopher in Residence" at a prominent liberal New York City think tank.

In the fall of 1994 a new, short book by James Barron appeared. The massive recent publicity about James, though derogatory, helped to make it a bestseller because his name was now widely known not only among progressive intellectuals of his own kind but also the general public. As with his earlier major work *The Metamorphosis of Philosophy: From Atheism to New Age,* Swenson Books received an advertising flyer from the publisher, and George and I read the book.

The book's name was *The Consolation of Philosophy.* It was comparable to C. S. Lewis's *A Grief Observed,* the autobiographical account of his rage against God whom he called "the cosmic sadist" in his despair after the death of his beloved wife Joy, and of his beginning recovery. The difference was that James was not raging against God but against philosophy, which "had no consolation for me when my whole private life was laid bare and then destroyed before my eyes." He wrote sarcastically that you could "read it, listen to it, talk about it, play mind games with it, teach it, analyze it, write about it, make a living with it, entertain yourself with it, kill time with it. You can also use it to suppress your thoughts about your suffering and grief. It can be an anesthetic for a while; it cannot be a consolation. I know—I have been there and done that."

James had borrowed the title for his book from a much earlier one with the same name by Boethius, a Christian philosopher living 470–525 A.D. This man, a Roman, served the Ostrogothic emperor Theodoric, was accused of treason, imprisoned and finally executed. He had written his book while in prison, but it did not really deal with consolation when in trouble. "And I believe this is true for all human philosophy," James wrote. "As I read the book, I was reminded of a quote from Augustine, who lived shortly before Boethius: 'I have read in Plato and Cicero sayings that are very wise and very beautiful; but I never read in either of them: 'Come to me, all you who are weary and burdened, and I will give you rest.' Philosophy does not promise rest; Christ does."

When I read this, tears came to my eyes. I remembered that tender moment when I had quoted Augustine's "Thou hast made us for Thyself, and our heart is restless till it rests in Thee" to young James, and he had answered me with the same quote he now used in his new book. Could it be that his trials had finally brought him to the faith? I warned myself not to hope too much too early; I knew his lifetime pattern to draw close to Christ only to draw back again before committing himself.

I read on. James said next that the best medicine human philosophy could offer to one who suffered with or for others was the advice of stoicism not to get too deeply involved emotionally. This, he felt, was good but not good enough if the suffering was one's own. Then he quoted the second stanza from the poem "Invictus" by William Ernest Henley:

> In the full clutch of circumstance
> I have not winced nor cried aloud,
> Under the bludgeonings of chance
> My head is bloody, but unbowed.

"These lines describe me today," James wrote, "as I look back on the last three years of my life. They do not describe me completely. I *have* winced under 'the bludgeonings of chance.' There were times when I considered putting a loaded gun to my head and pulling the trigger or jumping from the top of a tall building to stop the memories. Not only the recent memories of my son before the undertakers were done with him, of my daughter hooked to her ventilator, or of the man-woman who enslaved me so she could bring them into the world and who hated me. I could not bear these memories, but even less the good ones from long ago when none of all this horror had happened yet. The good memories cut deepest when you are in the pit of agony!

"What pulled me out of that pit in the end were Henley's words, 'My head is bloody, but unbowed.' My salvation was not in philosophy—it was in me! I myself am my ultimate anchor in this world, the only world there is, without rest. And even if there really were another world, the kingdom of God the Creator and Christ the Savior who gives rest, the price I would have to pay to enter it is too high. I would have to surrender myself, my ultimate anchor in this world. I cannot pay that price. And so I end with Henley:

> It matters not how strait the gate,
> How charged with punishments the scroll,
> I am the master of my fate:
> I am the captain of my soul.

29
The Work of Swenson Books; The MacPherson Family Reunion; Sylvia Draws James In

While James reached the zenith of his career and suffered the dreadful destruction of his private life, George and I were happy and blessed with our five wonderful children. All of them early became and have always remained dedicated Christian believers, encouraged by their parents, two sets of loving and beloved, involved grandparents, and the help of a large extended family and a caring church.

Swenson Books prospered and expanded along with our family. This was due in part to the growth of the creationist movement. Within the next three decades many more creationist materials became available to show the scientific bankruptcy of evolution. George saw to it that Swenson Books stocked them all in a separate section of the store where they could be previewed and creationist seminars and meetings could be advertised.

Another vital outreach of Swenson Books was its investment in educational materials for families who began to school their children at home in the early 1980s. Public education, based on ideas introduced by John Dewey at the turn of the century and propagated by leading American educators and philosophers like James ever since, had become woefully lacking in academic achievement and discipline. Christian parents were in the forefront of this movement because the public schools aggressively promoted an increasingly anti-Christian worldview in their teaching, beginning with indoctrination in evolution. More and more Bible-believing churches added schools to their ministries. Some, like our own rapidly growing church in Battle Hill, operated schools and also helped the home schooling families in our congregation. George and I home-schooled our younger children, and so did Robert and Neva. Colleges and universities accept home-schooled students because they are almost always much better disciplined and academically prepared than their public school peers. Besides, most home-schooled students grow up in intact homes, whereas a majority of their public school peers are children of divorce.

James, who had always been a keen observer of what went on in higher education and who occasionally bucked the "politically correct" opinions of the establishment, wrote an interesting article named "Passing the Torch," published in the spring of 1994. With his perennial prophetic insight he predicted that the torch in the race for scientific advances would soon pass from the Western countries, especially the United States, to oriental nations like China and South Korea. The main reason for this, he wrote, was these nations' proverbial diligence, hard work and dedication to learning. Already for some time the number of American college students in the "hard sciences"—engineering, math, medicine, physics—had been diminishing, and the number of foreign students, mainly from Asia, increasing. Within a generation, James predicted, these students would enable their countries to assume the leadership of the world not only in science and technology but possibly in politics as well. "And we must concede," James stated, "that our educational model of 'all play, no work' from kindergarten through high school is largely responsible for this result." This article was widely circulated and applauded among politically conservative people, a new first for James.

Swenson Books took part in yet another crucial effort to help college-bound Christian young people keep and defend their Christian faith against philosophical attacks. Our effort consisted in the dissemination of materials elaborating a biblical Christian worldview. A pioneer in this endeavor was the late Francis Schaeffer, whose ground-breaking book *How Shall We Then Live* was available at Swenson Books for many years. There was also a small but excellent ministry in Colorado named the "Summit Ministries." It was headed by Dr. David Noebel, a Christian philosopher who taught high school seniors and college freshmen in two-week summer seminars how to approach religion, philosophy, history, economics, sociology, psychology and related fields of human action from the biblical Christian perspective.

In the summer of 1994, George and I were also given the big task of arranging for the next MacPherson family reunion to take place in Battle Hill in June 1995. Our immediate family now consisted of our five children, two of them married with children of their own. Both our mothers, now in their eighties, were still with us. They, George's older brothers and sister, their spouses and extended families came to some sixty members. There were Swenson relatives as well; to our delight, one of George's "first cousins once removed" and his wife flew in from Norway to be with us for the occasion.

In addition there were the spouses of the younger generation and their families. Among these was Robert and Beth Barron's son Robert Jr., who had met our daughter Mary Anne, just a few months older than he, while both were attending a Christian college together. From the beginning they seemed made for each other and they were married to the joy of us all in 1993. Their beautiful little Karen Beth arrived in 1994. Thus the family relationship between the Barrons and the Margraves, which had failed to form when James and I broke up in 1965, became a most welcome reality after all. Robert and Neva, their spouses, their children and a couple of grandchildren were invited to the family reunion and gladly agreed to attend.

Because of this development James was now also in our extended family. We sent him an invitation but he declined, saying that he was already scheduled to be the keynote speaker at a regional conference of the American Educators Association. As we learned from local newspaper announcements, that conference would take place right here in Battle Hill. It would begin at 6:00 P.M. in one of the big ball rooms of our most prestigious hotel, at the same time and place as our family reunion. It was possible, though perhaps not likely in view of the past, that James might at least look in on us all before his own meeting.

George and I came to our reunion early along with our immediate family to make sure everything was ready. We sat at the head table next to our mothers, this reunion's matriarchs. We had an excellent observation post from which we could see the huge family stream in, decked in holiday finery.

We waved happily to Neva and David Ploughman and their children as they came to be at the "MacPherson Family Reunion" for the first time. Their eldest daughter Sylvia, the one born with Down Syndrome, was now twenty-five years old. Like most people with her handicap she was short and a little plump. Tonight she was gracefully dressed in a loose-fitting blue gown with little white flowers and a beautiful white lace collar. Her light brown hair was cut short, with part of it on top of her head brushed back and caught in a lovely ribbon of the same material as her dress. She was sitting beside Neva, and both were facing the wide open entrance door as we were. She also looked happily around the big ballroom. Whenever I saw her sweet little face with the slightly slanted eyes, she was beaming with joy.

Once or twice I saw Sylvia and her mother lovingly hugging and kissing each other. I remembered the deep struggle it had cost Neva to accept Sylvia with love before God had taken away her burden in answer to her prayer of Psalm 55:22. I also remembered how James had hurt David and Neva by telling them that Sylvia should have been aborted, and later that fortunately such children died at an early age. I silently shook my head at James' hardness of heart. I knew how hard it had been for David and Neva to forgive him, and that in spite of it all they had prayed with their children all these years that Uncle James might yet come to the Lord.

In that exact moment James stood in the door and looked in. Yes, it was he, tall, very slender in a dark pinstriped suit, his hair grey at the temples, his face grave. The next moment there was a loud, anguished cry, "Uncle James! Uncle James!" It was Sylvia, who remembered James from when he had attended the funeral of Lucinda. Her cry had been so loud and desperate that all noise in the room died down instantly. James stood rooted to the spot, not knowing how to react.

Sylvia got up and ran toward James. Neva made a movement to stop her, but she did not succeed. Sylvia halted before James, who loomed tall, dark and formal above her. She looked defenseless like a little child. She turned her face up to him and opened her arms wide as if to hug him.

"Uncle James!" she repeated, still in an anguished voice which shook with barely suppressed sobs, loud enough so we could all hear and understand, "I love you! We love you! We pray for you all the time! We love you so much! Please, please, come in! Come!"

James was still standing there looking at her, not moving. "Come! Please!" Sylvia repeated. Then she took him by the hand and gently pulled him forward. I held my breath in suspense as I watched; I think all of us who knew him did. Would he resist or pull his hand away?

Then we all breathed in relief. He left his hand in Sylvia's and walked in by her side. Both smiled through tears running down their cheeks. "I could not resist Sylvia," James told Neva later, "that total, unfeigned love! She was like Christ Himself to me."

30
"The Weakness of God"

We saw James sit down with Sylvia at the Ploughmans' table. Dinner was served and they ate it together, conversing animatedly all the while. George wondered whether he should go over and welcome James to the reunion, but decided against it; he felt he would be intruding in what was obviously James' homecoming on a much deeper level. After the meal James got up and hurriedly left the room; only now did we remember that he was supposed to be at the American Educators Association meeting as their keynote speaker.

Neva, flushed with excitement and joy, rushed over to talk to us. "I couldn't wait to tell you," she said, beaming and with tears in her eyes at the same time, "James has come to Christ! Sylvia brought him in! While he was walking with her to our table, he thought with horror that he would have had her aborted and had wished for her early death. But she just loved him unconditionally! He said he was so grateful for her little warm hand holding on to his hand with only love for him that it made him cry." Neva wiped tears from her own face before going on, "And so, James said, he gave in. He could not help himself. He was ashamed of himself and all the horrible things he had said and done all his life, but he was also full of joy. He smiled and said something I didn't quite understand, 'Certitude, certitude, feeling joy peace'."

"He quoted from the Pascal Memorial," I murmured, "Pascal's testimony of meeting with the Lord. So it stayed with him all these years."

"He also quoted from the Bible," said Neva, "'The foolishness of God is wiser than men; and the weakness of God is stronger than men.' He must have remembered it from our mother's Bible lessons. They stayed with him too! He said in awe, 'That's why He used Sylvia to speak to me. How wise is His foolishness and how strong is His weakness to use a Down Syndrome child to convict and convert me—me, the famous philosopher of our day.'"

After a moment of thought George said slowly, "Yes, Sylvia was God's final, decisive witness to James. But she was not the only one. Your mother sowed the early seeds. You, Neva, and Robert helped water them. You, Karen, added more seeds and your love."

"You had a part in it too, George," I put in, "after Robert and Neva's wedding you spoke to him of created reality as God's foot in the door to his heart. You told him Christ stood at that door knocking, and asked him to open his heart to Him. But then he refused. Evolution was his means of denying what he really knew was the truth."

George nodded. "I saw the struggle in him," he said, "remember how desperately he asked how he could not help but know that there is a difference between what it real and what is not, deny that anything really is, and how could he do a doctoral thesis about it? I knew God's Holy Spirit was wrestling with him then. I loved him at that moment too." After a brief pause he ended, "We all loved James with a perilous love, Christ's love, risking grief, abuse and rejection. We agonized over him as Christ did over Jerusalem: 'How often would I have gathered your children together, as a hen gathers her brood under her wings, but you would not!' For that agony, too, and His agony on the cross He deserves our everlasting love and worship."

"The trials James endured must have helped bring him in, too, with all their pain," said Neva.

George nodded. "All of it was needed in God's providence," he said, "so Sylvia could help James to give himself up to Christ tonight. Christ in her spoke to him." We all sat silent for a little while.

"Where is James now?" I asked.

"He had to go and speak to the American Educators Association," Neva answered. "'I am not ready for this,' he said, 'so soon after what has just happened to me. Pray that God will give me what to say and how to say it. I know I must say the opposite of what I came prepared to say. I must speak truth, but with kindness. Pray I won't speak with my clever sarcasm, or go off on tangents, or lecture them.'

"And one more thing," Neva added, "James asked us to pray that if the 'voice' spoke to him before his speech he would say 'No' to it."

"What voice?" we asked.

"He said it was perhaps just a thought in his mind or his own worldly ambition, but that it seemed to come from outside himself. He said he thought now that the voice came from Satan—he called him 'the serpent at Eden.' He said he first heard it when adopting evolution in high school, next when choosing philosophy as his career, and last before breaking off with you, Karen. 'It promised me total freedom to do all I wanted, and worldly leadership,' he said, 'but following it almost destroyed me. Pray that I will never listen to it again.'"

We could not talk any more because the reunion program and festivities were beginning. I am sure that the entire Barron family prayed for James almost constantly while he was gone. When he returned, he looked tired but victorious. He walked over to Neva's table. We saw Robert and Beth Barron join them. Of course we assumed James was now sharing the contents of his speech with his family. A day or two later Neva called me from Lonely Prairie and shared it with me.

James began by praising the educators for their desire to bring up their young student charges with freedom to inquire into the nature of reality and to enable them to live in it as wise stewards, neither abusing it nor neglecting its management. Each new generation, he continued, must examine its cultural inheritance, like a wise steward change or discard what might be obsolete or false, and adopt what agreed better with true reality. No generation, James said, fulfilled this task perfectly.

"Where we have gone wrong in our own generation, I believe," he said, "is that we have allowed our young people too much freedom. We have absorbed almost unthinkingly the idea of the 'noble savage' inherited from Rousseau that man is fundamentally good and needs no restraint. We have denied the reality of young people's rebellious hearts. In our reaction against earlier generations' sometimes unreasonable restraints on our personal freedom we have neglected our management responsibility for our young people. We have discarded absolute truth and absolute values. Our 'values clarification' courses are not helping our young people to face reality but rather encourage them to try to cheat it. We know, for example, that cheating on tests is now an epidemic. We really know our non-judgmental 'values clarification' does not help but harms our students in the long run.

"We really know our students need more factual knowledge in all subjects and are falling behind students from much less advanced countries. We really know that such innovations of our generation as 'learning by doing' or sex education are failures. Despite or rather because of our good intention of making learning more pleasant for them, our students now learn nothing thoroughly unless blessed by parents bucking our system. In our wish or resignation to let our young people do freely what comes naturally, we have abandoned all management of their sexual behavior. Now our children grow up oversexed and spoiled for mature, healthy family relationships; their children will suffer most from the consequences. We have allowed our young people's mass infection with sexually transmitted diseases, their pregnancies out of wedlock and their millions of abortions which may end in lifelong sterility and sometimes even death.

"We really know that the main ethical do's and don'ts our parents or grandparents drilled into us are not outdated but reality-ordained for our well-being. I suppressed my own knowledge of absolute ethical yeas and nays for years so I could be a leader of the new morality revolution. In the end I had to pay for my denial through the deaths of my children and breakup of my marriage.

"In the 1960s, the golden age of the youth revolution when I was a graduate student, I totally accepted the then current slogan 'Question Authority.' I wanted to do away with authority entirely as did many of my peers. I remember I had a black T-shirt made with 'Question Authority' printed on my chest in big red letters. I gave a speech in the student union center of Battle Hill University where I displayed it to the applause of the crowd. Now it is true that human authority is not absolute but subject to the absolute ethical yeas and nays true reality imposes. To the extent it refuses to be subject to these absolute yeas and nays, we may and should rightly question its actions.

"But we cannot question the very existence of authority. We ourselves as educators and parents exercise authority by virtue of being educators and parents. That is a fact of true reality which we deny at our deadly peril. Our students and children must accept it as well so that they and their children may prosper. We have tended to abdicate our rightful authority. We dread saying 'no' to our students and children. We should dread not saying 'no' to them when we know we should.

"Finally, in our rightful desire to make our schools and society safe and pleasant for the diversity of our people, we have virtually banished from our public life the very mention of the Creator of the reality by which we must live. We began with outlawing school prayers in 1962. We use the phrase 'separation of church and state' as our mantra to stifle any remotely Christian expression in our classrooms. That, too, met with my complete approval until literally an hour ago. I see now that it is indispensable for our welfare. I beg you to do what you can as educators to restore the freedom of our young people to acknowledge God."

"What a wonderful beginning of James' new life," I told Neva after hearing her report.

"Yes," she agreed, "that's what Robert said, too. Of course he was ready with a Bible verse right away which tells exactly what happened to James: *'Therefore if any man be in Christ, he is a new creation: old things are passed away; behold, all things are become new.'"* (2 Corinthians 5:17)

Postscript

The professional career of "James Barron" (but not his private life, set in the present) is partly modeled after that of the eminent American philosopher John Dewey (1859–1952) who fathered our modern system of public education. Dewey's philosophy is a detailed and consistent outworking of faith in a self-contained evolutionist universe in constant, endless flux, where we "learn by doing" without meaning, purpose, goals or rest. The supernatural, truth and absolutes are dropped as obsolete superstitions perhaps functional in the past but now expendable. Man's role is to control the world and its only and self-validating function, growth. His action is to be evaluated by its consequences according to the experimental method of the modern scientific laboratory. Ultimate immutable reality does not exist.

Dewey was born and raised in Vermont. His father was easy-going and somewhat indifferent with regard to his son's religious nurture. Dewey's mother Lucina, in part the model for "Lucinda Barron," visited a series of revival meetings with a friend, was converted and became a pious evangelical Christian. She taught young

John Dewey Bible stories, condemned dancing, card-playing, drinking and gambling, and forbade them to her son. She was deeply concerned about his salvation. John Dewey stated in later life that his mother's constant questioning him whether he was "right with Jesus" was especially repugnant to him. The family attended Burlington's liberal Protestant First Congregational Church, where Lucina's Bible-based convictions were not favored. In his forties Dewey discarded church membership altogether, believing with liberal Protestantism that the biblical difference between believers in Christ and "unsaved" unbelievers must be abolished. He also shared liberal Protestantism's belief in the basic goodness of man and repudiation of biblical law.

At the end of his junior year at the University of Vermont, Dewey, then 18, became acquainted with evolutionist thought through a textbook of physiology written by "Darwin's Bulldog" Thomas Henry Huxley. This was the most significant turning point in his life and transformed him from an indifferent student to sudden excellence, winning the highest grades in philosophy ever recorded at that school.

A year later when Dewey was teaching high school in Oil City, Pennsylvania, he had what he later called the one and only "mystic experience" of his life. He told a friend that one evening while he sat reading he received an answer to the one question still worrying him: whether he really meant business when he prayed. It was not a dramatic experience, just a supremely blissful feeling which came out like this: "What the hell are you worrying about anyway? Whatever is here is here, and you can just lie back on it." It stripped him of his last vestige of caring about God and freed him from all worry and all belief except a vague pantheism. This was his religion, and he said that he got it that night in Oil City.

Later Dewey taught philosophy at the Universities of Michigan, Minnesota, Chicago and Columbia from 1884 to 1939. Between 1895 and 1929 he traveled all over the world to lecture at famous universities and advise governments on modernizing their public education, receiving many honors along the way. Unlike the private life of "James Barron," John Dewey's long private life was morally unimpeachable, even admirable, like that of many of his generation who rejected Christianity but still practiced its moral customs. It was left to later generations to shake off the yoke of these customs as well, as did "James Barron."

Dewey was active in numerous influential professional associations, including the American Civil Liberties Union (ACLU) he helped found in 1920. He helped draft and signed Humanist Manifesto I. It rejected traditional religion in the name of evolution, modern science and man's intelligent inquiry. Dewey died peacefully at 93, is held in highest honor in the academic world as America's greatest modern philosopher, and still rules the world from the grave.

THEY SHALL *NOT* BE ASHAMED

Part 2

"A Place of Springs"

Blessed is the man whose strength is in thee;
In whose heart are the ways of them
Who passing through the valley of
Weeping Make it a place of springs.

Psalm 84:5–6—The Holy Bible (KJV, Updated NASB):

God often chooses those who had been the greatest sinners to receive His greatest grace, because this can reveal His goodness more dramatically.

—Brother Lawrence

Falls from which we return to the Lord are sources of humility, of light, of strength, and of comfort to others. **"All things work together for good to them that love God"** *Romans 8:28 (KJV). Augustine adds, "Even their sins."*

—Pastor Richard Wurmbrand

A Christian has only to be in order to change the world, for in that act of being there is contained all the mystery of supernatural life.

—Christopher Dawson

To the Reader

The following are the names of real people and organizations in Part 2, listed in alphabetical order. The names of very well-known people and organizations have been omitted (examples: John Calvin; the Salvation Army).
- Robert Bork
- Whittaker Chambers (*Witness*)
- Christopher Dawson
- John Dewey
- The Gideons
- Kurt Goedel
- Anita Hill
- Kenneth Scott Latourette (*A History of Christianity*)
- Brother Lawrence (*The Practice of the Presence of God*)
- George MacDonald
- Malcolm Muggeridge
- National Organization for Women
- Dr. David Noebel
- Blaise Pascal
- Josef Pieper
- Michael Ruse
- Lord Bertrand Russell (*Why I Am Not a Christian*)
- Andrei Sakharov
- Peter Singer
- Aleksandr Solzhenitsyn (*The Gulag Archipelago; Candle in the Wind*)
- Dr. Benjamin Spock (*Common Sense Book of Baby and Child Care*)
- The Summit Ministries (P. O. Box 207, Manitou Springs, CO 80829)
- Clarence Thomas
- Oscar Wilde (*The Picture of Dorian Gray*)
- Pastor Richard Wurmbrand (*Reaching Toward the Heights*)

All other persons and organizations are fictional, and any resemblance between them and actual persons or organizations is coincidental, except for "Fairfield University," lovingly modeled after Oklahoma Wesleyan University.

Table of Contents

1: Sylvia 111
2: My First Hours as a Christian 113
3: Interview on a Plane 117
4: A Glimpse of the Future 121
5: First Reflections, First Testing 124
6: Second Testing 128
7: Lisa Misses the Mark 133
8: The Radio Broadcast; All Hell Breaks Loose 136
9: First Date 141
10: Why They Must Kill Us 145
11: Transitions 149
12: In Praise of Bernard Gottlieb 154
13: Witness before Enemies 158
14: Strength, Goodness and Love 162
15: Stumbling Blocks 166
16: The Gag Order Works; A New Door Opens 170
17: The Greatest of These is Love 174
18: Lonely Prairie and Fairfield University 179
19: "Sister Poverty" 183
20: A Hateful Attack and Two Great Blessings 187
21: Descent into Hell 191
22: Kings and Priests 196
23: A Grown Man Does Not Cry 200
24: A Place of Springs 204

1
Sylvia

My new life began a little after six o'clock the evening of June 15, 1995. I was on my way to address a regional meeting of the American Educators Association in the grand ballroom of one of Battle Hill's most prestigious hotels. I had also been invited to the MacPherson Family Reunion, scheduled for that same evening in an adjacent ballroom of the same hotel, because my brother Robert's eldest son had married a MacPherson daughter and thus made me related to the MacPhersons too. I thought I would just take time for one quick look at that family reunion and stopped by the open entrance to do so.

That is when my sister Neva Ploughman's daughter, Sylvia, spotted me and cried out desperately, "Uncle James! Uncle James!" The noisy hubbub of the crowd in the big hotel ballroom suddenly stopped dead still.

Like most people with Down Syndrome, Sylvia is short and plump. That evening she was wearing a loose gown made of soft blue cloth with little white flowers and a pretty lace collar around her short neck. Her light brown hair was cut short, and part of it was tied back with a ribbon matching her gown. She looked like a little child, much younger than her twenty-five years, as she came running toward me. Her little pale, childlike face was lifted up to me with indescribable urgency, despair, and love. She seemed near tears.

Now she stood right in front of me, panting a little. Her light blue, slightly slanted eyes met mine, captured me and would not let me look or walk away from her. I felt awkward about my height, being over a foot taller than she and towering above her in my dark formal attire. In her complete innocence, she was totally unaware of the many people watching us. By contrast I, in my habitual preoccupation with myself and my appearance before others, cringed inwardly at the thought of being the object of their attentive scrutiny.

Sylvia opened her arms wide as if to hug me. It was an unmistakable gesture of welcome and overflowing good will. "Uncle James!" she repeated. Her voice shook with anguish and barely suppressed weeping. It was loud enough so all the people, still silent and hanging on every word, must have understood her.

"I love you!" Sylvia said. I thought with a pang of shame, she loves me while I would have had her killed in my sister's womb. She loves me, but I despised her and hoped she would die early. Sylvia, retarded, unworthy of life to me, who prided myself on my high I.Q., knew and lived true, unconditional love. I suddenly understood with agony that I in my chosen self-absorption had never truly loved anyone. I was the one who was unworthy of life!

"We love you!" Sylvia exclaimed. "We," I instantly understood, were all the members of my sister's family. They loved me. It did not enter my mind to doubt it even for a second. But I had rejected and despised them all these years, and Sylvia most of all! I stood guilty before the court of my own conscience, awakened at last by the witness of Sylvia's love and purity, and I abhorred myself.

"We pray for you all the time!" Sylvia assured me. They pray for me all the time, I thought, even though I have virtually disowned them. They keep praying for me to God, as my mother did with so much longing, and as my father probably did too at the very end of his life. But I rejected their prayers and love. God forgive me, I thought their love had been a fetter to bind me, to restrict my freedom!

"We love you so much!" Sylvia repeated. Everything in me suddenly wanted to cry out to her "I love you, too!" in reply; it was like a dam bursting in my heart. But outwardly I just stood there, looking at her silently, unable to move.

"Please, please, come in! Come!" Sylvia begged, and again, "Come! Please!" When I still stood there motionless, she reached out her little hand, grasped mine, and gently, so very gently and sweetly as only a little loving child knows how, she began to pull me forward. Her little hand around mine was warm and soft. Oh God, I thought and felt sudden tears well up in my eyes, thank You for that little warm hand! Thank you for Sylvia and her total, unfeigned love! It is Your love which does not count my rebellion, my hardness of heart and my many sins against me. I cannot resist Sylvia and her love. I cannot resist Your love. I cannot resist You, Lord—You ARE love. I can only love You back.   And so Sylvia and I walked in hand in hand to join our family reunion, both of us crying with joy.

I had never felt a joy like this in my whole life. It was not of this world. This joy was my token and assurance of the supernatural world beyond the here and now, which I had strained so long and hard to deny, and of the presence of God my Creator and Sustainer in my heart. I remembered Blaise Pascal's "Memorial" of his meeting with God; Karen Margrave MacPherson, out of God's and her love for me, had found and given it to me during our bittersweet relationship thirty years ago. It had almost brought me to God then with Pascal's jubilant words, "Certitude, certitude, feeling joy peace." So Pascal had felt when he met the personal, living God, "not the God of philosophers and learned men, the God of Jesus Christ" the night of November 23, 1654. So I now felt the evening of June 15, 1995.

As Sylvia and I reached the table where her family sat waiting for us, I said the words aloud. I meant them as confirmation between God and me that I had truly come home to Him at last, as had the prodigal son to his father. And our Father in heaven and I rejoiced together.

I immediately shared with my family what had happened to me thanks to Sylvia. I asked their forgiveness for having rejected them all these years. In particular I asked Neva and her husband David to forgive me for insisting years ago that Sylvia should have been aborted, and for my evil "comfort" that she might die young. How could I have displayed such hardness of heart in response to Neva's letter to me about how she had been tempted to kill Sylvia by suffocating her? I might as well have asked her, "Why didn't you?" and called her choice of life for her little handicapped baby foolishness—even though she had told me that Sylvia had become a great blessing of God to her and the family!

The word "foolishness" caught me up in the memory of my mother speaking of "the foolishness of God" at one of her family Bible studies: *"The foolishness of God is wiser than men, and the weakness of God is stronger than men"* was the New Testament verse. It had stuck in my mind because it seemed so irreverent. How had the apostle Paul dared to speak of God as foolish and weak? "But it's quite true," I said aloud, and quoted the verse to my family, "that's why He used Sylvia to speak to me. How wise is His foolishness and how strong is His weakness to use a Down Syndrome child to convict and convert me—me, the famous philosopher of our day." I suddenly laughed with glad admiration for God's "foolish" and "weak" way of bringing me home to Himself at last.

Then I became serious again as Neva said, "He made and kept Sylvia alive to do for you what she did tonight." I bowed my head as I realized with a shudder that if Neva had had Sylvia aborted, or had put that pillow on her head and killed her instead of letting her live, I might never have come to God.

2

My First Hours as a Christian

Dinner had been served and we had eaten it, all the while talking to each other. When the plates were being removed, I remembered with a pang of alarm that I had been expected for some time already at the American Educators Association meeting to give the keynote speech. I had forgotten all about it! Thankfully they, too, must have consumed their dinner while we were having ours, but by now they must be getting worried about my absence. I must join them right away.

I realized that I could not use the speech I had prepared for this occasion. It was a call to continue on the path the American public education establishment had been pursuing for most of the twentieth century, the path of "learning by doing" without God and without ethical guidelines mapped out by my philosophical predecessor John Dewey. I knew I must say the exact opposite. I, who had spoken to thousands of audiences all my adult life with unbroken success, felt that I was not ready for this first public address so soon after what had just taken place in my heart. I silently prayed a ragged and stumbling prayer to God that He might give me what He wanted me to say. I asked my family to pray that I might speak the truth without sarcasm, without going off on tangents, and without lecturing.

I also told my family of what I called "the voice" in my past life. It was like a thought in my mind, but seemed to come from outside myself. I believe that it came from Satan, the old serpent at Eden who promised Eve she could be as God and eat unharmed, even empowered, from the forbidden tree of the knowledge of good and evil. This had been its promise to me as well.

I first consciously heard the voice when I was still in high school. It told me to accept naturalistic evolution as my life's philosophy because it promised me unlimited freedom to do whatever I liked without ethical restrictions. I passionately embraced it. I heard it the second time when it promised me worldly leadership by choosing evolutionist philosophy as my career. I eagerly obeyed it, and it delivered.

I heard it the last time when I was in love with Karen Margrave. I strongly considered becoming a Christian so she would marry me. I somewhat reluctantly obeyed for the sake of my career, but it deeply hurt and in the end nearly destroyed me. Now I asked my family to pray that I would never listen to it again.

I hurried off to the American Educators Association. They welcomed me with relief and an enthusiastic standing ovation. After all, to them I was still the progressive atheist philosopher, the bold point man of untrammeled individual freedom, no matter what personal blows fate had dealt me. They thought they knew what to expect from me and were looking forward to it.

I stood at the lectern, watching their eager faces and waiting for their applause to die down. These top educators would be bitterly disappointed by what I was about to tell them. I had lived among them too long not to know that I would be making several influential, determined and powerful enemies among them if I went ahead with my new impromptu speech. God's truth, or my flattery of the powers of this world—which would I choose? I was afraid of what my choice of God might do to my worldly position. Dear Lord, be with me, I silently prayed.

My fear subsided. I delivered a speech totally opposed to everything I had ever taught in my life. I ended by calling for my listeners' acknowledgment of God as the Creator and hence Ruler of reality.

When I was done, the vast majority applauded politely but tepidly. The influential leaders of the AEA who had invited me did not applaud at all but stared at me with rigid faces and eyes full of hatred. My earlier fears had come true. These men were now my enemies. Surprisingly there were a very few men and one woman who actually stood up and clapped with enthusiastic abandon, their faces beaming with smiles of total approval.

I excused myself from the meeting in order to return to my family and walked away. Before I could leave the room the woman who had stood up to applaud me rushed to the exit to meet me. In appearance she strongly reminded me of my mother in the beauty of her younger years. She was about forty years old, fairly tall, slender, with dark brown, wavy hair and dark brown eyes. She was elegantly dressed and discreetly made up. Her demeanor was self-assured, regal and cool, with a touch of tired cynicism. A journalist of some sort, I guessed with the checkered experience of many interviews behind me and inwardly sighed. Please, Lord, no interview any more tonight!

I politely motioned for her to precede me as we stepped out of the meeting room. When the doors had closed behind us, she stopped.

"Thank you, Dr. Barron," she said in a low, soft voice, again much like my mother's. We walked on towards my family reunion's ballroom.

"I am Lisa Trent Harrison," she introduced herself; "you may have heard me speak on the radio or read one of my articles or columns in the press."

I nodded. I had never heard her speak, but I had read some of her articles and columns. So this was Lisa Trent Harrison, a prominent spokesperson of "extreme right wing" social and political conservatives. I had pictured her in my mind as a sour, narrow-minded old battle axe. How different was the real woman, exuding femininity, intelligence and informed engagement in all her words and looks!

Lisa looked up into my face and laughed. "I don't match your idea of me," she said. "That's all right. You didn't match my idea of you either in that speech you just gave. I came to the AEA conference to do an article about you as one of the chief destroyers of our way of life. You spoke like one of its would-be restorers. I have done my homework on your philosophical beliefs. Everything you said tonight was a total departure from them, especially the God the Creator conclusion. May I ask what prompted you to speak as you did?"

We had now arrived at the door of the MacPherson Family Reunion room. I half wanted to break off this unwelcome interrogation with a polite excuse. But some new honesty and I dare say God's love for Lisa beginning to work in my heart made me answer, "I had become a Christian just an hour earlier."

All laughter and every trace of cynicism disappeared from her face. I could tell she was totally taken aback by the straightforward simplicity of my answer. She thought it over but could find no way to doubt that I had told her the truth and nothing but the truth. Her perplexed and probing silence showed that she had never met God as had Pascal or even I. She might believe in conservatism's "Judeo-Christian principles" or "traditional family values," but was a stranger to their Author.

I took pity on her. "I understand you must want to ask me more about this," I said gently, "but it's getting late, and I need to rejoin my family now. Perhaps we could meet again in New York after we get back." I correctly assumed she came from New York, the capital of journalism.

"Or perhaps earlier," she said quickly, "What flight are you taking back? I am leaving here tomorrow morning on the first plane to Chicago and change planes there to New York."

"Why, so am I," I exclaimed. We agreed we would share a taxi to the airport and arrange for side by side seating on the plane where she could interview me at leisure. We parted agreeably, though a trace of perplexity and disbelief still lingered on her face.

I told my family about my impromptu address, and they were delighted. Then I took leave of them, promising to keep in touch, and went to my hotel room, looking forward to this night's rest. But it was not to be, or not the physical rest I had counted on. Something was missing. I was desperately hungry and thirsty for a Bible. I had not opened a Bible in many years and did not own one. Where could I obtain a Bible in the middle of the night? I suddenly remembered that a group named the Gideons used to distribute free Bibles to hotels; in fact I had once contributed money to an atheist organization fighting them in court. I looked in the drawer of the nightstand by the bed, and thank God, there was a Bible in the old translation my mother had used, faithfully provided for seekers like myself.

I snatched it up like a starving man would seize a hunk of bread, or a thirsty man a cup of water. Where ought I to begin reading? I thought that people usually begin reading a book with the first chapter and opened the Bible to Genesis 1. After reading it carefully several times and counting one particular phrase I said aloud, "This is God's word and it is true from the beginning. It says ten times in its first chapter that God made each creature 'after its kind.' That means evolution is false."

I remembered that my mother had always loved reading the Psalms. "They are person to person talks with our Lord," she used to say. I turned to Psalm 1 (KJV) and read it again and again to make it my own: *"Blessed is the man that walketh not in the counsel of the ungodly, nor standeth in the way of sinners, nor sitteth in the way of the scornful. But his delight is in the law of the LORD; and in his law doth he meditate day and night. And he shall be like a tree planted by the rivers of water, that bringeth forth his fruit in his season; his leaf also shall not wither; and whatsoever he doeth shall prosper. The ungodly are not so: but are like the chaff which the wind driveth away. Therefore the ungodly shall not stand in the judgment, nor sinners in the congregation of the righteous. For the LORD knoweth the way of the righteous: but the way of the wicked shall perish."*

I felt I could take spiritual nourishment from this one short psalm to last me for a lifetime. I prayed earnestly to God to help me never to walk again in the counsel of the ungodly, stand in the way of sinners, or sit in the seat of the scornful. "You have kept me from doing this tonight," I prayed, "thank You so much! Without You I would have given my prepared speech to avoid future trouble and been once again 'like the chaff which the wind drives away'—barren and worthless."

I went on to the New Testament, reading the first chapter of the Gospel of Matthew. The genealogy of Jesus through Joseph, Mary's husband, which begins this chapter seemed dry and boring at first sight but blessed me nevertheless because it showed me God's care to preserve the names of all the ancestors of "Jesus, who is called Christ." No name will be omitted from God's eternal list of remembrance! The names of little Sylvia and people like her whom this world despises and throws away will be there. I praised Him for this and again for bringing me to Him a short six hours ago.

It was now nearly midnight, and I needed to start the next day at five in the morning. But this last hour with meditation about the Bible and prayer had been the refreshment and rest I had craved and needed most. For the first time in my life You, Lord, were my last thought before falling asleep, and my first thought upon awakening the next morning.

My hunger and thirst for the Bible, completely absent all my earlier life, have never abated since that evening. Since then not one waking hour has gone by that I have not held You in my thoughts, dear Father. Brother Lawrence, like my beloved Blaise Pascal a French Christian of the seventeenth century, spoke of this as "practicing the presence of God." It is the most blessed part of my new life in Christ.

3
Interview on a Plane

The next morning dawned bright and early. I met Lisa Trent Harrison in the hotel lounge where we both had a cup of coffee before boarding our taxi to the Battle Hill Airport. There was no difficulty about arranging for seats next to each other on the plane.

No sooner had the plane taken off than Lisa, with cool, businesslike efficiency, pulled a neat indexed notebook and a slim silver pencil from her purse. She also produced a small tape recorder and asked my permission to switch it on during our conversation. I had done so many interviews before that I had come to think of the recording of my words as a mere formality. Only after I had already assented to Lisa's request did it occur to me that the recording of this interview might be much more problematic. It was my first interview after my radical change from atheist to Christian. It was a "scoop" for Lisa, the publication which would print it and the radio network which would air it. As such, and because I was well known as a leading contemporary philosopher, it was bound to become widely disseminated.

Slanted publicity would follow. Comments by the opinion leaders who mattered would be viciously hostile. It would be infinitely more damaging to me than the waves of news media bilge which had washed over me after my daughter Ecstasy's death by termination of life support in 1991, and my horrible year-long divorce from Nancy Berger, mercifully final in 1993. But my career had survived it all, including my son Dylan's earlier killing spree and suicide at the ultra-liberal Rousseau Academy.

But coming to God and Christ was totally different. In the eyes of my intellectual supporters and their news media allies, it was the worst treason I could have committed. Until last night, I myself had considered academic "failed atheists" my most despicable enemies, to be mocked, shunned, demonized, marginalized and silenced by any available means. Now this would happen to me. It was inevitable.

And Lisa Trent Harrison was about to start the process. She opened her notebook to a page filled with questions to ask me and pressed the starting button on her tape recorder. I took a deep breath and prayed silently, Lord, give me what I should say. I had no time for more preparation or fear, for the interview started immediately.

"In your keynote speech last night, June 15, 1995, to the American Educators Association in Battle Hill, Dr. Barron," Lisa began, "you totally repudiated your earlier atheistic and self-centered philosophy which has made you internationally famous. You defended the teaching of absolute ethical yeas and nays as necessary for our well-being, a teaching you rejected already when you were a graduate teaching assistant at Battle Hill University thirty years ago." She looked at me briefly and coolly, seeming hostile rather than friendly or impartial, before going on.

"In conclusion you asked your audience," she said, quoting from her notebook, "to 'restore the freedom of our young people to acknowledge God' whom you called 'the Creator of the reality by which we must live.' May I ask you again, Dr. Barron, as I did last night: what prompted you to speak as you did?"

I answered again as I had before, "I had become a Christian just an hour earlier." Now my words were on tape and irrevocable.

"Could you elaborate on that?" Lisa asked.

After a heartbeat of silence I answered slowly, looking past Lisa through the plane's window at the bright golden-rosy morning clouds outside (I can still see them in my mind in all the beauty of Your colors, Lord): "My family had a reunion in a ballroom near the AEA meeting. I stopped at the entrance for a look inside. I have a little niece who saw me and called out to me. She was born with Down Syndrome. Up to that moment I had strongly believed and even told her parents that she should have been aborted. She ran to meet me and told me she loved me. She said she and the family had prayed for me all the time. I just stood there," I stopped speaking in total recall of that moment.

"Yes?" prompted Lisa. Her latent hostility had been replaced by reluctant willingness to be open to what I would share with her.

"I suddenly saw myself for what I was and had been all my life," I said so softly that she mechanically pushed the tape recorder closer to me, "and I was ashamed. Sylvia, whom I had thought unworthy of life, loved me with total, unconditional, unfeigned love! I had never loved anyone. I thought that not she but I was the one who was unworthy of life."

Lisa wrote briefly in her notebook. I continued: "She begged me to come in. I couldn't move. She took me by the hand and gently pulled me forward. Her little hand was warm and soft. I was so grateful for that small warm hand around mine. I thanked God for it. That was my very first thank you to Him ever. I thanked Him with tears for Sylvia's and His love which did not count my past rebellion against me. I could not resist His love. I could only love Him back. Sylvia and I walked hand in hand into the room together. And then came the joy."

"The joy?" Lisa murmured, astonished. The joy I had known was totally new to her. I stopped caring about the tape recorder. I wanted to share the joy I now had with whoever might hear!

"The joy," I repeated, "a joy like none I had ever felt before in my whole life. Such indescribable joy! It came from God. He now lived in my heart. It was His joy in me and my joy in Him." I looked past Lisa towards the bright clouds again, reliving the memory of that joy, Your joy, dear Lord and Father.

I came down to earth again and said, "I am not the first or only one to have received this joy, you know. There was a French scientist named Blaise Pascal who met God the night of November 23, 1654. He wrote what we would call a memorandum—the so-called 'Pascal Memorial'—of the experience. He saw that God was not 'the God of philosophers and learned men,' a figment of men's thoughts.

God is really there. He is the personal, living God Who came to us in Jesus Christ. 'Certitude certitude, feeling joy peace' wrote Pascal, and 'Joy joy joy, tears of joy,' and 'Eternally joyful for one single day of renunciation on earth.'"

"All right," said Lisa thoughtfully after a little pause, "but some theologians would call your experience or Pascal's 'an interesting psychological event inside you' rather than a meeting with God. How would you answer them?"

I instantly remembered Reverend Dr. Brassfield under whose teaching I had grown up in my home town's liberal church. "I was taught by such a theologian in my youth," I said. "His teaching did not explain but explained away all evidences which might have brought me to faith in God. Of course it would define Pascal's or my experience in a reductionist manner as 'only inside you,' rather than meeting the transcendent God. Such theologians as well as modern atheist philosophers have reasoned themselves into a fictitious prison within their minds by denying that anything exists beyond this present world. I know. I was one of their leaders. I am no better than they. But I am out of that prison now."

"Why did you speak of God as the Creator of reality last night?" asked Lisa in a businesslike tone. This, I saw, was one of the questions she had listed in her notebook in advance. "Why your implicit attack upon belief in evolution?"

"Evolution has been understood since Darwin as naturalistic, self-starting and progressing from amoeba to man over billions of years in this, the only world there is. It is indispensable to atheism and the rejection of all moral absolutes," I replied. "I embraced this belief in high school and used it to substantiate my philosophy of man's totally unrestrained individual freedom to do whatever he likes. I was going to reaffirm it in my originally planned speech before the AEA. But after I came to God, I knew I must say exactly the opposite. Reality did not create itself. God did."

"How can you recommend the teaching of creation when science supports evolution?" asked Lisa.

"I never looked into the scientific evidences dealing with origins but uncritically accepted what I was taught in high school, a couple of undergraduate science courses and the popular news media," I answered. "I am not so sure true science really supports evolution. I read Genesis 1, the first chapter of the Bible, last night for the first time—remember, I have only been a Christian for less than twenty-four hours—and it says no less than ten times that God created all living creatures 'after their kind.' I will stick to that and believe true science does not contradict it. I also trust God for showing me evidence from true science when I need it—just as He showed me the Pascal Memorial."

"You say you have only been a Christian for less than twenty-four hours," Lisa said, "will you now call yourself a 'born-again' Christian and adopt a conservative position in political and cultural affairs?"

I stared at her nonplused for a moment. How could I answer such a question? I answered slowly and hesitantly, determined to be completely truthful.

"I have heard the word 'born-again' mockingly echoed among my academic colleagues," I said, "but I never knew what it really meant. If it comes from the

Bible and describes me, then I will gladly take this name as mine. As to political and cultural affairs, I have of course sided with what you and your friends call 'the radical left' since my undergraduate days in the 1960s, especially in the social issues like abortion, feminism, gay rights and the like. Doubtless, I will have to examine my views in light of the Bible and change them if necessary. I have already done this about abortion, which I now repudiate with all my heart. My speech last night is a repudiation of my former views on education. More such repudiations may well be in order. But as for across-the-board adoption of political and social conservatism, I cannot do so at this early stage of my new life in Christ, nor can I promise to do it later, or ever. I can only promise that I will examine it in the light of the Bible."

At this point our interview was interrupted by the announcement that our plane was now making the descent to Chicago's O'Hare Airport. We had about an hour between planes and decided we would just spend it in the waiting area by the gate.

I spotted vending machines in a corner and bought snacks and coffee for Lisa and myself. We sat down and consumed them somewhat tiredly without speaking to each other. Then Lisa asked me the first personal question since we had met.

"Have you ever thought about what harm you might have done to others by your philosophy?" she said accusingly. She obviously did not think I had ever had misgivings about my former teachings.

"It may surprise you, but yes, I did," I answered, "after what happened with my son and my daughter."

She looked distressed for a moment. "I am sorry, Dr. Barron," she said, "I forgot." Then she resumed with mounting anger: "But you didn't change your philosophy. You went on teaching all that lawlessness and self-absorption for, what was it—three or four years more? It got even worse. You switched from reliance upon your philosophy to undisguised reliance on yourself alone in that book you wrote, *The Consolation of Philosophy*. It caused my son to reject me, my values, and finally to die of an overdose of drugs."

I could not answer. She went on relentlessly: "That was about a year ago. I made a survey of all major opinion leaders today. You were the worst. I read all your books and most of your articles. I talked to people who had studied under you or used your *Metamorphosis of Philosophy* as a college textbook. I interviewed your ex-wife to get all the personal information about you I could. She still has a knife out for you, but I admit she is worse than you are—or were. I wangled an invitation to the AEA Conference to hear you speak so I could condemn you more convincingly." She sighed deeply. "And then I heard your speech," she ended softly, "and it was completely different from what I had expected. It was pure gold. I could only stand up and applaud with total approval. And you yourself, now—you are not the man I hated and wanted to attack in my planned expose´. At first I doubted your statement that you had come to Christ just an hour before the conference. I thought you might be making a fool of me. I believe you now."

4
A Glimpse of the Future

During our flight to New York Lisa switched her tape recorder on again, questioned me about various philosophical positions I had taken through the years and wondered whether I would now work out Christian responses to them. I said that such a program seemed incumbent upon me, but that I would not need to start as it were from scratch. I only needed to draw upon the Bible and the labors of earlier Christian philosophers like Augustine and Thomas Aquinas, and great Christian thinkers of our own time, such as Gilbert Keith Chesterton and especially C. S. Lewis.

"It is a shortcoming of our own generation," I commented, "that the study of Christian philosophers and thinkers is so neglected today. But then that, too, is done on purpose. It amounts to practical censorship. All my professional life I myself took part in it almost automatically, until last night. It's part and parcel of insuring the rule of atheist humanism in our academic establishment and society—that wonderful atheist humanism which does away with all ethical rules and grants us the freedom to do whatever we like. As Fyodor Dostoevsky said, 'Without God all things are permitted.'"

"He became a Christian," Lisa said, "after having been a radical revolutionary under Tsar Nicholas I of Russia. He was almost executed by a firing squad, but the tsar pardoned him at the last minute. Then he was sent to Siberia as a convict for years." She added, "I know this because I studied much European literature—older literature, not so much what passes for literature now."

The discussion turned next to my relationship with my ex-wife Nancy Berger, whom Lisa had interviewed extensively about our marriage and my early life. Nancy, Lisa said, was still extremely bitter about me and saw nothing good in me whatsoever. How did I feel about her?

I thought for a little while, then answered slowly: "If you had asked me this question before last night, I might have answered that I, too, was still bitter about her. I was especially angry about the unfair way she handled the divorce, as though the fault of it were all mine. I guess she still insists that this is the way it was. The memory of the actual court proceedings still rankles, though it all happened over two years ago.

"But last night is causing me to reconsider. Why did we tear each other down and sling so much mud at each other's reputations? Just to enjoy each other's pain and shame? I know I did. I never loved Nancy but only used her to further my career. Perhaps she did love me when it all began between us in 1965. How hurt she must have been by my self-centered exploitation and unfaithfulness through the years! I ought to ask her to forgive me."

Lisa did not continue the interview beyond this point. She felt that together with the earlier research she had done on me, she now had more than enough information for her planned write-up. "It will be fairly lengthy," she said, "I talked to my editor on the phone last night about it, especially your speech before the AEA. He told me to write it up as fast as I could so it can be the lead article of the next issue of *News in Depth.*" Noticing my questioning glance, she added, "It's the country's leading conservative magazine." She said she would send me a copy of it so we could discuss it later.

"I would also like to hear," she said, "of the personal reaction of your liberal colleagues to your change of heart. I expect they will be furious and vindictive. Liberals preach a lot about tolerance but are completely intolerant themselves. You ought to know that from within better than I."

"Yes," I agreed, "I have already thought of that. Speaking and writing against me after the publication of your article will be only the beginning. Unless I reject Christ, retract my statements to you and somehow gloss over my speech before the AEA—and so help me God, I will never do that—they will set out to destroy me professionally. And they are powerful. They may well succeed."

"Like what the British liberals did to the late Malcolm Muggeridge," nodded Lisa. "He started out as a prominent socialist and rose to becoming a top news reporter, comparable to our American Tom Brokaw or Walter Cronkite. Then he did a story on Mother Teresa's work in India titled *Something Beautiful for God.* It was the beginning of his Christian conversion. He was named Chancellor of the University of Edinburgh, where he strongly opposed, I think even forbade, the distribution of condoms to the students. This meant implicitly that he condemned extramarital sex. That was the last straw! He was booted from his position and banned from the British liberal establishment. His books written after his conversion are virtually underground publications chiefly promoted by conservatives.

"Here is another example from our own United States—maybe you even took a part in it. Remember the nomination and final confirmation of Clarence Thomas to the Supreme Court a few years ago?"

"Yes, I do," I said, "Our side pulled out all the stops. Of course you know what was done earlier to Supreme Court nominee Robert Bork. Our line of attack against Bork was so successful that it gave us the verb 'to Bork' for destroying the reputation and political career of a conservative applicant for high office. When Clarence Thomas was nominated, the National Organization for Women publicly vowed to Bork him. I wasn't in the forefront of either battle, but I certainly cheered our side on behind the scenes. I thought our strategy to use Anita Hill to slander him as a womanizer, unfaithful and treacherous both to his wife, a dedicated Christian, and to Hill herself was brilliant. We almost stopped his nomination due to the continuous news media publicity."

"They wouldn't have any difficulty finding an Anita Hill to destroy you," said Lisa, "and this time it wouldn't be slander."

"No," I agreed, "all that came out during my divorce when Nancy saw to it that my dirty laundry was thoroughly displayed and washed in public. The scandal sheets had a field day with it." I cringed inwardly at the memory. "However, because I was on the liberal side then, the mainline news media treated it with some reserve. My career was not affected."

"Well, this time it will be," said Lisa, "unless they think an attack on you along those lines won't work because it's 'old news.' In Clarence Thomas's case, the Hill story was effective because it was supposedly 'revealed' for the first time. In reality, of course, it never happened. They probably won't dig up your old dirt again, especially since you were given your present prestigious position at the Bertrand Russell Institute when they already knew about it all." She chuckled with bitter irony. "With you it will be done quietly behind the scenes. They will find a way." I nodded in agreement. We sat silently, thinking it over.

"In a way it serves me right," I mused. "Ever since I started to teach philosophy as a graduate teaching assistant, I used to ferret out the Christians among my students. Young people raised in Christian homes and churches were my meat! I used every trick in the book and out of the book to confuse them and if possible persuade them to give up their beliefs. I was very good at it and knew it. Sometimes I mocked Christian students in class in front of everyone. Sometimes I graded down their papers and tests due to their Christian content. Of course I failed now and then, especially with . . ." I stopped; the memory of Karen still hurt. I saw Lisa hanging attentively on my lips and completed the sentence, " . . . a Christian girl I was in love with. I broke up with her because she came very close to bringing me to her faith and my future career hung in the balance. Nancy, then my faculty advisor, had a large part in the breakup, but the final responsibility was mine."

I laughed wryly. "Yes, it serves me right," I repeated. "If I had stopped resisting God then, I would have lost only the first few rungs on the ladder to worldly success and still had many other options. Now I will fall from the very top with far fewer options left at my age."

"I see," said Lisa. After a thoughtful silence she added, "I have mixed feelings about what is happening to you. Part of me, the part still vengeful because your writings caused my son to die, is glad because you will pay for what you did. I know you already paid when your children died, but somehow it didn't seem enough." She swallowed and looked away, then turned back to me and said softly, "That was wrong of me. Please forgive me."

"Of course I forgive you," I said, "and if you can, please forgive me too."

"I know I should, and I will try," she answered. "That's the best I can do now." We exchanged our first glance of sympathy with each other. Lisa went on, "Another part of me is glad because now the stream of poison from your mouth and pen will dry up. It was a broad stream, and stopping its flow will make a real difference. And lastly," she said earnestly, "believe it or not, I feel very sorry for you, so sorry that I could wish I had not started doing research on you and interviewed you for the article. I am even tempted to tell my editor to forego publishing it, but it's a spectacular scoop. He wouldn't consent to do that even if I did plead with him to drop it in order to spare you the consequences. It's too late."

"I understood that," I said, "right after I had given you permission to start that tape recorder, and especially after my statement about when I came to Christ was down on tape. Strangely enough, I have no regrets. I was so glad to speak to whoever would listen about the joy that came to me right after I met God. No, don't feel sorry for me. If even one person comes to share that joy, it's worth any price I may have to pay."

Lisa looked at me with a quizzical smile. "I hope you still feel that way once you have started paying," she said. Then she asked me to excuse her for a while as she needed to do some work before our arrival in New York. She pulled a sleek laptop computer from her overnight bag and began typing away on it with furious speed.

I watched her for a little while from the side, admiring her concentration and studying her intent face. I never thought I would come to like you, Lisa Trent Harrison, I thought with a smile. Then physical fatigue took hold of me. My whole body relaxed, my head sank back in my seat, and soon I knew no more.

I awoke when our descent to New York was announced over the intercom. I felt warmer than before and very comfortable. To my surprise I was now covered with a light blanket, the kind flight attendants keep handy for passengers wanting to sleep. I knew I had not asked for it and doubted that the flight attendant had done it on her own initiative. I sat up straight and looked questioningly at Lisa. She smiled half gently, half mischievously.

"Yes," she nodded, "you looked exhausted and uncomfortable. I thought a blanket would help, so I asked for one and put it over you. You were so tired you never felt it or budged. I've got good news for you, too: you don't snore when you're asleep."

I could not help laughing. "That's good news indeed," I said, "and thanks for taking care of me. The last person that covered me with a blanket after I fell asleep was my mother."

"Don't mention it," she replied, also laughing. Our eyes met. Then suddenly both of us became serious, even a little awed and afraid. Unexpectedly, a barrier between us had been crossed, and what might come of this for our lives?

5

First Reflections, First Testing

After landing at New York's JFK Airport Lisa and I exchanged addresses and parted. We both lived in Manhattan but not close to each other, she in its more luxurious upper west, I near New York University for convenience's sake. She repeated her promise to send me the issue of *News in Depth* with her article about me as soon as it came off the press, and to contact me afterwards so we could discuss it together.

It was now late in the morning. Bright sunlight streamed down upon the congested traffic and the hurrying crowds. On my way home I watched the people around me in a completely new and different way. Something had changed in me. I no longer scanned them mechanically, detachedly and impersonally as I had before I set out on my trip to Battle Hill a scant two days ago when my heart had been absent from them in my former constant preoccupation with myself. No longer did I see them in the abstract as the "masses" or "populations" of academic sociology. I saw them as unique, individual men and women, each having their own burdens, each with their joys and sorrows, each dear to God Who had made them and loved them. I began to love them myself and wondered how many among them knew God and His unconditional love, certitude, joy and peace.

I reached Greenwich Village where I lived within walking distance of the Bertrand Russell Institute, the liberal think tank where I had held the position of "philosopher in residence" for the last two years. It was named for the late Lord Bertrand Russell of Liverpool, a contemporary British mathematician and philosopher of leftist persuasions. He had published his atheistic anti-Christian views in his well known book *Why I Am Not a Christian.* When I still taught philosophy at Herbert Spencer University before my divorce from Nancy, I had often assigned this book to my students as collateral reading.

The institute was lavishly financed by the heir to a vast industrial fortune. He had acquired his radical leftist worldviews in the 1960s while a student under equally radical professors. The chief purpose of the institute was to help destroy the remnants of Judeo-Christian beliefs and practices in the United States. Dr. J. Pierce Knightley, the institute's director, hated Christians with a passion. Whenever Christianity was mentioned, he was fond of saying that Christians were either idiots, insane, or both and good for nothing but garbage hauling. I felt sure he would not hesitate to pronounce this judgment on me when he found out about my conversion and to fire me, if not immediately then after my present contract ran out in a year.

Another goal of the Bertrand Russell Institute was the replacement of American-style free enterprise capitalism by a global economy governed by the United Nations and run along socialist-communist lines. I reflected on the irony of this scheme, for if it was successful, it would mean government control of our financial benefactor's own business empire. I supposed he knew this and did not care; he was reported to be a total idealist eager to sacrifice whatever it took for the causes he embraced. Although not all of us staff members agreed with his stand in this matter—we had several libertarian anarchists among us—we applauded his attitude. After all, it guaranteed our generous salaries which were indispensable for living in expensive New York.

The staff members of the institute did research and prepared speeches and position papers for prominent politicians and opinion leaders of the far left. They also wrote thoroughly nasty articles attacking "right wing extremists." I recalled several campaigns launched by the institute against Lisa Trent Harrison; I had almost written against her myself once or twice when her clever verbal arrows had been aimed specifically against my own work.

As a not inconsiderable perk we were permitted to use the institute's well equipped facilities to write books and articles for our own purposes and benefit. We had all been hired with the institute's implicit trust that what we would speak and write privately under our own names would agree with what we spoke and wrote officially as representatives of the Bertrand Russell Institute. This was not an explicit condition of being hired, nor a written clause of our contract, but it was clearly understood by both parties.

I now realized that I had broken this implicit commitment when I spoke as I did before the American Educators Association. At the time I had not even thought of this aspect of what I was doing. All I had thought of was that I could not deliver my prepared speech because it was in total agreement with my own lifelong philosophy of lawlessness and self-absorption and therefore totally opposed to God and Christ, and totally in line with the policies of the institute.

By the time I reached my apartment, I had come to some conclusions about what would happen to me soon, and what I must do. I would probably have a few days of calm before the storm until news of my speech before the AEA reached Dr. Knightley. When he questioned me as he was sure to do, I must tell the truth and prepare myself by prayer and strength from the Bible. My hunger and thirst for it leaped up in my mind and heart as urgently as it had the night before. "I must buy a Bible before I do anything else," I said aloud.

I also decided to ask my family to pray for me and to send me the most helpful Christian books they could think of or at least a list of them so I could buy them here. I smiled at the thought that they might fulfill my request through Swenson Books in Battle Hill, the great Christian bookstore owned and operated by George MacPherson and his wife Karen—dear "little Karen" who almost brought me to Christ thirty years ago. It occurred to me that God's great joy which had filled my heart—only last night, I thought with awe—had already spread and multiplied to others, the people nearest and now dearest to me. God's wonderful, unconditional love had reached me through Sylvia. It would now reach others through me.

Oddly enough the first person that came to my mind as I thought this was Dr. Knightley. "When I meet with him after he learns of my conversion," I thought, "may I be to him what Sylvia was to me. I saw her as a retarded idiot unworthy of life—he will see me as an idiot, insane or both, unworthy of esteem. May I show God to him as He really is." I realized this had been a prayer. It had been a spring of God's life welling up in my heart.

By now it was about noon. I found some snacks in my refrigerator, sufficient for a light lunch for me who could never eat much at any one time due to my stomach ulcer. Then I hurried out to the nearest bookstore and bought a Bible, making sure it was in the old translation my mother had used. I was astonished to see how many new translations had been published since my childhood. Upon the advice of the sales clerk, I also bought a concordance. It would help me to compare Scripture with Scripture about particular words or subjects.

The young man, eager to please and encouraged by my acceptance of the concordance, recommended several commentaries to me as well as Bibles with commentaries printed right along the biblical passages themselves. I gently but firmly declined. I did not want to let the commentaries guide me rather than the Bible itself. This was due to my lifelong torment of uncertainty resulting from my root sin of starting with man and his thinking—with me—rather than with God. Commentaries might be good and biblically sound, but they could only be below, not above, the Bible, God's own Word, itself. They might also be misleading or denominationally slanted. Better to abstain from them! Yes, I might not understand this or that Bible passage immediately or ever, but I would wait and trust that God would give me the understanding I needed in His own good time.

I returned to my apartment and eagerly opened my new Bible. I read Genesis 3, the record of the serpent in Eden and Eve and Adam's fall. I saw that the serpent's first weapon had been to sow doubt and uncertainty in Eve's mind: "Yea, hath God said?" Philosophers without God had been doing the same from antiquity to our own time. I read Psalm 2 and rejoiced because "He that sitteth in the heavens shall laugh" about the rulers—and that included godless philosophers—rebelling against Him. I read Matthew 2 and saw how Herod was foiled in his wish to kill the new-born King Jesus. I took away from my reading that no one can defeat God; the final victory is His.

I walked the few blocks to the Bertrand Russell Institute and stopped by the central reception desk in the lobby to ask about any messages for me. Lorena, our curvaceous young receptionist with the elegant clinging clothes, the red lips and fingernails and the artificially platinum-blonde curls, was on duty. She had let me know for some time that she would not turn me down if I asked her to go out with me. I, too, had given her to understand that our relationship might be more than being fellow employees of the institute. There was no reason why we couldn't spend a night in bed together; everybody did it nowadays. I had been told that as recently as twenty years ago one did not date or sleep with people in one's own office, but that was another quaint, old-fashioned taboo discarded by my own "me" generation.

All this went through my mind as I looked at Lorena and realized that she represented my first testing as a Christian. I felt the old physical lust rise strongly within me. How fatally easy it would be for me to "love her and leave her" as I had done with so many young women of her type before.

And then, just as when I had no longer seen the people on the sidewalks as merely masses or crowds but individual men and women whom God had made and loved, I suddenly looked at Lorena in a new, different way. God had made and loved her, too, so much that He had sent His only Son Christ to be mocked, tortured and crucified for her. How could I treat her as a mere object to serve my lust and then throw her away? That was not love—it was sin.

"Good to see you back again, Dr. Barron," Lorena greeted me with a warm, inviting smile, "can I do anything special for you today?"

"Good to see you again too, Lorena," I answered, friendly but somewhat impersonally. "Are there any messages for me?"

She turned to the pigeon-holed cabinet behind her and extracted a few letters and message slips which she handed to me in a way that made our fingers touch. I quickly withdrew my hand, thanked her and turned away toward my office. I knew I had done enough to let her know I wanted to put some distance between us. The wave of lust which had assaulted me a minute ago was ebbing away. It had been possible for me to resist and overcome it.

I knew, not with pride but with humility, that I had passed my first test. I had not even prayed for God's help, but He had helped me anyway by showing me the true nature of what I was tempted to do. He in me had overcome the temptation, or I in Him, only in Him. That particular temptation would assail me again and again because its appeal had been part of my old life so strongly and so long. It seemed almost like cutting off a part of my body to give it up, but give it up I must.

I could never give it up in my own strength! But He would be with me. I thanked Him and praised Him for giving me Himself the evening before and with Himself all things I needed as His free gifts. The sudden temptation, laying in wait for me like a concealed trap, frightened me in retrospect. I saw in a kind of reverent fear that from now on I must walk with Him step by step, moment by moment, clinging to Him as long as I would live.

"I cannot even promise You I will do this," I murmured, "just help me each moment to call on You so I can do Your will and not mine." His instant answer was His overflowing joy and peace in my heart. I saw that my new life was impossibly hard in me alone but totally easy and joyful in God. "That's all right," I assented and rejoiced as I stepped into my office.

6

Second Testing

I worked for a while at my desk, opening and reading my mail. One letter was an invitation to speak before a prestigious conference of leading North American philosophers to be held in Toronto, Canada in the fall of 1996, over a year from now. If my professional future turned out as I anticipated, my conversion to Christ would have become known by then and I would no longer be associated with the Bertrand Russell Institute. I was sure the organizers of the conference, whom I knew well as enemies of Christianity like myself until the day before, would never have invited me if they had thought me a Christian. Should I decline their invitation in view of these circumstances, or accept it and witness to them of the change in me? Should I write them, frankly explaining what had come to pass in my life, and leave the final decision in their hands? I put the letter aside for later decision in the light of the Bible and prayer.

What about the numerous other speaking engagements I had already accepted and put on my schedule? I looked at my appointment calendar. My next speech was coming up right here in New York at the annual conference of the National Federation of College Women on Friday, July 14. That day, my birthday, was and always would be painful for me because it was the anniversary of my son Dylan's killing spree and suicide at the Rousseau Academy as his "birthday gift" to me. He must have known that the timing of his rampage would brand it into my memory for the rest of my life. He had explained why he hated and despised me so much in a lengthy and detailed diary found among his belongings after his death.

Nancy had made extensive public use of his diary during our horrible divorce right after the death of our daughter Ecstasy. Once again I inwardly saw Ecstasy lying motionless and pale in her hospital bed beside the hissing ventilator. Once again I saw Dylan's bloody head, mutilated beyond restoration by the bullet he had fired upward through his mouth. Would this nightmare never end but haunt me forever?

I had tried to put it all behind me by writing *The Consolation of Philosophy*. I had proudly thought of myself as very high-minded and heroic, and the book had sold many copies. One of them fell into the hands of Lisa Trent Harrison's young son and led him to suicide. How many other people did I lead astray or kill? Oh yes, your ideas had deadly consequences, James, I told myself, and you cannot annul these consequences even after you did come to God and Christ. Your sorrow cannot change nor make up for what happened. You can only confess your sins to God and ask for His forgiveness and healing.

I did just this, and the sharp knife point of agony in my heart was dulled and gradually withdrawn. I trusted that God would forgive me even as I now forgave Dylan and Nancy with all my heart. I asked God to have mercy on poor little Ecstasy and to let her know I asked her forgiveness for having forced her to undergo the abortion which killed the baby she loved and led to her own death. Yes, she should not have had sex with Edison Aldridge, the baby's father, but we, her parents, had not taught her this absolute truth, nor had the amoral educators at the Rousseau Academy to whom we had abandoned her. She had sinned far less in her ignorance than we, I, had sinned against her on principle in our self-centered, proud lawlessness.

I resolved that God willing I would speak to the National Federation of College Women as scheduled and share these insights with them. Perhaps at least the mothers among them would listen. Perhaps Nancy would be there, relent towards me, and even receive comfort from what I would say. It was she who had desired our children in the first place. Doubtless she had suffered as much as I or more when they died so young and so terribly. I prayed that some good might yet come from all our horrible past.

At this moment the telephone rang. I picked up the receiver. To my surprise I heard the low, warm voice of Lisa Trent Harrison. She came right to the point.

"Hello, Dr. Barron," she said, "have you made plans for this evening yet? If not, could we have dinner together? I have something important to share with you."

We agreed to meet at one of the nice Italian restaurants in mid-Manhattan at six o'clock. I walked to my apartment, showered, shaved and changed, and drove to the appointed place. Lisa arrived shortly afterwards, dressed more informally but still as smoothly elegant as in the morning. She had reserved a secluded booth for us. I received her provident efficiency with grateful recognition but also thought that normally I was the one who took care of such details. I remembered how Lisa had covered me with a blanket this very morning while I was asleep on the plane. Accepting care from others is apparently part of my new life, too, I thought as we took our seats across from each other.

I looked at my watch; it was a few minutes after six. "I have been a Christian for twenty-four hours now," I told Lisa, "a whole day like no other in my life! And you took part in it almost from the start, and now again at the beginning of the next day."

She nodded. "That's what I want to talk to you about," she said. The waiter came with water and the menus. Lisa knew what she wanted and spent little time dallying over her choices. There was no coyness about her but rather a cool maturity which I liked.

While we waited, she gave me a sheaf of typed papers. "This is an advance copy of my article about you," she said. "There may be a couple of editorial changes or brief deletions, but it's essentially as it will be in *News in Depth.* I thought you might wish to read it before others get hold of it. I warn you—most of it isn't favorable to you."

"That's all right, Lisa," I answered, and then apologized, "sorry, I shouldn't call you by your first name."

"That's all right—James," she replied, laughing a little, "'Ms. Trent Harrison' is a bit awkward, I am sure, or even just 'Ms. Harrison.' Besides, we'll have a lot more contacts with each other, so it's much better to be informal. But here's the food. Let's eat first before we talk business."

Remembering my mother's custom I silently prayed, giving thanks for the meal. We ate, conversing about everyday matters. Lisa noticed how little and how slowly I ate and asked me about it. I told her how careful I had to be about my stomach ulcer, which had started vexing me thirty years ago. "It is especially bothersome at times of extreme stress," I explained, "but normally I can manage it by eating as I do right now. It's been an excellent help in staying thin."

"I can see that," she said, looking me over appraisingly, "and with as many public appearances as you make, it's been a real help indeed. I describe you briefly in my article. That is one part of it you won't mind."

I couldn't help smiling at the compliment. I knew, of course, that I was looking well for my age, fifty-four on my upcoming birthday. As a young man girls had found me very handsome as I was, tall, slender, with rich dark hair and dark brown eyes, resembling my mother, a great beauty in her youth. Women continued to find me attractive, for I went on all these years looking much the same as I did in my twenties and thirties. The only visible changes have been the graying hair at my temples which actually added a touch of scholarly distinction to my appearance, a few wrinkles around the corners of my eyes, and having to wear glasses when reading small print.

The waiter came, removed our dishes and gave us our separate bills. No sooner had he left that Lisa launched into the business she had come to discuss.

"I spent part of the day talking to my editor at *News in Depth* about you," she said, "and he is interested in publishing articles by you on the philosophies of our day as you will now see them from your changed perspective as a Christian. In the beginning you could just take your own earlier articles and respond to them. Later you could write original new presentations. We understand that you will need time to work out your positions as you become, well, better equipped. We would pay you as we pay our other comparable contributors. In a way no one else is exactly comparable to you, for no one else is, or will have been, the leading atheist philosopher of our time. That is why we are so interested in having you write for us. But we could surely come to an agreement about your honoraria. What do you think?"

I was stunned. Here was an offer which would help me bridge the gap between employments both financially and professionally when I left the Bertrand Russell Institute. Doubtless my income would be less than the top salary I was earning now. I might have to downscale my lifestyle considerably. But I could probably remain in New York and continue to study and write in my lifelong profession. If necessary I could even move to the Midwest with its much lower cost of living and write my articles for *News in Depth* from there.

But was it all right for me to write for *News in Depth?* I had been so accustomed to think of all staunchly conservative publications as beneath contempt that it was difficult for me to imagine myself associated with it. All my present colleagues would become my furious enemies when they saw my name as one of its contributors on the cover. Well, of course by that time they would already be my enemies due to my conversion, so I would already be ostracized and vilified in their own publications.

So much for the reaction of my former supporters—I concluded that it really did not matter. More importantly, could I write for *News in Depth* as a Christian? Suppose I found that biblical Christian beliefs clashed with political and social conservatism on certain issues. Worse, suppose we diverged on basic principles? I did not know enough yet about either conservatism or biblical Christianity to answer this question.

"Would I have full freedom to write from the biblical Christian perspective?" I asked.

Lisa stared at me. "Of course," she said, sounding somewhat offended, "conservatism and Christianity are virtually one and the same."

"Forgive me," I answered, "I am not yet familiar enough with either to be convinced of that. I don't much trust the word 'virtually'—I used it myself many times to allow myself some leeway to waffle on philosophical issues. I guess what I am getting at is that I cannot compromise my faith in God in any way. I don't want to write or speak a single word He would not approve of. If that is possible for me at *News in Depth,* I would be willing to discuss your offer with your editor."

"Okay," said Lisa, "I will pass this on to him. I don't see any difficulty about it. You will hear from him directly in a day or two. Now I have another proposal for you. How would you like to appear on the radio with me some time soon? Tomorrow night I will air the interview of you I did this morning on the plane. It will be on my special Saturday night program from ten to ten-thirty P.M. You might have heard of it—'Weekend Talks' with Lisa Trent Harrison. It's broadcast over several hundred radio stations across the country. I would like to have you on in person a week from tomorrow. The format would be another interview like this last one, only I might include asking you about any repercussions you might have experienced already about your conversion."

She looked at me, her face serious, her eyes pleading. "It would make you famous instantly," she said, "among conservative people all over the USA. It might lead to speaking invitations at venues you have never reached before." She became enthusiastic: "My goodness, James! Think of it! You are famous already. You are intelligent. You are an excellent speaker with a fantastic background and thirty years of experience. You know the enemy from within as do few others. Think how much you could do to counteract the false ideas you preached, and to halt their consequences which have done so much harm!"

All this was quite true. A few hours earlier I had agonized over being unable to undo the deadly consequences of my ideas. Now I thought it might be possible for me after all and rejoiced at the opportunity. Suddenly I remembered the unwritten clause of my contract with the Bertrand Russell Institute committing me to write or say nothing contrary to the institute's views and policies on my own time. I had genuinely forgotten that clause when I gave my speech before the American Educators Association. I could not plead that excuse now.

"I can't, Lisa," I said miserably but firmly, "I can't be on your radio show or write for your magazine as long as I am still employed by the Bertrand Russell Institute." I explained why. Lisa looked at me uncomprehendingly.

"But it's just an unspoken, unwritten, implicit understanding," she argued. "They can't hold you to it legally, can they? What could they do to you if you spoke out anyway?"

"It's deeper than a legal technicality," I said. "I would be guilty of duplicity if I used their facilities and abused their trust by working against them while I am still on their payroll. I cannot do it. Before I agree to write for *News in Depth* or to be on your radio show, I must resign from the institute. It's Friday evening now, so I will do it first thing Monday morning."

I felt a sudden tremendous, joyful relief as one released from being chained in an underground prison. "What a strange testing you put me through, Lisa," I said in awe, "first the welcome news of paid work doing what I should and would like to do, second, the offer of a platform from which to attack my former false and deadly teachings, and thirdly and finally the necessity of separating from the enemy honestly and immediately rather than after a period of false peace! I think I am most grateful for the third."

7
Lisa Misses the Mark

We left the restaurant. I walked Lisa to her car, a fairly new, expensive model. She unlocked it by remote control but did not immediately enter it. For several moments we stood silently beside it in the parking lot, reluctant to part from one another.

"I don't want to say good-bye yet, James," she finally said hesitantly, almost shyly. "It's been a most unusual evening for me. I have never met anyone as—," she stopped, searching for the right word, "—as transparent as you. If you put on an act, you are not only a philosopher but also a very talented actor, politician or diplomat. But I don't think so. I believe you never for one moment wore a mask before me." She had looked me full in the face but now averted her eyes. "And that's been true for you ever since we met last night," she reflected. "It was true while you gave your speech before the AEA. It wasn't intentional either. It's simply the way you were and still are."

She took a deep breath before going on, still not looking at me, "The James Barron whose life I researched and whom I hated was totally different. He wore a mask all the time, the mask of the self-absorbed, career-minded intellectual seducing simple people like my poor son by turning truth into lies with his high-flown rhetoric. It was that James Barron whom I describe in my article. The James Barron who wears that mask no longer—the transparent James Barron whom I met face to face last night and today—the James Barron whom I cannot hate any more—is not described at all. The only part of the article that might point to you as you are now is your statement about your coming to Christ, and it is largely eclipsed by my comments about how that might affect your career and our cultural and political climate." She looked up at me half ashamed. "Oh James! I angled the article to center upon the effect of your defection from the extreme atheist left. I see now that I completely missed the most important point—the change in you yourself. I am so sorry."

I did not say anything in reply. I hoped that when Lisa called me "transparent," she meant that she now believed I had never lied to her, and I was grateful. I was not surprised about the political emphasis of her article; it was to be expected from a secular political journal. When I heard her last words and felt her sadness about how she had written about me, I was strongly tempted to put my arm comfortingly around her shoulders. But I did not. We were not close enough for that, or not yet.

We parted content in knowing we would meet again soon. I drove home through the never ceasing tumult, lights and noises of night-time Manhattan in its incomparable splendor. How it had delighted me when I first moved here, and how accustomed, blasé and almost indifferent to it I had become in the two years since!

As soon as I arrived in my apartment I took out my advance copy of Lisa's article, sat down and read it carefully word for word and page by page. Its working title was "A Leading Atheist's Defection." She had done her homework very thoroughly, quoting from my many major writings over the years to prove that I had been the leading prophet, pioneer and spokesman of today's most radical atheist, self-centered, lawless philosophical thought in America if not the entire Western world. Her quotes were well chosen, in context and profusely footnoted. She aptly called me the John Dewey of my generation, comparing me to the famous philosopher John Dewey (1859–1952) who was the father of modern American education and had been hostile to biblical Christianity since his youth. She named other philosophers espousing similar lines of thought such as Nietzsche, Sartre, and most recently Michael Ruse and Peter Singer. She even found parallels between their philosophies and the ill-famed sophists of ancient Greece. I saw that Lisa as well as *News in Depth* wrote for a well informed and culturally advanced readership, not the ignorant right wing rabble of "redneck yokels" and "yahoos" of liberal name-calling.

Lisa spoke of John Dewey's morally unimpeachable private life and made a few references to the flaws in mine. On the whole, however, her narrative was limited to my professional career. It was clear and concise, captured the reader's interest and flowed well. It was sharply hostile throughout to me and all my philosophy, but then that was its declared intention.

The only neutral, even grudgingly favorable passage in Lisa's whole paper was her physical description of me. I could not help recognizing with a smile that she had found herself attracted to me in spite of herself. I remembered how unfavorably I myself had pictured her before meeting her face to face, and how I had had to revise my idea of her looks. I realized that I had been attracted to her, if the truth be told, from the very first moment we met when she reminded me so strongly of my mother.

The most important section of the article still remained to be read. It was Lisa's description of my conversion and her prediction of how it would affect the political and cultural climate of our time. This was the only part of the article which would hurt me in the eyes of my colleagues and the powerful radical academic left.

Lisa began with my speech to the American Educators Association. From its very first paragraph she had understood with delighted surprise that what I said was the repudiation of what I had taught all my professional life. The "dead giveaway," as she called it, of my totally changed position was my concluding paragraph about reinstating the freedom to worship God the Creator of reality in our schools. "Through the years Dr. Barron occasionally bucked the liberal establishment by opposing isolated trends in philosophy or education," Lisa wrote. "His politically incorrect article challenging the lenient child-rearing methods of Dr. Benjamin Spock comes to mind. Another politically incorrect example is Dr. Barron's recent article 'Passing the Torch,' which shows how China, South Korea and other Asian nations may soon surpass us in the hard sciences due to our lax educational methods. But Dr. Barron always remained a staunch atheist evolutionist till the evening of June 15, 1995 at the AEA conference in Battle Hill. I immediately confronted him after his speech to ask him what had caused him to speak as he had about God the Creator. Without hesitation he answered that he had become a Christian just an hour before. I suspected at first that he might be making a fool of me. However, he reconfirmed his statement in a taped interview he gave me the next morning during our return flight to New York. He knew the publication of his conversion would be a bombshell to his erstwhile fellow radical left wing atheists. He knew it might cause him deep and lasting professional harm. I believe he was sincere."

So far, so good, I thought. Lisa went on to describe what she believed would be the dismay and reduced public influence of cultural and political liberals due to my surprise defection from atheism, and my defection's encouragement for conservatives. I flew through the last remaining pages of her paper and shook my head. I could not remotely share Lisa's optimism. She grossly overestimated the effect of the loss of just one leader, even one as famous and prominent as I, upon the liberal atheist establishment.

I myself had been a well-known and brilliant forecaster of future social developments because I correctly estimated the strength of unbridled lawlessness multiplying all around me. As I saw it, already for many years there had not been a popular majority in western society on the side of traditional morality. Before his conversion to Christ a few weeks before his death, my own father, for example, had paid lip service to "traditional morality." However, his widely known shady business deals and suspicious relations with government officials who counted, his many one-night stands outside of marriage and his long affair with his secretary Fern Lowrie gave a different answer. The same was true for my grandfather the generation before. "Traditional morality" or the much acclaimed "Judeo-Christian values" were like a tree inwardly ravaged by termites and ready to crumble into dust. I remembered the scandal about Dorrie Fisher, the girl I had got pregnant in high school back in 1957 or '58. I had not been particularly reprimanded by my father, grandfather and most of the older generation. "Boys will be boys," and "Let James sow his wild oats," were their usual comments. And all this was customary in my rural Midwestern home town forty years ago, doubtless not yet as far gone from traditional morality as our large cities.

Christians like my mother, my brother Robert and my sister Neva, and the Bible-believing Christians who were their friends were a despised and stifled minority at Battle Hill University and everywhere in the influential academic world where I moved. Conservatives, too, were a dwindling minority and had lost battle after battle in their hopeless culture war to restrain the surge of lawlessness which finally broke loose openly in the 1960s. I was astonished that an informed conservative like Lisa overlooked this fact, which had seemed so obvious to me even then.

Even then I had already seen how academicians opposing the liberal establishment were made ineffectual or silenced. Mock them. Marginalize them. Demonize them. If they don't have tenure, fire them. If they do, let them vegetate on the lowest rung of the academic ladder as "assistant professors" till they are old and grey. It had happened to Dr. Francis S. Freeman, mockingly known as "Saint Francis," the only Christian in the department of philosophy at Battle Hill University. He had died long ago after years of retirement and had lived on the pension of an assistant rather than full professor. I bowed my head for a moment; I wished I could apologize to him for the many times I had mocked him behind his back and showed him blatant contempt to his face.

But Lisa's overestimation of the effect of my defection was not the only flaw in her article. To me a far more serious flaw was her all too brief description of my conversion to Christ. She had omitted almost all of it! There was not a word about Sylvia and her unconditional love, not a word about how she had shown me my sin and led me to God. There was not a word about the great joy, God's own joy that had filled my heart immediately afterwards. Lisa herself had been sad because she had not said one word about the change in me she had seen for herself—my no longer wearing a mask of self-absorption and being what she called "transparent."

I sighed as I laid the sheaf of papers aside. Yes, in her great eagerness to use my conversion to further the conservative cause Lisa had missed the mark deeply and entirely. I decided to talk the matter over with her the next time we met, but feared that the article was probably at the printer's already and it was too late to amend it.

8

The Radio Broadcast; All Hell Breaks Loose

I awoke early Saturday to a brilliant morning. I stepped to the window and enjoyed the spectacular view. I might not enjoy it much longer. I was about to resign from my position at the institute, and giving up my pricey high rise apartment must inevitably follow. The prospect made me sober but not sad or afraid, probably because I had never faced unemployment or lack of money before. I might need to endure that experience in order to become what God wanted me to be. "Lord, do with me what You will," I murmured.

And then a gentle voice said within my mind, "I am your *Father.*" It emphasized the word "Father." I understood He wished me to call Him Father rather than Lord, because He was my Father and He loved me. Yes, He was my Lord too, but his lordship was exercised within His Fatherhood. He was also assuring me that whatever He would send or allow in my life would come from His love for me and work out for my good. How could He love me like this, me who had despised and rejected Him so long? "Dear Father, I love You," I said, "I will call You Father in my prayers from now on."

He had spoken four words to me that fed me forever. It took but a fraction of a minute. I will never stop treasuring it in my mind and heart.

I dressed and fixed myself a simple breakfast. Perhaps I ought to learn to cook; I would eat a more healthy diet and save money. I chuckled; cooking "from scratch" might be quite an adventure for me. In the wealthy home of my childhood we had always employed cooks. Later there had always been prepackaged meals, fast food places, cafeterias or restaurants. During my marriage neither Nancy nor I had wanted to bow to the domesticity of home cooking, she because she was a feminist, I because I was a man. I saw that both of us had been equally "sexist," or rather put ourselves first in everything. Was that the deepest reason why our marriage had failed?

I needed to talk to my family and dialed Neva's number. Soon I heard her cheerful voice and began to tell her about all that had happened to me since our family reunion. She called Sylvia to the phone, who kept repeating "Uncle James, I love you!" It might be all or nearly all she was able to say to me, but it was more than enough, and this time I could tell her that I loved her too.

Then Neva got back with me. "So you gave an interview to Lisa Trent Harrison," she said excitedly. "What is she going to do with it? Will it be on her radio show?"

"Yes," I said, "tonight at ten P.M. Eastern time."

"I'll tell everyone I know," Neva promised. "Most everyone here has heard of Lisa Trent Harrison and will listen to the program. And everybody in our church will be so glad to hear that you finally came to the Lord!"

I warned Neva that Lisa might not play my interview about my conversion in full. "Her main concern is the conservative cause, not how people come to Christ," I explained.

"Oh well," Neva comforted me, "there will be enough in the broadcast to let people know what happened to you. I wish Mother could still be with us to hear it! She prayed for you ever since she became a Christian in 1956. But she is not grieving any more! There are no tears in heaven. The Lord will have told her that her prayers have been answered. She walked through a long valley of weeping over you, but now He has made it a place of springs."

"What beautiful words! Where do they come from?" I asked. And that is how I first learned Psalm 84:5–6, my second great blessing that day and now one of my most beloved Scripture verses.

We talked about my resignation from the Bertrand Russell Institute and possible future work. Neva thought that I might apply for a position as professor of philosophy at Fairfield University, the Christian institution from where she, her husband, my brother and some of their children had graduated. "Now that you are a Christian," she said happily, "they could use you and would welcome you! Keep it in mind." I promised I would.

Neva told me of one or two Christian radio ministries I could listen to until I found a local church to attend. "Most mainline Protestant churches are like First United Church at Lonely Prairie," she warned me, "stay away from them. Oh, how I would love for you to come back to the Midwest! Finding a good church and

Christian fellowship is so much easier here." On this we hung up.

I did some errands, had a snack and later a light dinner. Then I turned on the radio to my favorite classical music station, stretched out on my couch and listened. My mind and heart were at peace, soothed and blessed by the beautiful music of Handel, Bach and Vivaldi, my best loved composers. I was grateful that I did not need to reject this beautiful music which had given me my rare moments of rest and peace during the years of wandering in my godless wilderness. Thank You, dear Father!

When it was almost ten o'clock, I turned my radio dial to the station carrying Lisa's broadcast. I heard her low, soft voice announce the interview with me, the leading atheist philosopher of our time who had abandoned his atheism and surrendered to God and Christ. The entire interview followed exactly as I had given it and could be clearly understood throughout. It took almost the entire half hour of the program, leaving Lisa only enough time to say that she hoped to have me speak personally on a later program in the near future. The usual promotional sound bites followed, and that was the end.

A little later Lisa called me. "This time I let people see you as you now are," she said abruptly.

"Yes," I answered, "thank you."

"All hell will break loose for you," she said, her voice trembling, "if someone who has power to harm you and hates Christians heard the program, or if you resign from the Bertrand Russell Institute." I told her not to worry; what would come to me would come, and I must face it one step at a time under God's protection. We agreed to meet Monday evening after I would have submitted my resignation from the institute to Dr. Knightley.

I began my first Sunday as a Christian by listening to one of the Christian radio broadcasts Neva had recommended. It was based on the third chapter of the Gospel of John where Christ tells Nicodemus that one must be born again to see the kingdom of God. I now understood that what had happened to me was my new birth. This was confirmed, I thought, by the great joy in me right afterwards; by my delivering the opposite of my prepared speech before the AEA; by the radical change and the new "transparency" Lisa had seen in me; and most of all by my new love and longing for God and His Word.

The new birth came from above this present material world. I used my new concordance to look up the word "world" and found John 18:36 where Jesus tells Pilate, "My kingdom is not of this world." Of course not, I thought. This world is not and cannot be the only world there is. I remembered Austrian mathematician Kurt Goedel's famous theorem that a mathematical system cannot be logically explained from within that system itself but only from above and beyond it. So it is for this present world as a whole, I thought. Only God, who is above and beyond it as its Creator can explain it and its origin.

I spent most of that Sunday in writing my resignation from the institute. I described my conversion as fully, truthfully and gently as I could and reported that it had been broadcast on Lisa Trent Harrison's program the night before. I read the resignation over and over again, weighing every word, and prayed earnestly that it might be exactly as God wanted it to be. At last I had peace about it and slept with the comfort of David in Psalm 4:8 (KJV): *"I will both lay me down in peace, and sleep, for thou, LORD, only makest me dwell in safety."*

The next morning I walked over to Dr. Knightley's office, handed my resignation to his secretary and asked her to give it to him right away. She did so as I waited in his anteroom. Within a few minutes "all hell broke loose" as Lisa had predicted. The door of Dr. Knightley's inner sanctum burst open as he stormed out and shouted: "Get the hell in here, Barron, you s.o.b.! What the devil is the matter with you?"

I followed him back into his office and remained standing until he had flung himself into his own seat behind his desk, pointed to a chair across from him and barked "Sit down!" He launched into a furious tirade filled with a multitude of cuss words. Had I gone crazy? How could I turn my whole successful life upside down and kiss all further professional advancement good-bye because a retarded idiot had told me she loved me? How could I have allowed that right wing extremist nutcase Lisa Trent Harrison to interview me and play that unspeakable tape (he used a foul word to describe it) on her radio program? Had I gone stark-raving mad? Was I so dense that I didn't know she would only exploit me for her own political ends? Had I lost all common sense? What had become of my loyalty to my colleagues and the principles of progressive thought? What in hell did I mean by wanting to resign from the Bertrand Russell Institute? Was I already in the pay of the g******** opposition? Had our enemies plotted this whole happening to embarrass us? How could I have taken part in it? Could something yet be done to deny it, cover it up, or spin it to suit our agenda?

He went on in this vein for some time until he realized he had begun repeating himself. Then he gradually calmed down and finally stopped speaking. We looked at each other silently for a little while. I thought that this balding, pudgy man of about my own age and background had been pretty well a friend and then my colleague for years. I owed him my employment at the institute, which had enabled me to leave Herbert Spencer University and thus put distance between me and Nancy after our divorce. Much the same thoughts must be going through his mind. He sat up more straightly, squared his shoulders, shook his head slowly in regretful puzzlement and sighed deeply.

"I suppose you must really be in earnest about resigning from the institute, James," he said, "and that means that cockamamie conversion experience you describe in your resignation must have been real for you." He used a vile swear word. He couldn't help himself; foul language and cursing when upset had become his second nature. "It's the last thing I would have expected from you. D*** it, James, you have been a sound atheist all your adult life! You don't think it's still due to the hell you went through with your kids' deaths and your divorce? But all that was years ago! You even wrote your bestselling *Consolation of Philosophy* afterwards! Confound it, now you'll probably want to publicly repudiate it and most everything else you have ever said and written!"

He had talked himself into a fresh outbreak of anger and now had to stop for a moment to take a breath. I used it to say, "Yes, J. P., I do and I must. It's the reason why I cannot in good conscience continue to work for the institute."

"And I suppose that bitch Lisa Trent Harrison will see to it that your changed views get publicity through her right wing channels," he said. "I warn you! We have a lot more clout in the news media than they. You'll go in no time from being the honored top philosopher of our age to being a deranged religious fanatic and then a forgotten nobody."

I suddenly felt great pity for him. I prayed, "Father, help me speak to him of You," and then I answered, "Yes, J. P., but that's nothing compared to my new life with God. In Him I have the certitude I longed for all my life. In Him I have His great love—He *is* love. He loved me when I was still his enemy. He loved me so much He died on the cross for me. He loves you just the same right now. In Him I have peace and great joy. If you could only come to Him too! He is ready to give all this to you in Himself if you will only give yourself to Him."

His expression softened as he heard me out. Finally he said slowly: "You *are* different, James. You are different not only from the way you were before, but also from the so-called Christians I have known. Perhaps you know I grew up in a so-called Christian home in the South. To me Christianity was all nitpicking rules and regulations, arguing endlessly against other so-called Christians over petty theological issues I could never understand, and rabid racial prejudice against 'niggers' and 'kikes'—that's what they called Jews. I escaped it as soon as I could and swore I would never return to it no matter what."

I nodded sadly. His story was not unique. I saw how hard "Christians" like the ones Dr. Knightley had encountered in his youth had made it to win him to Christ. I also understood that I must bear the reproach rightly raised by unbelievers against counterfeit Christianity. I had not anticipated this burden.

Dr. Knightley seemed to understand what was going through my mind. After a brief pause he said, "I will speak to Paul Reynolds about what has happened to you and what we should do about your resignation. (Paul Reynolds was the wealthy benefactor financing the institute.) He will want to talk to you himself. You should hear from him within the week. Meanwhile, consider yourself on leave and don't accept any invitations to speak about your, uh, conversion or changed views. Agreed?"

I agreed. We stood up and shook hands. All hell had broken loose, but its fury had been restrained. Above all, I thought, J. P. Knightley had not dismissed me out of hand and might even want to talk to me again about the faith. Lastly, I now had an opportunity to witness to Paul Reynolds.

9

First Date

Being now on leave from the institute, I was free to do what I liked the rest of the day until I met Lisa again in the evening. I took a leisurely stroll through my neighborhood and eventually wound up at the bookstore where I had purchased my Bible. I had always been a voracious reader and could not resist going in and browsing. This store was well stocked with books of scholarly interest, including fiction by major European writers. Lisa had talked of Dostoevsky and her study of foreign literature. I myself had little knowledge of it. Now that I had time, I might learn more about it.

I soon found shelves loaded with the classical works of Pushkin, Tolstoy, and Dostoevsky as well as many books by Aleksandr Solzhenitsyn, the famous anti-communist Russian writer. In the 1970s he had shaken up the world by his harrowing description of the Soviet concentration camp system, *The Gulag Archipelago*. The liberal news media had been lukewarm about his no-holds-barred opposition to the Soviet regime; they had much preferred Andrei Sakharov, another well known dissident Russian of far more liberal leanings. Waning liberal support for Solzhenitsyn in academia and the press turned to strident hostility when he became known as a devout Christian and especially after his commencement address at Harvard University June 8, 1978.

I bought the three hefty volumes of *The Gulag Archipelago* and *One Day in the Life of Ivan Denisovich*, Solzhenitsyn's only work legally published in the Soviet Union before its demise in 1991. I leafed through Solzhenitsyn's play *Candle in the Wind* and came to a page where Aunt Christine reads from the Gospel of Luke 11:33, 35 (KJV): *"No man, when he hath lighted a candle, putteth it in a secret place, neither under a bushel, but on a candlestick, that they which come in may see the light. . . . Take heed therefore that the light which is in thee be not darkness."* I took this as an admonition to myself and bought the book.

The young clerk who had sold me my Bible and concordance saw my interest in Solzhenitsyn. He showed me another thick book, *Witness* by Whittaker Chambers. "It is the autobiography of a Communist who became a Christian," he said, "and one of the most important and best books of the twentieth century." I bought the book because it might parallel my own story.

I brought my new treasures home and started reading, beginning with *Candle in the Wind*. I could well relate to the elitist pride and self-absorption of some of the characters; I had been just like them before my conversion. I also saw myself in Alex, the play's hero, who must begin a new life in totally unfamiliar and generally hostile circumstances. But I was most impressed by Aunt Christine, a poor old woman, called foolish because she rescues hurt, abandoned cats. It is she who makes the sign of the cross and reads from the Bible over the dead body of rich, worldly Professor Maurice Craig. Keith Armes wrote in his foreword that "lonely, ragged Aunt Christine redeems a world which devotes all its spiritual energies to accumulating material possessions." She moved me to tears. If only I could be more like her, like Sylvia, like Christ!

I thought the last four days over and saw that they had been full of great blessings. Even this morning's hellishness had been among them. I felt so happy and blessed! I could have sung with joy. I saw that my joy was an earthly reflection of Your joy, dear Father. (And later You confirmed this to me when I read in Zephaniah 3:17 how You "rejoice with singing" over us, Your children.)

The rest of the afternoon I read *Ivan Denisovich,* a very realistic and moving account of one day in the life of an average Soviet concentration camp prisoner, until I left to meet Lisa. Both of us arrived so simultaneously that we could park next to each other. We walked into the restaurant together like old friends and headed for the same booth we had occupied before. The same waiter greeted us with a smile of recognition and brought us our water and menus.

We had planned to get together impersonally to discuss the reaction of the institute to my resignation, but the meeting seemed much more like our first personal date. If this was so, and I soon doubted it no longer, it was the first serious one I had had since my divorce. I sensed that it was Lisa's first serious date in a long time as well.

As we ate, Lisa asked me about the institute's reaction to my resignation. I described Dr. Knightley's initial anger about it, omitting his expletives, and how he had calmed down in the end after I had asked him to turn to God. I told her that he rejected biblical Christianity because he thought it was like the counterfeit Christianity he had rightly come to hate in his youth.

"I was sad about that," I said, "but I guess I shouldn't have been surprised. After all, I grew up within counterfeit Christianity too. Dr. Knightley saw bigotry against people of a different skin color and against Jews in the name of the Bible. I saw the denial of the Bible altogether in the name of 'higher criticism.'" I added slowly, appalled at finally recognizing a truth which had stared me in the face since my teenage quarrels with my mother: "In my case it was worse than a counterfeit. It was outright Anti-Christianity."

"In what church denomination did you grow up?" Lisa asked. I named the United Christian Church. After a moment of reflection she said thoughtfully, "I belong to the United Reformed Church. It is a member of the International Ecumenical Council of Churches, as is the United Christian Church. Conservative members of our church, including myself, have been concerned about our affiliation with the IECC because it has backed world-wide socialism and communism for many years. I have discussed its left-wing agenda in occasional articles and on the radio. I'll bet that Herbert Spencer University and the Bertrand Russell Institute never oppose it or even praise it every so often. Isn't that right?"

"Come to think of it, yes," I agreed, "but more so at Herbert Spencer U. than the institute. The institute prefers to treat Christianity as if it didn't exist at all."

"And that is why your conversion is so hateful to them," said Lisa. "What's your status now after your talk with Dr. Knightley?"

I informed her that I was now on leave, and that Paul Reynolds would talk to me and then presumably make the final decision. I thought he might simply accept my resignation effective at the end of June.

"So you can start writing an article right away for *News in Depth,*" Lisa said briskly. "I take it you have thought about our proposal and are willing to accept. I should think you could contribute an article every month, like I do. My editor will call you and settle the details with you. Welcome aboard, James!" She smiled happily.

I smiled in return, but with a touch of hesitancy. The talk with Paul Reynolds still hung over me. Suppose he would attach strings to my resignation, like making me agree not to say or write anything against the institute for the original duration of my contract? If so, I would be silenced for a whole year. Lisa observed my reaction.

"Having second thoughts?" she asked. I explained that we needed to await Paul Reynolds' decision before finalizing a contract with *News in Depth;* there might be unexpected roadblocks. She thought it over and nodded, the joy in her face fading.

"You're right," she said glumly, "they wouldn't let you get away so easily. They would want to harm you and silence you. And what would you live on after you leave the institute? I had hoped that your work for *News in Depth* would help with that."

"Lisa," I said gently, "you mustn't worry! Even if no new work and income turns up for me right away, I can get along for a while, especially if I move to a less expensive apartment as I have been planning already."

"How can you not worry yourself, James?" she said with incipient anger, "don't you care that maybe you can't speak out against them right away or ever? It isn't just your writing articles for *News in Depth.* I wanted you to be on my radio show this coming Saturday, and on other shows after that. Now I have to wait—till when? The interview with you has already brought in a substantial listener response. There must be a follow-up right away, or the story of your conversion from atheism will be forgotten."

Dear Father, let me help her, I prayed. "You must have trust in God," I answered, "He will use that story in the best possible way."

Lisa suddenly chuckled. "How funny," she said, "*you* who were an atheist all your life till less than a week ago are telling *me* who have been a church member all my life to have trust in God! Maybe I have been a, what did you call it? counterfeit Christian all this time." She became suddenly very thoughtful. I did not dare speak. She must ponder and answer this question in her heart by herself.

The waiter brought our bills, but we were not ready to leave and ordered dessert. After it arrived, I asked Lisa to tell me something about herself. "You know all about me," I said, "while I know very little about you beyond your conservative activities."

"That's not true," she said, "you know about my son. That's not 'very little.'

His life and death are the most important part of my life." I asked her gently to tell me more, and she did, haltingly at first and then in an outpour of grief and guilt resembling a confession.

Lisa had been born in upstate New York in 1953 as the oldest child of hard-working middle class parents. There were three younger children whom she helped raise because her mother worked outside the home to increase the family income. Pressure was on Lisa all the time to care for the other children, to keep the home clean and neat, to do well in school, to pass special exams for special college scholarships, to work part-time to help pay for her education and that of her siblings. Lisa had early shown talent for writing stories, interviews and reports of all kinds. It was natural that she chose journalism as her college major and English literature as her minor. She became a journalist and met her husband in a literature class.

Bill Harrison had been a good young man, she said, but he had "no drive at all." They were married in 1975 right after graduation from college and had their only son a year later. Bill was content to remain a life-long middle school English teacher, but Lisa had higher ambitions. While in college she had worked at a local television station; this led to a well-paid position with a national network which required her to spend most of her time in New York City. Lisa's mother assumed the care of Bill Jr. and wholeheartedly encouraged her daughter's blossoming career.

When Bill objected to his wife's almost constant absence, Lisa suggested he move to New York City and work there too. He refused, saying it was the husband's prerogative to choose where the couple should live and the wife's duty to live where he did, not the other way around. He intensely disliked large cities and believed Bill Jr. should be brought up as he himself had been, in a smaller, more rural town with a slower pace of life. "In all these things he was right and I was wrong," said Lisa with tears in her eyes. But she did not heed his wishes. After twelve years the marriage ended. Bill tried to obtain custody of his son, but the courts as usual awarded it to the mother.

Bill Jr. resented this decision. He loved his dad and greatly missed him. His school grades plummeted. He became alternately withdrawn or violent. He listened to the loud music with the lewd words and gestures, popular among his peers. Lisa, by now a rising star among the publicists of the conservative movement, began working from her home to be more available for him. She tried hard to teach him her work ethic and other traditional values inherited from her parents but failed, in part because public education taught the opposite. When he turned eighteen, Lisa bought him a car which he smashed up when he was stoned on drugs. Finally, he got hold of my book *The Consolation of Philosophy* and killed himself by an overdose of heroin. He left a note, copied in part from the end of my book, stating that he would kill himself and no one could stop him since he was the master of his fate and the captain of his soul.

"Now you know as much about me as I know about you," she said, pulling a tissue from her purse and wiping her eyes. "I haven't told it all together to anyone else except to a shrink six months after Bill Jr. died. I was very broken up and depressed about it and thought counseling would help. It didn't really." She looked up at me with a wan smile. "Telling you actually helped me more. I feel relieved somehow. You didn't just listen. You shared. You knew what I was talking about."

"Yes," I assented, "I knew." I thought how my own son had died, how he had blamed me for his suicide, how I had blamed myself ever since, and how God had forgiven me. After a brief silence Lisa said: "I told you earlier I would try to forgive you for your part in my son's death. I have realized that your part in it was no greater than mine. Who am I to hold it against you? I forgive you, James. It won't ever stand between us any more."

I thanked her. We got up to leave. I picked up the two tickets and left a tip. Lisa saw it and looked at me with a half mischievous smile. We had silently agreed that this had been a date, not a business meeting. When we walked to our cars, we set the time when we would meet again—the evening after my forthcoming talk with Paul Reynolds.

10

Why They Must Kill Us

I suddenly awoke out of a deep sleep at about four o'clock the next morning with a sense of utter urgency. I might be called in for the conference or interrogation with Paul Reynolds this very day and I was not prepared! I must clearly explain my conversion to him on biblical grounds. I must tell him of the wonderful joy, God's own joy that had come to me immediately after I turned to Him, based on the Bible. I must do it right now. I had no doubt that this message came from God.

I got up quickly, dressed and sat down at my desk, Bible and concordance at hand. I opened my concordance to the words "joy" and "rejoicing." I was amazed at the wealth of entries. There must be hundreds and hundreds of them, I thought. How important the place of joy and rejoicing was in the Christian life! No wonder God had made me get up so early. It would take hours to sift through all these passages, to choose among them and to relate them to my own joy and His joy in me. How dare I even attempt it, I, who had begun to study the Bible in earnest only four days ago? Father, I prayed with fear, if You want to tell Paul Reynolds of Your joy through me, all right. Only please be with me every moment and give me what to say!

I worked through the remainder of the night, daybreak and morning. The outline of a meditation on the joy of the Lord slowly formed in my mind. The timing had been perfect. I was just beginning to type the completed meditation when the phone rang. My appointment with Paul Reynolds had been scheduled for two o'clock that afternoon in the office of Dr. Knightley, who would also attend.

Here is what I shared with these men that day:

Enter into the Joy of Your Lord

The meaning of all things in creation is God's joy. This is why we read five times in Genesis 1 that God looked at what He had created and found it good. When He had finished all His work of creation, He looked at it all and found it "very good" (Genesis 1:31).

We human beings are uniquely created by God in His own image and likeness (Genesis 1:26, 28). Therefore, as originally created before the fall and when restored in Christ, we would have joy in all things just as God has. What pleases Him would please us. We would love God's righteousness and law and hate unrighteousness and lawlessness. Remnants of this original creation joy are ours even now: we have pleasure in lovely flowers, beautiful scenery, harmonious music, painting, architecture and other beautiful or beneficial human artistic and scientific creativity, good health and many other pleasures too numerous to mention.

Now God saw from all eternity that man would rebel against Him in Eden and all the horror, trouble, and pain man's rebellion would entail. So He permitted, and Christ His Son agreed, that Christ would die on the cross for our sins. It was the only way to redeem us from our self-centered rebellion against Him. Yet Christ bore the agony, shame and death of Calvary *"for the joy set before Him"* (Hebrews 12:2). God, to Whom all things are present in His eternal Now, also saw the glory which was to follow. Our glad Creator will have His good heart's desire fulfilled at last! *"The sufferings of this present time are not worthy to be compared with the glory which shall be revealed in us"* (Romans 8:18). *"Eye has not seen, nor ear heard, neither have entered into the heart of man, the things which God has prepared for them that love Him"* (1 Corinthians 2:9). How beautiful and liberating is the Gospel of Christ speaking of God the Creator's love, gift of eternal life, and joy with Him in His new heaven and earth!

The meaning, purpose and end of creation is God's joy, our joy, the joy of the whole creation (Romans 8:21). Many Scriptures confirm this, such as Zephaniah 3:17: *"The LORD thy God . . . will rejoice over thee with joy; He will rest in His love, He will joy over thee with singing."* In Isaiah 62:5 God tells His people, *"As the bridegroom rejoiceth over his bride, so shall thy God rejoice over thee."*

This is His joy, the overwhelming, indescribable joy like no other which I felt in me when I first came to Him. In the few days since then, my consciousness of it has varied in intensity, but His presence and the joy itself has never left me. It is the fulfillment of Jesus' words to His disciples at the Last Supper: *"These things have I spoken unto you, that my joy might remain in you and that your joy might be full"* (John 15:11). Again He prayed shortly afterwards that they might have His joy fulfilled in themselves (John 17:13). His joy and our joy together in us His disciples, His adopted children—what glory! Indeed the sufferings of this present time are not worthy to be compared with it!

I so much wish and pray that you could have it too! Become His children too! Be sad for having made Him sad. Love Him, not yourselves! Bring gladness to your heavenly Father's heart moment by moment from now on. You too were created in His image and likeness. You too were paid for by Christ. You too are created for His and your eternal joy. Praise Him with all His people, saying *"Thou art worthy, o Lord, to receive glory and honor and power: for thou hast created all things, and for thy pleasure they were and are created"* (Revelation 4:11). Serve Him faithfully so He can welcome you in the end with the words: *"Well done, thou good and faithful servant: enter thou into the joy of thy Lord"* (Matthew 25:21, 23).

It was now close to one o'clock. In my total absorption with the paper I had not eaten or drunk anything all day; yet my stomach ulcer had not caused me pain as it normally did when I skipped a meal or even a snack between meals. "Thank You so much for this freedom from pain today, Father," I said aloud. I heated up a bland prepackaged lunch, ate it and got ready to meet with the two hostile men who would so heavily influence my future. I prayed for myself and for them as I walked to the institute.

I arrived in Dr. Knightley's anteroom a little before two o'clock. The secretary gave me a brief look, pressed an intercom button, said, "Dr. Barron is here now," motioned for me to go on into the inner office, and quickly busied herself with some papers on her desk. Her reserve showed me that she knew everything that had occurred between Dr. Knightley and me the day before. Her unwillingness to look me in the face meant that what awaited me was not good. I went past her to the inner office and exchanged greetings with J. P. Knightley and Paul Reynolds. We sat down opposite each other.

"So you want to leave the institute, James," said Paul Reynolds quietly. He was a plain man in his late forties with thinning brown hair. His square, pale face was framed by a carefully trimmed graying beard. His piercing light blue eyes squinted at you from behind rimless glasses under thin brows. He wore an expensive grey business suit and a shiny silken necktie at which he tugged from time to time. He did not resort to cursing when losing his temper as did J. P., but his decisions were made with thoroughly thought-out finality, irrevocable and deadly.

"Yes, I do," I answered.

"Because you have become a Christian," Paul completed, still calm, looking me full in the face. I nodded wordlessly, unsure where he was going with his half-questions.

"I have read your resignation several times from cover to cover," he said, "and I also got a tape of your interview with Lisa Trent Harrison. I listened to it several times and still don't understand what really happened to you."

He leaned forward a little, his face perplexed. "I want to hear your story from yourself, James," he said. "This is the first time I have run into someone who had become a Christian just a couple of days before. And then it was you of all people! A man of your intelligence and academic fame! I must confess I would have thought you the very last person to turn from atheism to God. Your whole career was a battle to eradicate Christianity from public life. Your whole philosophy was an extension of historical atheism, skepticism, evolutionism, utilitarianism, instrumentalism, and existentialism. How could you turn all at once against everything you taught so successfully for so long? Are you sure it was not an aberration you already regret?"

He was offering me a chance to retract both my resignation and my testimony of my conversion! I had a strange feeling that he was offering it not to me but to someone else. And so he was: he still saw me as the man I had been before my new birth. That other man was dead now. The new I, in whom God Himself now lived, could not be tempted by Paul's offer.

"It is kind of you to offer me this way out of what you see as an aberration, Paul," I said gently, "but I don't see it that way. To me my aberration was my whole life before I said yes to God last Thursday evening. Since then I have certitude, peace, and joy, which I never had before. I will never again reject God Who loved me and gave them to me, me who sinned and rebelled against Him so long. He has especially blessed me with His joy. In a way God's joy in me *is* my story. You said you wanted me to share it with you."

"Yes," Paul answered. J. P. Knightley, too, nodded assent. I pulled out the meditation I had prepared, gave Paul and J. P. copies, and began to read, "Enter into the joy of your Lord," the title.

Immediately Paul yelled, "Stop right there!" I did, taken aback by his unusually violent reaction so soon. His face was distorted with rage; his hands fastened tightly around his copy of my paper, crumpling its margins; I thought he was going to tear it to pieces. J. P., too, stared at him in astonishment. Paul took a deep breath and controlled himself with an effort. "Okay, okay, go on," he muttered. I resumed reading my paper all the way to the end.

Both my listeners remained silent for a little while. I looked at them, awaiting their reaction. J. P. looked back at me with the ghost of a smile; I could not tell whether he thought my words the signs of my delusion or actually began to let them take root in his mind and heart. Paul looked both furious and distressed. Finally he said in a voice at first calm but later shaking with emotion:

"I'll tell you *my* story now. I grew up a 'cradle Catholic' in the Roman Catholic Church. I loved everything about it: the stained glass windows, the beautiful Gothic cathedral where we worshipped, the liturgy, the incense, the statues of the saints and of the Virgin Mary with the baby Jesus, and yes, its ancient, sacred tradition. I loved making the sign of the cross and kneeling during the liturgy in adoration of God. I was overwhelmed when I made my first communion and thought that I had been found worthy to partake of Christ's own Body. As a young boy I thought of entering the priesthood myself when I grew up, which made my parents very happy. Along with everyone in the church, I totally respected the priests in their saintly garments and their sacred chastity. They could do no wrong." He stopped momentarily and swallowed before going on.

"And then I became an altar boy. And then Father Ryan began to touch me where he shouldn't have. At first I couldn't believe it. Then I got used to it as a form of love. Then I got raped by him. Then I got used to being raped. Finally I *liked* being raped. I didn't call it rape any more. I called it a form of love. It went on for years. I found out he did it with other boys of the parish too."

He could not go on for a few moments. His face was distorted with shame, grief and rage. Finally he recovered himself and continued: "Eventually someone told the bishop about Father Ryan. The bishop transferred him to another parish in a distant part of the diocese where he continued as a priest in good standing. The whole affair was successfully hushed up. But I lost all confidence in the church, and not only the church. I lost all faith in its God who allowed such things to happen. I became an atheist and left Catholic University which my parents had chosen for me after my freshman year. I wound up at the University of California in Berkeley right at the time of the Free Speech Movement and other radical groups. I joined the most radical one I could find and decided that I would do everything I could to help destroy the church and the very name of its Christ and God. I hated them. I still hate them."

After another brief pause he added: "There was a deep private consequence for me too. I never had relations with women. I never married. I leave it to you to guess why." He took a deep breath. "And here you are, an atheist leader for many years, telling me to enter into the joy of my Lord. You are different from the way you were. You are dangerous! You could almost make me believe in your God and His joy."

And then Paul said something I would never forget: "When I still attended Catholic University, I read these words by Christopher Dawson, an English Catholic historian: 'A Christian has only to be in order to change the world, for in that act of being, there is contained all the mystery of supernatural life.' *And that is why we must kill you.* We must kill all Christians like you. Either physically, or by putting you into the gulag or psych wards as they did in the former Soviet Union, or at least by totally silencing you in public."

He ended: "And that is why I accept your resignation, effective immediately, and with the added stipulation that you will neither speak nor write publicly against the institute and any and all its works and policies for the remainder of your original contract, that is, until September 1996."

11

Transitions

Paul was not finished with me. He asked Dr. Knightley to produce a document made out in triplicate which he asked me to sign; Dr. Knightley complied with a trace of reluctance. It was my written agreement to the stipulation Paul had just explained. I paused to read it before signing.

"Sign, James," Paul said coldly, "or the institute will sue you over that speech you gave at the American Educators Association conference June 15. You didn't think we would find out about it so quickly, did you? Well, think again! Dr. Turnbull called me about it the next morning. He was furious, especially about your 'God the Creator' statement at the end." Dr. Turnbull was the AEA regional conference chairman who had invited me to speak. I was not surprised; I remembered his rigid, hostile face and refusal to applaud after the end of my speech.

"You can be glad you already resigned," Paul resumed. "If you hadn't, I . . . we," he looked aside at J. P. Knightley, who nodded but also gave a helpless little shrug, "would have fired you today, with the same stipulation of your public silence about the institute for the remainder of your contract, of course. We would not have allowed you to stay on and keep drawing your salary while undermining us behind our backs, as you did at the AEA meeting."

I pulled the document closer to me and quickly read it. Besides the stipulation about my public silence about the institute it provided for termination of my health insurance, forfeiting any accumulated vacation time, sick leave and retirement benefits, and stopping my salary the date of my resignation, June 19. The institute would cancel all speaking engagements I had received while still on its staff. The final paragraph forbade me to disclose any part of this document to any and all news media or to individuals affiliated with them. It was the institute's preventive strike against Lisa Trent Harrison lest she report the details of my departure from it in public. I looked up at Paul and J. P. for anything further they might say. They remained silent, Paul in frozen hatred, J. P. uncomfortably hunched back in his chair. I signed the document, got up, said good-bye and walked out of the room, my meditation on the joy of the Lord and one copy of the signed document still in my hand.

I went home, called Lisa and arranged for our meeting that evening. I passed most of the afternoon making inquiries about exchanging my apartment for a much less expensive one. I was relieved to see that this would be relatively easy. To take my mind off what had happened, I began reading Whittaker Chambers' remarkable book *Witness*. It was partly about the famous "Hiss-Chambers Case" of the late 1940s which dealt with Communist spies in high American government circles during the Franklin Roosevelt administration. Its chief subject, however, was Whittaker Chambers' road from faith in Communism to faith in Christ.

Chambers saw himself as a witness of his faith to the world. He understood that such a witness was not primarily a witness *against* something but a witness *for* something. He was a man whose life and faith were so completely one that when he was challenged to step out and testify for his faith, he did, no matter what the risks or the consequences (Whittaker Chambers, *Witness,* Random House, New York 1952, p. 5). Was I now a witness in Chambers' sense? I thought with wonder that in the five days since my conversion, I myself had already met at least four challenges to step out and testify for my faith, accepting the cost. The first had come with the AEA speech, the second with my interview with Lisa, the third with J. P. Knightley and the fourth with Paul Reynolds. I had not felt especially brave or faithful about any of them. I had simply "been there and done that." Only God could have made it possible. I thanked Him with all my heart.

I made a copy of my meditation on the joy of the Lord for Lisa and left to meet her. I told her I was no longer on the staff of the Bertrand Russell Institute but could not divulge any details.

"That bad," she said. "But I'll find out what you can't tell me yourself. Right now just tell me one thing. Did they forbid you to talk or write publicly about your conversion?"

"I don't think so," I said slowly, "as a matter of fact, Paul Reynolds asked me to tell him more about it. In answer I gave him and J. P. Knightley copies of this paper." I put it before her on the table. She read it slowly once and then again.

"I have never read anything exactly like this before," she said. "I have heard altar calls before at Billy Graham crusades on television. It's like an altar call, isn't it?"

"I wanted it to be like an altar call," I said sadly, "I wanted Paul and J. P. to be drawn to God. I was so sure God meant for me to tell them of the joy I had in Him and He in me right after coming to Him. I wanted God to be as glad with them as He was with me. But it didn't happen. What did I do wrong?"

Lisa did not answer right away. Our meals came and we turned to our food. "I don't see that you did anything wrong, James," she finally said. "You took decades to come to God. Does that mean that the people who witnessed to you earlier did something wrong?"

I shook my head. "No," I conceded, "I used to think my mother nagged me too much about 'being right with Jesus.' Now I could wish she had nagged me more!"

"Well, then, don't worry about Reynolds and Knightley. If they are among God's elect, He will bring them in. If not, not." She was quite cool, almost casual about it. I was about to comment on this when Lisa changed the subject.

"If no one at the institute forbade you to speak or write publicly about your conversion," she said, "you can do so in *News in Depth*. Not in the next issue, because that'll carry my article about you—the one that missed the mark." She smiled her mischievous smile. "But in the issue after that—the August issue—you could write about how your conversion really was and correct or complete what I wrote. My editor would love it, and you would love the honorarium."

"You never give up, do you," I said, "let me think it over."

"You should begin working on it right away," she prodded, "to be printed in the August issue we must have the manuscript in hand print-ready by July 10. July 15, tops."

"Less than a month," I murmured.

"You have already written several hundred words of it right here," she said, pointing to her copy of my meditation on the joy of the Lord. "Remember, you aren't working for the institute any more! You have time on your hands. Use it."

"I will pray about it tonight and let you know tomorrow," I said. "Or perhaps I ought to call your editor directly?"

"His name is Roy Mattingly," she said. She pulled a business card from her purse and handed it to me. "Here is his number." I took it and thanked her. "However, even if I write this article," I added, "I will have to find a full-time college level teaching position quickly. I'll have to begin right away calling on my university contacts and sending out resumes. With luck," I stopped and corrected myself, "God willing something will turn up before the fall semester begins."

"But your contacts would all be as you were before your conversion, and therefore unwilling to help you," Lisa said. "Plus, I am sure the institute will do its utmost to make sure you stay unemployed in your profession for a good long time."

I nodded. "I may have to find work away from New York," I mused. "My sister advised me to apply to Fairfield University. It's a Christian school from which several members of my family graduated. It's in the Midwest, not too far from Battle Hill and Lonely Prairie, the small town where I grew up."

Lisa looked at me in sudden fear. "Oh, please don't do that yet, James," she pleaded. "Please wait and see if something can't fall in place for you right here! After all, we've only just met."

She realized she had given herself away. The blood mounted in her face, but she kept looking at me in a sort of timid bravery. I looked back at her, unable to speak. I, too, understood that we had already become more than acquaintances or even friends. We had begun to love and think of each other as possible future life companions. I suddenly realized that I had yearned for a love like this for years, perhaps all my life. God had put it in my way at this perilous moment when my whole future already hung in the balance. I was grateful and fearful all at once.

Oh dear Father, I prayed, You allowed us to meet. Please be in charge of us both, especially me! I have never loved anyone as I should. Help me to love Lisa with Your love. May our love also become "a place of springs," joyful and fruitful as does everything You touch and transform.

I took Lisa's hands into mine. "Dear Lisa," I said, "I will not apply to Fairfield University at this time." And so that evening, just hours after my loss of status, work, and most probably my wealth, began my newness of life in love. That night I prayed and was given peace about the article for *News in Depth*. I called Roy Mattingly the next morning and set to work on it.

Later that morning I received a phone call from J. P. Knightley. He wanted to meet with me at a little neighborhood bistro over the lunch hour. I agreed. He arrived punctually and sat down with me at a corner table away from the lunch crowd.

After some desultory conversation he came to the point. "I wasn't completely in agreement with Paul about the stipulation document," he said. "I thought it was too harsh. And another thing. Paul has already made a lot of calls to influential people at liberal universities—and that means almost all universities in New York City and vicinity—and think tanks like the Bertrand Russell Institute to stop them from hiring you. I thought that was uncalled for. At any rate, don't bother sending resumes to them or contacting people you know there. You would only waste your money and your time."

"He wants to kill me," I murmured. J. P. overheard me and seized eagerly on my words.

"I know what he meant," he said, "he saw right away how different you are now. There is a spirit in you that simply shines out and convicts. That spirit was in your paper too. Paul saw this when you started reading it. That's why he screamed at you to stop." He fell silent, recalling that strange moment, then went on, "I saw that change in you too, both yesterday and the day before. The day before all I could do was rant and rave against you. I am sorry."

I could not believe my ears but saw that he really meant it. He continued, "I took your 'Joy of Your Lord' paper home with me and read it over and over again. James, it made me see that what turned me away from Christianity was pseudo-Christianity. What I saw in you was the real thing. I wanted your God, your 'glad Creator with His good heart.' I was sorry I had rejected Him based on a false, lying, damnable presentation of Him," he was on the verge of hot, righteous anger but caught himself and added with humility, "without checking whether it was true or not. I condemned Him without a hearing, and that was my sin. I told Him so. And He came in. And He gave me joy."

He took off his glasses and wiped his eyes. I felt my own eyes grow hot with tears. We looked at each other and smiled, then laughed with our joy, His joy which we both now shared.

"I want to say something else right away, too," J. P. said, "it's about your little niece who brought you to God. I prided myself on not being prejudiced against black people and Jews, but until last night I had a horrible I.Q. prejudice against mentally handicapped people. I am so sorry I called your little niece a retarded idiot and you crazy because you changed when she told you she loved you."

"I had a horrible I.Q. prejudice too," I said, "it comes with the society in which we live. I wanted Sylvia aborted years ago."

"If she had been aborted," J. P. said, "neither you nor I would have come to God." Then he said matter-of-factly, "I also wanted to talk to you about two projects in which you could cooperate and earn a little income. One is a catalog a relative of mine is putting together about philosophical books in a lending library he runs from his home. He needs someone qualified to write brief reviews of these books for the catalog. Who could be better qualified than you? Get in touch with him. Here is his address and phone number. The other project is the updating and re-editing of a major dictionary of philosophy by its publisher, Groton Books. It's just the job for you and the pay should be good." He gave me their address too.

I thanked him. He shrugged. "I had to do something for you after what you did for me," he said and added with a laugh, "Let's just hope Paul doesn't find out about it!"

J. P. had one more piece of significant news for me. "The institute cancelled all speeches that had been booked for you," he said, "except for the one you are to give before the National Federation of College Women July 14 here in New York and the one before the North American Philosophy Association in October 1996 in Toronto. The NFCW program chair is none other than Nancy Berger. She knew about your conversion and insisted on your coming nevertheless, or maybe just for that reason. The philosophers thought they would like to hear how your worldview had changed and how well you could present it."

12
In Praise of Bernard Gottlieb

The remaining days of June were very busy. I moved to a much smaller, much less expensive apartment in the center of Greenwich Village. I realized again as I had two years ago when moving from Maryland to New York how many superfluous things I had managed to acquire and hang on to. It would be impossible to take them all with me.

My past reckless greed for things astonished me. In accordance with my former left liberal mindset, I had flattered myself all my adult life with the thought that I was not materialistic; the multitude of my material possessions showed me how deeply materialistic I had really been. "Father," I prayed, "I do not really own anything. All I am and have comes from You. You even gave Your Son for me. You gave me Yourself in Your Holy Spirit to live in my heart. Let me be generous like You and show me what to do with all the things I don't need." In answer He gave me a relieved, cheerful heart as I gave away my excess furniture and other belongings to the Salvation Army which operated a thrift store near my new apartment.

I got in touch with Groton Books and agreed to edit and update a section of its dictionary, really an encyclopedia, of Western philosophy. The encyclopedia was arranged chronologically. They knew my name and professional background well and welcomed me as a friend of Dr. Knightley but did not seem to know about my conversion. They asked me which section I would prefer to work on. I chose the seventeenth century because it included Blaise Pascal. They were surprised at my choice and tried to dissuade me; they had expected me to choose the modern philosophers whom I had done so much to promote. But when I persisted in my choice, they did not pressure me further. My pay would cover a good part of my newly reduced rent. I thanked God for it and for J. P. who had steered me to it.

I began to draft the speech I had been asked to give before the National Federation of College Women on July 14. I was very uneasy about the fact that it was Nancy who had insisted that this engagement be kept. The National Federation of College Women was a radical feminist organization. I thought that whatever I might say as a new convert to Christ would provoke them to wrath. I anticipated being heckled, booed, shouted down, prevented from speaking altogether and pelted with refuse. Was that what Nancy planned to have in store for me? Many members of the NFCW were militant veterans of picketing, protest marches and violent demonstrations with no inhibitions about how to express their views. I prayed for God's protection, for release from fear, and for giving me what I should say.

Last but not least, I made contact with J. P.'s relative with the private lending library. His name was Bernard Gottlieb. I found him in the penthouse of a quietly sumptuous apartment building in upper Manhattan, and he welcomed me literally with open arms. He was a tall, slightly stooping, fatherly gentleman with snowy white hair and a clean-shaven wrinkled face with merry brown eyes. I liked and trusted him immediately.

"So you have just become a believer, James," he said as we were walking toward his living room. "J. P. called me and told me all about you. Do you know what? I told him for the first time that I was a believer too! I had never told him this before because he had always been so hostile toward Christianity. Then he told me he had just become a Christian too because of you. We had a sort of family reunion over the phone."

We entered his living room. My host indicated two comfortable armchairs facing a wide window through which the afternoon sun was streaming in. We sat down. All the while he kept talking joyfully. "Now he'll have to bring his wife and children to the Lord. And the people around him at the Bertrand Russell Institute! Can you imagine the upheaval there when he starts speaking out about the faith? He won't be able to keep quiet about it, you know. We'll need to keep him in prayer constantly."

It was like we had been family forever. I couldn't help laughing with joy like a child. Bernard Gottlieb happily laughed with me. In earthly years he could have been my father, but I felt he was as young as I, no, younger than I at heart; only his body was getting old.

"That's right," he said as if he had read my mind, "go ahead and laugh, James! Become a little child again. I did too. Jesus says that the kingdom of heaven belongs to little children, and that you and I must receive it as little children or we shall not enter it. He also thanked the Father, Lord of heaven and earth, because He had hidden those things from the wise and prudent and had revealed them to babes. Become His little child, be meek and lowly in heart as Jesus is, and you will find rest for your soul." He became earnest as he said these words.

"You will find these words of Jesus in the Gospel of Matthew, Chapters 11 and 19," he explained. "I take it you have a Bible?" I said yes, and that since my conversion I had read the first ten chapters of Genesis, the Psalms and Matthew. "That's good; that's very good," he said. "Never skip reading the Bible even for a day. You have read Matthew 4 then, the record of Satan tempting Jesus three times in the wilderness. You remember the first temptation and how Jesus answered: Man shall not live by bread alone, but by every word that proceeds out of the mouth of God. If you do not know the word of God, how can you live? God knows this, and this is why He gives His children great hunger and thirst for His word right after they are newly born. He did this for you, didn't He?"

"Oh yes," I confirmed, "the night right after my conversion for the first time in my life I wanted a Bible very much. I desperately longed for one, but I didn't have one. So He provided one for me through the Gideons in the nightstand of my hotel room. I learned that very night from Genesis 1 that evolution is a lie, from Psalm 1 not to be found in the way of sinners, and from Matthew 1 that He remembers the name of every one of His children in eternity."

My host looked at me with joy. "It is well," he said, "you are on the way—the highway of holiness, Isaiah 35:8. The whole chapter of Isaiah 35 is wonderful; learn it by heart, and as many other Scriptures as you can." After a brief silence he added slowly with fatherly concern, "You are going to have to face much hostility on your road ahead, James. At times you will be afraid. I think verses 4 and 5 of Isaiah 35 will help you: *'Say to them that are of a fearful heart, Be strong, fear not: behold, your God will come with vengeance, even God with a recompense: he will come and save you. Then the eyes of the blind shall be opened, and the ears of the deaf shall be unstopped.'"*

I asked my host about how he was related to J. P. He chuckled; their connection was quite remote. J. P. had discovered it and Bernard himself through genealogical research, his hobby. It seemed there had been a marriage some generations ago between a Knightley great-aunt once removed and a Gottlieb man. "He was my great-grandfather," said Bernard, "and he was Jewish. So were my grandfather and my father. My father was not religious but agnostic as so many Jewish people are nowadays. As for me, I am a Messianic Jew, that is, I am a Jew who believes that Jesus Christ is our Messiah. My Jewish relatives don't know how to handle that so they avoid me."

He chuckled again: "J. P. and I didn't have any personal contact until J. P. moved to New York, and not much then, but he would have avoided me too if he had known of my faith! To be Jewish was fine with him, but just like many Jewish people, he hated Christianity because he thought it hated Jews. Of course that wasn't true Christianity as he now knows."

Next we went to his "lending library." He called his extensive collection of philosophical and theological books by this name because he gladly and regularly shared his books with inquiring friends. He wanted me to catalog the books and write a short introduction to each. I would need to spend an hour or two in the library as often as I could until the whole catalog was completed. "And that may never happen," he said jokingly, "because I add books all the time. For instance, here is a growing section of books on creation and evolution, written from the literal biblical perspective, of course. So you can look forward to a permanent part time job. I can pay you the going rate for your work." He named a figure, and I agreed.

As we walked past the book shelves, my host suddenly stopped and pulled out a volume by Josef Pieper, an author whose name I had never heard before. "Pieper is a German Catholic philosopher following the thought of Thomas Aquinas," he said. "He is now over ninety years old. He opposed the Nazis and therefore did not begin his academic career until he was over forty years old. He wrote about fifty books, among which are *On Faith, On Love,* and *On Hope,* considered his master work. I understand from J. P. that you were especially grateful for the joy you received from God right after you came to Him, and that your meditation on the joy of the Lord brought him to Christ. Well, based on a statement by Thomas Aquinas in his *Summa theologica* Pieper has written the following beautiful words about God. I think you would like to hear what he wrote. It fully supports your meditation based on the Bible which you gave to J. P." He turned to a page in his book and translated from the original German (he was fluent in several foreign languages as I learned later):

The religious sense of our time allows little if any room to the thought that perfect happiness is one of the attributes of God. We can almost say that this concept is foreign to us. In the Summa theologica of St. Thomas, on the other hand, we read that not to conceive of Him as the perfectly happy being would be to miss the reality of God. . . . The sense of this affirmation is not only that God is happy. The intention and the terms are rather that 'God is His own happiness'. Every human being who is happy has a part in a happiness which is not from himself. But for God to be and to be happy are identical; God is happy by virtue of His existence.

This idea immediately gives birth to a disturbing consequence. If the happiness of God does not depend on anything that happens, He cannot be diminished or augmented by any event whatsoever in the kingdom of Creation and in the historical world of man . . .

If this unalterably solid being were not the source of that which is real, we could not even conceive the idea of a possible healing of the empirical evils of creation . . . This belief means that 'the terrible words written by Paul Claudel, 'When all is said and done, the truth is perhaps sad' fail to describe the reality which undergirds the world; on the contrary, the great joy of God is the only reality.

I asked him to read it to me again so I could write it down. He gladly complied. "It's wonderful, isn't it," he said quietly, "how God in His goodness, grace and love showed His great joy as the only reality to men as far removed from each other in time and personal circumstances as the writers of the Old and New Testaments, St. Thomas, Josef Pieper, me and you—and doubtless countless others in between."

"Like Blaise Pascal," I said. It turned out my host did not know of the Pascal Memorial, which I could now share with him in return. He went back to the library, pulled out another book, this one very small and thin, and gave it to me to keep. It was *The Practice of the Presence of God* by Brother Lawrence, written in the seventeenth century and in print ever since. I love it. I have given dozens of copies to others.

Bernard Gottlieb also invited me to a Bible study he taught weekly in his home. I thought of Lisa and asked him whether I could bring her with me to the Bible study. Of course he gladly agreed. Lastly, he encouraged me to call him between meetings with any questions I might have. "And you will have questions, James," he said, "they come with growth in Christ and deeper study of the Scriptures. I would be honored and blessed to help you all I can." After a moment he added, "I came out of philosophy too—the wasteland of man's independent thought."

In Bernard Gottlieb God gave me an indispensable beloved mentor and teacher, almost a father, as I began to live out the faith.

13
Witness Before Enemies

I asked for Bernard Gottlieb's help in preparing my article on my conversion for *News in Depth* and especially my speech before the National Federation of College Women. I had him read Lisa's *News in Depth* article on me; its title appeared along with my picture on the cover of the magazine's July issue, now on the newsstands. I sat across from him in his living room and watched him read the article. Up to now he had only known enough facts about me to understand that I had been a determined enemy of God all my adult life; now he saw the depth of my chosen self-absorbed lawlessness, diligently unearthed and thoroughly revealed by Lisa in all her early hostility against me. He never said anything, but he visibly shuddered at some of the details she had described; I could hardly bear to see his pain and revulsion.

Next I had him listen to the tape of my interview with Lisa about my conversion. He heard it through to the end and took a deep breath of relief. "That was a terrible story, James," he said, pointing to the magazine. "You were an evil man who had a big part in making the world more evil. And then unfortunately Lisa missed the main point, the change in you. Oh thank our dear Father in heaven that you aren't that man any more!"

He looked at me with love and joy as the father in Christ's parable must have looked at the prodigal son upon his return. "Brother Lawrence rightly says that God often chooses those who had been the greatest sinners to receive His greatest grace, because this can reveal His goodness more dramatically," he said. "That is what He did with you, that and sharing His joy with you when you returned to Him. These are the two chief marks He set upon you. These are what He wants you to share with others. He has already used you to witness in this way to J. P. and Paul Reynolds. It was an example, a pattern He wants you to follow."

Bernard had also learned from J. P. that I was the subject of a nasty little news item in the *Gotham Review,* a thick glossy scandal sheet for elite opinion leaders wishing to know the scuttlebutt about each other dredged up by society columnists. It had reported that Dr. James Barron, philosopher in residence at the Bertrand Russell Institute, "had been let go" from his position due to sudden strange deviations from the institute's policy. Rumors had it, the *Gotham Review* hinted, that I might soon appear on the payroll of extreme right wing publications, "attracted by the greener financial pastures provided by conservative monopoly industrialist fat cats." Of course the simultaneous appearance of my photo on the cover and Lisa's lead article about me on the pages of *News in Depth* could only lend credence to this bit of liberal journalistic slanting.

I knew that similar slanted reports would soon appear in university house organs, nationally read magazines, and the culture sections of leading newspapers pursuant to the directives to destroy me from powerful people behind the scenes like Paul Reynolds. I thought that if conservatives had their "monopoly industrialist fat cats," so had the liberals. However, I knew I would not argue this point in my own writing or public appearances, for that would only show the enemy how much this hypocritical, lying blow had hurt me and encourage him to use it over and over again.

With Bernard Gottlieb's approval I decided I would respond to Lisa's article in *News in Depth* by admitting that everything she had said about me was true, that I was indeed a man who had sinned most deeply, but that God had convicted me, allowed me to receive His grace which was greater than my sin, and even given me His great joy right after my surrender to Him.

My meditation on the joy of our Lord, which I had already shared with J. P. and Paul Reynolds, would be the next and concluding part. Bernard thought Paul would surely read this article and thus again be confronted with the testimony I had already given him. "That second confrontation is God's additional grace to him," Bernard said, "even as He showed you grace after grace through all the people in your life who loved you and witnessed to you time after time. He is no respecter of persons—He loves Paul Reynolds as much as He loves you." I knew this was true and joined Bernard in praying for Paul's salvation.

Full preparation for my speaking to the National Federation of College Women still lay ahead. It took another meeting with Bernard for me to be inwardly ready for it. What burdened me most was almost shameful for me to confess to him. It was my fear of a physical attack against me instigated by my ex-wife Nancy Berger. Bernard agreed that such an attack might be possible and saw no way in which I might absolutely prevent it or physically guard against it. "We must just pray for our Lord's protection," he said, and we did. He also encouraged me just to speak the truth to the women present at the conference, essentially repeating what I had written for *News in Depth* in my response to Lisa's article.

Bernard also said I should not look at these women as a mass of violent feminists or under some other stereotype but see them as individual persons, each created by God in His own image and likeness. "Think of yourself as speaking to each one of them alone, or just to Nancy alone," he advised. "Yes, that would be best, because you have hurt Nancy in the past and might need to ask her forgiveness, in public if necessary. Scripture tells us that 'a soft answer turns away wrath.' Your asking forgiveness should turn away Nancy's wrath against you and through her the wrath against men in general of other women in that conference." I thought this was excellent advice and promised to follow it.

Lisa, on the other hand, argued that I should not be a sitting duck for Nancy or her feminist cohorts. At least, she said, I must have someone come with me who could be an independent witness to whatever might be planned or done against me. I understood immediately, of course, that she intended to be that someone. She was motivated by her growing love for me but also by her newshound instinct; here might be just the right story or scoop to keep the public's interest in my defection from atheist liberalism alive! I was afraid that if I came to the NFCW conference accompanied by Lisa, Nancy's still smoldering resentment against me might burst into yet greater hate and fury. I even said half in jest that it was dangerous to be with me on July 14, because it was not only my birthday but also the fifth anniversary of my son Dylan's "Rousseau Academy Massacre." Lisa knew what that was as she had thoroughly investigated it and described it in her article. But nothing would deter her. In the end I gave in and took her with me to the hotel where the conference was held.

Nancy stood behind the registration table and came forward to greet me. It was the first time we had seen each other again after our divorce, now over two years ago. We looked each other over, she with hostile curiosity, I with genuine pity, for she had greatly aged. Being my senior by eight years, she was now sixty-two years old and looked a good many years older. She was still stocky and still dressed in a mannish navy pant suit much like the ones she used to wear when we first met at Battle Hill University. Her hair, which had been a mousy brown then, was now a mousy grey, still cut short and still untidy. Her face was lined and sallow, with deep rings below and sagging upper eyelids above her squinting eyes. I was fully and almost apologetically conscious of the fact that I looked much more handsome, fitter and younger than she, and that Lisa who stood by my side was obviously much more attractive and much more suitable as my companion.

I introduced Lisa as the author of the article about me now running in *News in Depth* and gave Nancy a copy of it. "I have already met Ms. Harrison and I have already read the article," Nancy said as she accepted the copy, "a lot of the information in it came from me. You did a good job with it, Ms. Harrison. Did you come tonight to hear what James might say for another write-up?"

"That's right," Lisa answered, "and also to observe the audience reaction. Are the ladies aware that James has changed his views radically since you first invited him to speak?"

"He can speak for himself, Ms. Harrison," Nancy said. "Any comments you want to make on that subject, James, before the meeting starts?" She began to walk towards the head table, expecting us to accompany her.

I fell in step with her, walking by her left side as I always had in the past. "Yes, I have changed my views, Nancy," I confirmed, suddenly totally free from fear, "not only in philosophy but about the way I led my life. I know I did you much wrong from the very start, just as you told Lisa when she interviewed you for the article. Please forgive me if you can."

I stopped speaking because Nancy had stopped walking. We stood still opposite each other. She looked up at me out of her age-ravaged face with those squinting eyes of a sad old woman. After clearing her throat, she said in a hoarse voice: "Oh James! If you could only have asked me that when the children died! Or even during the divorce . . ." Her voice failed. Tears welled up in her eyes and ran down those sallow, wrinkled cheeks. She took me by the arm and led me a few steps away, doubtless so Lisa could not hear what she wanted to tell me.

"I read about your conversion in the article," she said, "I thought you must be pulling Ms. Harrison's leg. *You* becoming a Christian? Give me a break! But then

I heard your interview with Ms. Harrison when it was rebroadcast last Saturday." I stared at her, surprised; Lisa had not told me about this. Nancy went on: "And now you ask me to forgive you. You have really changed! You are different! Ms. Harrison did not mention that in the article." She wiped away the tears on her cheeks roughly with her hands. "I want to tell you something I never told you before, James, but don't laugh at me."

I shook my head that I would not. "I fell in love with you soon after we first met," Nancy began, "I couldn't ever let you know or tell you then! You would only have laughed at me, the plain older woman. I could only manipulate you by working on your career ambition, promoting you, smoothing your way before you, and yes, getting you to break up with your little honey-blonde girl friend. I was so happy when we went to Herbert Spencer University and things finally fell into place between us. I knew you still didn't love me. You never loved me! But I settled for less to have children. Not just children because 'my biological clock was ticking.' Children from you."

Again she couldn't speak because tears choked her voice. Finally she said almost in a whisper: "And then you wanted nothing to do with me or the children. Our beautiful little boy who looked so much like you and our little girl with the blonde hair and the serious face! If I had only stayed home and been a full-time mother to them! But I was a feminist who despised 'homemakers.' I had been a feminist for years, ever since my stepfather abused me as a young girl."

She took a deep breath. "Feminism gave me my self-esteem and my identity. I had to prove I could do anything a man did. Furthermore, my profession had helped me get you. If I gave it up, you might leave me. And then you threw me away anyway, over and over again, for your one-night stands with younger women. And I had to pretend to fellow faculty members that it was okay with me when in reality I lay alone night after night and cried. I loved you so much that I finally began to hate you. That's when Vivian Sims came into my life."

She started weeping aloud. I put my arms around her and let her lean her old grey head against my breast. "I am so sorry, Nancy," I said softly, "I didn't ever know or dream that you were in love with me. Forgive me that too. Forgive me about the children. I didn't know what they meant to you." I thought, and perhaps she thought, too, that our marriage might have been rescued if only we had had this exchange before our divorce. Now it was too late.

Finally Nancy sighed and stepped away from me. "We'll have to go to the podium," she said briskly, wiping her face dry with her hands once more. "They are waiting for your speech. Tell them—let them know what you are now, after your conversion." We walked ahead, with Lisa a few steps behind us.

I gave my speech just as Bernard had advised me, admitting who I had been and trying to explain who I was now after You, dear Father, finally reached me through little Sylvia. I told them about Your wonderful joy. They applauded heartily at the end. I thought everything had gone well beyond all expectation.

And then a woman in the front row stood up, pulled something from her purse, stepped forward and threw the thing she held straight at me. It hit me in the face just above my left eye. I cried out with terrific pain and raised my hand to my forehead; blood ran through my fingers across my eye and down my cheek. The missile fell to my feet and broke into shards. It had been a small perfume bottle made of glass. The perfume was trickling along the floor. Some had leaked into my wound, burning like fire.

The woman stepped to the podium. "You had that coming to you, Dr. Barron," she said. "You had a one-night stand with me back at Herbert Spencer University. I hope it leaves a good deep scar to remember me by." Then she walked away. Security had not come yet, and no one stopped her.

14

Strength, Goodness and Love

Lisa and Nancy were by my side instantly. I had pressed a handkerchief to the wound, which still hurt but had stopped bleeding. I did not think it was serious and wanted simply to go home, but the women insisted that we go to the nearest hospital for emergency checkup and treatment. "It will need cleaning up and stitches," said Lisa. Nancy agreed. I finally gave in to them to placate them.

We drove through the late evening traffic, Lisa at the wheel of my car, I by her side and Nancy in the back seat. As the minutes went by, my ulcer began to throb, its increasing pain soon exceeding that of the wound above my eye. My tension during the weeks before and especially during the meeting, the unexpected shock afterwards, and the emptiness of my stomach hours after my last skimpy meal before I set out for the hotel had done their work. I put my hands over my stomach, hoping their warmth would deaden the pain as it sometimes did, but it did not help. Lisa glanced at me a few times with concern but said nothing. When we arrived at the hospital I was almost doubled over with the pain and could walk upright only with an effort.

"Your ulcer," said Nancy. She had not forgotten how it had plagued me during the years of our marriage. Lisa looked at her, aghast, then at me with love and pity. Nancy saw it, pressed her lips together and slightly shook her head. For some reason it reminded me of my father's reaction to my love for little Karen many years ago. "He has got it badly," he had said, comparing my love for her to a bad sickness. So Nancy seemed to feel about Lisa's love for me. And perhaps she is right, I thought; was it good for Lisa to be in love with me? Me with my horrible past? Me with my wound caused by one of the many women I had used and thrown away? Me who had just lost prestige, position, and financial security? Me who was twelve years older than she and not in the best of health?

My pain cut short this train of thought. Oh dear Father, I prayed in my heart as we walked into the emergency room, please stop this ulcer from getting worse. Don't let it perforate my stomach wall. I don't even have health insurance any more. Please don't make me stay in the hospital. Please, please stop this awful pain!

The pain from the ulcer stopped. I could not believe it at first. I tentatively straightened up a little as I took the next couple of steps. I took a deep breath and contracted my abdominal muscles: the pain was not there any more. Both women noticed the change in my movements.

"What happened?" asked Nancy.

"You are better now, aren't you?" said Lisa.

"I prayed," I said slowly, "and He answered. He stopped the pain." The women looked at me doubtfully. "He really did," I reaffirmed, and repeated in awe and stunned joy, "He really did!" I thanked Him with joy restored in my heart.

I was not permanently healed from my ulcer trouble then, nor do I believe that His Word promises us healing upon every request. He gives us doctors and medicines; Luke the Evangelist was a "beloved physician," and St. Paul told Timothy to use a little wine for his stomach's sake (perhaps an ulcer?) and his frequent infirmities. Later a doctor treated my ulcer with antibiotics which helped greatly. But I learned that evening in my own body that He can and does heal directly in answer to prayer when it pleases Him in His good and perfect will.

The cut on my forehead was cleaned and closed with several stitches. There would be no permanent damage except a scar. "You were lucky," the young intern doctor told me. "You might have lost the vision in your left eye or even the eye itself if that perfume bottle had hit you there." He told us that he had never treated anyone at whom someone had thrown a perfume bottle. "Beer bottles, yes, but perfume bottles, no," he chuckled. I laughed with him but Lisa winced and said a beer bottle might have killed me, making us men laugh again.

While we drove Nancy back to the hotel, with me back at the wheel this time, Lisa asked me who the woman was who had attacked me. I had not recognized her and felt badly about it; it proved how little she had meant to me while our brief affair had left her grieved and enraged for years. "Do you know who she was?" Lisa asked Nancy, who said no, but falteringly. "Are you sure you don't know?" Lisa, experienced journalist that she was, insisted. Again Nancy asserted she didn't. I guessed that she knew the woman well but did not want her to suffer bad consequences from what she had done.

"If you remember later who she was," I said to Nancy, "tell her I will never sue or retaliate for what she did to me. I promise it. Tell her I am sorry for the past and for not even recognizing her." Nancy said she would. She also gave me a check as honorarium for my speech before the NFCW. As it turned out, the check almost covered the bill I later received from the hospital for my emergency treatment.

A day later I was called in by Groton Books' chief editor of the philosophy encyclopedia I had been hired to help revise and update. He told me that my services would not be required for the revised encyclopedia after all, and gave me the one month notice required by our contract. Groton Books would pay me through the end of August. I asked him why the company had changed its mind about me. At first he demurred, but finally he said that Lisa Trent Harrison's article about me in *News in Depth* and the news item about me in the *Gotham Review* had something to do with it. "We don't believe you would correctly represent the firm's viewpoint," he ended. "We were already wondering about that when you chose to edit the section about philosophy in the seventeenth century rather than in our own time." I knew further discussion was useless, thanked him for his time and left.

This was very bad news for me. After *News in Depth* would have paid me for my article I would have only the work and income provided by Bernard Gottlieb, plus what might come in from book royalties and interest from investments. Father, I put it all into Your hands, I prayed. You know my circumstances and my needs. I trust You! Help me to keep trusting You as You lead me where I dread to go. The worry about to engulf me lifted, and I was at peace.

That evening I had a date with Lisa and told her what had happened. She listened quietly, but it did not seem to phase her.

"We could see this kind of persecution coming and now it has come," she said. "By the way, I know now what Reynolds and the Bertrand Russell Institute made you sign. I have it on good authority—Dr. Knightley's secretary. Secretaries always know everything that goes on in their work place. There isn't much we can do about it directly, as they are legally within their rights. We'll have to make an end run around it, as we did with your present article. I'll take it up with Roy Mattingly."

She became more agitated as she continued: "But you should have stood your ground more firmly, James! You should have held out for being released from silence about the institute and its policies six months after leaving it, not twelve. You can't just lie down and let your enemies run over you. They only despise you for it."

She sat up straighter and looked at me with exasperation. "That's one thing we need to talk about, James. You are too gentle! You are leaning over backwards to be good to everybody. It's your weakness! I have seen it now time after time, beginning with your interview with me. I have seen it when you talked to Nancy Berger before that NFCW conference. She took you aside so I wouldn't hear what she said, but I have excellent ears and as a news reporter I have learned to listen well. She told you a great sob story, but the fact remains that she manipulated you for years."

"And I went along with her willingly," I interrupted. "I thought we had simply exploited each other, but I more than she because my career benefited from it more than hers, and because of my affairs. That's why I felt guilty about Nancy after my conversion and wanted to ask her forgiveness. Then she told me her story. I saw for the first time that she did what she did out of love, largely selfish as it may have been, and later to have my children. How could I hear that and not feel even guiltier? I went along with her out of sheer ambition and self-absorption. No, Lisa, I was not weak when I asked her to forgive me. I did not lean over backwards to be good to her. I only did what was right under God."

"Love? She did it out of lust for a good-looking young man!" Lisa exclaimed. "And what about your son?" she asked, unconvinced and with rising anger. "He wrote in his diary that he saw you as his mother's weak slave and believed that you had the affairs to assert your manhood. I think there is truth in that. A man wants to assert his manhood and resents it when his wife manipulates him for any reason. I know that because my husband was fed up with my bossiness. That's why our marriage broke up."

"So you think like Dylan that I was weak all my life with Nancy, or just weak, period," I said. "I considered that too after his diary was brought into our divorce. It's certainly possible. I was so completely self-absorbed that weakness would have been quite acceptable to me if it got me what I wanted."

"And you might be weak now, too, James," Lisa insisted. "Why would your conversion have changed that? Look at that woman who attacked you. Why did you let her get away with it? That's not goodness but weakness! Her attack was completely lawless. You encourage such acts when you don't enforce the law against them. Sue her, even yet. I can find out who she is."

"No," I said, "I have remembered who she is, and I have all the less desire to take action against her. There was this girl I went to bed with a couple of times when I was on the faculty of Herbert Spencer University. When I dropped her, she was all broken up. I had no pity but mocked her by telling her that what I couldn't stand about her was the perfume she used. Throw it away, I told her, before going to bed with someone else. It was absolutely heartless of me. That's why she threw a bottle of perfume at me."

"I see," said Lisa, stunned. "It's amazing that I didn't hear this story when I did my research on you, but I still think she shouldn't get away with what she did."

"We are to love our enemies, do good to them that hate us, and pray for them who despitefully use us so we may be the children of our Father in heaven and be perfect like He is," I said. "Christ says so in the Sermon on the Mount. And besides, I began the lawlessness when I slept with her, committing adultery as well. It was wrong of me, and I paid. Do not look for her, and do not bring it up again."

Lisa looked at me in silence. Her face reflected first perplexity, then resignation, and finally loving acceptance. "You are not weak, James," she said wonderingly, feeling her way from word to word, "on the contrary, you are stronger than I thought. But your strength is different. It is as though your weakness were your strength! It is part of the way you are now—a gentle strength, a righteous strength." It is Your strength, Father, I thought, remembering again His word that His weakness is stronger than men.

Lisa took a deep breath as though making a momentous decision. For the first time since we had met she told me, "I love you, James."

"I love you too, Lisa," I answered, "I love you for all your initiative, drive, energy and zeal to find ways to fight the enemy. I love you for all your impatience with my patience. I love you because you love me even though you know what I was like before. I love you because you love me now that I am different. But do not call me strong or good. Only one is good, God Himself. Whatever may be strong or good or loveable in me is of Him."

They Shall *Not* Be Ashamed

15
Stumbling Blocks

I took Lisa with me to the Bible study at Bernard's the last week in July. I told her a little about it in advance. It had been meeting for many years. Led by a Messianic Jew, it included former unbelievers like me, Protestants from various denominations, Roman Catholics and Eastern Orthodox. "It's representative of the universal Church," I said, "which is truly one. Jesus prayed that His people should be one as He and the Father are one."

Thanks to my virtual unemployment and resulting free time I had by now devoured all the Gospels and most of the rest of the New Testament. I especially loved the Gospel of John where the above prayer is recorded. I went on happily, "I am so grateful God gave me this Bible study as my first fellowship with other believers! He removed the first stumbling block a new Christian faces today—the disunity of the visible church."

I remembered how J. P. had raged against the endless arguing among professing Christians over "petty theological issues he could never understand," and told Lisa about it. She became very thoughtful. "The United Reformed Church in which I grew up put doctrines first," she mused, "and it excluded anyone who did not accept exactly the same doctrines we did. Yet we joined the International Ecumenical Council of Churches to show unity with denominations who did not share our doctrines! So it certainly isn't *doctrinal* unity which unites the IECC. It's just outward *organizational* unity. But Christ prayed that His people might be one as He and the Father were one—*inward unity* in spirit and love, in their very being. Of course doctrinal unity and outward unity in all essentials would come with that inward unity, as they did in the early church. I see that now. I am also beginning to see that doctrines can become stumbling blocks to people considering Christianity."

"Yes, they can, but we must test doctrines," I said. "We can't help it. It's a little like philosophy, Lisa, where I was taught to 'doubt all things.' But doubting is not testing! To test, you must have a standard to test by to begin with. As St. Augustine said, you must have truth to test whether something is true or not. We Christians have truth—God Himself and His word." His joy rose up in me so strongly as I saw this that I could not help exclaiming, "I love Him because He Himself is the truth—the way, the truth and the life!"

As usual when His and my joy irrepressibly welled up in me, Lisa looked at me with some reserve and incomprehension. If only I could bodily transfer the joy of the Lord to her! I yearned so much in that moment for her to be open to receive that joy, and Him with it. I recognized with a pang of foreboding that we would not be one for life unless she did.

We arrived a little early at Bernard's place. About twenty people were present and visiting with each other, including J. P. who greeted me with joy. He had brought his wife Brenda with him and we all got acquainted.

"Brenda thought I might have gone off the deep end," he told me, "but she has noticed that I don't cuss nearly as much as I used to over every little thing that goes wrong. It's a change for the better, the first of many, we hope. It's a whole new beginning for us! We actually met in the church I told you about—the one where blacks and Jews were not welcome. And there was a hell of a lot," he amended a little sheepishly, "a lot of putting other churches down because of doctrinal differences."

"But we did hear the Gospel," said Brenda, a cheerful woman in her early fifties, "the minister preached it at the close of every service. You know, that all people are sinners and that Christ died for our sins so we would not go to hell. All we had to do to go to heaven was to accept Jesus as our Lord and Savior and then to be baptized for the remission of sins. I did that as a little child."

"But something must have been missing, because it didn't last," J. P. said. "I went forward at the altar call when I was fifteen. It made no difference in me. Then I was baptized to see if *that* made any difference in me. It didn't. Of course the preacher had an answer for people like me. 'Satan has slipped you a counterfeit,' he said. 'Rededicate yourself!' I did. It still didn't make any difference in me. But I was a church member and so Brenda's folks let me marry her. I had come to hate Christianity, that is, what I thought was Christianity. I wanted no more to do with it. Brenda didn't exactly hate it but gradually drifted away. We forgot what we had learned about the Bible. We raised our two kids as agnostics, with the help of the public schools. Now we'll have to undo that."

"At least I read Bible stories to them when they were little," said Brenda.

"And we put up a Christmas tree when the kids still lived at home," said J. P., "but we told them it was just a cultural habit. And so it was, for us. Well, we'd better stop chatting," he interrupted himself, "everyone else has sat down." We joined the circle around Bernard, who began the meeting with prayer.

The Bible lesson this evening was about Christ's messages to the churches of Philadelphia and Laodicea in Revelation, Chapter 3. Bernard told us to compare our churches with them. Those of us who were looking for a church home must know which ones to avoid. "Always try to apply what you find in the Bible to your own life," he said, "as you study these churches, think also of yourselves. Are you faithful to Christ, like Philadelphia? Are you lukewarm about your faith like Laodicea?"

We took turns reading Revelation 3 from our Bibles. Christ had only praise for the church of Philadelphia, which had a little strength, had kept His word and had not denied His name. The only other church among the seven churches of Revelation He had also praised without reservation was the church of Smyrna in Revelation 2 which remained faithful in the midst of tribulation, persecution and poverty. "Smyrna and Philadelphia are the shining examples for all churches to follow," Bernard said, "and also for all us individual Christian believers."

Finally there was the church of Laodicea, "the worst of them all," Bernard said. "Christ told it that 'because you are lukewarm and neither cold nor hot, I will vomit you out of my mouth.' This church thought itself rich and in need of nothing and did not know that it was really wretched, miserable, poor, blind, and naked. Christ told it to buy from Him gold tried in the fire and white clothing to hide the shame of its nakedness, and to anoint its eyes with eye salve so it might see.

"And then comes our Lord's final invitation," Bernard ended, "'Behold, I stand at the door, and knock: if any man hear my voice, and open the door, I will come in to him, and will sup with him, and he with me. To him that overcometh will I grant to sit with me in my throne, even as I also overcame, and am set down with my Father in his throne. He that hath an ear, let him hear what the Spirit saith unto the churches.' If anyone here has not let the Lord come into his or her heart till now, or is not sure whether he has or not, ask Him to come in now."

Afterwards we briefly reviewed the main faults of the five Revelation churches Christ had reprimanded. Ephesus had left its first love of Christ; Pergamos had tolerated those who taught false doctrines; Thyatira had allowed a false prophetess to teach and seduce Christ's servants; Sardis had not been watchful to keep what it had received and heard from the Lord; lukewarm Laodicea prided itself on being rich and perfect and did not even know its own wretchedness, blindness and nakedness. These were among the "stumbling blocks" even within the church itself which we must overcome.

The descent always begins with leaving our first love for You, dear Father and Jesus, I thought. Help me always to put You first. Help me never to leave my first love for You! Don't ever let me tolerate or be seduced by false teaching! Let me be like Smyrna and Philadelphia, faithful in tribulation and never denying Your holy and perfect Name!

Before we left, I asked J. P. how he was getting along at the Bertrand Russell Institute. He chuckled but was serious as well. "I am not as widely known as you, James," he said, "my doctorate is in business administration, not philosophy. I am the administrative director, not a 'philosopher in residence.' That means I will have much less trouble than you finding another job if Reynolds discovers what's happened to me and boots me out. I am putting out confidential feelers now about working somewhere else. Until I do, I am doing Christian termite work on my secretary and a couple of others in the institute and elsewhere. Thank God Brenda is with me all the way. Pray for me." I promised to do so and asked him to pray for me to find other work soon, especially since my contract with Groton Books had been rescinded. We parted closer friends than ever.

As I was driving Lisa home, I recalled our conversation on the way to Bernard's. The maxim "Doubt everything" of secular philosophy struck me again, this time with an extrapolation I had not thought of before.

"What else can man without God do but doubt everything?" I wondered out loud, "the highest guarantee he has for evaluating anything in the world correctly is his own thought. Descartes was right after all! But if evolution is true, then what confidence can man have in his thought coming from a brain evolved from an ape's? Darwin already asked this question. It is man's last humility to admit he cannot truly know anything by himself."

Lisa heard me out with a smile. "Once a philosopher, always a philosopher, James," she said. "You ought to write a paper about what you just said, with the title 'Man's Last Humility.'"

"And which shows that his 'humility' turns into pride and becomes sin," I added, "if man willfully closes his mind and heart to the knowledge that God *is*. I did that until six weeks ago. When I stopped doing that, I could not help knowing that God exists." On that thought we arrived at Lisa's apartment building.

I walked her to the entrance. For the first time since we had known each other she invited me for a nightcap in her apartment. After a moment of inward struggle, I declined. I think we both understood that I did not trust myself to resist the temptation, sure to come if I went with her, to want to be intimate with her. After agreeing where we would meet the next time, we parted with a hug and kiss. As I drove home, I realized that I had acted towards Lisa like a very young man towards his very first love. And that is true, I thought, for I am a very young man in Christ, and Lisa is my first love since my new birth, perhaps my only love for the rest of my life. This is why You restored my innocence, dear Father, I prayed; thank You and keep me like this. I remembered that Lisa as yet did not share my heart knowledge of You nor Your joy and might never share it (but I could hardly bear this thought and dismissed it quickly). I prayed that she might share it soon so that she might become my wife and companion "till death do us part." "But do what You will with me, Father," I prayed, "You know what is best for me. I say yes to You if I must live alone the rest of my days on earth."

A day or two later I received a phone call from a Dr. Gerrit Van Houten who identified himself as the founder and director of the Van Houten Foundation. I had never heard of it before. He said it was an offshoot of the United Reformed Church, though no longer with organizational ties to it. The foundation published a thick quarterly magazine simply called the *Van Houten Journal.* It featured articles, critiques, and book reviews on theological and philosophical issues. Dr. Van Houten had read the recent article on me by Lisa Trent Harrison in *News in Depth.* He had also received a personal phone call from Ms. Harrison with further information about me. Could I meet with him and discuss possible future contributions from me for the *Van Houten Journal?* I agreed to a time for us to meet and smiled, admiring Lisa's never failing ability to sense and seize career opportunities. Just one thing bothered me: the theology, or "doctrines," of the Van Houten Foundation, doubtless derived from the United Reformed Church, might yet prove a stumbling block in the way of my working for it.

16
The Gag Order Works; A New Door Opens

Before my meeting with Dr. Van Houten, Lisa and Roy Mattingly got together with me for lunch to discuss how we might "make an end run" around the stipulation document I had signed for the Bertrand Russell Institute. Roy was a capable, handsome man in his mid-forties. I watched his special attention and courtesy toward Lisa and became sure that he was very interested in her apart from their professional relationship.

No sooner had we settled down in our restaurant booth that Roy launched into a mini-lecture on his conservative beliefs to educate me. He praised the virtues of minimal government interference in society. He explained how economic competition kept prices down and stimulated the invention and production of better and technically more advanced goods. "That is why people are so much better off economically in our society than under socialism and communism," he said. He inveighed against the explosive growth of government bureaucracy, the "soak the rich" transfer payments of earned income through taxation for welfare and social security programs, and the "dumbing down" of public education. He resented the liberal bias of most news media and deplored the apathy of so many citizens about public affairs. "Many of them don't even vote," he said sadly and quoted statistics to prove his point.

I asked him how Christianity fit into his beliefs. Like Lisa, he felt that Christianity and conservatism were almost the same thing. He was concerned, however, about the growing influence of liberalism in the church. I asked him whether he thought that Christianity and the visible church organizations were the same. This question stumped him; he had never thought about it. He thought his work as a conservative journalist was to influence the "church"—and he now added, "that is, the visible church organizations"—to adopt conservative positions about society. He was worried because this was becoming more and more uphill work. For example, the "church" was going soft on traditional conservative positions on abortion and now homosexuality.

I suggested that conservatives had originally received their positions on abortion and homosexuality and related ones like divorce and feminism from biblical Christianity. Roy agreed this might be so. "Of course conservatism is primarily a political movement, just like *News in Depth* is largely a political and cultural magazine," he said. With this statement he had abandoned his earlier view that conservatism and Christianity were almost the same thing. I had doubted this all along, but by now my reading of the Gospel of John had completely convinced me that Christianity was not a political movement. "My kingdom is not of this world," Christ had told Pilate.

"You mentioned divorce," said Roy. "A lot of conservatives are divorced. I was divorced myself just a few weeks ago." He looked quickly at Lisa as though he wanted to make sure she heard this information.

Armed by my intensive reading of the New Testament and the Bible study on the churches of Revelation under Bernard Gottlieb, I told Roy that the visible church organizations and the true church were not the same thing. Visible church organizations and the merely nominal Christians in them might abandon biblical commands and principles. But the true church consisted of the Christian believers who overcame such backslidings and betrayals and would never take part in them.

"What do the overcomers have that the others don't?" asked Roy. Lisa, too, listened intently as I answered, "Their faith is not just head knowledge of teachings about Christ. Their faith is much more. *It is the substance of things hoped for, the evidence of things not seen—Christ in them, the hope of glory,* Colossians 1:27. It is their love of God with all their heart, mind, soul and strength. They are completely sold out to God and trust Him totally. Historical facts bear this out. May I quote, as best I can, a passage from the Christian historian Kenneth Scott Latourette?"

"My heavens, James," said Roy, "how can you have studied so much already since your conversion?"

"Well, God used my unemployment for a crash course in Christianity," I said, "and He also gave me access to a wonderful private library. Here is the gist of what Latourette says: 'The exceeding greatness of the power of God was displayed primarily in the transformation of the men and women who put their trust in Christ. They could die to sin; they could walk in newness of life. They showed forth the fruits of the Holy Spirit Who dwelled in them: love, joy, peace, long-suffering, gentleness, goodness, faith, meekness, and temperance. They were, in Jesus' words, 'the salt of the earth and the light of the world'. In them the exceeding greatness of the power of God has been palpably at work." (adapted from Kenneth Scott Latourette, *A History of Christianity* (New York: Harper & Row, 1953, pp. 263, 264).

"Perhaps you could write an article for us on the Christian worldview as you see it," said Roy. "That wouldn't conflict with the gag order placed on you by the institute, would it?"

"I am afraid it would," I said, "because the Christian worldview begins with biblical creation, which attacks the worldview of the institute and all its cohorts at its very root."

"What *wouldn't* violate the gag order of the institute, then?" Roy asked somewhat impatiently, "they seem to have silenced you very effectively."

Because they must kill me as Paul Reynolds said, I thought, but I did not say it. Roy would not understand that nothing less would do for the enemy. He had to kill the human vessels who bore Christ in themselves, the people whose mere being in the world changed the world. I trembled because God now counted me as one of them, me who was totally unworthy. Like Peter I wanted to sink down at Christ's knees and cry out, depart from me, for I am a sinful man, o Lord. And He answered me through my remembering His answer to Peter, "Fear not, you will be a fisher of men." But how can I endure to the end, Lord? I am afraid, I said. And He answered me through His word in the Sermon on the Mount and at the end of the Gospel of Matthew, "Do not worry about tomorrow, for tomorrow will care for itself. I am with you always, even to the end of the age." And I left my life in His hands.

My mind returned to Roy's question. The answer seemed clear.

"I am afraid, Roy," I said, "that there is nothing I could write or say in public which would not violate the gag order, except something purely personal like describing my conversion, and I have already done that. For Christianity touches everything, and there is no area of neutrality or dialog between it and the godless thinking the institute represents. The institute knows that fact better than its opponents, including, forgive me, conservatives. The line of separation and irreconcilable enmity is drawn in the sand."

I shrugged resignedly. "*News in Depth* won't be able to make an end run around that line. The only places where they might possibly let me be published till the gag order expires are in-church or denominational news organs or magazines—the Christian underground. Within the year I'll be as good as dead as far as general public recognition is concerned, which is their goal."

"In that case it's no use discussing your writing for us any more," said Roy Mattingly regretfully but decisively. And that ended my active contact with *News in Depth*.

A few days later I went to western Long Island where Dr. Van Houten lived in a stately, secluded mansion from which he ran his foundation and the *Van Houten Journal*. He was a tall, handsome patriarch in his early sixties, with rich graying hair and beard and steely blue eyes. We passed his huge library and another large room which served as his office. As we turned to the living room, a grey-haired, motherly lady came toward us. "Margaret," Dr. Van Houten said, "this is Dr. James Barron. Dr. Barron, my wife." She shook hands with me and looked at me with warm friendliness. I liked her at once. She said good-bye and left us to ourselves.

In the living room, brightened by the sun streaming in through many windows, we sat down at a big round table. Dr. Van Houten lost no time coming to the reason for his inviting me here.

"Ms. Harrison's article on you in *News in Depth* wasn't the first time I heard of you, Dr. Barron," he said in a stern tone of voice and sitting up straight and stiff like a judge presiding at a trial, "I follow news about contemporary philosophy closely because the *Van Houten Journal* discusses philosophy in every issue. You were one of the leading Western philosophers today, perhaps the foremost among them and certainly the most hostile to Christianity. According to Ms. Harrison and some bits and pieces I had already learned about you from earlier news reports, you were also what I must call an evil man in every respect. I was very surprised about the news that you had become a Christian. Is it true?"

I had wilted under this stern summary of what he knew of me. "Yes," I said, hardly daring to look him in the face, "all you said is true. I am a Christian now."

"What makes you think you really are?" he inquired the same stern tone. I described as briefly as I could how Sylvia had brought me to Christ by her unconditional love, how I had recognized myself as a sinner worthy of death, how God had shared His great joy with me, how I had immediately spoken what He laid on my heart and mind before the AEA, how hungry I had been for a Bible, how I had told Lisa of my conversion in the interview she later broadcast on the radio, and how I had paid for it through the loss of my position at the Bertrand Russell Institute and related benefits.

"And you paid through the institute's gag order," Dr. Van Houten added when I thought I was done, "Ms. Harrison told me about it." His stern face relaxed and he sat more comfortably on his chair. He said with the first hint of a smile, "All right, James. I believe your conversion was genuine. You didn't mention that you already brought your friend Dr. Knightley to Christ. I understand it was through a meditation you wrote on the joy of the Lord."

I nodded. "His joy is my greatest joy in life," I said haltingly, "He Himself *is* my life." I stopped. I felt I neither could nor should say anything else. Yes, there was one more thing I needed to share with Dr. Van Houten! "He is my Father," I said, "He told me to call Him Father two days after my conversion. I had called him 'Lord' when I prayed to Him before. He said to me 'I am your *Father*,' emphasizing the word 'Father.'"

Dr. Van Houten's face turned stern again. "Do you mean He spoke to you?" he asked in his judge's voice, ready to accuse me of an error or a lie, "you mean you heard an audible voice?"

"No," I answered, "not audible. Like a gentle thought in my mind."

"The still small voice speaking to Elijah," he murmured. "Tell me more," he said, his voice now hushed. I tried to recall all the fullness of that moment so I could share it with him. "I understood He wished me to call Him Father," I said slowly, "not Lord, because He was my Father and He loved me as His son. Yes, of course He was and is my Lord, too, but His lordship is part of His Fatherhood. I was about to resign from the institute and knew it would cost me. He assured me that whatever He would allow in my life would work out for my good. I didn't know it then, but now I know that's in Romans 8:28."

"And you didn't know the Lord's Prayer yet then, either, did you," he said.

"Well, I had heard it years before from my mother," I answered, "but I had forgotten it. I certainly had not seen it or thought of it between my conversion and right before He told me to call Him Father." I suddenly saw where he was going. "Jesus tells us to call our Father 'Father' in the Lord's Prayer. Since I didn't know it, He told me. Oh, thank you for showing me this!"

"And thank you for telling me all this," he said, "It was a joy to me. I have been extremely leery all my life of people's claims that they had received direct communications from God. It's at the root of many heresies and anti-Christian movements. But I do believe you really heard His still, small voice as His people did in the Bible because what you heard is supported by Christ's own words in Matthew 6:9."

After a brief silence Dr. Van Houten warned me: "Always test everything by His word, the Bible, even what you believe to be His own voice within you. He tells us, 'Beloved, believe not every spirit, but try the spirits whether they are of God.' Don't ever neglect or twist the teaching of the Bible." I nodded. His voice grew sad and harsh as he went on bitterly, "That's what the United Reformed Church did. That's why I left it. It had been the church of my grandparents who took the Reformed faith with them from their native Holland and raised my father in it. I grew up in it and loved it till it abandoned its heritage. It is a bitter thing to have to leave a church you once loved. But you wouldn't know that, James. I'll talk about it another time."

He proceeded to discuss the work I might do for the *Van Houten Journal.* He hoped I could do peer review of papers submitted by Reformed contributors or others of acceptable theological persuasions. Pastors, teachers, philosophers and historians were among them. Many had run afoul of the "new Reformed political correctness" as Dr. Van Houten called it.

"If this interests you at all," he said, "I will need to meet with you to acquaint you with correct Reformed theology so you can spot deviations from it in the papers you review. There won't be too many papers, so this is only part time work with part time pay. But I think it's interesting and should widen your Christian horizon. Think it over and let me know next week what you have decided."

After talking it over with Bernard Gottlieb and Lisa, I called him the next week and agreed to his proposal.

17

The Greatest of These is Love

Dr. Van Houten had asked me to meet with him for three sessions before my actual work would begin so he could introduce me to Reformed theology. When Bernard Gottlieb heard this, he became visibly concerned.

"Didn't you tell me once that when you bought your Bible, the salesman wanted to sell you commentaries as well?" he asked. I said yes, remembering how I had decided against such a purchase. The Bible itself was to be my only standard and guide. I had especially wanted to avoid a denominationally slanted commentary so as not to read the Bible through denominational glasses.

"Well, Reformed theology is a particularly strong and logically plausible denominational theology," Bernard said. "It goes back to John Calvin with his strong logical mind. He was insistent that God's sovereign lordship over all things should be emphasized foremost in Christian teaching. From this starting point he developed a theology which was later summed up in the famous 'Five Points of Calvinism,' represented by the acronym T.U.L.I.P. The T stands for total depravity, the U for unconditional election, the L for limited atonement, the I for irresistible grace, and the P for perseverance of the saints. Can you see anything here at first sight which raises questions in your mind?"

I reflected for a while. I did not want to disagree too quickly with a theological system developed and defended by seasoned Christians for hundreds of years. Who was I, the rank newcomer with my atheist background and no theological training, to do so?

I confess that I also did not want to oppose Reformed theology in particular because if I did, Dr. Van Houten might terminate my employment with him before it had really begun. And I desperately needed that employment. I had just been informed that there would be no more royalties from the sale of my book *The Metamorphosis of Philosophy;* all the universities which had used it as a textbook in their philosophy courses had cancelled whatever purchase orders in the hands of my publisher were still unfilled. As to my other bestselling book *The Consolation of Philosophy,* my publisher informed me that its planned reprinting had been put on hold "for the time being." I knew that the Bertrand Russell Institute at the behest of Paul Reynolds was behind this latest blow to my financial security.

But my financial security could not be my first concern under God. To consider it as such was a temptation which I must overcome. I was preparing myself to do so before Dr. Van Houten if necessary as I now slowly and gropingly answered Bernard: "If I understand these five points correctly, they *all* raise questions in my mind. If 'total depravity' means that man has totally lost the image of God in which he was created and is therefore unable to have any part in his salvation, not even a response to God's love and grace, I disagree. I should know. I was well on the way to being totally depraved. But I could recognize and respond to God's love and grace when Sylvia showed Him to me. If I did not respond myself, who did?

"I guess 'unconditional election' means that God elected me without any conditions I had to fulfill. It's true that no *works* can earn our salvation. Salvation is His free gift to us. But I know, none better, that I had to *respond,* to say yes to God, to hand myself over to Him, to receive His gift. That wasn't 'work'—the work comes *after* salvation—Ephesians 2:8–10.

"Can 'limited atonement' really mean what I think it means—that Christ did not die for all men but only for some? The New Testament is overflowing with verses which say He died for us all! John 3:16 says God so loved the *world*—that surely includes all men!—that He gave His only begotten Son that 'whosoever' believes in Him should not perish but have everlasting life. There are many more verses like it."

"The Old Testament, too, speaks of God's salvation offered to all men," Bernard said with a smile, "Ezekiel 18:23 and 32 instantly come to mind: *'Have I any pleasure at all that the wicked should die? says the Lord GOD, and not that he should return from his ways, and live?'* and *'For I have no pleasure in the death of him that dieth, saith the Lord GOD, wherefore turn yourselves and live ye.'"*

"I had trouble with 'irresistible grace' too," I went on, "Jesus Christ speaks to Jerusalem in Matthew 23:37 with great grief: *'O Jerusalem, Jerusalem, thou that killest the prophets, and stonest them which are sent unto thee, how often would I have gathered thy children together, even as a hen gathereth her chickens under her wings, but ye would not!'* If that was not grace resisted, what was?"

"And the LORD spoke to Moses in Deuteronomy 5:29 about the Israelites," Bernard said, *"'Oh that there were such an heart in them, that they would fear me, and keep all my commandments always, that it might be well with them, and with their children for ever!'* The 'weeping prophet' Jeremiah grieves because the Lord offered the people rest for their souls by walking in the old, good ways He had established, *'but they said, we will not walk therein.'* He set watchmen over them to call them back to Him, *'but they said, we will not hearken*—Jeremiah 6:16–17. Oh yes, His grace can be and is resisted over and over again."

"I, too, am an example of this," I said, "how often I resisted His grace all the years of my life!"

Lastly we spoke about "perseverance of the saints." "I suppose this says that true Christians will persevere in the faith till the end," I said, "and that is possible only with God's help. If it means that, I could accept it. The only question that would remain is how we can tell in advance, so to speak, who is or is not a true Christian."

"In answer to this question," Bernard said slowly, "remember, for Him there is no past or future. As you wrote in your meditation on His joy, He exists in His eternal Now. That is why C. S. Lewis could write in his novel *Perelandra* that God's predestination and man's freedom are apparently identical."

I listened spellbound, knowing I was receiving the preparation I needed for my impending discussions with Dr. Van Houten. Bernard continued: "As I remember it, C. S. Lewis also says in *The Screwtape Letters,* supposedly written by a senior devil to his underling, that the reason *why* God's creative act leaves room for giving us human beings free will is God's love for us which desires that we love Him back. If we were robots, we couldn't respond to Him in love! But *how* God does this isn't a problem, for God does not *foresee* us making our free choices for Him or against Him in the future, but *sees* us making them in His own unbounded Now. And of course to *watch* us doing something is not to *make* us do it. That is where you must weigh in when Dr. Van Houten tries to persuade you of Reformed teaching. Do not speak to him only of your experience with our Lord; Reformed theology does not look favorably on experience."

"Oh Bernard," I said, "I did nothing else when we first met. He asked me to tell him what made me think I was a Christian now, and I described my conversion. What else was my conversion but experience?"

"How did he receive it?" Bernard asked.

"He began calling me by my first name," I said, "and told me he believed that my conversion was genuine. And then I felt I should share with him how God told me to call Him 'Father.'" Bernard nodded; I had spoken of this to him early on in our acquaintance.

"Hmm," Bernard said, "what was his reaction then?"

I told Bernard how Dr. Van Houten had first asked me whether I had heard an audible voice and become reassured when I said no and explained my thoughts about the experience in more detail. I told him how we had both thanked each other when we saw with joy how my experience was in accord with Romans 8:28 and the Lord's Prayer.

"That's good—that's very good," said Bernard. "It shows you can and do have true fellowship in our Lord with him, even though some doctrinal differences may divide you."

After a short silence he added: "Do not engage in theological arguments for which you aren't qualified anyway, James. Instead, obey First Corinthians 13! It says: *'Though I speak with the tongues of men and of angels and have not love, I am become as sounding brass, or a tinkling cymbal. And though I understand all knowledge and all faith, so I could remove mountains, and have not love, I am nothing. Love suffereth long, and is kind; love does not envy; love vaunteth not itself, is not puffed up, seeketh not her own, is not easily provoked, thinketh no evil, rejoiceth in the truth; beareth, believeth, hopeth, endureth all things. Love never faileth; all else, prophecies, tongues, or knowledge shall vanish away. For we know only in part, and when that which is perfect is come, that which is in part shall be done away. And now abideth faith, hope, and love, these three; but the greatest of these is love.'* Pray that God would give you His love for Dr. Van Houten. He is your brother in Christ. Doubtless he, too, is praying to have God's love for you. I believe both your prayers will be answered."

I repeated this conversation to Lisa at our next date. As I had thought, she had been taught the five points of Calvinism in the United Reformed Church. She said she had recently reflected more deeply on this teaching.

"I have come to the conclusion that it's totally unjust," she said. "According to TULIP our salvation depends totally on whether He elects us or not, and He elects only a few of us and condemns most of us to hell. It's called 'double predestination.' So our eternal damnation is His fault, not ours. What an unjust God! It also leads to indifference about the eternal fate of others. That's why I told you a while ago not to worry about the salvation of Paul Reynolds or J. P.—if they were among the elect, God would bring them in, and if not, not."

'Yes, I remember,' I said, "I thought it a bit flippant and wanted to comment on it, but we started talking about something else."

"Yes," she said, "about your article for *News in Depth*. That's past history now, but how are you getting along financially?"

I told her the bad news about no longer receiving royalties on my books. "Will you be able to go on living in New York, James?" she asked, fear in her voice.

I said I could draw on my savings and investments for a while, but it could not go on forever. I would have to look immediately for a full time position outside New York with its sky-high living expenses. In fact, I was thinking of flying to Battle Hill to see my family in Lonely Prairie over the Labor Day weekend and to visit Fairfield University to ask about a possible position there. I had enough frequent flyer miles left from my previous traveling to afford the trip. I asked Lisa whether she would like to come with me.

"I would like you to see the Midwest for yourself," I said. "It's not as boring and behind the times as people here make out. You might even like it, especially the people."

"I don't suppose the Midwest is too different from upstate New York where I grew up," Lisa said forlornly, "but I can't come with you, James. It would imply a commitment to you I am not yet ready to make. I love you. I trust you. I sometimes, well, often, fantasize about us being together the rest of our lives. But the better I know you, the more I realize how different I am from you. I love living in New York. I love my career. I have neither your faith nor your joy nor your peace when things go wrong, like your gag order or your loss of royalties. The bottom line is, to be with you I must be a Christian like you, and I am not."

I said sadly, "It's like it was between me and little Karen Margrave thirty years ago, only the other way around. She was the Christian, and I was after my career. At least you don't have someone in your life to draw you away from me as I had Nancy in my life to draw me away from Karen."

"But I do," Lisa said, "didn't you guess the other day? I have Roy Mattingly. Now he is divorced and free to marry someone else. If I encouraged him, I could be that someone else. We would be a good match in every way—professional, age, looks, income, and even religion. He's a nominal church member too."

This was a stab to my heart. I could not say anything at first. Finally I asked Lisa whether she wanted to end our relationship.

"No!" she exclaimed immediately, and repeated very softly, "no, James. Never ask me that again. I want to be with you, to see you as often as possible, as long as you are here. Beyond that. Always. I can't imagine not seeing you again. It's as though you were the first man I ever loved. Oh God, I love you so much! Pray for us that we can be together always. He'll listen to you."

"Let's both pray for that together, Lisa," I said. She nodded. She soundlessly cried as I prayed that we might be together always. I know You were there and listened.

Later that week I began to meet with Dr. Van Houten. He discussed TULIP with me gently, not dogmatically, nor did he dismiss me when I told him I could not subscribe to it. He said he would examine the incoming papers for the *Van Houten Journal* himself for doctrinal correctness; I was merely to check them for factual accuracy, style and format. He told me he would still pay me as we had agreed at first although my work was far less demanding. He acted towards me as though he were an elder brother.

In late August the Van Houtens had me come to lunch and questioned me closely about my financial situation until they knew the exact details, including my relationship with Lisa. "We want you to understand, James," Mrs. Van Houten said, "that you could live with us here and pay only room and board if your situation demanded it." "You could also do work around the house and garden," Dr. Van Houten added, chuckling, "I could show you how. I'll bet you have never done it in your life!" I thanked them for their gracious, generous, truly loving offer. I knew I might have to take them up on it if I wanted to stay in New York beyond the end of the year for Lisa's sake.

18
Lonely Prairie and Fairfield University

Lisa drove me to the JFK Airport the morning of Thursday, August 31. I planned to spend three days with my family in Lonely Prairie. The morning of Labor Day, September 4, was reserved for an interview which Robert had obtained for me with Dr. Michael Wood, the president of Fairfield University. The interview would decide whether the university would invite me to join its faculty in the fall of 1996. Robert thought there was a good possibility of this because Fairfield's current professor of philosophy was retiring in the spring. By now my family knew about my resignation from the Bertrand Russell Institute, its subsequent gag order and my loss of almost all paid employment. Robert had passed on this information and a tape of my radio interview with Lisa to Dr. Wood.

Lisa prayed with me that the interview might go well. I felt this was the first time in her life that she freely put her own wishes for the future below a man's. She would pick me up when I returned late Monday evening.

As the plane took off, I tried to put all anxious thoughts about Lisa and my future employment out of my mind. At first they kept plaguing me, but then I pulled out my new pocket Bible which had a list of "God's promises" in the back. I read its entries on "anxiety" and was soon comforted and relieved. First Peter 5:7, *"Cast all your care upon Him, for He careth for you"* was especially helpful.

A bearded young man in the seat next to me observed me with curiosity. We began a conversation. He was a college student about to visit his family over the Labor Day weekend much as I was. Moreover he was majoring in philosophy! I told him I was a philosophy professor; immediately he asked me whether philosophy could ever assert anything with certainty. I prayed inwardly that I might clearly point him to You. Then I told him that philosophy without God could never give him certainty and explained why, starting with creation according to the Bible. He listened with total attention. No one had ever told him this, he said; his parents were not "religious" at all, nor were any of his teachers or fellow students.

He asked me how I had come to believe in God. I told him how I had become a Christian just two and a half months ago, emphasizing my former self-absorbed, amoral life, my recognition of its worthlessness, and how God had come into my heart and shared His great joy with me. He just drank it all in with no questions. He asked me who I was and recognized my name, for he had studied my philosophy textbook, *The Metamorphosis of Philosophy,* in one of his courses.

And then You gave me Your joy more fully than ever. He asked me how he could really know You too! I told him to pray to You, telling You he had sinned against You and asking You to forgive him for the sake of Jesus Christ Who had died on the cross for him. He could open the door of his heart to Jesus Christ, Who was even now knocking at that door, and let Him come in to live there as his Lord and Savior.

He immediately bowed his head and prayed as I had suggested. Then he looked up at me, his face shining with joy. "Oh thank you, thank you, Dr. Barron," he kept saying. He looked longingly at my Bible, and I gave it to him. We exchanged addresses. I now have the joy of corresponding with him and seeing his rapidly growing faith. He left the plane in Chicago while I continued on to Battle Hill with joy in my heart. Dear Father, next to receiving You in our hearts it is the greatest joy in the world to help bring someone else to You!

My whole family was awaiting me when I arrived at the Battle Hill airport. Sylvia hugged and kissed me before anyone else did; everyone knew she had first claim to her Uncle James as he now was, thanks to her. She insisted on sitting beside me and put her little warm hand into mine as we got settled in Robert's big van and set out on the one hour drive to Lonely Prairie.

It was late in the afternoon. The sun was slowly sinking in the fiery orange-red western sky. How beautiful is the wide, clear, majestic Midwestern sky! I looked forward to seeing it break out in countless stars when night came. I was glad beyond expectation to see again the endless prairie of my youth, its rolling hills and its small towns dotted about here and there, their tall water towers and grain elevators announcing their existence. It seemed to me that I was seeing it all with new eyes and certainly with new joy. I was perfectly happy. I wondered whether Lisa would love it all as I did, but dismissed the thought as premature. First I must secure a position at Fairfield University, and Lisa must become a Christian.

On Friday we enjoyed a wonderful picnic with all the extended family and a number of close friends in Lonely Prairie's public park. I was also given time for rest and a blessed hour with Robert late in the evening when we sat on the front porch, watched the stars, and spoke of You. His knowledge of Scripture was extensive and always uppermost in his mind and conversation. I had despised him for it before my conversion; now I could not hear enough of it, and he was very glad to share.

On Saturday, however, the serious counseling about my financial situation with Robert and Neva I had hoped for was constantly interrupted by visits from their friends and neighbors who had heard of my visit and wanted to meet me. One of our visitors was Tim Smith, my family's senior pastor at Grace Baptist Church, who asked me to give a short testimony of my conversion at the church's two Sunday morning services. Robert and Neva were delighted and encouraged me to say yes. I did, but with some trepidation; I was a little afraid to speak to the people of my hometown who personally knew my past.

Pastor Smith told us he had just read a short article about me in the latest issue of *News Messenger,* a national weekly magazine. He had clipped it out and gave it to me. "If I had not already heard your conversion on the radio, James, and talked about it with Robert and Neva, I would have come away from that article with an entirely false picture of you," he told us.

The institute has been busy again behind the scenes, so what else is new? I thought with little emotion as I read the clipping. Then I remembered how heavily influenced the general public was by the secular mass circulation media. I had often gloated about it with my former colleagues. Oh yes, the institute knew what it was doing by planting slanted information against me in *News Messenger!* The average reader would now remember my name as that of a formerly respected, rational opinion leader who had regrettably become a deranged religious fanatic. I had foreseen such defamation, but foreseeing it and actually seeing it were not the same. What scar would that lying article leave on my life?

On Sunday I went to Grace Baptist Church with all my family. I was surprised at the church's enormous growth. A large new sanctuary had been built adjacent to the old structure which now housed the church's administrative offices, Christian school and pre-school. When the service began, I had another surprise. The congregational singing consisted largely of little repetitive choruses set to music which seemed to have no melody line. Some of it reminded me of "New Age" tunes then very popular on the radio. Some of it was accompanied by drums and deafeningly loud. For me, a lover of classical music, none of it was pleasing except the occasional older hymns with their much deeper messages of the faith, but I shrugged; who was I to judge the music now popular in church?

Pastor Smith had me give my testimony at both services. I delivered a short version of what I had written in answer to Lisa's article in *News in Depth.* The people listened to me with rapt attention; when I came to the part about the joy of the Lord, I was interrupted with applause a couple of times.

After the services Pastor Smith had me stand at the exit from the sanctuary to meet the people as they left. Some of the older ones remembered me as a boy and young man and told me how glad they were that I had finally "come home"; they meant my homecoming to You, dear Father, and I thanked You and them. I was greeted by Mrs. Margrave, the mother of "little Karen" who told me Karen and her husband George were doing fine. She said she was very glad I was now a Christian.

And then a slender, timid blonde woman of about my own age stood before me, a sturdy suntanned man, obviously her husband, by her side. "Do you recognize me, James?" she asked softly. I looked at her carefully, but I had no idea who she was.

"I recognized you right away," she said, "you haven't changed much since we were in high school together." She paused. "You still don't know who I am, do you," she said sadly, "I thought you might. After all, we knew each other real well then." When I still remained silent, she said with a little embarrassed giggle, "I used to be Dorrie Fisher. I'm Mrs. Hank Peters now. This is Hank, my husband."

Dorrie Fisher! I had gotten her pregnant when we were both seventeen. She had been the first girl in my life I had "loved and left" as my sister put it. I had shown no interest in the baby either. I could feel the blood mount to my face, and my heart seemed to stop beating.

I finally found my tongue. "I am so sorry," I said, bringing out the words with difficulty, "I am so desperately sorry for what I did to you. Please forgive me."

Dorrie smiled. She looked sweet when she smiled, much like the young timid girl I now remembered. Her husband and she were holding hands. He looked at her lovingly.

"I forgave you a long time ago, James," she said, "you see, I was saved at the unwed mothers' home where my folks sent me. It was run by the Salvation Army—such good Christian people!" Suddenly tears came to her eyes. "It hurt to give up the baby. It was a little boy—he looked like you," she broke off and wiped the tears from her eyes. "The Army found a good Christian couple to adopt him. I'm sure he is okay. And God gave me Hank. He loves the Lord, too. That's all that matters."

"We farm near Riverton, about two hundred miles west of Lonely Prairie," Hank added, "We are visiting Dorrie's mother over Labor Day."

"Mom was sick and couldn't be in church this morning," Dorrie said. "We'll tell her all about you. She'll be so surprised to hear you've become a Christian after all these years!" She added with pity, "Your life hasn't been so good, has it, James? Losing your children the way you did, and your divorce. It'll be better now that you know the Lord."

I nodded, too choked up to speak. She said gently, "God bless you, James." Hank said, "Good-bye, Dr. Barron," and they turned and left.

I had little time to regain my composure, for another man who had been directly in line behind Dorrie and Hank stepped up to me. He was perhaps sixty years old, dressed in a somewhat worn business suit, fairly tall, with receding grey hair. He studied me attentively from clear grey eyes looking larger than natural behind heavy glasses. His pallor showed that he spent most of his days indoors; a teacher of some kind, I thought. He introduced himself as Dr. Michael Wood, president of Fairfield University.

"I attended church here this morning in hopes that you might give your testimony, Dr. Barron," he said. "Your brother told me you would be here for the Labor Day weekend. Pastor Smith is always alert and eager to book a testimony from someone like you. After all, you are Lonely Prairie's most famous son. You are a fine speaker." I slightly bowed and thanked him for his compliment.

"I know we have an appointment to meet at Fairfield University tomorrow morning," he continued, "but I already know all I need to know about your background and your precarious circumstances. I also came here this morning to spare you, if possible, any unnecessary suspense. Fairfield University will offer you a position as full professor of philosophy, beginning the fall semester of 1996. The faculty must vote on it to make it official, but you may be sure it will once it is informed of your story."

He took me by the arm and led me a few steps to a little bench in the church foyer. We both sat down. Dr. Wood went on, "You see, Dr. Barron, Fairfield University has a special concern for Christians who suffer persecution for the faith. Most of them live in restricted nations like China, the Sudan or North Korea, but some are here where the persecution is more subtle. You are one of these Christians. The little vicious article in the latest *News Messenger* proves it, besides the gag order the Bertrand Russell Institute coerced you to sign, and its other chicaneries."

I looked at him, unable to answer. Finally I replied with difficulty, "I don't deserve your help. Just a moment ago I met a woman—a girl—whom I hurt terribly years ago. I didn't even recognize her. She was the first of many . . ."

He interrupted me. "I overheard the whole conversation." I stared at him in horror. He went on unheedingly, "You said all you should have said, and no more. You told her you were sorry and asked her to forgive you. It is because I overheard that conversation that I decided to offer you the position today. It totally confirmed to me that you have truly come to the Lord, Who loves you and gave you a new heart. Dorrie forgave you. God is as forgiving as she. Put it behind you." He ended by telling me to keep my appointment with him Monday so he could show me the campus of Fairfield University and settle the conditions of my employment.

19

"Sister Poverty"

The next day I drove to Fairfield in Robert's car for my appointment with Dr. Wood. He received me with friendly formality and then took me on a walking tour of the campus. "Before you sign a contract with Fairfield University, you should know much more about us," he said as though he did not know that I had nowhere else to go. I gratefully recognized his respect for my dignity and promised You I would try to show the same respect to others. My encounter with Dorrie had reminded me once more that contempt for other people had been the chief evil fruit of my former self-absorption, ironically along with the philosophical pretense of "helping them find themselves."

As we walked across the campus, Dr. Wood told me that Fairfield University belonged to the Bible Wesleyan denomination and was attended by some four thousand students. Its chief purpose was to prepare teachers for the denomination's and other Christian schools, including in foreign countries for the children of missionaries. It offered most subjects normally taught at universities, including business administration, the natural sciences, and the fine arts and music. It was renowned for certain innovative and unusual Christian study programs; one of these, dedicated to persecuted Christians around the world, was unique in the country. "I am hoping you will develop a course on Christian worldview positions in our time, James," he said, using my first name as though I were already on the faculty. "Perhaps you could prepare such a course and teach it next fall, or even already in the summer." I gave him a quick look of hope; how much I would welcome this opportunity! He smiled and said we would talk about it when we discussed my contract.

The campus was peaceful and extremely beautiful. Its buildings, all designed in the same style and meticulously maintained, looked simple, unpretentious, clean, fresh and inviting with their soft beige stucco walls, cheery red trim, and tiled roofs. They were surrounded by wide expanses of well kept lawns and framed a large, quiet pond. As we were walking there during Labor Day, there were few students on the sidewalks. They greeted Dr. Wood politely and were dressed cleanly, neatly and modestly.

The largest building was the combination chapel, concert hall and fine arts building which featured the only tall structure on campus, the chapel's bell tower. Dr. Wood had me enter it so I might see its beautiful stained glass window of Christ rescuing Peter when he attempts to walk to Him on the water but becomes afraid of the boisterous waves and is about to sink (Matthew 14). "How often it is like this with us," Dr. Wood said. The morning sun was shining through the window and showed all its details in their full glory. I thought I would almost want to work at Fairfield University for no other reason but that I might see this window every day.

Dr. Wood told me that an alumnus of the university had donated the window some years ago. "Our Lord has blessed us with a few very rich and generous patrons," he said, "though most Bible Wesleyans are in moderate circumstances. John Wesley, who lived from 1703 to 1791 and founded the Methodist church from which we separated years ago over its growing apostasy, said, 'Earn as much as you can; save as much as you can; give as much as you can.' Our people live like that." He stopped walking and looked into the distance. "That is what holiness is," he said softly as though to himself, "to live as Jesus Christ lived, moment by moment, always doing what pleases our Father."

He turned to me and smiled. "None of us does that perfectly, James," he said, "but the next best thing is to ask Him to forgive us for our lapses, have Him help us get up again as He did for Peter on that window, put the forgiven past with all its shame behind us and walk on by His side. That's what you did yesterday. Now it is today, and His sun of joy is still shining on you."

We walked on a few steps in silence. Then he added, "I have learned much from a dear Lutheran pastor named Richard Wurmbrand, a great hero of the faith. He spent fourteen years in prison under the Communists in Romania, three of them in solitary confinement. We use many of his books in our courses on persecuted Christians. In his daily devotional book *Reaching Toward the Heights* he wrote: 'Falls from which we return to the Lord are sources of humility, of light, of strength, and of comfort to others. *All things work together for good to them that love God'* (Romans 8:28). Augustine adds, 'Even their sins.'"

"Even their sins," I repeated. It was a source of immense comfort to me.

After visiting the library, student center, dining hall and other common buildings, we returned to the administration center and Dr. Wood's office to discuss my contract, as well as the possibility of my teaching a special Christian worldview course during the summer. "If you agree to do that," said Dr. Wood, "I would like to have you submit a course outline and syllabus so I can look them over with Dr. Raymond, whose position you will assume after he retires next spring. Can you have them ready by the end of February so possible changes can be incorporated in them before the course begins?" I thought I could, with the help of Bernard Gottlieb and perhaps Dr. Van Houten, and agreed.

We discussed my salary for the summer course and afterwards. It was of course far less than I had earned at the Bertrand Russell Institute, but so were the living expenses. I would be assured of a modest but sufficient lifestyle, living in my beloved Midwest, working on this beautiful, peaceful campus, and doing what I greatly wanted to do, teaching philosophy beginning with God. What more could I ask for? What better choice, indeed what other choice did I have? I thanked Dr. Wood and signed the contract.

As I drove back to Lonely Prairie, I thought of Lisa. If she did not become a Christian, marry me before the move and consent to accompany me here, our relationship would probably end—and what about the nine months of unemployment between now and next June? My total income was simply too small to cover my expenses in New York, even in my new smaller and cheaper apartment in a poorer, noisier, rougher, more unsafe neighborhood. The next four months in New York might consume all my savings, let alone nine months. If I wanted to stretch my resources until my new full employment began, I must leave New York right away and move to the cheapest place I could find in Lonely Prairie or Fairfield. If I did that, I would just barely make it till June 1996 without going into debt. I reproached myself for having spent so much and saved so little in the past. If only I could already have been a Christian and lived according to John Wesley's maxim Dr. Wood had shared with me!

But if I left New York now, how could I continue my relationship with Lisa? I groaned as I realized that though she loved me, she was still too enamored with her career and even with the glamour and excitement of New York life to commit herself to me and to the quiet backwaters of the Midwest. If I wanted to keep her in my life, I must stay in New York.

Finally, I must prepare the Christian worldview course I was to teach in June. It would require much help from my elders in the faith, Bernard Gottlieb and Dr. Van Houten. Without them, and without access to their wonderful Christ-centered libraries, how could I with my atheist background put together such a course? This was another valid reason for staying there, at least until the outline and syllabus for the course were finished.

I remembered the Van Houtens' invitation to room and board with them. Perhaps I should take them up on their offer. I thought of this course of action as humbling myself unbearably to the status of a beggar. How could I ask people I hardly knew and whose theology I had already rejected to do so much for me? I suddenly thought of Saint Francis of Assisi whose name we had mockingly bestowed at Battle Hill University upon Christian professor Dr. Francis S. Freeman. The original Saint Francis had actually spoken lovingly of his penury in God's service as "Sister Poverty." He and his monks had begged for their living. It had seemed another example of quaint medieval foolishness to me, but now I began to think about it in earnest.

I had never known "Sister Poverty" myself and never even remotely feared I might have to beg for my living. If the truth be told, I had despised the poor; oh, not openly of course, that was not politically correct in the circles where I moved, but inwardly as too lazy, too weak, or too stupid to obtain more of the world's goods. But how about the long term sick and old, or the mentally handicapped like Sylvia who could never be independent but had to live on charity? How about workers who had lost their jobs with no way of instantly finding other employment—like I myself now?

The liberal answer which Roy Mattingly had attacked in the name of conservatism was government largesse by transfer payments of taxes from the rich to the poor. I supposed I could apply for government unemployment relief. But was that the Christian answer? Christ had said we had the poor always with us, "and when you will you may do them good." We Christians ourselves were to help the poor among us when we met them face to face, and Christ told us that "it is more blessed to give than to receive." Many passages in the Bible spoke of the poor and blind begging for help. So why could I not go to the Van Houtens, fellow Christians who had already expressed their willingness to help me, explain my situation and ask them to do so? It was much more right and just than to take aid acquired by government decree from people I did not know at all. I did not like having to beg the Van Houtens to help me because it meant humbling myself before them, but that was not a sufficient reason not to do it. I saw from my own situation that the Christian way did not only teach the givers Christ's love, but also taught the would-be recipients Christ's humility. Both teachings were lost in the modern impersonal government-imposed and bureaucracy-administered redistribution system.

I suddenly saw that this entire train of thought had led me to recognize an important part of the overall Christian worldview. Conservatives like Roy Mattingly had been right to disagree with the liberals' poor relief by government coercion but had not promoted the only true alternative, voluntary doing good to the poor for Christ's sake. Meanwhile "Sister Poverty" was still standing at the door begging and liberals at least "did something" about it, although their "something" killed true charity from the Christ-like loving heart. It also relieved the government-assisted poor from doing anything for their benefactors in return. Their sense of gratitude and obligation towards the people who helped them was destroyed when they came to regard government handouts as their due and right and forgot that government money originates with private people who have worked for it. I could hardly wait to write down all these thoughts for use in my summer course outline.

My family was very glad to hear I had been offered and accepted the position at Fairfield University. "Now you will live close to us," said Neva happily. Robert asked when I would leave New York. I told him it would not be till the next summer, explaining about Lisa, the summer course outline I had to prepare, and my decision to room and board with the Van Houtens. My family heard this silently but did not try to dissuade me, though Neva said a little sadly that I must love Lisa very much. "She is your main reason for not moving here right away, isn't she?" she said, and after a moment of reflection I nodded in agreement. After all, I might have asked Bernard and Dr. Van Houten to loan me the books they thought I should have for my course outline, and we could have communicated by letter or telephone. Neva chuckled mischievously, said, "I guess you won't just love her and leave her!" and when she saw I could not laugh about her joke she earnestly promised she would pray for us. My heart ached as I parted from my family and boarded my return plane to New York.

20

A Hateful Attack and Two Great Blessings

Lisa was there waiting for me after I got off the plane. "You got the job," were her first words; the news must have been written on my face. As we walked to her car and drove away, she asked when I would have to move away; when I told her not till the end of next May, she sighed with relief. I told her about the rest of my trip and of my plan to take the Van Houtens up on their offer to have me stay with them, paying only for my room and board.

"If that doesn't work out," I said, "I may have to move away earlier."

Her face clouded over with anger. "It's outrageous," she said, "that there should be no suitable work for you in this big city among all these millions of people!"

"The key word is 'suitable'," I replied, "what suitable work is there in academic New York, a stronghold of atheist liberalism, for a famous atheist professor of philosophy who betrayed the atheist faith and deserted to God? Above all else, they don't want me to teach students what I believe now. Students might be open to it." I told her the story of the young man on the plane.

"The key word is 'famous,'" she shot back, "if you hadn't been so famous before, you'd find a job here."

I laughed. "It serves me right," I said, "all my past life I did all I could to be famous! But look at the blessing from it, too! My fame is part of the reason we met. Remember, you came to hear me at that AEA meeting because I was that famous atheist whom you hated! God timed my conversion to take place right before that meeting so you would hear my speech and feel differently about me. He opens our way before us step by step."

Lisa thought this over. "I can't contradict you," she finally answered, "but I always vaguely thought God determined all things in advance from the beginning. The step by step part is new to me."

"His determining is different from ours and much greater because it allows our freedom to choose," I said, "He foresees all things, but for Him it's not 'foreseeing' but just seeing. He doesn't live in a timeline like we do. For Him all things are now. I already learned that with so much joy when I wrote my meditation on the joy of the Lord. Just trust Him! Not even a sparrow falls to the ground without His providence—how much less you and I."

"Just trust Him," she said, "you make it sound so easy, and you seem to really live that way, but for me it's the hardest thing in the world. I can almost take that step when I am with you, but the very next thing that goes wrong sends me right back to mistrust."

We were now driving through my seedy neighborhood and approaching my apartment building. I had left my car parked near the front entrance. I expected to see it as it had been four days ago, but instead of its familiar shape, I saw a battered wreck. It had been demolished beyond repair. Whatever had been made of glass now lay in splinters and shards on the pavement. The inside had been thoroughly vandalized, the radio and cassette player removed, my little box of treasured classic music cassettes smashed to pieces, and the upholstery ripped up. It was destruction beyond mere gang violence; it bore the imprint of personal fury. Other cars were parked nearby; they had not been touched. It looked like the attack had been directed specifically against me.

Who could hate me like this? I wondered. And then, as clearly as when I first heard him, Paul Reynolds again spoke these words in my mind: "Here you are, telling me to enter into the joy of my Lord. You could almost make me believe in your God and His joy. A Christian has only to be in order to change the world. And that is why we must kill you." I was suddenly sure that Paul Reynolds had wrecked my car, or rather had hired some neighborhood thugs to do it. My witness to him had been so powerful that he was still fighting it and me in uncontrollable fury, almost in madness, after all these weeks and months.

"There! You see?" Lisa interrupted my thoughts, "no sooner do I hear you tell me to trust in God that He allows something like this! Now you don't even have a car to get around in!"

"Not until I get another one," I said, "come on, honey. It's only a car. I'll buy another one in the next few days. It'll have to be a used car, not as nice and new as this one was, but it'll do. You wouldn't be ashamed to be seen in it with me, would you?"

She had to laugh in spite of herself. "No, James," she said, "I'd even ride the subway with you if it comes to that." She became serious again. "Why your car among all the others?" she asked, her journalistic instinct asserting itself. "Is this perhaps part of the institute's campaign against you? At least it means a lot of hassle and inconvenience for you, plus having to replace an almost new car by a much older, inferior one. It's another financial blow from them against you, I tell you!" She stood before me like an avenging fury, her eyes flaming, her hands balled into tight fists. "I will find out who did this if it's the last thing I do," she said grimly, "I will have the full support of *News in Depth*. Finding out that they did this to you would be news in depth, indeed. And don't bend over backwards again trying to be meek and mild, James, as you did with that woman and her perfume bottle," she lashed out at me. "This is in my hands now and I'll see to it that whoever was behind this will pay for it!"

I made no objections because this time the attack against me had not been provoked by my own sin. Dear Father, I prayed, if Lisa succeeds in tracking this violence to Paul Reynolds, let me witness to him of You one more time by forgiving him even as You forgive him, and by showing him that Your joy in me was not destroyed along with my car. Let him see that even killing me would not defeat Your kingdom!

I reported the vandalism to the police, obtained a settlement from my insurance company and bought a mechanically sound used car. Then I drove out to the Van Houtens and told them all my news since they had offered me to room and board with them. I asked them whether I might accept their offer, probably till the end of May 1996, and shared with them my reflections on "Sister Poverty." I told them what had happened to my car and was surprised when they immediately wondered whether the institute might be behind it. I told them Lisa was investigating it.

Dr. and Mrs. Van Houten looked at each other and nodded. "You are welcome to stay with us, James," said Mrs. Van Houten. "I will show you your room and the rest of our home, which is now yours as well." "I think your payment for reviewing the papers sent in for the *Van Houten Journal* will pretty well cover your room rent and food," said Dr. Van Houten, "so just do the reviews and we'll call it a fair exchange. There'll be other work in my office or in the yard you might help me with from time to time." I said I would be only too glad to help in any way I could. Mrs. Van Houten said that I was free to use the laundry facilities as well. "And you can park your car in our garage," said Dr. Van Houten.

He then told me peremptorily to move immediately. "Rent a trailer van, load everything you have in it, and drive out here tomorrow," he ordered. "We have a big shed attached to our garage. You can store your furniture and anything you don't need in your room in the shed till you move to Fairfield. There is room enough; our children recently moved a lot of their things out to where they live." I thanked him but was puzzled why he seemed in such a hurry to have me move. He guessed my thoughts. "Don't you understand, James?" he said impatiently, "they wrecked your car. They might maim or kill you next." I mildly objected that "they" might not have wrecked my car after all. "Why take chances?" he countered, "I think someone is behind this who really hates you. Someone connected with the institute. Just take my advice and move here tomorrow." I thought he was way too alarmed but said I would do as he said.

I spent the next day loading a rented trailer van with the help of a couple of young neighborhood men, drove it out to the Van Houtens and unloaded my belongings in their shed with the help, and very efficient help it was, of Dr. Van Houten himself. He had plenty of opportunity to observe my general clumsiness. "I *knew*, James, that you hadn't done much physical work, if any, before," he chuckled, "we'll change that. We'll make a Dutchman out of you yet." It was an introduction to the wonderful months which followed.

That evening I had my first dinner with the Van Houtens as a member of their household. I was aching from the physical work of the day, but I was also exceptionally hungry and had helping after helping of the good home-cooked food my hosts pressed on me. They loved to see me eat! I forgot all about my ulcer, and it forgot about me. In between eating they asked me about my childhood and youth. I gladly told them of my mother who had tried so hard to win me to Christ, of my father who finally came to Christ on his deathbed, of Robert, Neva, and of dear little Sylvia who had loved me to the Lord. I even told them of Dorrie Fisher and the words Dr. Wood had quoted from Pastor Wurmbrand and Augustine about Romans 8:28. "Even our sins," yes, even our sins work for good to us who love You, Father!

Finally I was talked empty and fed full. I felt like a very young son or brother at home on vacation. I had not felt like this in many years, not since before my poisoning with evolution teaching in early high school. "Thank you so much," I said to my benefactors, "for the food and for everything. I haven't felt this good and at peace in years."

"Thank you for being so open with us, James," said Dr. Van Houten. "We enjoyed listening to you. My younger brother lived with us for a while. It was like having him back with us again." That night I slept a deep and refreshing sleep undisturbed by apartment neighbors and traffic.

The next morning I woke early as had become my habit, read my Bible and made out a work schedule for myself. I must prepare the outline and syllabus for the summer course and the permanent basic and advanced philosophy courses I would teach. Dr. Wood had given me copies of the philosophy textbooks now in use at Fairfield University; I would need to read them carefully and make notes of how to present and enrich them based on my personal background. The summer worldview course gave me the most concern. "Not even most Christians today seem to be united or even informed about their own worldviews," I thought, "how much less I who only know the worldviews of our enemies! At least my past experience will help me recognize what Christians must *not* believe."

I also decided to get all the advice I could from Bernard Gottlieb. I called him and he agreed that I could spend our entire weekly Bible study day at his home to continue cataloguing his library, to study books in it he recommended and to counsel with him on worldviews. He spoke of this project as a one on one post-graduate course and told me he would assign me written papers from session to session. I learned that he had taught such courses before; as he had told me earlier, he too had come to Christ from the wasteland of godless philosophy. "You could even mention this course on future resumes," he said, "I am adjunct professor of philosophy at Shalom Israel Seminary, a small school for Messianic Jews preparing for the ministry." He told me that my cataloguing of his library would be my payment for the course. This arrangement exactly met my needs and was Your blessed answer far exceeding anything I could have wished for, dear Father!

The other immense blessing You gave me during those wonderful months, dear Father, was to learn from the Van Houtens how to be a good steward over my private life and goods. I became a better man as I stopped being merely a chair-bound intellectual in his ivory tower and priding myself on my masculinity or high

IQ. Under Mrs. Van Houten's gentle care I learned for the first time in my life how to cook "from scratch," to shop wisely and economically as she would send me out to get the family groceries (I saw how much money I had wasted in the past on prepackaged meals), to scrub floors and to do minor home repairs.

Dr. Van Houten was true to his promise that he would "make a Dutchman out of me." He taught me the routine upkeep of my car, gardening and yard work, and some basic elements of plumbing, electrical repairs and even roofing after a fall rainstorm. It would all come in handy later when I moved into my own home. I became physically stronger and much more adept at manual labor, and thanks to the healthy meals I could now help prepare, I put on a little weight and felt healthier than in many years.

Lisa, who became a frequent guest at our dinners, noticed all these changes with astonishment and admiration. She told me she had almost found out who had been behind the destruction of my car, and once the final evidence was in it would be a spectacular piece of news. Our relationship became more and more solid and comfortable but Lisa's lack of true faith and trust in You still prevented our permanent commitment to each other. The Van Houtens quietly observed us and told me they were praying for us to become one in You.

21

Descent into Hell

Lisa had found out from the police and through a private investigator she sent into my neighborhood that the vandalism of my car had indeed been unusual. It had been carried out not as first supposed by a gang of local black youths but by a group of several adult white males who had arrived and left in two cars. Lisa's private investigator had found and talked to a woman who lived in my own apartment building and knew me slightly. Once I had carried a sack of groceries for her to her apartment door and spoken a few words about Christ to her when I noticed the little cross on her necklace and guessed she was a believer too. She had been sitting up with a sick baby late in the night of September 2 and watched the attack on my car from her apartment window.

The woman, an excellent observer, had especially noticed one of the attackers, the one who was the most violent. He had taken a little box out of my car, opened it, pulled out the contents, she thought audio cassettes, and removed one of them. Then he had put the box on the pavement and given it several blows with a baseball bat. She had seen the attackers leave and could roughly describe their cars, like mine fairly late, expensive models. She even remembered several of the license plate numbers of the car in which the most violent attacker had left. She had not shared her information with the police because her husband was in prison and she did not want to get involved. But now she had second thoughts because she learned the destroyed car had been mine, "and Mr. Barron loves the Lord," she told the P.I. The license plate number was eventually traced back to a car belonging to Paul Reynolds.

Lisa was ready and burning to make this information public. "The only thing we are not sure of," she said, "is whether the men in the cars were just hired by Reynolds, or whether he himself was with them and took part in the attack." I thought that Paul had been with them but said nothing; efficient Lisa was in charge and would find the answer. She did not disappoint me.

"I will find out whether he and his car were at his home that night," she said, "if not, he has no alibi." A few days later she knew Paul and his car had been gone precisely during the time the attack on my car had taken place. Moreover, as she found out from a secretary in Paul's company (secretaries always know everything that goes on in the work place), he had played an audio cassette tape with a strange kind of medieval music and words in a foreign language sung a cappella by a choir of male voices over and over again in his private office the day after the Labor day weekend.

"Gregorian chant," I said, "it was my cassette with Gregorian chant. They sang it in Latin." It was one of my very favorite cassettes, the nearest to other-worldly, heavenly music I knew. I, too, had often played it over and over again in my car and at home. How strange that Paul Reynolds should share my love of it; well, perhaps not so strange, for he had come out of the Roman Catholic Church.

"That settles it," said Lisa triumphantly, "not too many people have cassettes of Gregorian chant. It's the proof we needed to expose him publicly! It's just a question of how best to proceed from here. I'll talk to Roy about it."

"Maybe I should talk to Paul about it," I murmured, the will to do so taking root in my heart.

Lisa whirled around. "I told you to stay out of this, James!" she upbraided me, "I know you! You want to bring him to Christ by being good to him. You want to go and tell him you forgive him for all he has done to you all these weeks and months and for wrecking your car. That's right, isn't it? Well, it's crazy, and I won't let you do it."

"You cannot stop me, Lisa," I said, "I love you, but you have no authority over me. I will counsel with Bernard and Dr. Van Houten and pray about it. Then I will do what I believe God wants me to do and say to Paul what He wants me to say." Suddenly I felt a crushing pity for Paul and added slowly, "Most of all I will listen to Paul. He needs so much to have relief from all his hatred and guilt."

She knew me well enough to stop arguing. "If you decide to go," she said more calmly, "go as soon as you can and let me know how it went. I will wait with a write-up for *News in Depth* or a radio broadcast until after you have talked to Reynolds."

I agreed. Dr. Van Houten advised me not to call on Paul. He thought it would only increase Paul's hatred against me. "He might even attack you personally if you see him in his home or office," he warned, "you can forgive him later when he has been brought to book for what he did." Bernard Gottlieb, on the other hand, first prayed with me and then encouraged me to go. I called Paul's office to make an appointment with him; his secretary called right back and told me he would see me the next morning. I found little sleep that night in my homey room at the Van Houtens but prayed off and on until it was time to drive to Paul's office in the Empire State Building. As I rode up in the elevator a cloud of darkness seemed to surround me. I called on You in sudden fear; You gave me the sure certainty that You were with me, and the cloud lifted. Still that ascent to the heights of the building seemed like a descent into hell. I knew a deep darkness was awaiting me above.

I entered the anteroom to Paul's office right on time. His secretary buzzed him on the intercom and he came out, received me with a silent nod and led me back into his inner office, then pointed to the chair across his desk. We both sat down. Still no word had been spoken. I was determined to let Paul have the first word, and finally it came.

"You are looking good, James," he said in a hoarse voice, "better than the last time I saw you—stronger, younger, healthier." He cleared his throat. "I had a dream of you the other night," he said in that same hoarse voice and cleared his throat again before going on. "You were sitting across from me cringing and begging me to stop persecuting you. I was enjoying it. But now here you are, and I see you haven't suffered at all. Nothing I did to you has really hurt you! Deep down you still have that same joy you spoke about at our last meeting. A greater joy because you have overcome all I did." He stopped, only to give in to a prolonged coughing spell.

"It's nothing," he said when it stopped, "just something that I catch every fall." He leaned forward in his chair in anger, ready for attack. "What do you want to tell me?" he said, "that you and your right wing girlfriend have found out that I helped wreck your car? Quite a newshound, Ms. Lisa Trent Harrison, I'll admit. I take it she can prove I did it. So what—I've got the money to pay for the damages, and for emotional pain and suffering too. Go ahead and sue me, or have your lawyers and mine arrange for a settlement. You didn't need to see me personally about that. And it won't help restore your career, James. That's over, no matter what sensational stories your girlfriend might cook up for her conservative followers in connection with my little bit of vandalism. You are a deranged religious fanatic now for the general public, and soon you'll be nobody at all." He paused to take a breath, and again a coughing attack shook him. I waited till it subsided.

"It doesn't matter," I said. "As a matter of fact, it has been good for me. You meant it for evil, but God meant it for good. I have learned to walk with shame and with poverty and to rejoice in Him. Even the disunity among Christians is overcome by His great love. His wells of His living water are still springing up in me and in all believers, especially under persecution. You will never stop that living water from flowing."

I stopped for a moment to let Paul take it all in and continued, "I came in part to show you that through me. Even if you attacked me instead of the car and killed me, you would accomplish nothing. All you can do, you and all the people who hate God and take it out on us Christian believers is to kill our bodies. You can never kill Him and the real us in Him. His Holy Spirit in us is greater than the evil spirit from hell that is in you."

"But you are not perfect in God's sight," Paul said angrily, "underneath all that joy you are still that old self-centered sinner who slept around and would do anything for his career."

"That's where you are wrong," I answered, "and that's part of the reason why your campaign to hurt me can't succeed. I am born again and God is no longer my angry judge but my dear Father. Christ took my sins on Himself when He suffered and died on the cross. I may be tempted, but temptation is not sin. I may give in to temptation and sin, but then I can come to Him, ask Him to forgive me and renew me, and He does. Oh Paul," I implored him, "it doesn't matter who I was or am. You are the one who matters right now! You wouldn't have let me come here—you wouldn't listen to me now—if God were not reaching out to you right now with His love and grace. Let Him come into your heart as your Lord, your Savior, your Healer, your Giver of joy! He will not force His way in—He is waiting for you to say yes to Him."

He stared at me half convinced, half resisting. His resistance won out. "Why can't I overcome my sins by myself?" he asked. "I was taught to do that and tried hard to do that all through the years. Stay chaste. Close your eyes to temptation. Say prayers. Confess and do penance. How much penance I have done already! But my sin—that special sin which took hold of me through that pedophile priest—kept coming back. I kept welcoming it. Damn it, James, I must try harder!"

"It won't work, Paul," I said, "don't torture yourself that way. I learned that the very first day after my conversion when I came back to the institute from Battle Hill and saw Lorena again."

"Oh yes," he said, "our luscious receptionist. I'll bet half the male staff has slept with her at one time or another."

"And so would I have," I said, "if God had not shown me that He made and loved her, too, and that He had sent His only Son to be tortured and crucified for her. I could not just 'love her and leave her' as though she were good enough only to be used by me and then thrown away. It was sin. And I could not give it up by myself! I had practiced it too long. I could only call on Him to help me over and over again whenever the temptation reared its head—like a little child clinging to his dad, or like Peter clinging to Jesus when trying to walk on the water in the storm and about to sink. Jesus helped Peter. Jesus helped me. Jesus will help you, moment by moment. Your part is to ask Him! Don't try to walk on the water in your own strength. If you do, you *will* sink."

Paul got up, walked from his desk to the window to look away into the haze of the sky and returned to his seat. "You suppose *that* is my sin?" he muttered, "not to want to ask Him? I don't want to, you know. Is that because deep down I want to go on sinning, or is it even deeper down, coming from the pit of hell? Is it pride?"

I hardly dared answer this, the deepest question he could ask about himself. Oh dear Father, please give me what I must say and how to say it, I prayed.

"God alone knows the deepest secrets of your heart," I said, "I dare not analyze you from the outside. I only know this—you must humble yourself to ask Him to help you. He loves you. He will deliver you from your will to sin, and your pride. Pride is to want to be your own lord and master. But God is your Lord and Master, and your loving Father too if you will have Him. Humble yourself and let Him be your live goodness in your heart."

"It's too easy," he said, "I have sinned too deeply. Let me tell you why I took your Gregorian chant cassette with me after I helped wreck your car."

"I don't really need to know that," I said, half afraid of what he might tell me.

"But I want to tell you," he insisted, "consider it a confession. Can't any Christian hear a confession and forgive the sinner?" He leaned forward. "I took it, of course, because I knew you must love it. No one buys this music unless he loves it. I took it because to me, and I suppose to you also, Gregorian chant is of all music the most heavenly. I took it just so you could not hear it again. At least for a few days you would miss it. You would have to find and buy another one. Anything would do to hurt you! You had almost drawn me back to God. The memory of you and your joy was still drawing me to God months after you left the Bertrand Russell Institute."

Paul stopped. For a moment he seemed unable to continue. I realized that the worst part of his confession was still to come. Finally he went on, "I took the cassette to my house. I played it over and over again and imagined you in my mind on the pavement under the blows of our crowbars, like that car. I think if it had really happened it would have killed you. I enjoyed it all so much that I brought the cassette with me and played it while I repeated my fantasy right here at the office the day after Labor Day."

He had another coughing spell. When it abated, I said: "Now I know why remembering my joy in the Lord still draws you to Him. You have no joy! No one can have joy who lives the life you live and thinks the thoughts you think. Come out of that life of blackness and bitterness! All you have to do is pray to Him to deliver you! The Bible says Christ went down to hell to set the captives free. He will descend into your hell and set you free. Do it now! Let us pray for it together right now."

Paul shook his head. "I will think it over," he said, "and now go. I have talked and listened to you long enough. And here is your cassette back. I won't need it any more."

He found the Gregorian chant cassette on his desk, pressed it into my hand and showed me to the door. I was about to leave when he asked me, almost as an afterthought, whether I forgave him for what he had done to me. I assured him I had; he nodded and closed the door behind me.

The next day we read in the newspaper and heard on television that he had shot and killed himself there in his Empire State Building office a few hours after I left him.

22
Kings and Priests

Paul Reynolds' funeral was held a few days later. I thought it my duty to attend. J. P. was there to represent the Bertrand Russell Institute and said a few words of gratitude for Paul's support through the years. He spotted me quickly and joined me after the service. He was about to leave the institute to work for another think tank in New Jersey, this one dealing strictly with economics from a conservative perspective. He could be a Christian there openly. He thought the days of the institute might be numbered because Paul's heirs and corporate successors opposed the institute's ultra-liberal views and would stop supporting it financially. I was glad to hear it.

J. P. also handed me a sealed letter addressed to me in Paul's handwriting which an attorney for Paul's estate had asked him to pass on to me. Here is his letter:

James,

This is the last letter I write before killing myself, in part to escape the shame of being pilloried by your girlfriend over a certain car, in part because I have been diagnosed with AIDS and would rather die as quickly and painlessly as I can.

If I hadn't seen you again and half believed that your indestructible joy was really God's joy He shared with you, I might not have found my own life of darkness so utterly intolerable. I haven't had peace or joy in many years and won't take it any more.

You told me to pray to God, but I stopped saying prayers after what that priest did to me. I would rather approach God with the sacrifice of suicide. It's less cheap and less humiliating than prayer and accepting Christ's sacrifice for me on the cross as His free gift. If that means I am going to hell, so be it. I will not be humiliated any more.

Paul

He had remained proud to the end. It grieved me deeply. It still grieves me to this day because it left me no further possibility to pray for his salvation.

I had been steadily working away at the outline and syllabus for the projected worldview summer course at Fairfield University when I found out from Neva at one of our phone calls that the Summit Ministries in Colorado, headed by Dr. David Noebel, had produced an excellent worldview course for high school and freshman college students. Several of Neva's and Robert's children had taken the course and been most satisfied with it. I ordered the Summit Ministries textbook and student workbook and thoroughly reviewed them. They seemed to be ideal for the purposes of my course. I contacted Dr. Wood, told him of these ready made teaching materials and recommended that we use them instead of what I had been preparing. He had me send him a set of the books, vetted them together with Dr.

Raymond and informed me in January 1996 that I could use them in the summer. This relieved me of further work on my own outline and syllabus and left me more time for my other tasks.

I continued with Bernard in the one on one post-graduate course he was teaching me. He told me with a twinkle in his eye that my homework papers improved markedly after my work on the outline and syllabus ceased. I also made much headway on cataloguing his books. By working on it one whole day per week and without the addition of new books, I might just finish cataloguing them all by the end of May. However, there certainly would be new books! Bernard's pet weakness was to browse in all kinds of bookstores where he could not resist buying what interested him, including books in other European languages. "I'll have to teach you at least French and German, James," he told me, "when you come back to visit me in 1997." What was really at the bottom of his language teaching idea was his desire to have me back with him from time to time. I finally understood this and promised him I would certainly visit him in the future even without language lessons.

I also attended Bernard's Shalom Israel Messianic Jewish congregation with him on their long Saturday night services in addition to the little Bible Reformed Church the Van Houtens hosted in their home on Sunday mornings. I could not sleep much Saturday nights, but it was well worth my tiredness Sunday afternoons.

Shalom Israel fed what Dr. Van Houten called my "mysticism," his name for my great love of Bible passages about God's felt, heard and seen presence with His people. One of my best loved Bible verses is Psalm 27:8, where God says to David, *"Seek ye My face,"* and David answers Him, *"My heart said unto thee, Thy face, LORD, I will seek."* It is also Your call to me, dear Father, which I first really heard at long last at my conversion. And now, hearing it, I can answer You as David did by my heart's longing to see Your face, the final joy of all joys.

The Bible Reformed Church gave me a much needed store of well organized Bible knowledge. It prepared me to explain and defend my faith to inquirers and opponents. Although my "mysticism" made me resist its tendency to compress all biblical teaching into a logical system, its method of thorough verse by verse explanation and study were invaluable to me. I made life-long friends in both congregations.

When the Bible Reformed congregation learned in early November that the lady who was their pianist would have to move away, I asked the Van Houtens whether I might try to replace her. I had learned to play the piano in my early youth and was willing to restore and expand my skills. It took hours of practice before I could play at sight the many old hymns, so familiar to my friends and alas, so unfamiliar to me. Thanksgiving came, and among other songs I was able to play and sing the beautiful Dutch hymn "We gather together to ask the Lord's blessing" especially requested by Mrs. Van Houten. When she told me I sang well, I was no longer shy but gave in to my desire to sing when I practiced the hymns between services.

The words and music of these beautiful old hymns, one of the church's greatest treasures, became a comfort and refuge to me very soon when my relationship with Lisa began to deteriorate. She had been very upset when Paul Reynolds' suicide ruled out the pursuit of a legal case against him. All her journalistic detective work after the destruction of my car had been in vain as far as she could see, and she resented it. Although I never showed her Paul's letter, she correctly believed that if I had not gone and spoken to him he might not have killed himself later that same day and thus escaped legal punishment. She was angry with me about this, but even more so because I could not hate him but only pitied him. Lisa had no pity for him whatever; all she could think of was what he had done to hurt me, and that he was now beyond retribution.

On the morning of December 15, I was struck by Revelation 1:6 and 5:9 which said that Christ had made His people "kings and priests" to His God and Father. I felt I knew the meaning of kingship under God as being His servants and overcomers, but what was it to be a priest? I found First Peter 2:9: *"Ye are . . . a royal priesthood . . . that ye should shew forth the praises of Him who hath called you out of darkness into His marvelous light."* I read in Hebrews 3 and 5 that Christ is our High Priest, and in Hebrews 7:25 that He now lives forever to make intercession for us. Chapter 17 of my beloved Gospel of John was Christ's final prayer of intercession for His believers. I saw that *showing forth His excellence* and *intercession* were my priestly calling. It was to show forth Your excellence, dear Father, that I yearned so much to speak to others of You and of the excellence of Your wonderful joy. It was to intercede with You for others that I prayed for them. I also saw how totally evil it was to abuse one's priesthood under God like the priest who had abused Paul Reynolds, and I felt sorry for Paul anew. Dear Father, I prayed, please take into account what was done to him when You judge him. It was my final intercession for him, and I was given assurance that You would, for You are just and right in all You do.

And we all who belong to You are your kings and priests! Little handicapped Sylvia had been Your priest to me, interceding for me for years and proclaiming to me the excellence of Your great love. And not only she who had always been innocent was a priest to You, but even I with all my past sins. It all was a staggering revelation to me, almost as great as six months ago when I was born again.

Later that day Lisa called and said we had to talk. She asked me to meet her in a Long Island seaside restaurant where we had never dined before. "I don't want any memories to intrude on what I want to tell you," she said.

It was a raw winter evening. I found the restaurant, which obviously catered to people of more financial means than mine. I was grateful that I had dressed well. A head waiter received me at the entrance and led the way to where Lisa was already seated at a table for two beside a window from which we could see the deserted beach and the darkening waters of Long Island Sound in the distance. It was the most joyless evening I had known between us since we first met.

We made meaningless small talk about the weather and the roads. I felt we were regressing to a much earlier, more formal stage of our relationship. The menus came. We ordered. The food arrived. We began to eat, picking at the expensive delicacies before us. To my dismay I felt the ulcer beginning to twinge inside me, and I could make myself eat only about half of my meal.

Lisa put her fork down with a little clank and pushed her plate away. "All right," she said, "let's talk. I can't get over what happened to my investigation of the vandalism to your car, James. Do you know how much thought, effort and money I and *News in Depth* invested in that? Do you know we had Paul Reynolds exactly where we wanted him? Don't you see that if we could have exposed him, it would have hurt the Bertrand Russell Institute as well? And then you go and 'witness to him,'" she almost spat out the words, "causing him to commit suicide, which ruined all our work."

"Well, not all of it," I said, "J. P. told me that the days of the institute may be numbered because Paul's successors will stop financing it."

Lisa thought this news over for a moment. "Okay, so something good came out of our investigation after all," she finally said. "It's too bad we—I—don't get any credit for digging up the truth and no refund for our expenses. But my problem with you goes deeper than your unwanted interference in our investigation. That's only an outgrowth of the difference between us. We have touched on it before, but this time we need to get to the root of it. And don't tell me we have this problem because I am not a Christian, James. I accept the Nicene Creed, the common formulation of the Christian faith, the same as you do. You have no right to sit in judgment on me—oh, not in words, but in your whole being."

She took a deep breath and launched into another accusation. "I am a professional journalist and radio personality, and I am darn good at it," she said. "I earn a good living and don't take charity from anyone. You haven't earned a living now for nearly six months. If I hadn't pointed you to the Van Houtens, you would have had to go back to Indian Prairie or wherever and live on the charity of your family. It's wonderful that you have learned to cook and to run Dr. Van Houten's lawn mower, and whatever other chores you do for them."

She stopped, feeling she had been too hard on me, and said more softly, "I admire you for having the humility to do it. I guess you do the best you can in exchange for their hospitality. Both you and the Van Houtens are happy with each other, but it's simply not the way I look at life. I would be totally ashamed of myself if I were in your situation. I suppose you do a lot of Bible study and prayer and whatever else someone does who has turned from a completely worldly lifestyle to being a pious Christian. The amazing thing is that despite it all, I am still in love with you." She smiled at me for the first time that evening. I could not smile back; her attack had hit me too hard. She saw it but would not retract any of it. However, she did not want to end the evening on this note but by our reconciliation. This was the time, she felt, of asking me for my opinion of what the problem was between us, and she did.

"So what do you think about all this?" she asked.

I sat still, unsure whether or how to answer. The ulcer in my stomach throbbed with pain. I prayed. The pain did not lessen, but the answer to Lisa's question came into my mind.

"You are a doer and achiever, Lisa," I said gently. "I am quite different. I just learned today that when I became a Christian, I was called to become what the Bible calls a priest. All of us Christians are called to be priests. Priests' work is to show forth God's excellence to other people and to intercede for them in prayer. I did that for Paul Reynolds. He had free will and rejected it and I interfered with your doing and achieving, although God may be bringing down the institute by my work and Paul's rejection of it without your doing and achieving. His ways are marvelous and as high above our ways as heaven is above earth." And as I said this, Your great joy, Father, sprang up again like a fountain in my heart.

23
A Grown Man Does Not Cry

Lisa and I knew that defining the difference between us would not bridge or resolve it. Our conversation, or rather her angry attack against me, had only made that difference stand out in sharper focus. And while she might claim to be a Christian on the basis of accepting the basic doctrinal beliefs of Christianity, we both knew that her Christianity was different from mine. I sensed that she had been repelled rather than attracted by my new view of life in Christ as priesthood; it had been too otherworldly and "mystical" for her, much like Gregorian chant.

I needed to give Christmas gifts to my near and dear ones, and Lisa was at the top of my list. What gift could I give her? I consulted with Neva who came up with a beautiful suggestion. "Why not put together a photo album with pictures from your earlier life," she said, "we have lots of pictures we can send you, complete with dates. You can choose from them which ones to share with Lisa. To receive such an album will be intimate enough between you two, but it won't commit her to you as some other gift might." She added wistfully, "I guess she still isn't ready for that. I'll keep praying."

Neva sent me dozens of pictures from my childhood to my Labor Day visit to Lonely Prairie and Fairfield. I completed the album just before Christmas. It was a bittersweet pleasure to see and choose between the pictures. Here I was as a child with my young, beautiful mother. I had inherited her looks, as had my brother Robert, my son Dylan and apparently my son with Dorrie Fisher. God had bestowed a dominant gene of physical beauty on us over several generations. Lisa looked somewhat like my mother too. If we ever married and had a child together, he or she would be blessed with good looks from both parents. I brushed the thought aside quickly; I was now fifty-four, Lisa forty-two, and we weren't even married yet.

I looked at my high school graduation picture and the later ones from Battle Hill and Herbert Spencer University. There was increasing hardness on my face as the years passed by, especially after my marriage to Nancy and during the zenith of my academic career. Finally there were a couple of photos taken over the Labor Day weekend in front of Robert's house, and on them I looked somehow younger, softer, gentler and more vulnerable. Neva had noticed this and mentioned it to me on the phone. "Your conversion is showing on those photos," she said, and I had to agree with her when I saw them. There were also pictures of Lonely Prairie, of Fairfield and one of the beautiful campus of Fairfield University. "Lisa should see where you will live and work after you leave New York," Neva said.

Lisa spent Christmas in upstate New York with members of her family, but I gave her my Christmas gift when we met for a New Year's Eve celebration at the Van Houtens. We watched the pictures together. And sure enough, as she came to the last two photos of me, she studied them with special care and finally said: "You look different here, James—I can see the change in you from before." Then she, the former English literature student, said thoughtfully:

"There is a famous novel by Oscar Wilde, *The Picture of Dorian Gray*. Dorian Gray is a very beautiful young man, of whom a painter friend paints a lifelike picture. There is a magic spell on the picture so that it bears the mark of every sin and indecency Dorian Gray commits. The picture becomes more and more hideous while Dorian himself remains young and handsome despite all his debaucheries. In the end he looks so unbearably vile on the picture that he begins to slash and destroy it. Later a servant finds his dead body, almost unrecognizable in its hideousness, beside the picture restored to the beauty of Dorian as he originally was."

"Why do the photos of me remind you of Dorian Gray?" I asked.

"Well," Lisa mused, "the older photos of you showed the outside changes in you as you grew older and harder inside. These last two, after your conversion, show the opposite changes. Before tonight I had only seen the old hard photos of you, like the publicity photo we used on the cover of *News in Depth* with my article about you. Today it wouldn't do you justice any more at all. That's kind of magical, too, like Dorian Gray's picture, isn't it? So I was wondering where your old hard look went when you became a Christian."

"It went to Christ and was nailed with Him to the cross," I said, "together with the old, hard me. There was an exchange between us, like the exchange between the picture and Dorian Gray. It's not a perfect similarity, of course: Christ is incomparably greater than any picture. But as the picture bore the sinful likeness of Dorian Gray, Christ bore my sinful likeness, and I will bear His sinless likeness at the resurrection. *'For God hath made him to be sin for us, who knew no sin; that we might be made the righteousness of God in him,'* Second Corinthians 5:21. *'As for me, I will behold thy face in righteousness: I shall be satisfied, when I awake with thy likeness,'* Psalm 17:15."

"I never understood that," said Lisa softly, "for that matter, I don't remember ever hearing it. Now you explain it to me by, of all things, an analogy with *The Picture of Dorian Gray*. I must admit I am learning much about Christ from you I never knew before, and in a brand new way."

We finally turned to the pictures of Lonely Prairie, Fairfield and Fairfield University. "So that is where you will move in May." Lisa said, "It is beautiful." She added slowly after a moment of silence, "Yes, I can imagine living and working from there. . . ."

Her voice trailed off. I was thinking of asking her right then to marry me, but did not. She might now be willing to live with me in the Midwest, but she had still not come closer to Christ than her head belief of the Nicene Creed. She still lived her life and made her decisions according to her will rather than seeking and submitting to Your will first of all.

January passed, February arrived and with it Valentine's Day. I had looked forward to a date with Lisa that evening, but she cancelled at the last minute and postponed it to the following day. We met at a little lower Manhattan pizzeria. I brought Lisa a box of chocolates she especially liked.

Lisa was excited in a somewhat furtive way. I knew she must have special news that concerned both of us. When we had finished our dinner, she could not constrain herself any longer.

"Last night Roy Mattingly made me stay overtime to discuss something about the layout of the next issue of *News in Depth*," she said, "that's why I had to cancel our date. I told him I had a date with you, but he insisted that what he had to discuss with me was too urgent." And now came the bombshell. "After some business discussion which wasn't really all that important Roy whipped out a gorgeous bouquet of roses and proposed to me."

I was not totally surprised. After all, Roy's name had come up earlier between us as a possible marriage partner for Lisa. I also knew that Lisa would not have told me about Roy's proposal if she had accepted it.

"What did you tell him?" I asked.

"I said I appreciated his interest in me but would have to think about it," she said. "He said he and I were made for each other and gave me several reasons why. He also said," she stopped and broke out in her mischievous smile, "that he knew I was still carrying a torch for 'your ex-atheist philosopher friend who is too much into religion to grab you while he can.' He had a point."

She leaned forward. She had never looked more desirable. "James," she said, no longer mischievous but in dead earnest, "it's only three months or so until you leave for Fairfield University. We will have to make a decision before then. We are in love with each other, and I know we have both thought about marriage. It is customary that the man is the first to propose. Roy has made his move. How about you?"

I looked at her in distress. "You said Roy gave you several reasons why you and he were made for each other," I said with a forced smile, "Let me give you several reasons why you and I are perhaps *not* made for each other. I am twelve years older than you and not in perfect health." "I don't mind about your ulcer," Lisa muttered.

"I will teach at a small Christian college for low pay and prestige. We would live a modest, quiet life. You might not be able to continue your career. You . . ."

"Will you get to the real point?" she interrupted me. "All these reasons are secondary and you know it. I would not necessarily have to give up my career if I moved to the Midwest. The real point is our difference about religion. Can you really mean to tell me you won't ask me to marry you because of *that*?" Angry tears were spilling from her eyes. She picked up a napkin from the table and wiped them away.

She had narrowed my dilemma down to the ultimate choice. The temptation to give in to her almost overwhelmed me. I cried out in my heart to You, Father, to be my strength. I did not want to sound judgmental or act "holier than thou" but there was no way to soften the sharp edge of what I must tell her.

"I would marry you this instant if I could," I said, "my greatest desire is to spend the rest of my life with you. But I want our marriage to be right and good. That is possible only if we both submit to God as our Ruler and Guide in everything. Not to submit to Him was the gist of my godless philosophy before my conversion as you well know.

"But you have bought into that philosophy yourself, Lisa. You hold two separate beliefs side by side—a head belief in Christianity according to the Nicene Creed and the belief you actively and passionately live out: belief in yourself and your own doing and achieving, a subset of my former godless philosophy. Only Christ Himself living in your heart can cast it out. Until He does, it is better for us not to marry."

She heard me out silently. I was tortured by the mixture of sadness and rebellion against my words I read on her face. Finally she stood up and picked up her purse and gloves.

"I still think we could make a go of it," she said dully. "My doing and achieving hasn't been all that bad for you, has it? I don't accept that it is part of your former philosophy. Unless and until I accept that, I had better not see you—it would hurt me too much. If you change your mind about anything you said, let me know. Good-bye, James." She came around to me, kissed me on the cheek with a suppressed sob and quickly walked out of the restaurant.

I drove home through the glitter of the city barely able to restrain my tears. I kept telling myself sternly that a grown man does not cry. You have just wrecked your relationship with a beautiful, brilliant, faithful lady who loved you and whom you loved, a mocking mental voice kept tormenting me. And for what? Because she is resourceful and diligent in her profession, more so than you if the truth be told. Maybe it wasn't your Christianity which made you do it but your male ego. She was even willing to go to "Indian Prairie or wherever" with you. But no, you just wanted to lord it over her and threw it all away by harping on her submission to your God.

And that is where the voice went too far. I knew that I had been right in my insistence that You, dear Father, must be first in Lisa's life. I had fulfilled my priestly function by showing her Your excellence above all other excellences. I was still very sad but no longer reproving myself for what I had done when I arrived at the Van Houtens.

Mrs. Van Houten was awaiting me and told me there had been an urgent phone call for me from Dr. Wood at Fairfield University. He wanted me to call him back no matter how late. Now you are about to lose your job too, the little voice said, but I gritted my teeth, went to the phone and called him back. He told me that Dr. Raymond had had a heart attack and would be unable to serve out his final term at Fairfield University. Could I come right away and take over? The university would pay my air fare, and I could stay at its guest house on the campus until I found lodgings of my own.

There was now no reason why I had to remain in New York any longer and I immediately said yes. I told the Van Houtens all that had happened, called Bernard Gottlieb to do the same and packed what I needed to take with me. Dr. Wood called me again about midnight and gave me the needed information about my flight. I left the next morning with a dull emptiness in my heart about Lisa but also beginning to look forward to my new professional start.

Everything went very well as I settled in. While still in New York I had already gone through the textbooks of all the courses I was to take over from Dr. Raymond, who was slowly recovering and able to discuss them with me as I started my class work. The students accepted me warmly and I loved to teach them. I had always enjoyed my interaction with my students and did so even more in this caring and relatively small place where we were all family. My colleagues welcomed me unreservedly despite or perhaps even because of my background. Older Christians seem to have a special love for us who are recent converts to You, dear Father.

My family, of course, was very happy to see me back months earlier than expected. Neva and Robert asked me about Lisa and sadly but silently received the news that we had separated. I was grateful that they did not question me about it in detail but simply did not bring up the matter any more. Robert scouted the real estate firms in Fairfield and soon found a perfectly suitable two-bedroom house near the campus for me to buy. Since I now received a regular salary again, I could afford it. After I moved in, I asked the Van Houtens whether they could have all my belongings shipped to me, and they did me their last great kindness by agreeing. In April 1996 I celebrated my first Easter as a Christian with new roots and security in my native Midwest.

24

A Place of Springs

I had of course maintained my connection with my friends in New York. Bernard Gottlieb had insisted that we complete the one on one post-graduate course he was teaching me. I occasionally chafed at still having to write weekly assignments for him, but You, Father, are faithful in Your promises to us and so we are to be faithful in our commitments to others, especially beloved elders in the faith. He sent me news of my Bible study friends and greetings from the Shalom Israel fellowship when he returned my papers, which always bore helpful corrections and comments. He told me that he counted on me to finish the cataloguing of his library, now getting larger than ever.

I heard from Dr. and Mrs. Van Houten as well. They frequently called me on the phone. Dr. Van Houten chided me about leaving for the Midwest just when I was becoming really useful to him—"I had almost made a Dutchman of you," he said—and as the gardening work around his house was just beginning in earnest. "Good timing for moving away, James," he chuckled, "but use what you have learned in your new house. We might visit you someday, and your place better be kept up properly." Mrs. Van Houten, ever like a motherly elder sister to me, never failed to ask whether I was keeping up my cooking skills and eating properly. On the whole I could assure her that I was.

Mrs. Van Houten had also learned that ulcers could be treated with antibiotics. I asked my family's doctor about this, and he prescribed antibiotics for me which really helped. From then on I did not need to be quite so careful about small, frequent, bland meals. The ulcer was still there but no longer the cause of rather frequent sudden, horrible stomach pains. After my many years of enduring such attacks, this was a most welcome relief.

I also had news from J. P. Knightley. He was very happy in his new position at the Frederic Bastiat Foundation, named for a very conservative French economist of the nineteenth century. He and Brenda had had the joy of seeing their daughter turn to Christ and bringing the little grandchildren with her. "Our son-in-law will be next," J. P. said confidently, "and we are working on our son. You are having grandchildren and great-grandchildren in the faith, James, and we can't thank you enough for starting it all. I have shared your meditation on the joy of the Lord with my children and many others. It still brings me joy every time I read it again."

J. P. also told me that the Bertrand Russell Institute had reduced its staff and moved to smaller headquarters. "They are running out of money now that Paul Reynolds isn't around any longer," he said. He added that Paul had neglected to make a will before his suicide, and therefore his entire estate would go to his blood relatives and none of it to the institute. This news reminded me of Paul's vandalism of my car and Lisa's "doing and achieving" to bring him to book and injure the institute. You, dear Father, were fulfilling her purpose by means she had not wanted and without her efforts, just as I had told her shortly after the event.

I also received regular letters from Jeff Jensen, the young student who had come to You on the airplane on my Labor Day visit to Lonely Prairie and Fairfield. He had no one else to turn to with questions about the faith and the Bible, and I spent many hours answering them and praying for him. Sometimes I would have to ask other Christians for help, including my brother Robert with his seasoned and extensive knowledge of Scripture. Jeff studied philosophy at Columbia University and was now trying to share his faith with his friends there. I had the impression that his questions to me often included theirs, and that the answers I sent him from the combined scriptural treasure store available to me fed a whole study group of young inquirers.

A few students at Fairfield University asked me to be their faculty sponsor for a new philosophy club. "We want you," their spokesman said, "because you know what it's like on the other side." More and more my atheist background turned out to be an asset to me in my professional and Christian work. You, dear Father, now used my former enmity to You according to Your good purpose. I saw with deep joy that I myself was becoming more and more "a place of springs" for seekers after You.

The only black and barren spot of sadness in my life was the seemingly total and permanent separation from Lisa. I hardly dared admit to myself that I hoped for a letter from her every time the mail was delivered to my house. I always answered my phone with the secret longing that I might hear her low, soft voice again, the voice like no other which I had loved so much. It was always a sting of disappointment to me when the caller was someone else, much welcome as he or she might be.

My love for Lisa drove me to study the many Bible passages dealing with Your love for us. I so much wanted to be a good husband to Lisa, to provide a home for her, to be there for her in times of need, to make her feel cherished and secure in my love. It was a deep and painful frustration for me not to be able to do that. I saw that this is Your own desire in relating to us as well; You call Yourself our Bridegroom and us Your Bride in the Song of Solomon. *"I have loved thee with an everlasting love,"* You say to Israel through Jeremiah, *"therefore with lovingkindness have I drawn thee."* You loved us so much that You gave Your only Son for us. I knew my love for Lisa was only like a dim sputtering candle compared to the burning sun which You created to give light and warmth to the whole earth. But if even my earthly love could almost consume me, how much more the Consuming Fire of Everlasting Love which is You Yourself!

A day came shortly after Easter when I was ready and willing to give up my hope that we might be man and wife. "Only bring her fully to Yourself, dear Father," I prayed, "I only pray for her, not also for me any longer." I saw that this was part and parcel of priesthood in Christ as well.

The time between my separation from Lisa and that day was my most severe testing and cleansing since I became a Christian. You had to lay it on me, dear Father, for You knew better than I how little if anything I knew about true love. Now You taught me true love, which "does not seek its own." I had never truly loved anyone in all my godless years unless it were myself, and self-love is not love at all, for love requires more than one person. In teaching me true love, You also taught me why You, our God Who is Love, are not one as in Islam, but Three Persons in One.

Late in the evening of Monday, April 15, 1996, I was sitting in the living room of my little house in Fairfield working on a lecture on the treatment of Christians believing in biblical creation in American public schools and colleges. It demanded concentrated attention and the use of many sources. I do not know how much time elapsed before I noticed a repeated knock on my front door which was becoming louder and louder. Finally the late visitor was pounding on the door with his fist. I wondered why he was not calling out to me as I got up and walked to the entrance to see who it might be. I switched on the front porch light and peered through the small glass window of the door. And then I could not unlock the door fast enough, fumbling in my haste as I inserted the key, turned it and stepped across the threshold.

Lisa and I stood there facing each other, unable to speak or move. I saw tears well up in her eyes and stream down her face and knew my tears could not be stopped either. After looking at each other like this for a long time in our mutual blessedness, we finally put our arms around each other and walked into my house.

"I came as soon as I could," she said solemnly, like a confession of faith made before You, "it took me these two months to think over our entire relationship from the beginning. From the AEA speech to my interview with you, to our flight to New York when I covered you with that blanket because I had already begun to fall in love with you, to everything that followed. I thought how changed and transparent and gentle you were after your conversion, and of everything you went through afterwards without hating anyone and without losing your joy and your trust in God. I thought especially hard about how you asked forgiveness from Nancy Berger and how you accepted your punishment from the woman who attacked you with the perfume bottle. I thought about your effect on Paul Reynolds. I knew your conversion was real. That meant God was real, not just part of a creed to be believed in my head, true as it may be. He is my living Lord, Savior and Father Who loves me."

She took a deep breath before her final words, "You became my 'place of springs,' James. Your life matched your words. I saw Christ in You. Therefore, I now submit and say yes to you and to Christ. I accept my 'doing and achieving' as part of your former philosophy of putting oneself first in one's life. I will no longer put my own will above God's. "

"God used these two months," I confessed to her before You in return, "to teach me to love truly, not seeking my own. Now I love you as I should, seeking only your good."

She looked up at me with the first mischievous smile dawning on her lips. "So now are you ready and willing to ask for my hand in marriage, James?" she asked.

And I did.

THEY SHALL *NOT* BE ASHAMED

Part 3

"They Shall Not Be Ashamed"

*Wherefore we receiving a kingdom which cannot be moved,
let us have grace, whereby we may serve God acceptably
with reverence and godly fear: For our God is a consuming fire.*

—The Holy Bible: Hebrews 12:28–29

*O my God, I trust in thee:
let me not be ashamed, let not mine enemies triumph over me.
Yea, let none that wait on thee be ashamed:
let them be ashamed which transgress without cause.*

—The Holy Bible: Psalm 25:2–3

*I thy God am with thee! I have heard thy call!
I have blest thy labor! Thou shalt never fall.
Seven thousand others I have kept for me
Who will not to idols bow their knee.
In my name and promise claim the victory!
Then in pow'r and glory reign with Me! Amen!*

—Adapted from The Holy Bible:
1 Kings 19 and 2 Kings 2

To the Reader

The following are the names of real people and organizations in Part 3, listed in alphabetical order:
- Frederic Bastiat
- Henri Bergson (*Creative Evolution*)
- Aleister Crowley
- Mark Crutcher (*Lime 5*)
- Paul Ehrlich
- G. F. W. Hegel
- Lambeth Conference
- George MacDonald
- Dr. Henry Morris (*The Genesis Flood*)
- Bernard Nathanson (*The Hand of God*)
- Planned Parenthood
- Roe v. Wade (U. S. Supreme Court abortion decision of January 22, 1973)
- Margaret Sanger
- Pierre Teilhard de Chardin
- Gerhard Tersteegen

All other persons and organizations are fictional, and any resemblance between them and actual persons or organizations is coincidental.

Table of Contents

1 Our Wedding; Enter Jonathan Wood 212
2 We Were Greatly Blessed. 215
3 Pantheism and Philosophy. 218
4 Termination of Pregnancy? 221
5 A Fateful Omission 226
6 About Dr. Nathanson; You Forgave my Sin; Abortion and the
  Dominion Mandate 229
7 Probing the Abyss 233
8 Dwelling with the Consuming Fire 237
9 Bioethics; A Painful Illness; An Unexpected Joy 241
10 More About my Son; Helping Dolly Hernandez 245
11 Being There for Dolly Hernandez 249
12 Spiritual Warfare 254
13 "The Little Brothers of Saint James". 258
14 Reconciliation at a Funeral 262
15 God's Love Includes God's Justice 267
16 Treasures of Darkness 271
17 Promoting the Death Culture 275
18 There Are No Accidents with God. 279
19 "It's Over and You Have Lost" 283
20 "Claim the Victory" 288
21 "Rejoice in My Joy". 292
A Letter to Bernard Gottlieb 298

1
Our Wedding; Enter Jonathan Wood

When I met and fell in love with Lisa Trent Harrison immediately after my conversion to Christ, it had seemed to me that I, the James Barron who had "loved and left" woman after woman during my years in the desert of my godless philosophy, was being transformed into a young, innocent man in love for the first time in his life. Lisa, also self-centered before her surrender to Christ, but less so than I, had spoken similarly of her love for me. Thus it seemed to both of us that our marriage to each other was our first one ever. It was a brand new, utterly serious commitment for us to God and to each other before the world. We were determined to put You, Father, and Your will first in our lives together moment by moment, each other second, and ourselves last.

We wanted to be completely truthful before You, Father, and our elders in the faith. Therefore, we frankly confessed our past histories, so painful for Lisa, so painful as well as shameful for me, to Pastor Benjamin Wood of Fairfield Bible Wesleyan Church when we asked him to marry us. Pastor Wood was a brother of Dr. Michael Wood, President of Fairfield University whose faculty I had joined as professor of philosophy in February 1996. I had been attending Fairfield Bible Wesleyan Church ever since, not because this was required of me as a faculty member but because Your love and holiness were there. Lisa began to attend with me after she moved to Fairfield in May. We wanted our marriage to be blessed before this community of believers.

Pastor Wood listened attentively to all we had to tell him. First he ascertained that remarriage to our previous spouses, the biblical and best way in situations like ours, was impossible. Then he agreed to perform the marriage according to the traditional Christian rite, totally unlike the contract in which my ex-wife and I had exchanged the meaningless promise "to give each other comfort and assistance as long as our mutual affection should endure." It would be a small ceremony attended by members of our families, some of my fellow faculty members including President and Mrs. Wood, and a small number of other invited guests including my old friend J. P. Knightley and his wife Brenda who had flown in from New Jersey for the occasion. A goodly number of members of the congregation also honored us with their presence.

We were married in the afternoon of Saturday, June 15, 1996, the first anniversary of my new birth in Christ and just two months after Lisa had first shared her own conversion with me. My brother Robert served as my best man, and Lisa's father was on hand to give away his daughter. Pastor Wood reminded us and the assembled witnesses that we were about to be joined in "holy matrimony," which was instituted of God, signified the mystical union between Christ and His Church, was beautified by Christ's presence and the first miracle He wrought in Cana of

Galilee, and commended of Saint Paul to be honorable among all men. Upon Pastor Wood's unanswered question whether any man could show just cause why we could not lawfully be joined together, we finally pronounced our marriage vows.

I took Lisa's right hand into mine and pledged, "I, James, take thee, Lisa, to be my wedded Wife, to have and to hold from this day forward, for better for worse, for richer for poorer, in sickness and in health, to love and to cherish, till death us do part, according to God's holy ordinance." You heard my pledge, dear Father, and knew I meant every word of it. Then Lisa took my right hand into hers and likewise pledged her life to me in our Lord. Then we exchanged our wedding rings, putting them on the fourth finger of each other's left hand, and we each repeated after Pastor Wood, "With this Ring I thee wed: In the Name of the Father, and of the Son, and of the Holy Ghost. Amen."

Then Pastor Wood joined our hands together and said, "Those whom God has joined together let no man put asunder," pronounced us man and wife in the Name of the Father, and of the Son, and of the Holy Ghost, and blessed us in Your name. We received it all gratefully and with humble hearts. I prayed, dear Father, let me never be ashamed because I took Your great blessing lightly. And You in Your great fatherly love recalled to me a Scripture I had recently found in my study of the word "ashamed": *"Fear not; for thou shalt not be ashamed: neither be thou confounded; for thou shalt not be put to shame; **for thou shalt forget the shame of thy youth*** (Isaiah 54:4)." I could not stop smiling for a long time. Lisa looked at me and smiled, too; no words were needed for us in our deep unity for her to rejoice with me in my joy.

The church had prepared a reception for us in their parlor. How good it was for us to welcome our families and friends! The first to hug and kiss us was Sylvia who had led me to You a year ago with her unfailing, unconditional love, Christ's own love in her for me. We hugged and kissed her back, and Lisa said, "Thank you, Sylvia, for helping to bring your Uncle James and me together!" My sister Neva, Sylvia's mother, beamed as she stood by.

"I can't believe I was ashamed of Sylvia right after she was born," she murmured to me, "to have a mentally retarded child seemed such a stigma to me! How is it possible that I even thought of suffocating her with a pillow in my bed? Thank God He stopped me by letting me see that what I did to her I did to Jesus! *'As you do to these the least of my brethren, you do to Me.'* If I had done *that,* we would not be here today celebrating your wedding—your beautiful wedding in our Lord."

We also joyfully greeted our good friends J. P. and Brenda Knightley. They brought us up to date on what had happened in New York since I had left it in February. J. P. brought greetings from my dear old mentor Bernard Gottlieb and his Bible study circle. "We now live much farther away from them," J. P. said, "but we try to make it to their Bible study at least once a month. It's hard to find a good Bible-believing Christian church where we are! But our son-in-law is a Christian now, too. Maybe we'll start our own open fellowship in their home."

J. P. also told me that most of the Bertrand Russell Institute staff members had now left it "like rats abandoning a sinking ship," he chuckled. He felt it would soon be gone entirely, "and good riddance," he added. Of course he and I knew that the institute had been just one of a large number of similar powerful militant atheist organizations subverting our once Christian society. But we couldn't help being glad that at least this one tentacle of the enemy was being cut off.

And then the buzz of happy voices diminished as the parlor door was pushed open by a tall young man and a pretty young woman with dark eyes and dark hair, obviously his girl friend. He immediately made his way towards me, dragging her along by her hand. They were most inappropriately dressed in faded blue jeans and sweatshirts. I knew him well; he had attended the introductory philosophy class I had taken over from Dr. Raymond. He was Jonathan Wood, President Wood's youngest son, and he was almost certainly not a Christian.

I had had many private conversations with Jonathan about how I had come to the faith and why I continued in it. His principal question to me, which he would bring up again and again, was whether we, our own selves or egos, still continued to exist as separate entities after coming to Christ or were so to speak absorbed into Him. I suspected that he had had some exposure to New Age beliefs permeated by Hinduism. Time after time I affirmed our continued separate existence to him as taught by the Bible, but this question continued to occupy, even torment him. We had developed a sort of friendship through our discussions, and he was in my daily prayers. Now here he was coming to stand before me, a smile on his face, his girl friend, a little awkward and shy, by his side.

The people around us stood by, curious. Among them was Dr. Wood, a frown of embarrassment and resignation on his face, looking at me in mute appeal. I instantly understood that I must do whatever I could to make his son's unexpected, uninvited appearance with his girl friend and in his inappropriate apparel acceptable to all the wedding party. I stretched out my hand to Jonathan in welcome with a smile, and he shook it, smiling in return. "It's so good of you to come to my wedding reception, Jonathan," I said, putting my arm around his shoulders, "and who is this pretty young lady?" He introduced her as Dolly Hernandez. I knew she must come from the western part of Fairfield where most of our growing Mexican-American population resided. Dolly limply shook hands with me and looked up at me timidly. Our eyes met. Her glance pleaded for my acceptance much as Jonathan's father had done before. I put my other arm around her and led them both to the refreshment table, where I gave each of them a little plate with a piece of the wedding cake. The buzz of the other guests' voices resumed its earlier volume.

"Thank you, Dr. Barron," said Jonathan, and "thank you," whispered Dolly. I understood they both meant more than just thanks for the cake. They had dared, or rather Jonathan had dared, to invade our party uninvited, and I had made it all right. I was happy about it, thinking You approved.

2
We Were Greatly Blessed

Lisa and I soon found out that our whole lives changed drastically as we began endeavoring to be truly one in marriage under You, dear Father. We knew we must rid ourselves of our previous notions of marriage in our increasingly anti-Christian society. Marriage as the world thinks of it nowadays is merely a joint housing and sleeping arrangement of two single people who continue to live side by side as though they were still single and independent of each other. They think of this arrangement as a temporary contract, to be cancelled by either party at will. Lisa and I had been true moderns in this respect, she without full awareness, I quite explicitly.

Along with most of our generation, we had also been stupid enough to assume that married people do not need to spend much time with each other. Both of us had been almost continually away from our spouses to lead or attend conferences, lectures, courses, news media events and gala celebrity meetings all over the country or even abroad. We loved our careers and our excessive busyness which largely defined our identities. We enjoyed our prestige, our conspicuous spending of money for the latest clothes, cars and gadgets, our streamlined surroundings and perks. We virtually forgot our spouses, dropping in on them only between our other far preferred activities for occasional pit stops of ever less satisfying sex.

We saw now that our chosen absence from our spouses had been our own virtual "putting asunder" of our marriages. You Yourself, dear Father and Jesus, bestow Your continuous presence on us as part of Your great love! Even so we, made and being restored in Your image and likeness, should be lovingly present with our spouses and loved ones as much as humanly possible, and faithfully remember them in our hearts and minds when unavoidably absent. We should also firmly and vocally resist the increasing tendency of corporate business to preempt our time for their use, stealing it from our families.

From the first day of our married life, we put all our assets into joint ownership, from our little house in Fairfield to all our financial accounts and investments to that final testing point, a joint checking account. Each of us would know how much each of us spent, and for what purpose. We agreed to adopt John Wesley's maxim "Earn as much as you can; save as much as you can; give as much as you can" as our own. The "saving" admonition was the hardest to obey! It brought about some major changes in our spending habits. Some of these changes were painful and revealed how much of our old egos, especially mine, were still left untouched beneath our slowly growing new identities in Christ. It sounds ridiculous to me now, but I never realized how little sales resistance I had to new neckties matching my dark dress suits, new white dress shirts and new shoes until after Lisa and I were married!

On the other hand, we had much more money than ever before to give to people in need and causes worthy of our support in our Lord's good will. We agreed that everything we had really belonged to You; we were the stewards, not the owners of Your property. Support of our good local church came first in our giving. The next cause which greatly appealed to our hearts and minds was the teaching of biblical creation and uncompromising Christian worldviews. Next came financial support of Christians persecuted for the faith around the world. Lastly was our deep desire to help persuade expectant mothers, the babies' fathers and our whole culture sunk in materialism and self-absorption that babies are God's gifts to us and should be allowed to live rather than to be aborted. We began by supporting these causes financially, but true to Your Word that *"where your treasure is, there your heart will be also"* we became more and more actively involved in them. Eventually, both Lisa and I would regularly take part in demonstrations and prayer vigils at the nationally famous abortion mill in Battle Hill run by late-term abortionist Derek Hellmann.

As I had to learn about other areas of my life, Father, walking with You in marriage is impossibly hard on our own, but easy and joyful with our hand in Yours step by step as a little child with his father. In marriage You, dear Father, are our "third partner." It is one of Your excellent but hard schools, teaching Your children to live out Your love in them for each other day by day! We are to be one single organism joined together for the remainder of our lives on earth, which no one and least of all we ourselves may "put asunder."

We had some run-ins about cooking and household chores. I had learned to perform them and to cook during my blessed months of living with Dr. and Mrs. Van Houten. Even before we were married Lisa had had trouble reconciling herself to my new readiness to do whatever menial everyday tasks needed to be done *"as unto the Lord"* (Colossians 3:23). She never put it in these words, but I had sometimes wondered whether she was much more willing to accept me as professor of philosophy (and a famous one at that in my atheist days) than as working around the Van Houtens' house and yard and even cooking and grocery shopping in exchange for my room and board. She had been brought up by her parents with the firm conviction that men should not be doing "women's work." She believed that it was her sole responsibility to take care of our home and meals, and when she saw me pitch in, she felt somehow criticized and ashamed. We finally talked it over and agreed that I would restrict myself to the upkeep of the yard and help in the house only in emergencies.

Paradoxically, it was hardest for me to obey the inner voice of love when it came to little things, like picking up dirty clothes and putting them in the laundry basket or doing dishes after a meal. Lisa at least had learned to limit her natural selfishness as an unconverted sinful human being by having to help care for her three younger siblings when she grew up, and later by trying to be a good mother to her son. But I had grown up as the proverbial selfish, spoiled "rich kid," expecting everything I wanted to drop into my hands without even feeling obligation or gratitude. I talked to Lisa about this, asked for and received her help and forbearance. Dear Lisa, if you ever read this, know that I thank you for all your love and patience with me. The success and joy of our marriage is mostly due to you!

After we were married, Lisa greatly diminished her journalistic work for *News in Depth.* She no longer traveled around the country for news investigations and almost ceased her public speaking before conservative audiences. She also reduced her radio talk show from six days a week to Saturday evenings, preparing its programs in advance at a local studio. She did all this because she accepted her care for me and our home as her chief duty and joy under You, dear Father.

How often had we and our professional peers publicly recognized and praised our spouses in our pre-Christian lives? The answer for me and Lisa, alas, was "never"; we would not make that mistake with each other. Now I always listened with undivided attention to Lisa's broadcast with her and praised it as we sat hand in hand on our living room sofa; those Saturday evenings are among my fondest memories of our early life together. I was openly proud before my family, colleagues and friends of being the husband of "Lisa Trent Harrison," the name she retained in her professional circles. Lisa also often referred to me with pride as her husband on her radio program and in her articles. She also often asked for and used my input from the Christian perspective about philosophy in general and ethics in particular. We made the second bedroom in our little house into an office for her and put in a separate telephone for her use only.

I said earlier that in marriage according to Your good will You are our "third partner" and always lovingly present with us. This was true for us especially in our intimate relations as husband and wife. Dear Father, thank you so much for Yourself as the wellspring of our love which always transcended its mere physical expression. Thank You that You allowed no faintest remembrance of others who had been in our past lives to intrude upon our loving, tender union. Thank You for giving us the great grace of willingly abstaining from using any means to prevent the conception of a child when we knew each other in the biblical meaning of the term.

When my beloved wife told me in September 1996 that we were expecting a child to be born to us in April 1997, we took it that You had wiped away "the shame of our youth," rejoiced and thanked You with all our hearts. With our joyful anticipation, of course, came our rush to prepare for the arrival of the new member of our family. For me it was all a brand new experience, for in my former complete self-centeredness I had been a deliberate absentee father for all my children from the beginning. I had totally missed the joy and happy excitement of preparing for them; my one concern had been not to be bothered. Now I knew that children are a gift from You, dear Father and Jesus (Psalm 127:3–5). Therefore this new child You gave us made me completely joyful and altogether willing to take part in his or her life from the very start, yes, beginning with conception. So much joy comes from You, dear Father!

Lisa on the other hand had been through this experience before with her first husband. She wisely refrained from talking much about it or telling me exactly what they had done, but her memories must have helped her make good choices as she and I went shopping for a baby bed, baby clothes, a dresser to store them in, a car seat, and other more or less indispensable things. I wondered sometimes whether we were really obeying John Wesley's directive to "save all we could" as we did our baby shopping, walking around the stores as in a happy dream with happy smiles on our faces, but we couldn't help being joyful all the time and I felt You were smiling with us.

We also decided that we would have our attached garage rebuilt for use as Lisa's office and laughed happily as we went to work again to change our second bedroom, only just remade into Lisa's office, to become our baby's room. By October this project was finished to our satisfaction, and hardly an evening went by that we did not first stand hand in hand in this newly prepared room for our child and fondly looked at everything in it before going to bed. Oh yes, dear Father, we were greatly blessed!

3

Pantheism and Philosophers

My summer had been particularly busy with the new Christian worldview course developed by the Summit Ministries. In the fall semester of 1996 I taught the history of Western philosophy from antiquity to scholasticism, a course on ethics with emphasis on the bioethics of our own day, and offered directed readings tutorials, always the most intense and time consuming part of my work load.

Jonathan Wood registered to take one of these tutorials and wanted to have me assign him my old atheistic textbook *The Metamorphosis of Philosophy: From Atheism to New Age* as his directed reading. He briefly talked to me about it ahead of time. I told him it had begun as my doctoral thesis written in the late 1960s when I was in my late twenties and a passionate atheist-evolutionist, but that I now repudiated everything in it. Jonathan demurred, wondering whether some of my former beliefs could be defended. He wanted to search the book for such defensible beliefs and discuss them with me in our tutorials. It was an unusual request coming from the son of the Christian president of a strongly Christian school. I agreed, hoping that You, Father, would help me defeat Jonathan's latent or perhaps not so latent leanings toward my former anti-Christian views.

I was also beginning to prepare for the address I was scheduled to give to the North American Philosophy Association in Toronto, Canada on October 31, 1996. This was the last leftover from my former work as "philosopher in residence" at the Bertrand Russell Institute. My peers who had invited me in June 1995 insisted on my keeping this engagement when the institute was about to cancel it due to my conversion and resignation. They wanted to hear the details of my conversion and defense of my new beliefs. The Scripture You gave me for my address was 1 Peter 3:15–16, exhorting me *"to give an answer to every man that asketh you a reason of the hope that is in you with meekness and fear, having a good conscience; that, whereas they speak evil of you, as of evildoers, they may be ashamed that falsely accuse your good conversation (behavior) in Christ."*

Lisa and I thought of attending the Toronto meeting together. Because of my continuous teaching schedule, we had not gone on a honeymoon after our wedding. Why not use the Toronto trip as our honeymoon? Our trip expenses would be partly covered by my honorarium. We could rent a car and drive from Toronto to New York City via the suburb of Schenectady where Lisa's relatives lived. We would visit them, look up our friends Bernard Gottlieb and the Van Houtens in New York, and then fly back home. By the end of October Lisa would start her fourth month of pregnancy and no longer be subject to her present morning sickness bouts. Dr. Raymond, now pretty well recovered from his heart attack, might cover my classes for me. We made the necessary arrangements.

My directed readings sessions with Jonathan Wood challenged me deeply. He was especially interested in pantheistic "emergent" evolution as presented by the unorthodox Catholic priest Pierre Teilhard de Chardin, briefly described in the latter part of my old textbook. It was therefore this part that I must rethink, explain and refute as a Christian. To my distress I also had to read the works of Teilhard, an almost impossible task due to their nebulous, wordy vagueness and high-sounding mysticism which could mean everything and nothing. I saw that I must cut through the outer verbiage of Teilhard's pantheism to its essence if I was to overcome it in Jonathan's mind by Christian theism.

After much reflection and prayer I explained to Jonathan that pantheism is the "spiritual" reverse of the coin whose "materialist" front is atheism. Both pantheism and atheism deny the God of Christianity, Who is personal (in fact three persons in one), transcendent, that is, apart from and above and beyond this world, and immanent, that is, present everywhere. The god of pantheism cannot be the God of the Bible; I thought he was Satan, whom the Bible calls *"the god of this world"* (2 Corinthians 4:4).

After digesting all this, Jonathan asked me whether people who tried to connect with the god of pantheism took a step toward occultism or Satanism. I became very concerned and asked him whether he had tried to take that step. He denied it, but I was sure he was lying. Unfortunately this was our last discussion before my Toronto trip. I told him we would take this matter up again after my return.

Lisa and I flew to Toronto on October 31, arriving in the early afternoon. We rented a car and used the rest of the afternoon to do some sight seeing before getting ready for the evening's event. As we examined ourselves together in our hotel room's big mirror before leaving, we were pleased with our appearance. We were a tall, well matched, handsome and distinguished-looking couple, formally but not ostentatiously dressed and smiling because we took so much joy in each other. I was especially joyful in you, dear Lisa, every time I saw the new slight swelling of your body where our child was growing, as yet unnoticed by most people.

We entered the ballroom where the conference took place. I knew a good number of the attending philosophers from previous meetings over the years. Most of them had shared my former views and therefore now greeted me with reserve, but there were also a few who had avoided me in the past and now welcomed me warmly, including the conference chairman, a French Canadian professor in his late thirties named Andre Lavigne. After we had talked together for a few minutes, we knew we were brothers in You, dear Father, and became instant friends. Andre taught philosophy at a university in Quebec and had become a believer after obtaining tenure. "They wouldn't hire me now, but they can't fire me," he said, and also explained that he had been chosen as conference chairman before his conversion. Christians were as little welcome in Canadian academia as in the United States.

Andre wanted to know what had really happened to me after I left the Bertrand Russell Institute. He had read some of the slanderous news items and heard the contemptuous gossip of his atheist colleagues about me. "But I knew it was all lies," he said. Now I could tell him the truth, since the gag order the institute imposed on me when I left it had expired in September. Andre had also heard of Lisa and was pleased to meet her, though her conservative radio show was as unpopular among Canada's liberal news media as among ours.

Finally the time arrived for me to speak. Andre gave me a most complimentary introduction and I launched into my address, prepared many weeks in advance with much prayer. Pursuant to the wish of those who had invited me I started with describing my conversion. "It began at the door of a hotel ballroom much like this one where my family had a reunion," I said and told the philosophers how Sylvia, my niece with Down Syndrome, had cried out to me and stopped me from walking on to another room where I was to speak to an audience much like ours here.

And then my prepared address fell away from me as though it had never existed. Instead of it You, dear Father, took me back to that moment when I first saw myself as a loveless, self-absorbed, lost sinner unworthy of life and thanked You for Sylvia's little warm hand taking my hand and leading me home to You. It was as real to me there in Toronto as it had been when it actually happened, and just as then tears came to my eyes, both of shame and of joy. Yes, dear Father, it was as if I was being converted again right before these philosophers! I relived the shame, I relived willingly surrendering myself to You, and I relived receiving Your great and everlasting joy just as I had received it that night in Battle Hill. And all the while that I relived it I heard and felt myself speaking of it to the philosophers who were listening spellbound. You also gave me the gift of sharing it with them by my tears which I could not stop, and by my simple words, stammering a little but bringing them out audibly and in Your sequence given to me as Your vessel and Your spokesman, Your priest and Your king. You were there and I was there before them, and we were one, an "I-You" or a "You-I."

I stopped speaking. There was a total, prolonged silence. Lisa and Andre Lavigne were crying soundlessly and unashamedly, perhaps not even aware of the tears streaming down their faces, yet they also smiled with joy. They were not the only ones; here and there in the audience others were touched in their hearts, weeping and smiling just like them.

Finally Andre stood up and thanked me. "Your testimony transcended philosophy," he said, "it was as if you were converted before our eyes! In particular we were allowed to share your joy, coming to you from beyond yourself. We will never forget it." He then opened the meeting to questions. There were a number of questions about my life after my conversion and my views regarding the policies of the Bertrand Russell Institute. I was delighted to be asked and to be free to answer them according to the faith. No one asked me to formally defend it; Your and my earlier description of my conversion was itself its all-sufficient defense.

And then a white-haired, bearded man sitting in the front who had stared at me stonily all through the meeting raised his hand and was recognized. He stood up. I recognized him as Thor Ericson, a strident American atheist. Before my conversion we had cooperated on several radical left-wing atheist projects, but now he was my enemy. I prepared myself for a figurative blow.

"I take it you and Ms. Lisa Trent Harrison are married now," he said sarcastically in a loud voice so everyone could hear, "the last time I checked, you weren't. Both of you are sort of old to start a family. My question is, haven't you two ever heard of birth control?"

He had noticed that Lisa was pregnant and wanted to shame us! The blood rushed to my face and my hands balled into fists. His attack against me did not matter, but everything in me wanted to fight him physically for insulting my wife. But You, Father, restrained me, telling me Lisa and I had no reason to be ashamed. You also reminded me again of 1 Peter 3:15–16 which exhorts us to be gentle and reverent so that not we but those who falsely slander us may be ashamed. I took my place at Lisa's side and put my arm around her.

"Yes, Thor, we know about birth control," I answered him, "but we didn't use it. We wanted to be open to God if He would bless us with a child, and He did. We thank and praise Him for giving us this joy."

And suddenly that audience of philosophers, including those most likely hostile to me as a Christian, broke into the applause they had been too stunned to give after seeing my conversion to You reenacted before their eyes. Andre Lavigne told me later that one of them was converted that very night. In the months to come he wrote me of other men and women among them who came to faith in You.

4

Termination of Pregnancy?

The next day we drove from Toronto to Hilton, New York, a suburb of Schenectady where Lisa's parents and relatives lived. I noticed that she became more and more thoughtful and withdrawn as we came closer and closer to her hometown. I finally gently asked her if anything was wrong. Her reaction of strong, angry unhappiness surprised me.

"Oh James," she burst out, "I wish we could skip this visit to my family! And for a whole day and night, no less! I hate it. I wish we had never planned on it. Can't we just drive on to New York City and give them some excuse later why we couldn't see them?" She looked up at me pleadingly.

I could hardly believe my ears. She had never given me the slightest indication that she felt this way about her family.

"I had no idea you didn't get along with your folks," I said.

"I did get along with them just fine," Lisa explained bitterly, "until they saw that I was getting serious about you. If it had been up to them, and especially my mother, we would never have married. 'Are you still dating that ex-atheist religious maniac of yours?' she asked me when I visited them last Christmas. She had swallowed all that garbage about you she read in *News Messenger, Celebrity Update,* and *Present Trends.* She 'knew' more about you than I who saw you face to face almost every day, only all her information was false!"

I silently congratulated myself in retrospect. I had foreseen the news media campaign against me from the moment I had let Lisa record my conversion to Christ on tape for her radio interview. After all, when I was still a leading left-wing atheist, I had taken part in such campaigns myself. Therefore, I had spared myself useless and impotent anger by not reading the leading news magazines any more after becoming a Christian.

Lisa had grown angrier and angrier as she spoke, but now she shrugged resignedly. "Nothing I could say would convince her otherwise," she said more softly, "the Bertrand Russell Institute had done its lying publicity work well. Not only did it wreck your career, but it poisoned my family against you, especially my mother. People are so ignorant and brainwashed! They really think that if they read it in the *New York Times* or *News Messenger* it must be true."

I couldn't resist teasing her a little. "And then there was that early article 'A Leading Atheist's Defection' about me by Lisa Trent Harrison in the July 1995 issue of *News in Depth,*" I said, "which painted me in solid black and said almost nothing about my conversion."

Lisa punched me playfully in the arm. "Will you stop bringing up that article?" she said. "It was about the old James who doesn't exist any more." Her journalist's nature asserted itself. She added more soberly, "Maybe I should do an article about the new you for *News in Depth.* The new James would be painted in solid white—well, almost solid white. I would have to mention his attempts to dodge doing the dishes when it's his turn, and never picking up his socks for the laundry." I punched her back lightly. We laughed out loud together.

I returned to the matter of concern before us. "Surely by now your mother is reconciled to our marriage," I said comfortingly, "Your dad seemed to accept me all right when he attended our wedding. He is a nice man, your dad. I liked him. I'll bet he did his best to make the rest of your family accept me, too."

"His best wouldn't be good enough," Lisa said somberly, "I never told you much about the relationship between my parents, but I suppose now I should. My mom wore the pants in their marriage. Her will was the law in our home. That's why she went to work away from home when we children were still small. My dad didn't like it, but she overruled him. I followed in her footsteps when I left Bill to take that television job in New York. She made it possible by assuming the care for Bill Jr., and my dad just gave in to her. They are now in their sixties. He retired last year; that's why he could come to our wedding. She is still working and looking down on him as she always did. I learned from her to look down on Bill because he 'had no drive.' 'You have no drive, Jack Trent' my mom used to yell at my dad many times as I was growing up. I can still hear her in my mind."

Lisa sighed deeply and remained silent for a while. I compared what she had told me to what I knew about my own family. My mother had borne with my father's faults for many years after coming to the faith when I was fifteen. She had never put him down before us children or contested his leadership as the head of our family. Her humble and faithful submission in obedience to Christ had held the family together, spared us the disgrace and disaster of divorce and helped bring her husband to the faith at last. For that I was profoundly grateful. Oh Father, how crucial it is for us to have good examples in our parents and to be godly, loving parents and spouses ourselves!

I also realized more fully how hard it must have been for Lisa to submit to a husband after observing the faulty relationship between her parents. In fact, she could not do it in her first marriage. You faced her with this test again and gave me grace to insist that her submission to me must include, nay, be based on full submission to You, Father. And now all was well between us—in You, dear Father, only in You.

"Maybe your mother still isn't happy about me," I said, "but we ought to visit your folks nevertheless. For one thing, we told them we would, and we should keep our promise. Besides, if we never try to get them to accept me, how will they ever do it? It is up to us—to me perhaps—to take the first step. And third, we don't want to make up a reason afterwards about why we couldn't visit them. It would be a lie."

"Okay, Okay," Lisa said, lifting her hand and counting on her fingers, "one, we made a promise; two, we—or you—should earn their favor, and three, we mustn't lie. Four, it's only for one day and one night. You win, James." With this agreement of sorts we completed our travel to Hilton, where we arrived in mid-afternoon.

Lisa's parents welcomed us politely enough. I saw that Lisa's father genuinely liked me. When he had been at our wedding, he had told me to call him Jack; now he said why not call him Dad Trent. "And you'll call me Grandpa Trent or just Grandpa soon, James," he told me as he helped me carry our overnight luggage to the upstairs bedroom. I gave him a quick questioning glance, and he chuckled. "I know what to look for," he said, "Lisa is pregnant, isn't she? About three months along, maybe a little more, I should say. She looks wonderful, so happy and in good health. Congratulations, son! I am real happy for you all." He clapped me on the back. I could have hugged him with pleasure.

It was quite different with Freda, Lisa's mother. Dad Trent had easily and gladly spoken to me when we were by ourselves upstairs. Now he did not open his mouth while we all sat around their living room table and Freda made small talk about the recent cooler weather, the higher cost of living at the East coast, the upcoming election (she would vote for President Clinton) and other indifferent topics. After a while she asked Lisa to come with her to the kitchen to help fix dinner. Lisa's siblings and their spouses were coming to see their oldest sister again "and meet Dr. Barron." I did not like that sentence much; could she not have said "and meet her husband" instead?

When I was alone with Dad Trent, he said in his wife's excuse that she had not wanted Lisa to marry me. "Freda's main objection," he said, "was that you lost your good position in New York. She felt you should have been more, uh, diplomatic about your change of views. Later she believed everything she read about you in the news. She was surprised to hear from me that your church where you and Lisa were married was just a regular church with regular services, not some strange cult."

He added hesitantly, "People are driven too much nowadays, with no peace and rest. You probably didn't have any peace when you still had that good position. Peace doesn't come with worldly success. But now there is peace all about you, James. Give Lisa your peace. Freda has drive enough for two, but she has no peace. Lisa was just like her before she met you. Now she is more like you. Make her like you all the way."

I was touched to the depth of my heart. "Dear Dad Trent," I said, "my peace and all that may be good in me comes from God and Jesus Christ. Without Him I would still have my 'good position' and be altogether worthless. Please pray to Him for me that I would be a good husband to your daughter and father to your grandchild. He loves you and will hear you. And thank you for all you said."

"Pray for me too," he said sadly, "pray for Freda and our whole family. Pray I will be patient."

At that moment Lisa burst into the room, with Freda right on her heels. "I won't stay here any longer, James!" Lisa exclaimed. "Let's leave right now! She told me I should be ashamed to be pregnant at my age! She asked me just like that atheist at the philosophers' conference whether we hadn't ever heard about birth control!"

"Well, you obviously didn't use it," Freda said in cold anger, "and neither did he." She couldn't bring herself to call me Lisa's husband. She turned to me, her eyes flaming. "How could you do this to her, Dr. Barron? I was disgusted enough when Lisa married you, but getting her pregnant is below contempt! If she has the baby, she won't be free again to live her own life until it's too late for that. You, of course, can go on footloose and fancy free, teaching and doing research just as before! Men can't do women's work and wouldn't if they could—you least of all. Your past record as a father is totally despicable to say the least."

I wanted to say that I would and could help with all "women's work" including, of course, the care of my child, but Freda disregarded my attempt to speak. She went on furiously, "Having a baby at your age is such poor stewardship over your finances, too! You wouldn't want your child to study at your little Bible college, would you? Well, your income is not enough to pay for more than that. If you go through with this pregnancy, you condemn your child to a third rate life—just as you did to yourself when you broke with the Bertrand Russell Institute."

"What do you mean, Mother, 'if you go through with this pregnancy'?" asked Lisa, dawning horror in her voice. She walked to my side and clung to my arm.

"Well," Freda answered coolly, "termination of pregnancy wasn't allowed before 1973, but it is a perfectly legal option today. The earlier in the pregnancy it is done, the safer it is for the mother. You ought to have it done right away. He," she pointed at me with her thumb, "has no legal right to interfere. He has no moral right either. As you know, he had it done for his own daughter before he became religiously unhinged."

After a brief pause she added, "Keep in mind also that children of older mothers like you are often born with Down Syndrome or other severe handicaps. Believe me, Lisa, termination of pregnancy would be best in your situation. I say all this only because I love you and am concerned for your welfare first of all."

Lisa and I put our arms around each other and stood straight and tall before Lisa's mother, with Dad Trent sadly and silently watching us. We looked at each other, wondering which of us should speak first. Finally Lisa whispered, "Go ahead, James—you speak for both of us."

"We are very sorry you feel this way about our child, Mrs. Trent," I said, "we both left ourselves open to receive this wonderful gift from God if He would grant it to us. He did, and we thank Him with all our hearts. We are not ashamed.

"We would not prevent our child's birth any more than we prevented his or her conception. We trust God to give us the child who is best for us in His good will, including a handicapped child. It was a little Down Syndrome girl who led me to Christ, Who loved me and gave His life for mine. Without that little Down Syndrome girl, Lisa and I would not have met, loved each other, or be married now with great joy.

"We will leave now, but we pray the day will come soon when we all can welcome each other lovingly as we should. I personally pray I may behave in such a way that you will forget my past and accept me as the husband for your daughter and father of your grandchild. Till then, may God bless you and all your family."

I went back upstairs, fetched our luggage and loaded it into our car with Lisa's help. Mrs. Trent stood in the front door and watched us with a stony face; Dad Trent accompanied us outside and hugged both of us good-bye. We drove away without looking back.

"Was that visit worth stopping for?" Lisa asked after a while.

"We did what we thought we should do," I answered. "It must have been worth it because God allowed it. And it was good that you asked me to speak for both of us, darling. Thank you." And we were more one in You and Your joy, Father, than ever.

5
A Fateful Omission

We spent that night in a nice motel near Albany, New York. We called our friends Bernard Gottlieb and the Van Houtens and told them we would arrive in New York City a day earlier than anticipated. Both were delighted to hear it and ready to welcome us the next day.

After our severe testing the day before, we relaxed and enjoyed our scenic drive through the late fall landscape. Lisa was overflowing with a childlike joy I had never observed in her before. I stole glances at her repeatedly to see her smile and the sparkle in her eyes when they met mine. It was as if a tremendous weight had been rolled away from her heart and mind. Every now and then she sighed deeply with relief. Moreover she credited her deliverance to me.

"I never thought anyone could stand up to my mother," she said, "until you did yesterday. And if you hadn't insisted that we go through with the visit, I wouldn't have seen it. I would rather have avoided the confrontation with her altogether. Of course you couldn't have had any idea how horrible it might be. I did. I saw and heard it many times since I was just a little girl. She would upbraid Dad as she upbraided you yesterday, only even more furiously with no holds barred. My brothers and sister and I would hide. Sometimes when Dad couldn't bear it any longer he would leave the house and wander or drive around in the streets for hours, even in bad weather. My poor long-suffering dad! I wonder what he had to bear from her for attending our wedding."

Lisa choked up for a moment. She finally continued with an effort:

"He kept quiet yesterday when she attacked you because if he had said anything at all she would have turned her fury against him as well as you. It would only have heaped more shame on him in front of us. He is gentle by nature, and very patient, and now he is cowed as well after all these years." Tears of compassion for her father welled up in her eyes. She wiped them away, smiled at me and went on, "And then you stood up to her as no one ever had before. And you did it quietly and gently, yet with total authority! You did not apologize for what did not require an apology. You were respectful yet did not yield an iota of what was right. You said all that needed to be said and no more. You gave honor to God and Christ. I was so grateful you were there, able and willing to speak for us both!"

"That's what a husband is for under God," I said, "and again, thank you for asking me to do it. I could not have spoken with total authority if I had not been sure my wife stood with me. In relying on me and honoring me, you too gave honor to God and Christ Who made us one and gave us our child." After a few moments of reflection I asked, "Why didn't you tell me before how it is with your parents?"

"I was too ashamed," Lisa murmured, "even before you I was too ashamed. I wanted you to think I came from a respectable family that got along well without any problems. What would you think of me if you knew . . ." Her voice trailed away.

"Well, now I know," I said, "and I love you just as much as ever or more. Don't ever be afraid again to trust me or to lose face before me with anything like this, which wasn't even your fault, or with anything else. And who am I of all people to put you down, you who know all my horrible past and love me anyway? We are supposed to be transparent with each other and love each other like our Heavenly Father, Who knows us completely and yet loves us."

I stopped the car, hugged my wife and she hugged and kissed me. "I love you, James," she said, "I have peace now as never before. It was worth visiting my folks to have all this out in the open." She repeated, "Yes, it was worth it." And so it was; we trusted each other with everything from then on.

We drove on. "Out of curiosity," I asked Lisa, "what work does your mother do, and does it have anything to do with her political views?"

"Oh that," Lisa answered, "I never dare bring up politics with her. She started out as a social worker with the Health and Human Services Administration in the 1960s. At first she was still pretty conservative; she was actually proud of me when I started writing for *News in Depth* and doing my radio show. But she became more and more liberal as she advanced in her career. Now she is a department supervisor and as far or farther left-wing in politics as you ever were."

"Like I was before my conversion," I repeated, "I understand! She might perhaps have tolerated me as your husband if I had remained as I was, complete with my good position at the Bertrand Russell Institute."

"That's right," Lisa agreed, "if you hadn't taken the heat yesterday chiefly because we are expecting, you would have taken it chiefly because you became a Christian—a 'fundamentalist, Bible-thumping, bigoted, judgmental religious maniac,' as she puts it." Lisa looked hurt as she quoted her mother's words, but I had to laugh. I had used much the same epithets for Christians before I became a "failed atheist."

"She wasn't far from the truth," I said, "our expecting our child is part of our faith and trust in God. Let's not be hurt about her rejection of me, darling! Let's just pray for her. If I changed in God's good time, so can she."

Having started out early in the morning, we arrived at Bernard Gottlieb's residence in upper Manhattan early in the afternoon. I had known my dear fatherly friend and mentor almost from the day I became a Christian. He was my first teacher of the Bible in the "mystical" way I have always loved most deeply. By "mystical" I mean rejoicing above all in Your presence with us, Your speaking to us, Your planting by Your own longing for us, the longing in our hearts for You which causes us to say, *"As the hart panteth after the water brooks, so panteth my soul after thee, O God. My soul thirsteth for God, for the living God: when shall I come and appear before God?"* (Psalm 42:1–2)

Lisa had begun to come with me to Bernard's weekly Bible study group soon after we began to love each other. And now we came to see him again after we were man and wife. It was a truly blessed reunion for us all.

There had always been peace for me in Bernard's presence. This time was no exception. In his constant search for Christian writings of lasting worth he had come across a collection of poems by an eighteenth century German "mystical" poet named Gerhard Tersteegen. He was totally enthusiastic about these poems and could hardly wait to tell us about them. Most of Tersteegen's works were available only in German, accessible to Bernard with his knowledge of all major European languages but not to us. However, he had found one little volume of Tersteegen's poems translated into English, sat us down on the sofa of his living room and joyfully read some of them to us. One of them immediately took root in my mind and heart:

> Man earthy, of the earth, an hungered feeds
> On earth's dark poison tree—
> Wild gourds, and deadly roots, and bitter weeds;
> And as his food is he.
> And hungry souls there are, that find and eat
> God's manna day by day;
> And glad they are, their life is fresh and sweet,
> For as their food are they.

"That is you, James," Bernard told me lovingly, "both before and after you came to our Lord."

Lisa nodded and put her hand on mine. "Yes," she said to Bernard, "I only know him as he became afterwards, and it is true. The last four lines of the poem certainly describe him as he is."

I heard them, bowed my head and thought, it is true and yet not true. Yes, You give me Your manna from heaven, dear Father; yes, I am glad, and yes, my life is fresh and sweet. But—how often I neglect or even forget to pray, how little time I take to help others, how often I think about things that do not help me serve You as I should, how often I still spend Your money as though it were my own.

How often I hesitate, delay and postpone tasks You put on my heart! How much I am like Jonah with Nineveh, unwilling to confront people as Your spokesman and warn them to turn away from their sins! As I thought this, as it were an inner voice was calling to me, listen! It is not quite time yet for something you must do, but listen and be ready!

I returned to my earlier stream of thought. I am an unprofitable servant and an ungrateful son, Father, I prayed. How can they say that I am like Your manna from heaven? Please, Father, do not let those who love me make me proud! Do not let me take credit for anything good that I do. As George MacDonald taught me, "*Am I going to do a good deed? Then, of all times—Father, into thy hands; lest the enemy should have me now.*" Always let me remember that without You I am and can do nothing, indeed I can only fail. I should always be on fire for You, but I am not. As Brother Lawrence says, *Thus I will always do if You leave me to myself.* Dear Father, do not leave me to myself! Always be with me and let Your will alone be done in me.

When Lisa and Bernard asked me for the reason of my silence, I shared only that if I was in any way like "God's manna" it was solely due to God.

"Of course," Bernard said. He added: "The young Christians who called themselves 'Jesus Freaks' in the sixties would raise their index finger and point upwards saying 'One Way,' meaning Jesus, and '*He* does it' when they were praised for something good they had said or done. I liked that gesture. I liked a lot about the 'Jesus Freaks.' Before coming to Christ they had been radicals for wrong or evil causes, sold out to rebellion, sex and drugs. Some even sought out the occult and Satanism."

Listen, listen, the earlier voice in my mind spoke up again. Who does this remind you of? Instantly Jonathan Wood appeared before my inner vision, dressed as he had been at our wedding in his faded blue jeans and grey-white sweatshirt, his timid little girl friend by his side. You need to call him, the voice said. He is about to do something that will hurt him and Dolly for life. Call him now. Just talk to him! You don't have to know what it is he wants to do. He is drawn to you as the only Christian in his life who was once Christ's radical enemy. He will listen to you, only you. You can talk to him as no one else can. You can tell him that you heard an inner voice which asked you to call him. He will understand, better than some Christians that there is such a thing as direct communication with the supernatural, God, or Satan and his demons. Call him now!

Father, forgive me! I looked at my watch and saw it was only about five o'clock, which meant it was only four o'clock in Fairfield. I would have to reach Jonathan through Dr. or Mrs. Wood. How awkward it would be to explain to them that I wanted to speak to Jonathan at four o'clock Saturday afternoon because a voice in my mind had told me to, and I didn't really know why. They would think me a little strange to say the least. Forgive me, Father, I even wondered how my phone call would affect my professional standing in Dr. Wood's eyes—after all, he was the president of Fairfield University. It never occurred to me that Jonathan himself might answer the phone.

The long and the short of it is that I never made that call. I planned to talk to Jonathan after our return to Fairfield on Tuesday, "only" three days later. By then it was too late.

6

About Dr. Nathanson; You Forgave my Sin; Abortion and the Dominion Mandate

The Messianic Jewish Shalom Israel congregation met at Bernard Gottlieb's that evening at six o'clock. We gladly attended. Bernard had called the Knightleys to tell them we were there and they came in from New Jersey to be with us. Brenda recognized that Lisa was pregnant and announced it to the group. We were celebrated with hearty applause. It was a most welcome reception especially after what had happened to us the day before.

"In Scripture children are always welcomed as a gift and great blessing from the Lord," Bernard said, "His very first command to our first parents was to be fruitful, multiply and fill the earth. In Israel it was considered a shame to be barren, as we see from the stories of Rachel, the patriarch Jacob's wife, Hannah, the mother of the prophet Samuel, Elizabeth, the mother of John the Baptist, and others. In our culture most people stand these values on their head; they praise barrenness and want few if any children."

"This reversal began in the 1920s with Margaret Sanger's campaign to make contraception acceptable," chimed in J. P., "but it really took hold when the 'pill' hit the market in the early sixties. Now you are considered a freak if you have more than two children. And Brenda and I bought right into that! We are sorry now that we did." Brenda nodded.

"Four would have been much better," J. P. continued, "but it's really too late now for us. Plus," he leaned over to me and murmured into my ear, "I had a vasectomy." He said more loudly to everyone: "If you add the numbers of marriages with sterilized partners or women whose abortions made them unable to bear children, our country's prospects for the future aren't the best. It's the same for the entire West and spreading to the rest of the world as well. I recently prepared a study of world population trends for the Frederic Bastiat Foundation and found that we are facing a world wide birth dearth, not a population explosion as Paul Ehrlich and his followers would have us believe in the sixties."

Our congregational service began, but afterwards when we had refreshments we resumed our conversation, which now turned to abortion. Bernard told us the story of Dr. Bernard Nathanson who had overseen the abortions of some 60,000 babies as director of the Center for Reproductive and Sexual Health in New York City. In addition he had personally aborted some 5,000 unborn children, including his own. He wrote later that he had had no regrets whatever while doing this, sharing "the mentality of the abortionist: another job well done, another demonstration of the moral neutrality of advanced technology in the hands of the amoral" (*The Hand of God,* Life Cycle Books, P. O. Box 420, Lewiston, NY 14092–0420, p. 81). But when ultra-sound photography was invented, he watched an ultra-sound film of an abortion. It radically changed his convictions and made him a zealous pro-life activist.

Later Dr. Nathanson observed pro-life Christians protesting at abortion mills in freezing weather. He was impressed by their gentle, peaceful, confident attitude while being mocked, called filthy names, lied about by the press, opposed by police, the federal judiciary and municipal officials. What gave them their strength? In his spiritual autobiography *The Hand of God,* published 1996, he wrote that for the first time in his adult life he began to consider seriously the idea that God might exist, because it gave him a shining ray of hope as he came to believe that Christ had died for his sins and evil two thousand years ago. He joined the Roman Catholic Church in December 1996.

His moral conversion came at a high cost. He had to leave his position of virtually unlimited authority. His former friends saw him as a traitor and responded with scorn, hate mail, and even death threats. They refused to engage in public debates with him in their arrogant knowledge that they had the power of the ruling opinion setters behind them.

How similar Dr. Nathanson's story was to mine! Both of us were former lifelong atheists. He had aborted his child with his own hands; I had forced my daughter to have an abortion which was botched and led to her death. Both of us had had to pay a steep price for our changes of heart. But there were differences too. Apparently he had not received any Christian witness in his younger years, as I had. His conversion had been by gradual steps, mine had struck me like a bolt of lightning.

You dealt with each of us after our separate identities and needs, dear Father, I thought, and thanked You. But as I spoke to You in my heart, it seemed that You were not as close to me as usual. My joy in You, my most prized treasure, was diminished because somehow I had diminished Your joy in me. What had I done or failed to do to deserve Your displeasure?

I thought about this again after we left Bernard Gottlieb and drove through the late evening to Dr. and Mrs. Van Houten. The only failure on my part I could come up with was my decision not to call Jonathan Wood as the voice in my mind had told me because I had been afraid or rather ashamed to acknowledge that voice as Yours before Dr. Wood.

I saw now how foolish and disobedient I had been. Dr. Wood was my seasoned elder in the faith who knew You far longer and far better than I. What had made me fear that he would think me strange or despise me professionally for acting upon what I believed to be Your call to me? Regardless of whether this fear had come from my own cowardice or from the enemy to stop me from helping Jonathan, I ought to have called on You for strength to overcome it. Replacing obedience to You by my own plan to speak to Jonathan face to face three days later had been sin, yes, "stubbornness, which is as iniquity and idolatry," as the prophet Samuel told King Saul in 1 Samuel 15:10–23. It was not a little thing to be taken lightly. It had grieved You and now it burdened me almost unbearably.

Oh Father, I prayed with Psalm 51 which I had memorized in the early weeks after my conversion, please hide Your face from my sin, forgive me and blot it out. Please make my heart clean and renew a steadfast spirit within me. Please do not cast me away from Your presence and do not take Your Holy Spirit from me. And please, dear Father, for Jesus' sake restore the joy of Your salvation to me and sustain me with a willing spirit. I added on my own, please, Father, be close to me again as before! I cannot stand being separated from you even a little.

And as Psalm 130:4 tells us, *"there is forgiveness with thee, that thou mayest be feared."* You restored the closeness between us, and Your joy and Your peace returned with You to me more fully than ever. I had sometimes worried that I loved Your joy and Your peace more than You Yourself; now I saw that You Yourself *are* joy and peace, even as You *are* love (1 John 4:16).

Nor was this all that Your great love and grace gave me in reply. You took me back to Psalm 51:12 where I had ended praying it and let me cite verse 13, *"Then will I teach transgressors thy ways, and sinners shall be converted unto thee."* I believed it was Your preview of things to come in the future for Jonathan Wood and me. Though I had spoiled Your intention of keeping him from whatever evil he had been about to commit, You would still use me to help him overcome it. After tasting the bitterness of failing You, I would be doubly careful not to taste it again.

We arrived at the Van Houtens. They gave us the same upstairs room I had called mine while staying with them. We sank into my old firm, comfortable bed wide enough for two and soon slept the deepest, best sleep of our honeymoon trip.

Of course I had not forgotten that the Van Houtens hosted the weekly service of the little Bible Reformed Church in their home, and I made sure we were up and ready for it on Sunday morning. We came downstairs and found them in their roomy kitchen, where I helped Mrs. Van Houten with fixing and serving breakfast. Lisa tried to object and to help herself, but both Mrs. Van Houten and I told her that I must prove I had not forgotten everything she had taught me during my stay with them.

When we sat down to eat, Dr. Van Houten who had watched me said jokingly that I was getting rusty. "You'd better keep in practice, James," he added. "When your baby arrives, Lisa will appreciate your help with cooking and around the home. Let him fix you a meal once in a while, Lisa," he admonished her. "When we were expecting and raising our children, I would always serve Margaret breakfast in bed Saturday mornings and help with other household chores. And it's better for James to give such service than only to receive it all the time."

"He gives me all I need," my dear wife immediately said in my defense, "It was I who felt awkward about his help around the house and insisted that he stick only to taking care of the yard."

"Well, that's good to hear," said Dr. Van Houten. "At least he won't forget all he learned from me while he lived with us. You mustn't let him revert to being fit only for lecturing or writing about philosophy as he was before I took him in hand. A man must be a good steward under our Lord not only of his mind but also of the strength and skill of his body. It's part of his dominion mandate given him at creation, Genesis 1:28."

The church service followed in the living room. All the people were my friends and greeted us with joy. The service and the hymns were familiar to Lisa and to me also since my stay with the Van Houtens, at the end of which I had even served as the group's pianist. The group remembered this and asked me to play for them now. I had not touched a piano since leaving New York and hesitated, but they insisted and I finally did. My joy of doing it again was so strong that I thought about having a piano in our home in Fairfield after our return. I would play and sing all these beautiful old hymns whenever I could. Later our child would learn to play the piano, too, just as my mother had me do as a boy. Once again, dear Father,

I thanked You for all my dear mother had done for me and was sorry for having been so ungrateful to her while she was still on earth.

Dr. Van Houten preached a sermon on First Samuel 8, where Israel asked the prophet Samuel to appoint them a king to judge them so they might be like the other nations around them. Samuel did not like their request and prayed to the Lord, Who told him that the people were not rejecting him, Samuel, but the Lord Himself from being king over them. The Lord also told him to warn the people about what a king would be like. He would take their sons and daughters, the best of their fields and vineyards, their servants and flocks, and their own selves for his own service. *"And ye shall cry out in that day because of your king which ye shall have chosen you; and the LORD will not hear you in that day"* (1 Samuel 8:18). But the people refused to listen.

"And so it has been in our own country for a long time," said Dr. Van Houten. "And so, I am afraid, it will be this coming Tuesday, November 5, 1996, when we must choose our modern king, the President, and other elected officials at the polls. For God's sake we Christians must choose the men who follow biblical precepts most closely. Today a candidate's stand on abortion, the murder of innocent children still in their mothers' wombs legalized by the Supreme Court January 22, 1973, must be the decisive issue for us. Many millions of children have been legally murdered in our country since then. As Christians we dare not endorse anyone who supports abortion. In America we ourselves are the ultimate government according to our Constitution. We must at least be salt and light to our elected government officials. It's part of our dominion mandate under God. I trust every eligible voter among us is registered to vote. Let us faithfully discharge this responsibility under our Lord this coming Tuesday."

Dr. Van Houten's sermon, coming as it did right after our testing by Lisa's mother and hearing the story of Dr. Nathanson from Bernard Gottlieb, persuaded Lisa and me to become much more actively involved in the right to life battle after our return to Fairfield.

7

Probing the Abyss

We flew back to Battle Hill early Monday afternoon and drove back to Fairfield. We had barely arrived at our home and unloaded our luggage when the telephone rang. I answered. It was Dr. Wood. He sounded very perturbed.

"I realize you must just have returned from your trip, James," he said, "but Mary and I are faced with a crisis involving Jonathan. We believe you are the only one we know who can help us, because due to your background you are the only one of his teachers—really the only person we know—Jonathan has ever been drawn to and confided in, as much as he ever confides in anyone. Could we come over in a little while and talk to you? We know he has his next directed readings course meeting with you tomorrow, and we want you to know before you see him what we have just learned. We would really appreciate it."

After talking to Lisa I agreed that they could come in about an hour, which allowed us to hurriedly stash away our suitcases, freshen up, eat a quick snack and have a few moments of rest and prayer to prepare for the meeting. They arrived exactly on time. We sat down together in our living room. With some embarrassment Dr. Wood asked Lisa whether they could talk to me alone. "It's not that we don't trust you to keep what we say in confidence," he explained, "it's only that it would be easier for us to talk if only one person heard us—and it has to be James." Lisa brought us cups of coffee, excused herself and went to her office.

"Already when Jonathan was eleven or twelve and still in our church school," said Dr. Wood, "he began to fight his teachers about every biblical teaching against union or compromise with unbelievers. Because God is merciful, everyone will go to heaven in the end, he argued—the heresy of universalism. Because he is so intelligent, he made the teachers look foolish before the class. Finally the headmaster called us in and told us that unless we could prevail upon Jonathan to change his behavior and give up his universalism, he would have to leave the school. We tried hard but couldn't; all we accomplished was that he refused to discuss his beliefs with us any longer. He transferred to public high school, graduating with honors but no longer a Christian if he ever was one. In public school his universalism was praised as politically completely correct."

"Of course," I agreed, "it's right in line with our culture's belief that all truth is relative and that everyone should be allowed to do his or her own thing." And I helped spread that belief myself until a little over a year ago, I thought ruefully.

"We think," said Mrs. Wood, "that lately he has turned to the occult. He began by saying there are ways to contact the spirit world, and that the pagan religions with their shamans and witch doctors were acquainted with them. He said it meant 'probing the abyss.' The abyss!" She shuddered. "According to Revelation 11 that's hell—the bottomless pit where the evil spirits are. It is so terrible that even the demons themselves whom Jesus cast out from the possessed man in Luke 8 begged Him not to send them there."

"All this," said Dr. Wood, "is only the background to what we really came to tell you. Part of it happened on Halloween night and part of it the night of November 3, this last Sunday. He spent Halloween night in the company of several friends he has made in the Mexican community. He probably met them through Dolly Hernandez, his girl friend whom you met at your wedding reception."

"The pretty, timid little girl," I murmured, "I so much wanted her to feel accepted."

"They were all dressed in black and must have attended an occult ceremony or celebration of some kind," Dr. Wood went on, disregarding my words. "We feared it was part of 'Sonda Infernal,' or 'Probing the Abyss,' a satanic cult widespread among our Mexican population. The next two days he seemed stunned and frightened. We knew something very horrible must have happened at that Halloween party."

"He disliked it when we asked him questions about what he did—he wanted to have total independence and to shut us out of his life," said Mrs. Wood. "But we were so concerned that we asked him anyway. He wouldn't answer at all except to murmur that he had 'probed the abyss.' His face was contorted with horror but also with some resolution slowly forming in his mind. We thought he might be thinking of suicide."

"We had an unavoidable engagement Saturday afternoon," said Dr. Wood, "and had to leave him home by himself from about three to six. We were very afraid and prayed all the time we were gone that he would not kill himself. We thanked our Lord that we found him alive and seemingly better when we came back."

"From three to six Saturday afternoon," I repeated. A great sadness overwhelmed me. It had been right at the time You had urged me to call Jonathan from New York, dear Father, but I had deliberately disregarded Your voice. Yes, You forgave me and restored me to full fellowship with You, but my disobedience had hurt Jonathan, I did not know yet how much, and his good parents whom I loved.

"Why, what's the matter, James?" asked Mrs. Wood. I told them of my omission to call Jonathan Saturday afternoon and asked them to forgive me. They did, adding that it meant much to them to learn that You had remembered them and wanted to help Jonathan through me.

"And now we come to Sunday night," said Dr. Wood. "Again Jonathan's Mexican friends came to pick him up, bringing Dolly Hernandez and a couple of other young women with them. Again the young men were dressed in black from head to foot. They all left in the friends' cars. Again as at Halloween they were gone till way past midnight. This time we sat up waiting for Jonathan to return. They finally dropped him off at our home at about three o'clock this morning. He looked like death warmed over. His face was white as a sheet, his hair tousled wildly, his shirt unbuttoned, leaving his chest uncovered. In the light of our hallway we saw that his pupils were widely dilated—that meant he had taken drugs of some kind. He swayed a little as he walked, as one does with drugs in one's system. 'Where have you been? What happened to you?' we asked, but he wouldn't answer, except to say, 'I was probing the abyss, and it is too deep.'"

"He staggered to his room and didn't come out till this afternoon," added Mrs. Wood. "He was silent and pale. I urged him to eat something, but he wouldn't. 'I can't just eat as though everything was all right,' he told me, 'I did something terrible, and I want to pay for it.' Then Michael came home and we both sat him down and tried again to find out what had happened."

"He said it was too terrible for us to hear," said Dr. Wood. "He said the only person he might talk to about it was you, James. 'He has been there, or at least close enough to it that he will listen without instantly condemning me,' he said. And that's why we are here. Please talk to him and listen to him tomorrow when you see him."

I promised I would. We prayed together. I asked them to pray for me, especially the next morning when Jonathan and I would meet. They seemed to have lighter hearts when they left. When their car pulled out of our driveway, Lisa rejoined me. I told her only that something very bad had happened with Jonathan, and that his parents wanted me to talk to him about it at our next class.

Tuesday, November 5, 1996 arrived. I stopped by our polling place and voted for Robert Dole, the Republican candidate for President, because he opposed legalized abortion. Next on my schedule was the meeting with Jonathan Wood. I realized that I dreaded it. I looked up some Bible passages against anxiety and was especially helped by Hebrews 13:5–6, *"He hath said, 'I will never leave thee, nor forsake thee. So that we may boldly say, 'The Lord is my helper, and I will not fear what man shall do unto me.'"*

I also prayed for a verse to use with Jonathan, recalling what he had told his parents about "probing the abyss." You, dear Father, put verses about "darkness" in my mind for an abyss, a bottomless pit, must be dark beyond imagination. My beloved Gospel of John told me long ago that "the Light—Your life, Lord, which is the light of us men—shineth in darkness, *and the darkness comprehended it not*" (John 1:5).

And then there was the knock of his hand on my door. I said, "Come in" and he entered. I had a strong urge to stand up to welcome him and I did, stretching out my hand to him as I had when he crashed my wedding reception. He looked haggard, and his eyes seemed sunken in their sockets. I thought he might not have eaten, drunk or slept since that horrible Sunday night and its unspeakable secret.

He came nearer, looked at my outstretched hand and shook his head. "You don't want to touch me, Dr. Barron," he said hoarsely, his head bowed.

"Do you want to touch me, Jonathan?" I asked, still standing and keeping my hand within his reach.

At that he lifted up his head. He understood what I meant; if he touched me, I would of necessity touch him as well, and I was willing. Suddenly tears came to his eyes. He took another step forward and grasped my hand.

"Thank you," he said softly, "I know my parents talked to you about me last night. I couldn't tell them what I did because I was too ashamed. I wasn't sure I could tell you either—but now that you let me touch you perhaps I can. After all, you were once probing the abyss too." We let go of each other's hands and sat down at my desk across from each other.

The abyss was hell. I knew well the shame Jonathan now felt—the shame of standing naked in Your sight and recognizing myself as I was while probing it, with my many sins. But I also knew the relief of confessing my sin and seeing it covered by Your blood, dear Jesus Christ, my Savior and Lord. And I knew the liberation of receiving You into my heart, You, my Joy and my Peace, my Goodness and Love.

Jonathan launched into his story. At Halloween he and his friends had gone to the home of a *brujo*, a sorcerer adept in the ways of "Sonda Infernal." They had slaughtered a rooster as a sacrifice to the "god of the abyss," drained its blood and drunk it. They had also decided that they would come together again the third night afterwards, which fell on Sunday, a good omen. They would entice Dolly Hernandez to come with them because she was a virgin. They would give her drugged wine to drink so she would more or less lose consciousness, and then—Jonathan began to weep.

"I drank of that drugged wine, too," he added when he had recovered, "and I waited till Dolly was spaced out enough that she hardly knew what she was doing. Then she let me have sex with her, but I had no joy in it because it was just physical. Where was our real love for each other? By the time we drove home I was horrified at what I had done." He looked at me in despair. "My little Dolly," he whispered, "how can I ever look her in the face again? I threw my love—my very first love in my life—into the abyss. It was a sacrifice to Satan all right. I probed the abyss and it was too deep. I have sunk too deep ever to come out of it again."

"But you can," I said, "our God is not the god who eats the flesh of bulls or drinks the blood of goats or roosters. The true sacrifice a covenant with Him requires is the blood of His Son Jesus Christ, and He has shed it for you and me. You have been taught the Bible. You know the Gospel. You have heard it many times. Call on Him in your terrible trouble. He will deliver you, and you will glorify Him." You gave me Psalm 50:5, 8, 13 and 15 for this hour.

"I have never heard the Gospel presented like this," he said, "starting with Psalm 50. The blood sacrifices of the Old Testament really point to Christ! Jesus Christ is the Lamb of God, which takes away the sin of the world—John 1:29. Chapters 9 and 10 of Hebrews about Christ as both our sacrifice and our high priest clearly confirm it. Yes, I see that now."

"And now make *your* covenant with Him by *His* sacrifice," I said. "Do it now." He nodded. I led him in prayer to You to forgive him his sins and grant him Your salvation in Your Son Jesus Christ for the sake of His sacrifice of Himself for us. I praise You, dear loving Father Who abundantly pardons, that Jonathan said it with me from a penitent, believing heart. I promised to stand by him as he began his new life. We hugged each other as brothers in You, and he went on his way comforted.

8

Dwelling with the Consuming Fire

"Wherefore we receiving a kingdom which cannot be moved, let us have grace, whereby we may serve God acceptably with reverence and godly fear: For our God is a consuming fire."—Hebrews 12:28–29

You made me Jonathan's mentor in the faith, then, Father, and it was the holiest and hardest service to which You called me since my conversion. I had to teach him to dwell with You, the Consuming Fire. It was possible only if I dwelt there myself moment by moment.

I have said earlier that my conversion had struck me like a bolt of lightning. Now I understood more deeply what You did in me then and continue to do in me now. The moment I finally said yes to You, You the Holy Spirit, the Consuming Fire of Isaiah 33:14 and Hebrews 12:29, entered my heart and consumed the core of my old rebellious nature all at once. Now You dwell within me, and I willingly submit to You moment by moment and welcome Your purifying burning, the sure proof that You truly love me. For unless Your true love were burning away my dross and thus perfecting Your purity in me, how could You and I ever dwell together?

I understood all this also from my own lack of love for my own children. I proved that I did not love them by allowing them their lawless "freedom" so I could pursue my own selfish goals undisturbed. If I had truly loved them, I would have brought them up to know, love and obey Your holy and just law, for obeying it from the heart is man's true and perfect freedom.

Dear Father, I prayed, please help me to be there for Jonathan, just as You are always there for me. May I truly love him as You love me. Let me never tolerate any wrong beliefs in his mind and any wrong desires in his heart just because tolerating them would be easier for me than laboring to correct them. And be patient with me and keep burning away any wrong in me which might stand in the way of Your love for him.

I called on Dr. and Mrs. Wood to tell them that my meeting with Jonathan had led to his genuine profession of faith. They were overjoyed but also asked whether I had learned from him what had happened to him at Halloween and the following Sunday. I said I had, and that a satanic ritual of "Sonda Infernal" had taken place which involved both Jonathan and Dolly Hernandez. However, I thought Jonathan himself should be the first to tell them the details when he was ready. I also said that what had happened ought to be reported to the authorities, and that Dolly might have done so. "I will counsel him to ask you to forgive him for all the grief he has caused you," I said, "I will also assure him that you will do so, based on your gentleness with me, Dr. Wood, when I applied for the appointment to the faculty." Dr. Wood smiled in remembrance, and he and Mrs. Wood nodded in agreement. They hoped that I could establish some sort of mentoring relationship with their son. I felt honored, thanked them for their confidence in me and promised I would never encroach on their God-given parental authority.

I then set regular weekly times for Jonathan and me to study the Bible and grow in the faith together. We met in my home in the early evening. I liked it that Lisa would be nearby. I could hear her steps in the kitchen and the homely sounds of pots and dishes being stashed away as she tidied up after dinner. Occasionally she would have to walk through our living room and wave to me with a loving smile.

Lisa also faithfully prayed for me and Jonathan while we met and our meetings went well. Just as I had been irresistibly hungry and thirsty for the Bible after my conversion, so now was he. He began to attend our church regularly. He asked me about my devotional practices, especially prayer, told me he would do the same, and I could tell he really did. Because he had been conscientiously brought up in the faith by both his parents and in his Bible-believing church, it took him much less time than it had taken me in my early Christian walk to memorize, or memorize again, many Bible passages and to recall them as needed in our study.

In our third mentoring meeting in late November I confessed to him my omission to call him from New York the Saturday before his descent into the abyss and asked his forgiveness. I did this to show him that I too was a sinner saved only by Your grace and needed Your consuming fire to burn away my sins just as he did. I had noticed that he was beginning to develop a sort of hero worship of me and wanted to stop it. He must never think of me more highly than he ought to, for his own sake and for mine as well. I also wanted to show him by my example that we must never shun the shame of confessing our sins to God and to each other, for only thus can we put them and their shame behind us.

"You have been so good to me, Dr. Barron," said Jonathan, "why would I need to forgive you for anything? Besides, I would probably have gone ahead anyway."

"All my other goodness does not cover this particular sin I committed against you, and against God too," I answered, "just as the ninety-nine percent of purity of a poisonous plant do not cover the one percent of poison in it. We must not minimize our sins because we have not sinned in other respects and as if that excused us. We need to confess them to Him."

"Still," Jonathan said, "I don't think your phone call would have kept me from—" he stopped. The memory was still too raw and painful for him to put into spoken words, and perhaps always would be.

"You had free will to listen to me or not," I agreed, "but that's not the point now. God told me to warn you as He told the prophet Ezekiel to warn Israel. God said that if he did not warn the wicked and the wicked did not turn from his wickedness he would die in his sin, but God would require his blood from Ezekiel. On the other hand, if he warned the wicked and he would not turn from his wicked way, he would die but Ezekiel would have delivered his soul—Ezekiel 3:18–21. I did not warn you and therefore I have a part in what you did. I have confessed it to God and He forgave me, but I hurt you too by my neglect and ask your forgiveness. Please forgive me."

Jonathan looked at me in silence for a while before he hesitantly answered, "I forgive you gladly, Dr. Barron, if you insist, but you didn't need to—have to—lower yourself before me like this. I don't want you to be ashamed because . . ." He stopped, embarrassed.

"Because you like me and don't want to hurt my feelings," I said gently. He nodded with a smile. "But you see, Jonathan, when we truly like, or I should say love, another person, we sometimes *must* hurt their feelings. It comes out in small things, like telling them there is a dirt spot on their face. If we love them, we want them to be clean. How else can they wipe it off?" I stopped to let him take this in and then went on, "Other dirt spots are deeper and bigger, like mine before you now. Suppose you had found out in some other way that I had not warned you.

You could have told me then that if only I had warned you, you would not have done it. As a matter of fact, that's a real possibility, isn't it? You keep saying you would have done it anyway, but you don't really know that, do you? You have free will and either choice was open to you. Therefore the person who could warn another but doesn't, bears part of the responsibility for the other's wrong choice. God Himself lovingly and faithfully gave us His law and warns us over and over again against choosing what is wrong. If He did not, He Himself would be at least partly to blame for our sins."

"I always hated to have to tell my parents about anything I had done wrong," Jonathan mused, "because I hated so much to be ashamed before them." He actually shuddered at the thought. "Why does God insist that we feel so much shame about admitting our sins?"

"The shame isn't some extra punishment He lays upon us," I answered. "It's just part of seeing ourselves as He sees us, as sinners, which is as we really are without Him." I stopped, remembering my shame when You struck down my pride by making me see the worthlessness of my loveless self compared to Sylvia's unconditional love. And yet, I thought with joyful gratitude, my shame was immeasurably truer and better than all my previous self-esteem!

I continued, "Without acknowledging our sins and accepting the shame that comes with them, and without His forgiveness and cleansing, we can't have fellowship with Him. He can't have joy in us as long as they are not confessed and dealt with. If you love Him truly, you can't bear not being in full fellowship with Him. Compared to that, shame is as nothing! That's true in principle for our fellowship with other people too, like between you and your parents."

I prayed Jonathan would see this when he now asked somewhat stubbornly: "Don't you hate being ashamed even more than having wronged someone? Don't you wish to be forgiven without having to humiliate yourself? Can't God be generous enough—merciful enough—loving enough to spare us the shame?"

"It's not possible," I answered. "He would have to spare us the indispensable godly sorrow over our sins *'which worketh repentance unto salvation,'* 2 Corinthians 7:10. The shame is part of this godly sorrow, its cutting edge if you will. God is generous, merciful, and loving enough not to spare us the shame." I noticed that Lisa had quietly slipped into the room and remained silently standing inside the door listening.

As to our shame before other people, I remembered George MacDonald's teaching that we should be willing to bow our heads in hearty shame when we rightly ought to be ashamed. For MacDonald to be ashamed was a holy and blessed thing! Shame was shameful only to those who want to *seem* righteous, not to those who want to *be* righteous. He had deplored that people grieve over the defilement to themselves and the shame of it before others instead of hastening to make the confession and amends due them. He urged us to forget our own selves and our disgrace, and instead to turn our eyes to our Lord's glory, the only thing which can produce Christ-likeness in us. I repeated it all to Jonathan and told him to think it over.

I finally asked him outright that day, as I had hinted since the day of his conversion, whether he had talked to Dolly Hernandez and asked for her forgiveness. He stared at me as though I had taken leave of my senses.

"Talked to Dolly!" he repeated, aghast, "no way! I can't ever look her in the face again."

"Well, then," I amended, "at least write her and ask her to forgive you. That's what I should have done after I got a girl pregnant when I was seventeen. Instead I broke off all contact with her, totally abandoned her, and later our baby, a little boy whom she gave up for adoption. She said he looked like me. I couldn't have cared less then." I added regretfully, "Now I would be glad to know where he is and how he is doing. Maybe I have grandchildren through him whom I will never know. Your father knows the story. You can ask him about it some time. Anyway, write Dolly. Ask her to forgive you. It isn't right to just drop her as though she were to blame for what happened."

He picked up on only one thing in all I said. "My God," he murmured, staring past me, his voice filled with horror, "what if Dolly got pregnant by what I did? It's nearly a month since it happened. She might know by now, mightn't she? You are right, Dr. Barron. I must contact her right away. What if she is? What should we do then?"

I put my hand on his shoulder to calm him. "First of all," I said, "we must pray. Our heavenly Father loves us all. We must trust Him. He will make our darkness light before us and show us the right way." Lisa now joined us and we all prayed together. I know You were there and heard us.

9

Bioethics; A Painful Illness; An Unexpected Joy

In the fall semester of 1996 a surprisingly large number of students had enrolled in my ethics class with emphasis on bioethics. I encouraged them to ask questions, and to my delight they avidly took me up on it. Not only birth control and abortion but also passive and active euthanasia, withdrawal of life support, the triage type rationing of expensive advanced medical care, the emerging concept of "futile care" and the use of cloning techniques for the future practice of medicine were in the news almost daily. I had to do extensive reading of the latest philosophical articles, most of which were in favor of what I began to think of as our society's new "death culture." In addition I tried to keep up with the latest news in the field of medicine to satisfy my students' curiosity. I also followed political developments relating to bioethical issues.

I paid special attention to the voices raised in the Christian community about these matters. At least I did not have to bother about the anti-Christian opinions of the liberal, Bible-rejecting "pro-choice" leadership of mainline Protestantism.

Our Bible Wesleyan denomination, having separated from it long ago, published a blanket condemnation of its public pronouncements about bioethics. All I had to do was to hand out copies of this condemnation to all my students, read it to them and enjoin them to remember and comply with it. I was in total, heartfelt, emphatic agreement with this policy and made it a point to say so repeatedly in my class.

On the other hand, I found that among professing Christian groups the Roman Catholic Church provided the most active, consistent and uncompromising public defense of the God-given right to life of innocent human beings from conception to natural death, the orthodox biblical position through history. Catholics had led the fight against legalized abortion already years before the Supreme Court's January 22, 1973 Roe v. Wade decision sanctioning abortion. The only major difference between the Catholic stand on bioethics issues and that of our denomination was that we took no official position on birth control while the Roman Catholic Church allowed only natural family planning.

I thought long and hard about this issue. Bernard Gottlieb had told Lisa and me when we visited him after our Toronto trip and after our run-in with Mrs. Trent, that in Scripture children were always welcomed with joy as a gift from You, dear Father. We had unreservedly opened ourselves to You in trust and hope, which You rewarded with giving us our child. Had this merely been our private desire, or was it not rather Your norm for everyone professing the name of Christ as the Catholic Church taught? Actually every Christian church had taught the same until the Church of England broke ranks with them all at its Lambeth Conference of 1931 and made common cause with Margaret Sanger and her "planned parenthood" (barrenhood?) cohorts around the world.

I prayed about it, but not for long. I saw almost immediately that I really knew what Your answer was. If we were not just talkers about holiness, if we really meant business about entrusting our whole selves to You, if we were truly dwelling in mutual love with You the Consuming Fire, then You must have all of us with nothing held back, including our bodies' ability to beget and bear children within lifelong biblical marriage. From henceforth I would hold this position, live it out day by day, and defend it when asked by others as I had now put it into words in my mind and heart.

My reading preparation for the class often kept me up deep into the night. In addition I was teaching my other large class on the history of Western philosophy and four one on one directed readings tutorials besides the one with Jonathan Wood. Of course I continued my weekly mentoring session with him. It often drained my last mental and emotional reserves of the day because we were still struggling against his fascination with pantheism and universalism and concerned about what might come of what he had done to Dolly Hernandez. There was the new campus philosophy club which met only once a month but required my presence and occasional advice. This should have been more than enough work, but I had begun to be invited to give my testimony before area churches, radio programs and civic clubs, and felt I should not refuse. After all, these invitations allowed me to speak out against my former godless ideas and actions!

Lisa began to be concerned about my busy schedule, my sleep deprivation, and my inner tension which slowly mounted as I was turning into a workaholic. She warned me about it, but it seemed to me there was no way to avoid it if I wanted to do the very best job I could. I see now as I look back, I perversely prided myself on how much I was doing for You, dear Father, and how well I did it all. I totally disregarded Your gentle, loving call to Your apostles and to me through my wife to *"come apart and rest a while"* (Mark 6:31). I disregarded Dad Trent's diffident request that I give my peace to Lisa because I was not prizing my peace as Your gift and was gradually losing it. I was sliding back into the extreme busyness of my godless days as my chosen identity under the pretense of being very zealous in Your service. I was actually serving my own self-esteem, but I did not see it.

You in Your love and mercy had to pull me out of this blind alley, dear Father. You had to do it in such a way that I could not resist You, could not fail to see what I had been doing, would never forget Your chastisement, and would never do again what I had done. A few days before the Christmas break, You allowed me to be struck with a short but extremely painful illness.

I woke up that morning with what seemed like an incipient cold and did not pay much attention. I went to my classes and tutorials as usual. In the evening I had a slight fever. I took aspirin, tried to force myself to do some reading anyway, but my head ached and I gave it up. I slept very little during the night, for I felt hot and sick. I awoke around three o'clock with a burning pain across my face. I got up and checked myself in the bathroom mirror. A line of strange spots had erupted on my face, running from the left side of my forehead across my left cheek down to my mouth and chin. The spots were covered with ugly brownish scabs. They also burned like fire so intense that I moaned with the searing pain, worse than any I had ever felt in my life. I tried to soothe the pain with a little cold water on my fingers; it would help for the fraction of a moment, then burn again as strongly as before. What was it?

Lisa had woken up and joined me in the bathroom. She took one look at me and said with pity, "Shingles." She told me one of her siblings had had it at the age of fifteen. It is caused by the same virus which produces chickenpox, a fairly harmless childhood disease. The virus then lies dormant in the spine and may reemerge as shingles if the body's immune system is compromised by too much stress.

"We'll call our doctor in the morning," Lisa said comfortingly, "you'll need a prescription for a good strong painkiller. You'll have to stay home and cancel whatever engagements you have till Christmas. Thank God the scabs will be gone before Christmas is here!" She seemed on the point of saying more, but she caught herself and stopped. Some surprise about Christmas, I thought, but I didn't go into it. All I could concentrate on was the awful burning pain across my face and pray that it might lessen. I spent the rest of that night awake in an armchair in our living room so at least Lisa could get some rest.

Lisa got some strong painkiller for me the next morning but it only dulled the pain. I would have paid almost any price to have had a better one. I go into all this so thoroughly to remind myself never to risk having shingles again by my own stress-causing behavior. I had ample time during my enforced rest to think about what I had done. I came to understand that I had not walked with You hand in hand but run ahead of You out of self-will and ambition, a form of self-centeredness next to pride, which I must never again allow in my life.

Only two more sessions of my classes and tutorials were left before Christmas. I had already prepared homework assignments for them which Lisa transmitted when she called the university to inform them of my illness. Two days later we received huge get-well cards from each of my large classes signed by all my students, telling me they missed me and were looking forward to seeing me all well again after the break. We also received similar individual cards from my tutorial students. It did me good to know that they all thought me a good teacher and liked me personally, but now I took care not to take pride in it as if it were due only to me. Let me never forget again that You, dear Father, are the author and perfecter of whatever is good in me, including my teaching ability!

Jonathan visited me the last day of school. He showed me a letter he had written to Dolly, but it had been returned to him with a post office stamp saying that its delivery had been refused. How could he now get in touch with her? He dreaded to go to her home in person but was considering calling her on the phone or seeking her out at the Fairfield Business College where she was taking secretarial courses. I encouraged him to try any one of these options as soon as possible.

I asked him whether he had told his parents anything at all about what had happened. He said no but asked whether I would I be willing to come with him and help him talk to them. I said yes. We set a date between Christmas and New Year to do so.

Lisa got more and more mysterious and could hardly stop smiling as Christmas drew near. The day before Christmas a furniture delivery truck stopped before our home. Lisa was there to welcome the burly men knocking at our door and to direct them as they trundled in a beautiful upright piano and helped settle it in its permanent place in our living room. I recognized it; it had been my parents' and I had practiced on it as a boy.

Lisa told me it was a Christmas gift from Robert, Neva, and herself. "I watched you closely when you played the piano and sang the hymns at the Van Houtens," she said, "and saw how much you loved it. I talked to your family about it and we all agreed you should have your childhood piano, which they weren't using anyway. My contribution was to have a few keys repaired, to have it transported here from Lonely Prairie and later tuned. Now you can play and sing to your heart's content any time you want." She hugged and kissed me.

I could hardly speak to say thank you. I walked over to the old instrument and softly played a few chords. All about this gift spoke to me of Your love which had lain over and around me since my childhood. "And that's not the only Christmas gift you will get this year," Lisa said happily, "a much, much better one is on the way! You will get it on Christmas Day."

Christmas Day came. Our little Christmas tree sparkled in its multicolored ornaments. Our baby could now easily be seen under Lisa's clothes and felt moving in her body. We got up late, had a light breakfast and were unwrapping Christmas gifts. Lisa seemed to be listening for something outside off and on all morning. She perked up when a car entered our driveway. We heard its doors slam shut, the chatter of voices of adults and children, and steps on our sidewalk. Then there was a knock on our door.

"Go open it, James," my wife said with her most mischievous smile. I did. Outside stood a handsome, tall, slender dark-haired man in his thirties, a lovely blonde lady obviously his wife carrying a cute baby in her arms, and two children of elementary school age who were looking up at me with timid smiles. I noticed that he wore a little cross in the lapel of his coat.

"Merry Christmas, Dr. Barron," the man said, "I am Luke Albertson, and this is my family and really your family too. Albertson is the name of my adoptive parents who brought me up. Dorrie Fisher was my birth mother, and you are my birth father. If I may, I would like to call you Dad."

They say a college professor never runs out of words, but they are wrong. I stood there speechless, nailed to the spot, totally overcome by surprise and joy. Lisa realized she needed to take over the speaking for both of us.

"Come in," she said to our guests, "we are so glad you could come!" She turned to me. "Yes, James," she said, "a while ago I overheard you tell Jonathan that you wished you could know what had happened to your son from Dorrie Fisher, and that maybe you had grandchildren you would never know. Well, I wasn't the only one who heard you. God heard you too. And so He had me meet Luke at a Christian broadcasters' conference soon afterwards. I noticed how much he looks like you. So I asked him about his background and found out he was adopted. He checked his adoption records. And sure enough, he turned out to be your son and wanted to meet you! Isn't our Lord wonderful?"

"Yes, He is," I said and hugged my firstborn son for the first time in my life.

10

More About my Son; Helping Dolly Hernandez

My son, his wife Sarah with baby Martha asleep in her arms, and my grandchildren John and Lydia came in and sat down with us in our living room. Soon we adults were talking away at a great rate trying to bring each other up to date on our lives as quickly as possible. John, nine years old, and Lydia, six, were listening with rapt attention. Occasionally they politely contributed little details their parents had overlooked in telling Lisa and me their family story. They were bright and well behaved, taking part in our fellowship without becoming obnoxious. As I looked at my grandson, I saw with pleasure that my mother's good looks which Luke and I had inherited and which had helped Lisa bring us together had also come down to John. I praised You, dear Father, for Your trans-generational design for us laid down when You had us in mind before the creation of the world!

I asked Luke and Sarah where John and Lydia attended school. "Right in our own home," Sarah answered with a smile, "we have home-schooled them since they were five years old." "It's more and more the custom now with Christian parents," Luke added, "and it's catching on in Mexico too for Christian believers. Public schools are certainly not neutral but becoming more and more blatantly anti-Christian. Their evolutionist indoctrination alone is reason enough for us to avoid them."

"That indoctrination began in earnest when I was in junior high school," I reminisced, "it was the major means by which I was brought to my former self-centered, amoral, atheist philosophy. I am glad you have a way out of it, even though it demands a lot of work and commitment from you."

"We received the right values and commitment from our parents," Luke said. "They put us children first and set a good example for us." Of course he was speaking of his adoptive parents. I, his birth father, had never done anything for him and could not help but be hurt when I heard him praise them, knowing that they deserved his gratitude and I did not. Nevertheless, I thanked You with all my heart because You had amply made up for my neglect.

The Salvation Army, which had arranged my son's adoption, had chosen his adoptive parents well. They lived in a state next to ours in the Midwest and were dedicated believers. They had led him to You when he was five years old. His father was a school teacher and an elder in their Baptist church. Luke had committed himself to full-time Christian service in his early teens, attended a Christian college where he majored in Spanish, and a missionary training institute learning all about radio communications. He had met and married Sarah there, and she was as sold out to You as was he.

They had served as missionaries in several Latin American countries and finally settled in Mexico. They loved the Mexican people. They also told us that evangelical Christians were persecuted for the faith by the local caciques in the Mexican state of Chiapas. They were surprised and pleased that we had already learned this fact from Fairfield University's unique department offering a degree program for the study of the severe persecution of Christians around the world today (some 160,000 to 200,000 of us are killed every year, chiefly in Muslim and Communist countries).

The one great grief in Luke and Sarah's lives had been the miscarriage of a child they had been expecting between Lydia and baby Martha. "We would have loved so much to have and raise that child," Sarah said softly, "but we trust we will see him in heaven. I think of the child as 'him' and call him David in my mind, though of course it might have been a little girl. I still grieve for him." I had never realized or even thought about the deep, lasting pain of losing a child by miscarriage; now I wondered how Lisa and I would feel if we lost our much desired child in that way and knew that it would be almost unbearable! Luke tenderly took Sarah's hand in his. I was blessed to see how close and loving they were in their marriage.

Luke had served for several years as director of a Christian missionary radio station in Mexico City. He had done every kind of evangelistic outreach from street evangelism to decision counseling to being a traveling preacher on evangelistic tours. He had also counseled people in family crisis situations. Right now he was back in the Midwest on furlough and fundraising travels to support the ministry under which he served. He would return to Mexico City in May 1997.

Lisa had already told Luke before his visit that I had been the famous atheist philosopher James Barron until my conversion just a year and a half ago, and she had described the most important milestones of my life as a Christian. Thus we could discuss our current Christian concerns with each other without having to delve into my past. Luke told me of the needs of his ministry, chiefly for financial support but also for young people who might come to Mexico on short term missionary trips to help with hands-on labor projects of various kinds. I hoped I would be able to recruit some of them among Fairfield University students. In exchange I told him the outline of what had happened with Jonathan Wood and Dolly Hernandez. We brainstormed together for a while about how to help them.

"Do you know yet whether Dolly is pregnant?" he asked. I explained that thus far Jonathan's attempts to contact her had been fruitless.

"That's not so good," he said. "If she is pregnant, she may well want to abort the baby as soon as possible so her parents and family will not find out about it. In their culture shame before family and friends in a situation like this is overwhelming. Dolly would also desperately want to hide the fact that she was enticed by false friends to attend a satanic ceremony and then drugged and seduced to have sex by Jonathan whom she had loved and trusted. If she is pregnant and he wants to stand by her, as of course he should now that he is a Christian, he has no time to lose."

"He wrote her a while ago," I said, "but the letter was returned to him marked 'delivery refused.' He thinks she simply wants nothing more to do with him—and no wonder. He is heartbroken about it and afraid just as you and I are that she may have an abortion if there is a baby. I am sure he is willing to do whatever it takes to stop that from happening."

"Can he talk to his parents about it?" asked Luke.

"He will if I come with him," I answered. "We have set a time to do that this coming Saturday afternoon."

"What you need to establish," said Luke with the practical common sense due to his past counseling experience, "is, first, whether Dolly is pregnant, and second, what exactly Jonathan and his parents are ready and willing to do to help her. The Old Testament deals with situations like theirs in Exodus 22:16–17 and Deuteronomy 22:28–29. When rape of an innocent girl is involved, the man must make a payment equal to her dowry to her parents, or he must marry and stay with her for life. Since Dolly does not want to have anything to do with Jonathan any more—"

"—and Jonathan is too ashamed to meet her again either," I interjected,

"—it seems to me that the first alternative is the only feasible one," concluded

Luke.

He came up with another suggestion. We had a pro-life group in Fairfield which offered pregnancy testing free of charge. Dolly might seek its services. Why not ask the volunteer staff to let her know that there were friends who knew her personally, cared for her and stood ready to help her? He suggested that I could be the contact person, and my phone number could be given to Dolly along with this information. For that matter, Luke added, could I not ask Jonathan for Dolly's phone number and take the initiative in calling her myself to talk the whole matter over with her?

I considered it and thought that though she would not talk to Jonathan, she might well talk to me. I remembered her timid glance pleading for my acceptance and her whispered "thank you" at my wedding reception; I was sure she would remember me and not reject me out of hand. I saw that both these proposals, the second more surely than the first, would make me a catalyst or key person in bringing the drama of Jonathan and Dolly to a conclusion in accordance with Your good will. I instantly understood all this as Your call to me, dear Father, and knew I must not shirk it. I told Luke I would implement both his suggestions right away.

Finally, Luke and I agreed that we had to do all we could to stop Dolly from going through with an abortion, for that would only add the guilt of the sin of murder to what already weighed on her mind and heart. As a last resort we must be there and appeal to her one last time to let her baby live if and when she was about to enter the notorious abortion center in Battle Hill run by Dr. Derek Hellmann. His "Women's Drive-Through Clinic" was the only abortion place in our region. Hellmann did abortions at any stage of pregnancy on Fridays and Saturdays every week. A number of pro-life volunteers, including myself, kept vigil at the entrance to his facility, much harassed by his so-called security guards who dressed in black shirts with pictures of bright red and yellow flames and called themselves "Escorts from Hell." We prayed, held up posters with slogans like "Abortion Kills Babies," handed out tracts explaining how abortions were done and how they could permanently hurt women, leaflets listing Bible passages against abortion, and informing Hellmann's prospective clients what help was available to women with problem pregnancies so they could give birth to their babies. Each week one or two babies were saved from death by our efforts, and a continuing testimony was given to the community.

I had driven to Battle Hill alone or sometimes with Lisa to take part in these vigils on about a dozen Saturdays since our wedding. I did it in part to practice what I taught my students, in part impelled by the memory of my daughter Ecstasy, who had died from a botched abortion done on my order. Luke thought that from now on till his return to Mexico, he and his family could drive across the state line one Saturday each month to join us in front of the Hellmann clinic to help us demonstrate and save some babies—perhaps including Dolly's. We could provide pictures of Dolly to the other volunteers so they could recognize her and make a special effort to keep her from entering the clinic if we ourselves were not there.

At about this time a delicious smell of good food came to us from the kitchen.

Lisa had bought a fully prepared turkey dinner from our grocery store the day before and it was now heated up and ready to serve. We moved to our dining room and took our places around the dinner table.

I asked Luke to say the blessing, but he insisted with respect that I do it as his father and our host. I loved my son for granting me this respect and silently thanked You for it. Then I thanked You aloud, dear Father, for having preserved us and brought us together in Your great love and mercy to me after all these years. I thanked you for making us all believers so we could wholeheartedly rejoice in one another both as an earthly reunited family and as part of Your heavenly family, united forever. I thanked You for the children You had given us, including the little one in Lisa's womb and the little one already with You in heaven. I thanked You that You had made us kings and priests with You to serve You in Your Kingdom which is not of this world, to intercede for others and to show forth Your excellent virtues to them in Your love. I thanked You for the good food before us, for the hands that had prepared it ahead of the Christmas holiday, and for my dear wife who had so providently planned our reunion and this meal. "We pray it in the Name of Your dear Son Jesus Christ, Amen," I ended, and my whole family said "Amen" in reply.

We all were hungry and ate our fill. To top it all off, Lisa had bought gifts as from both of us for Luke and his family which she now brought in from her office with Sarah's help. Having the advantage over me of having raised a child, she had known what my grandchildren would like, and they did. I looked on happily as they were unwrapping their gifts. Lastly, as the afternoon sun was sinking in the west, we decided to end our time together with singing the old beloved Christmas songs for the last time this season. Sarah could have played them on our piano, but she turned to me and asked me to accompany us as we sang. "Lisa told us how much you love to play and sing the old hymns," she said, "please, Dad Barron, do it for us now. We want to remember it this way whenever we think of this wonderful day." So I did, and the old familiar music and the old familiar words about You our Immanuel, our God with us and our Savior, lingered in our hearts when we finally took leave of one another, knowing we would meet again soon.

11

Being There for Dolly Hernandez

I got up early the next morning to read my Bible with special attention and to pray. I was going to tell Jonathan that I believed Dolly Hernandez would let me talk to her, to ask him for her telephone number and to call her so we might meet face to face. What I was proposing to do might influence all her life. I knew I must never undertake such a crucial task without Your full direction and constant presence. Only You the Consuming Fire could burn her clean from false shame and from choosing the grave sin of destroying her child.

I also fasted that morning before You, dear Father. It is sometimes necessary to defeat an especially cunning or persistent spiritual attack (Matthew 17:21). I believe this is why you had me do it then in preparation for what followed.

Isaiah 58 with its clear teaching about false and true fasting came to my mind. The fast You choose includes, among other concerns, *"that thou hide not thyself from thine own flesh"* (verse 7). What else is abortion but our hiding ourselves from our own flesh? I decided to use this verse with Dolly Hernandez if needed.

Dolly remembered me from my kindness to her at my wedding reception and was willing to talk to me. She asked me to pick her up at the back entrance of the Fairfield Business College early that afternoon and added very softly that I should bring her to my home where we could talk unobserved. I told her my wife would be with us or nearby. "I don't mind you and your wife knowing about it—just other people," she almost whispered, the "it" including all that had happened to her. I thought she was afraid that some family member might overhear her as she took the phone call.

I met Dolly as directed and we soon arrived at my home. We sat down opposite each other in the living room. Lisa greeted us and offered to bring us hot chocolate and cookies. I thanked her and said that would be nice. We remained silent until she had brought us the snacks and left.

Dolly looked around the room, then back at me, and began to speak. Her first words to me were quite unexpected. "You live very simply, don't you, Dr. Barron," she said, sounding surprised, "your house isn't so different from ours. The only thing you have that we haven't is your piano. You could be living next door to us."

I understood that the simplicity of our lifestyle increased Dolly's trust in me. "We got the piano only a couple of days ago," I explained, "it used to belong to my parents. My family in Lonely Prairie and my wife gave it to me as a Christmas gift."

"I heard your brother is in the construction business," she said. She must have heard it from Jonathan who might have heard it from his father. "My dad worked construction before he died." She looked at me in mute appeal, expecting me to read as it were between the lines of her words. Help me understand her rightly, Father, I prayed. Then I understood: somehow she wanted me to be for her like the father she had lost. Poor timid lost little girl, I thought, what rightful authority and support have you had to lean on in your life?

I thought with a pang of terror that I was the last person on earth who could function as a substitute father for Dolly. As Mrs. Trent had shouted at me, my past record as a father was despicable to say the least. I cannot do this, Father! I cried out in my heart. You answered me with the truth of Galatians 2:20: *"You, the old despicable you, have been crucified with Christ. It is no longer you who live, but Christ lives in you; and the life which you now live in the flesh you live by faith in the Son of God, Who loved you and gave Himself for you."* You added the encouragement of Philippians 4:13, *"You can do all things through Christ Who strengthens you."*

I gently said to Dolly: "You must have had a very good father to work so hard for you. He must have loved you and your family very much."

Dolly nodded. A sweet, sunny little smile appeared on her lips. "Yes, he did," she confirmed, "and he didn't go and spend his wages on liquor or gambling or women like a lot of other men. He was always there for us. He would always have a bit of candy for us when we were little. He could fix anything that was broken around the house."

Suddenly she broke down crying uncontrollably. Her whole body shook with her sobs. I waited silently till her weeping slowed down and finally ceased. She pulled a couple of tissues from a pocket in her slacks and dried her face.

"I am sorry, Dr. Barron," she said, "I didn't mean to cry. It's just that—just that—" She stopped. Her face crumpled up as if she was going to cry again.

"It's just that you have needed to cry for a long time," I said as tenderly as I could. "Now you have finally been able to cry, and if you want to, you can tell me why. At least I can listen, and maybe I can even help."

She looked at me with some hesitation, but her trust in me overcame it. "I will tell you everything," she agreed. "I haven't had anyone to whom I could talk about it." She said bitterly, "Not my mother, and not my older sisters! They always think that if anything bad happens to me, it must be my fault. Not my girl friends either! They would only gossip about it and it would get back to my family. Certainly not a social worker from the government social services! The government would stick its nose into our lives and tell us what to do."

"Have you reported what happened to the police?" I asked. "A crime was committed against you. The community should be warned of this satanic cult."

"No!" exclaimed Dolly with fear, "I will never report it to the police! You mustn't either! They would find out some of our relatives are illegal immigrants. We can't risk it. And 'Sonda Infernal' is dangerous! They might murder me and my family."

After pausing for breath she resumed, "I couldn't even tell our priest. I didn't confess anything to him because I believe I was innocent. Yes, I let Jonathan go ahead with what he wanted. He didn't rape me. But I was drugged from that wine!"

Her eyes widened in horror. "I never really understood it till now," she said, "dear God, that's what their 'probing the abyss' really is! Turning everything upside down. Like the upside down crosses they had in their meeting place. Like saying the Lord's Prayer backwards. Like the words of a British sorcerer named Aleister Crowley which they repeated like a chant, 'Do what thou wilt shall be the whole of the law.' That really means there is no law! Like trampling on consecrated communion wafers when they can get hold of them or steal them. That's why they dress all in black when they go there. It was 'Sonda Infernal'! Black is the devil's color. It says in the Bible that at the final judgment the damned souls will be cast into the blackness of darkness for ever." I thought that the Scripture she might have in mind was Jude 13.

When she quoted Aleister Crowley, I saw more clearly than ever that in principle my own past "probing the abyss" had been just the same as his. I had not worshiped upside down crosses, burned black candles or stomped on communion wafers, but I had trampled on every norm of goodness You, Father and Lord, hold dear, and I had taught others to do so. What better capsule description could there be for my former philosophy and indeed for the beliefs and practices of our whole contemporary death culture than the satanic "do what thou wilt shall be the whole of the law"?

Dolly sighed. "I am sorry," she said. "I haven't told this very well, have I? I'll start over and tell you what happened in order from start to finish." She settled herself more comfortably in her armchair. This time she spoke dryly as though reporting on something which did not concern her at all. She began with Jonathan and his Mexican friends picking her up that Sunday night, bringing her to a house in west Fairfield painted all black inside, with lighted black candles as the only lights and the smell of incense everywhere. She had actually been looking forward to it.

"It was like some sort of strange party at first," Dolly said. "They gave me wine to drink that made me woozy very quickly. I recognized that they were trying to make me unconscious. That's when I should have gotten away from them! But I was still so stupid that I thought it was all a game. They were Jonathan and his friends. Surely they wouldn't do any harm to me! But they did." The rest of her story matched what Jonathan had told me earlier.

"You should report it to the police, Dolly," I urged again, "what Jonathan and his friends did should not go unpunished. Perhaps I should report it."

She bowed her head. "I don't want Jonathan punished," she whispered forlornly. "Deep down something in me said yes to him. Besides," she reiterated more loudly, raising her head, "we just can't risk it! And if it went to court, *I* would be the one on trial, especially if they saw that I went along with what he and the others did! I will not do it! It would be much more shameful for me than it is already." I knew this was true and reluctantly accepted her decision. Besides, this long after the event, a report from her or me on a seduction she herself would not call a date rape would have little if any effect.

"And now I am pregnant," Dolly ended, "I am sure of it. I got one of those little pregnancy testing kits they sell at the drug store, and it tested positive. I have already had morning sickness a couple of times. Pretty soon it'll begin to show. Oh Dr. Barron, what shall I do?" She began to cry again softly. The tears streamed down her wan face.

I got up, sat down beside Dolly and put my arm around her shoulders. Perhaps her father would have done the same, I thought.

"Don't be afraid," I said, "having a baby is not the end of the world. God will take care of you! Friends will help you! Psalm 127 tells us that children are a gift of the Lord, and the fruit of the womb is His reward." It was the first Scripture I thought of because Lisa and I had received it with much joy when we first knew we were expecting.

Dolly answered dreamily, "Sometimes I am glad I have a little baby growing in me. I am looking forward to holding it in my arms, nursing it, playing with it. I try to imagine what it will look like. Maybe more like me, a cute little Mexican girl with light brown skin, dark eyes and lots of dark hair. Maybe it will be a little boy and look like Jonathan, with his tousled brown hair, blue-grey eyes and energetic mouth. I would like that. I loved Jonathan so much!" She smiled at the thought. But suddenly she sat bolt upright.

"At other times," she said fiercely, "I hate Jonathan for what he did to me and never want to see him again! I don't want to have his child! I don't want the shame of having to face my mother and family as I am, pregnant without being married and without any fault of mine! I don't want to be a poor, unwed mother tied down by a child forced on me! I have a choice! I can go to Dr. Hellmann's Women's Drive-Through Clinic and have an abortion! I found out that they do it on an outpatient basis. During the first three months of pregnancy it doesn't cost too much either. It isn't as if it's a real baby yet anyway—it's only like a bunch of cells or a tadpole."

"No, it is not," I said, "it is a little human being from the moment of conception. It is your own flesh and blood! You really know that. Do not hide yourself from your own flesh."

"You talk like our priest," Dolly said. "You aren't Catholic, are you? The Catholic Church forbids abortion absolutely."

"No, I am not," I replied, "but I agree completely with Catholics on this point."

She bowed her head. "I really know abortion is wrong," she admitted. "I am all torn up about it. It would be so much easier to hide an abortion than to hide a baby."

"Only before other people," I answered, "not before God, Who sees you and your baby right now. Nothing is hidden from Him. All our days are written in His book when as yet there were none of them. He says so in Psalm 139. You may bear little or no responsibility for the conception of this child, *but neither does the child.* Do not become guilty of shedding his innocent blood! If you do, you may avoid shame here on earth, but you will stand far more deeply ashamed before God at His judgment seat in heaven. Let your baby live!" Dolly nodded, but I sensed that she had not finally decided what she would do about her pregnancy. With all her childlike timidity and vacillation there was a core of hardness deep in her heart which I had not overcome.

I asked Dolly whether we could pray together about her choice, and she agreed. I fervently prayed for her, for her baby, for all the people who knew and loved her to stand by her and help her to let her child You had given her be born. I spoke of Job who had said of You in the midst of his severe testing, *"When he hath tried me, I shall come forth as gold"* (Job 23:10), and prayed that Dolly might come forth with Your holiness from her present trial as had Job from his.

Our meeting seemed over. We got up to leave. "I will always be there for you and do all I can for you," I promised as we were walking to the door.

Dolly stood still and looked up at me timidly and imploringly just as she had at my wedding reception. "Please, please, Dr. Barron," she almost whispered, "I have no one else I can talk to. Could I call you or even come here again some time, like today?"

"Of course, Dolly," I immediately agreed. "In fact, let's set a time for our next meeting, and maybe regular times after that." We worked out a weekly schedule for me to pick her up and bring her to my home as we had that day, with Lisa present. I was relieved; in Your good providence Dolly would now surely make the right decision about her pregnancy. I thanked You for allowing me to have a part in it as Your faithful son and servant. I did not then remember that You reward faithful service with greater tasks, nor did I suspect that the greatest obstacles in Dolly's path to You lay yet ahead.

12

Spiritual Warfare

Jonathan and I had set our meeting with his parents for the afternoon of the upcoming Saturday, December 28. In the Catholic Church's calendar, December 28 is known as Holy Innocents Day. It is dedicated to the memory of all the babies two years old and under in the region of Bethlehem, whom King Herod commanded to be slaughtered in his effort to kill the Christ Child (Matthew 2:16–18). I thought it was a pity that we Protestants did not have such a day as well to help us remember and mourn the many millions of innocent children our own society had slaughtered by abortion.

After my meeting with Dolly, I called Luke to inform him that she was indeed pregnant and asked him to give me any advice he might have for me. Luke told me he had thought the whole matter over again and prayed about it since we had met. "I now wonder whether we weren't too hasty about rejecting reconciliation and the possibility of marriage between Dolly and Jonathan, Dad," he said. "I believe we should pray that our Lord will help them and everyone involved to bow to His wisdom of what is best for them all, instead of coming to Him with our own minds already half made up about what we plan to do."

"Of course much if not everything depends on Jonathan and Dolly themselves," I thought aloud. "If only Jonathan could humble himself to come to her and ask for her forgiveness! If only Dolly could forgive him from her heart! They need to do this anyway, whether they eventually marry or not. It will require God's great grace, especially for Dolly."

A memory came to my mind. "My wife and I faced a similar impasse early on in our relationship," I told Luke. "I had written a horrible book, *The Consolation of Philosophy,* in which I declared my rejection of God and my total reliance upon myself as 'the master of my fate and the captain of my soul.'"

"Lisa mentioned it to me," Luke said. "She said it became an instant bestseller."

"It did," I confirmed, "and a copy of it fell into the hands of her son, her only child. It led him to kill himself by an overdose of drugs. Lisa hated me for that when we first met. I had to ask her forgiveness, and she had to give it to me before our relationship could continue. God gave her the great grace to do it and even never to mention it to me again afterwards."

"She never told me that," my son said. After a little pause he added, "Thank you for telling me about it. I am learning much from you that can help me in my work. This story now about Lisa and you—it will help me counsel others about forgiveness. Forgiveness is one of the hardest matters to discuss in Christian counseling!" He sighed. "You wouldn't believe how often I have heard from my counselees, 'I'll *never* forgive my husband, or wife, or boy friend, or parents for what they did to me.' How much fury and bitterness they store up in their hearts, and they never heal because of it! I use the verse in the Lord's Prayer, *'Forgive us our debts, as we also have forgiven our debtors,'* and Jesus' parable about the kingdom of heaven and forgiveness of debts in Matthew 18. I use Ephesians 4:32: *'And be ye kind to one another, tenderhearted, forgiving one another, even as God for Christ's sake hath forgiven you.'*" I could almost see my son smile over the telephone as he ended, "Now I can use you and Lisa as examples of people who are living out this verse."

We briefly prayed together and hung up. I was grateful that You had given me my newly restored son to uphold me in this spiritual warfare over Jonathan and Dolly. You had also reminded me of the story of my reconciliation with Lisa so I might share it with them and help them reconcile as well. If Lisa had forgiven me my part in the death of her son, Dolly might forgive Jonathan for what he had done to her.

Saturday afternoon arrived and I drove over to Dr. Wood's home. Jonathan welcomed me at the entrance. "I am glad you are here," he told me in a low voice. "There is no way I could have talked to my folks alone about what happened."

We sat down and spent a few minutes talking about how we had spent Christmas. I told the Woods about the wonderful surprise of meeting my firstborn son. "The son I had at seventeen with Dorrie Fisher, Dr. Wood," I explained, "and his family for the first time. My son and his wife are strong Christians," I said happily. "He and I already share our concerns as believers. He plans to bring his family to Battle Hill once a month to help us demonstrate and save babies at the Hellmann abortion clinic." I added a few words about Luke's work in Mexico City, and that I hoped I might be allowed to recruit some of our Fairfield University students for short term mission trips to help my son's ministry there. Dr. Wood asked me to submit detailed information about the trips to share with the university's governing board. He felt sure the board would approve.

"We all have confidence that any projects you support are in line with our beliefs and policies, James," he told me, "and that goes for your participation in peaceful pro-life activities as well." He added with evident pleasure, "We all noticed how much our students like you and are willing to listen to you—for example, when they started the new philosophy club on campus with your guidance, and when they all signed and sent you those two big get-well cards when you were sick just before Christmas. We would like you to be in charge of our pro-life witnessing outreach. Take a busload of our students along when you go to the Hellmann Clinic in one of the university buses. It's good for our young people to become active in a totally biblical Christian effort like this. It's part of our spiritual warfare today. A number of our parents and financial supporters have already suggested that we do something like this in addition to our aid to persecuted Christians around the world." I thanked Dr. Wood and You with joy.

We now turned to the crisis between Jonathan and Dolly. Jonathan described the satanic ritual he had attended Halloween, and the much more horrible one the Sunday after it. Just before the end he looked at me in mute appeal to let him stop at this point, but I silently shook my head. He must fully confess his own part in what had been done, or how could he be fully forgiven and set free?

"I had sex with Dolly," he said miserably, his head bowed, "she let me do it when she hardly knew what she was doing from the drugs in the wine we gave her to drink."

He stopped and looked up at me again. "There is one thing more I didn't tell you, Dr. Barron," he said, "because I thought that if you knew it you would surely turn your back on me, even with your background, even with your willingness to let me touch you." I remembered our first meeting after the event when I had broken down the wall of shame between us by holding out my hand to him. Had not Sylvia done the same for me? Had not Christ done the same for each and every one of us fallen men stained through and through with the leprosy of sin?

"God's love is unconditional," I said, "the only unforgivable sin is to refuse His Holy Spirit, the Consuming Fire, to come into our hearts. Tell us everything. Hold nothing back."

Dr. Wood joined me. As with me after learning of my sin against Dorrie Fisher, he now lovingly told his son, "God will not turn His back on you, and neither will we. Cast your burden, all of it, on Him, and He will sustain you."

Jonathan looked at his father and mother and saw the deep, silent grief on their faces. Tears came to his eyes and started running down his cheeks.

"I did what I did," he said, "because I had asked Dolly earlier to have sex with me, but she wouldn't let me. She said that she had never done it and wouldn't do it because it was wrong outside of marriage. I resented that. I believed then with my Satanist friends that nothing is wrong, for 'do what thou wilt shall be the whole of the law.' I wanted what I wanted and was also pretty sure she wouldn't resist me if I seduced her the way I did. My friends knew what I was after and agreed. It fit right in with their ritual."

He paused briefly before going on, "I was terribly sorry for what I had done right afterwards. Dolly was the first girl I was really in love with. I still am. How could I have done what I did, even if she let me, drugged as she was? I wish with all my heart it had never happened." He bowed his head. His shoulders shook with his weeping.

Dr. and Mrs. Wood and I kept silent till he stopped. Dr. Wood then asked him whether he had truly renounced all his satanic beliefs and connections when he professed the faith with me. Jonathan looked up.

"Yes, I did," he said. "I was in dead earnest when I prayed with Dr. Barron. I followed up by destroying all my occult materials, the black clothes we wore to the ceremonies, everything. I told my friends that I was now a Christian and could never meet with them any more, and I haven't. I never want to return to that horror again."

He turned to his parents. "Now you know everything," he said, "I am so sorry for it all, and I was so ashamed. You can see why I haven't been able to tell you about it before. If Dr. Barron hadn't insisted that I do it and ask your forgiveness, and if he had not come with me today I might never have told you. Please forgive me for all the grief I have caused you."

"We forgive you, son," said Dr. Wood,

"Of course, Jonathan," said Jonathan's mother.

I looked on with joy as they lovingly hugged their youngest son, restored to them as the prodigal son of Scripture had been restored to his father. However, there was one more matter we must deal with.

"I am very sorry to have to bring this up," I said gently after a little while, "I have met with Dolly Hernandez, and she is expecting a child." They all looked at me, stricken.

"We must let her know right away that we will help her in any way we can," said Dr. Wood. "Can you tell her we will, James?"

"I will," I answered, "but I have to tell you that she is quite ambivalent about what to do about her pregnancy. At times she is looking forward to having the baby and even fondly imagines it might be a little boy looking like you, Jonathan." Jonathan looked at me with sudden hope in his eyes. I continued:

"But at other times she is seriously considering abortion. Her overwhelming concern is the shame she would have to endure once her pregnancy becomes apparent to her mother and family. She hasn't told anybody about it yet except me." Noticing the Woods' questioning glances, I explained, "Her father whom she loved died some years ago. I guess she sees me as a sort of substitute father. It goes back to when Jonathan and she crashed my wedding reception and I tried to make you both welcome."

"It's amazing what can come of a little kindness," murmured Mrs. Wood. I nodded. I now saw Mrs. Wood's motherly feelings strongly assert themselves as she mused aloud, "We must do all we possibly can to keep Dolly from having an abortion! This is our little grandchild, Michael. I liked Dolly, Jonathan—such a sweet girl, and so much in love with you too. Is there any possibility, even after what has happened, that you two might marry?" She stopped quickly and looked around at us all, almost afraid of having spoken this last word.

"You mean it, Mother?" Jonathan exclaimed immediately. "You mean you wouldn't object?"

His mother shook her head no as Dr. Wood intervened. "You are going too far too fast," he said, "first Jonathan must make amends to Dolly. You must ask her to forgive you, son. It won't be easy, I know, but it is just as imperative or even more so as it was between you and us. You are now a Christian and really know this in your heart. And she must forgive you, an even harder duty than yours." He quoted the Scriptures my son had mentioned to me over the phone. I supported him by telling the family the story of the impasse between Lisa and me over the death of her son.

Jonathan looked at us reluctantly but also in dawning readiness to do what was required of him. "Please pray for me," he asked us, "and please talk to Dolly, Dr. Barron, that she would find it in her heart to let me talk to her and ask her forgiveness—and that she would forgive me," he ended. Again, as with his parents, I promised I would try to persuade her.

"Lastly," Dr. Wood said, "it is true that Dolly is a sweet, lovable girl and essentially the innocent victim in what happened. It is especially praiseworthy that she was unwilling to compromise her standard of abstinence from sex outside of marriage. But we must be sure she knows the Lord in her heart as you now do, Jonathan, before we even think about marriage between you and her. It's absolutely essential."

Finally Dr. Wood wanted to inform the police about what had happened just as I had when first talking to Dolly. Like I he believed we had a duty to warn the community against "Sonda Infernal." He thought he, Jonathan and I should meet with Fairfield's chief of police whom he knew well as a conscientious public servant and tell him the whole story. I was glad to see that Jonathan agreed immediately, taking it as further evidence that his conversion was genuine.

Dr. Wood arranged for our meeting to be held right after New Year's Day 1997. The police chief had an official police record made of our report, to be added to their already voluminous file on the nefarious activities of "Sonda Infernal." Jonathan's name would now be part of the police records as well. The police chief sternly warned him never to be involved with any satanic cult again, nor even to think of seducing a girl as he had Dolly. "A conviction of date rape would stamp you forever as a convicted sex offender, young man, and ruin your whole life," he said. "Thank God He kept you from crossing that line this time."

13

"The Little Brothers of Saint James"

The spring semester of 1997 began with much work for me, but it all came from Your hand and therefore did not overtax my strength or make me tense. I taught the history of philosophy from Aquinas to our own time. I also taught another ethics class pursuant to student demand, but this time not with emphasis on the entire wide field of bioethics but only on abortion and euthanasia. I rightly felt that my previous attempt to cover all areas of bioethics had been a product of my latent worldly ambition and not Your good will for me (and please, Father, no more shingles ever again!).

I continued to assist with the monthly meetings of our philosophy club, conducted somewhat as C. S. Lewis had directed the Socratic Club at Oxford, England. No one on our faculty would defend atheism, agnosticism, or evolutionism against Christianity in open debate as had been the custom in Lewis's Socratic Society, but we chose students who played the part of such defenders so the audience or another student playing a Christian believer could cross verbal swords with them. This was excellent preparation for the real combat for the minds of men awaiting my students after graduation. It was a very interesting format and I enjoyed coaching my most promising students in either role. Again my background was almost indispensable in this work. After all, I had been a real live, passionate atheist-evolutionist most of my life and was now endeavoring to be a real live, passionate Christian.

The university administration did not let me teach more than two one on one directed readings courses because I was now also the coordinator for Fairfield University's pro-life outreach and in charge of a busload of students who would demonstrate at the Hellmann Abortion Clinic the third Saturday of every month. I had no trouble at all recruiting students for this ministry; on the contrary, we could easily fill two of our Fairfield University buses with the young people who volunteered. Among them was Jonathan Wood, who again took one of my one on one directed readings courses and whom I was still mentoring in the faith. In January and early February, I also met with Dolly Hernandez separately once a week, and we occasionally talked on the phone between meetings.

We decided that we would have students demonstrate at the Hellmann Clinic in two groups, one in the morning and one in the afternoon. To supervise both groups meant that I would spend the entire third Saturday of each month in Battle Hill. I was perfectly willing to do this, and to my delight Lisa went with me every time. We contacted Luke, who arranged to meet us with his family at the clinic in the afternoon so we could all demonstrate and then have dinner together in Battle Hill.

I got in touch with the pro-life people in Battle Hill who coordinated the demonstrations against "Hell-Man," as they called the abortionist doctor, to let them know they were about to receive regular sizeable reinforcements from Fairfield. Naturally they were glad to hear it. We began our student missions to the Women's Drive-Through Clinic the third Saturday of January 1997.

I had begun to take part in the pro-life presence at Hellmann's clinic already in May 1996, shortly after my move to Fairfield. I had become well-known among our own people and also among the self-styled "escorts from hell" guarding the site and doing their best to prevent our contact with Hellmann's prospective clients. They would vie with each other to come up with epithets and mocking names to shame us, insult us and perhaps even provoke us to answer them in kind or to attack them. Several of these security guards wore their untidy hair in hippy-style pony tails and sported wide, bushy beards.

One man in particular stood out among them, the tallest, broadest and heaviest, a veritable giant with a brutal face and big beefy hands. We called him "Tiny." Only the bravest among us dared approach the cars of incoming clients, hand a tract to the pregnant woman or girl inside or tell her to let her baby live when this man stood nearby. He had never as yet physically interfered with our efforts, but we felt sure he would if we ever disregarded the 100 feet buffer zone federal law had decreed between abortion clinics and pro-life activists.

The way we pro-lifers were treated reminded me vividly of the story of Dr. Bernard Nathanson which Bernard Gottlieb had told us. I shared it with our pro-life friends, especially the part where the beautiful witness of pro-life Christians protesting abortion despite harsh winter weather and the hostility of press, police, and municipal government authorities first drew Dr. Nathanson to Christ. We prayed that our witness be as winsome as theirs in converting our enemies to You.

For a while Hellmann's guards only called me "The Thin Man" after an old movie due to my height and slender build. It did not really bother me; I would shrug and laugh about it. After they had observed me with Lisa a few times, they picked up on the age difference between us and taunted me as robbing the cradle or her as being too young for an old man like me. When her pregnancy became obvious, their taunts and filthy insinuations sank to new lows, from the usual mocking questions whether we had forgotten about birth control, needed pills or condoms, or were ready to patronize the clinic ourselves to slurs and invectives about our relationship I will not repeat. By now they had found out that I had been the atheist philosopher James Barron who had become a Christian and would call me by the same names Lisa's mother had used against me and which I myself had used against Christians before I became one. I bore it all with relative indifference, but when Lisa came with me and heard them hurl their mockeries and insults at me, she could bear it only with great effort and would sometimes shed tears about it when we were safely back in our car driving home. I admit that hurt; offenses against our loved ones are much harder to bear than offenses against ourselves!

Then came February 1997 and with it a front page article in the Battle Hill newspaper. It was splashed in big headlines across its Sunday issue two weeks and a day after we did our first pro-life outreach with our Fairfield University students at Hellmann's clinic. It featured a large photo of me as the "ringleader" of a bunch of young religious fanatics bused in from a backwoods fundamentalist institution, and it gave a summary of my life equal to the most slanted and malicious screeds ever penned against me by the old Bertrand Russell Institute.

At first I took it with relative calm. What else could I expect from the regional liberal monopoly newspaper? But I became uneasy when I came to the concluding paragraph, "For his literalist Bible reading followers James Barron is no longer a lost sinner but a born-again saint. For the rest of us he is no longer a respected philosopher but lost in religious extremism." Having formerly engaged in similar attacks against "failed atheists" myself, I at once spotted the term the "escorts from hell" would most likely taunt me with from now on—"born-again saint" or just "saint." And sure enough, when I took my place with our pro-life group the following Saturday morning, I was greeted with a sneering "Good morning, Saint James!" in unison by a chorus of the "escorts from hell." They asked me whether I had said all my prayers this morning or the night before, whether I had knelt when saying them, whether I had prayed for the fetuses—they never spoke of babies or children—and so on, always prefacing their mocking questions by calling me "Saint James" and laughing at me and their own wit.

Of all the insults and foul language they had ever hurled against me, "Saint James" was the only one I found almost unbearable. I hated it. I winced inwardly and often outwardly when hearing it. Of course they noticed it, being always on the watch for what hurt us the most, and they used the hateful name as often, as mockingly and as loudly as they possibly could. That morning it took all my commitment to the cause and to my fellow pro-lifers for me to remain in my spot until it was my time to leave.

As I was driving back to Fairfield, I asked myself why this particular mockery upset me so much. To me a "saint" was a completely holy and righteous person. I knew all too well that I had no claim whatever to such a title, and that was why the taunt cut so deeply. Doubtless the newspaper article and the Hellmann "escorts" agreed with me about the meaning of the word "saint," about the fact that so understood it did not fit me, and that therefore, it would hurt me precisely where my conscience was most vulnerable and tender.

I cringed at the thought that I would have to run this gauntlet from now on every time I demonstrated at Hellmann's clinic. Dear Father, I prayed, please help me over this hurdle. If there is any pride in me that needs to be cast out, do it. If there is any answer to my predicament in Your Word or from brothers and sisters in You, please give it to me. While I was still praying for this, You assured me You would grant my request soon. You also reminded me of the years long ago at Battle Hill University when I was an atheist graduate student and had gleefully joined other students and even faculty members in mockingly calling Dr. Francis S. Freeman, the only Christian professor in the philosophy department, "Saint Francis," often within his hearing. It served me right to endure the same treatment now. I had been just as cruel then as those "escorts from hell" today.

Mocking others is actually a pleasure to people who do not know God, I thought. That's why they mocked Christ, blindfolding Him, beating Him and then asking Him to "prophesy" who hit Him. But He made no reply, and He even prayed for them because they did not know what they were doing. Did the Hellmann security guards really know what they were doing, assisting with the slaughter of innocent babies and taunting their would-be rescuers? I began to pray for them from that day on.

I talked about all this to Jonathan Wood at our next mentoring session. I shared my particular intense revulsion against being called "Saint James" with him, exclaiming at one point that I hated it so much because "I am not a saint, not remotely." And in Your good providence, Father, You gave me the help I needed through my young brother.

"But you are a saint, Dr. Barron," he said, a little surprised that I seemed to be ignorant of this truth, "all Christian believers are. It's clear from many Bible verses all through the New Testament. You just haven't applied the name to yourself. It means simply to be set aside, holy to our Lord. I learned that in Sunday School long before I became a saint myself." He laughed a little at the idea that he had received this knowledge long before receiving its substance. I considered once again ruefully how little if any Christian truth the apostate Bible-denying church of my youth had taught me.

"I thought that being a saint meant being especially good and pure," I said, "and I am not that. Of course that's what those escorts thought, too. That's why they used the word to mock me and shame me, and that's why they succeeded. Thank you so much, Jonathan, for clearing this up for me. I won't be hurt any more when they call me by what is my rightful biblical name, thanks to Christ."

Jonathan was pleased that he had been able to help me. Unbeknownst to me he also spoke to the other student volunteers in our pro-life outreach about my problem with being called "Saint James," and they all got together and carried out a special plan. When we set out on our next outreach the third Saturday in February, all the students wore blue T-shirts with the words "Children are a Gift from God" in back. The shirts also bore a big white inscription in front which read "The Little Brothers of Saint James" for the young men or "The Little Sisters of Saint James" for the girls. Their support of me could not have been plainer. I felt tears come to my eyes when I saw them in those shirts for the first time. They smiled, giggled and then laughed aloud as they watched my face. We all laughed together happily as we boarded the bus.

"That'll shut up those escorts from hell, Dr. Barron," said one of the students. "You just wait and see!" And it did. My tormentors were nonplused and stopped using the title "Saint James" for me when they saw that all our young people proclaimed their solidarity with me as a true saint. From then on all of us half humorously and half solemnly called ourselves "The Order of Saint James." That order still exists today and is now the semi-official name of Fairfield University's ongoing pro-life outreach. All the students who take part in it continue to wear T-shirts with the inscription "The Little Brothers of Saint James."

14

Reconciliation at a Funeral

The Monday after our February "Order of Saint James" outreach Lisa received a phone call from her sister Helen Wilson. Dad Trent had died of a stroke. The funeral was set for the following Thursday, and Helen told Lisa that her mother wanted us to attend.

"Me too?" I asked not unnaturally, recalling our last visit.

"Yes, you too," Lisa said, "Helen said Mother specifically told her to make sure that you came too. She was very surprised; she had heard Mother call you names and say nasty things against you many times before. Helen said you must be a very nice man indeed and that she is looking forward to meeting you." Lisa giggled a little in spite of our sadness over her father's death.

We flew to Schenectady the day before the funeral. We were met by Helen and her husband Randy. I liked them both at first sight. Helen looked much like Lisa and resembled her in other ways as well. She was the manager of the Schenectady branch office of a national travel agency and knew her way around the airport as if it was her home. By following her competent directions it took us virtually no time at all to find and be installed in the Wilsons' nice new car with Randy at the wheel and me by his side, so Helen and Lisa could visit in the back seat during our drive to Hilton.

Lisa had kept the Wilsons up to date about our lives in Fairfield. "It's only two more months now till your baby is born, isn't it?" asked Helen.

"Yes," Lisa confirmed happily, "the due date is in two months and one week to be exact. We can hardly wait!"

"What is it, a boy or a girl?" Helen asked.

"We don't know," Lisa said, "it doesn't matter to us. Either is most welcome, and by not finding out in advance which it is, we want to make a statement to that effect to everyone who knows us."

"You two," Helen said with a little laugh, "you are 'making statements' to the world all the time, aren't you?"

"What do you mean?" Lisa asked. It turned out that the hateful article about me in the Battle Hill newspaper after our first "Order of Saint James" outreach had been picked up by the Schenectady daily paper and therefore by who knows how many other local or regional newspapers across the country. The liberal grapevine as I well knew was very efficient.

Lisa and I took turns telling Randy and Helen about how the "escorts from hell" had taunted me by calling me "Saint James" after that article appeared and about my students' counterattack by their "Little Brothers of Saint James" T-shirts. They enjoyed the story very much. "Your students must like you a lot, James," Helen said and added with childlike frankness, "and so do we, don't we, Randy? We certainly back you all the way on the right to life issue." My brother-in-law laughed and agreed.

Helen became more serious as she told us how Dad Trent had liked me from the time he met me at our wedding. He had been looking forward very much to the birth of our child. In fact, his last quarrel with Mrs. Trent had been precipitated by that newspaper article and involved me, my faith and Lisa's pregnancy. Helen also said Mrs. Trent wanted Lisa and me to stay at her home until our return to Fairfield. I could hardly believe it and silently shook my head; I felt that it would be far better for Mrs. Trent and us if we stayed at a nearby bed and breakfast place or hotel.

By this time we had reached the Trents' home. Mrs. Trent stood waiting for us at the entrance. Her face showed the ravages of much recent weeping. I walked in last, wishing to give her a few more moments to decide how to receive me. It must be very difficult for her to interact with me after how she had treated me the last time we met. She welcomed Helen, Randy and Lisa with brief hugs and kisses.

When my turn came, she looked up at me with a pitiable expression of shame and apology. For a moment or two she was unable to bring out any words. Finally she said with an effort: "I am so sorry for the way I acted toward you the last time you were here, Dr. Barron. Please forgive me." She swallowed and added, "I should have listened to Jack." Tears came to her eyes, which met mine with total grief.

I remembered my mother's tear-filled eyes after my father had died. True, he had finally come to Christ and she knew she would see him again in Your blessed eternity, but even so she had deeply mourned his death. How much deeper must be Mrs. Trent's grief over the loss of her husband whom she had berated, shamed and cowed throughout their married years and whom she, an unbeliever, had no real hope of ever seeing again.

I suddenly understood why she might have wanted me to come to the funeral and even to stay in her home. Somehow she had not been able to apologize to Dad Trent for her abuse of him. He had died too suddenly for that. Somehow I, whom she had abused like her husband the first and only time we had met, might accept the apology she could no longer offer her husband and grant her the forgiveness she could no longer receive from him.

"Of course I forgive you, Mrs. Trent," I said gently, with Lisa and the Wilsons standing by as my witnesses, "and if you will, please call me James from now on."

"I will—James," she said a little shakily, timidly smiling and added, "and call me Freda like my other in-laws do." She proceeded to tell Lisa and me which room we would occupy. It was the same room we would have stayed in if her furious attack against me and her attempt to have Lisa abort our child had not compelled us to leave back in November.

We carried our overnight bags upstairs and stretched out on the double bed for a little while of rest, facing one another and smiling. I saw a slight movement under my wife's skirt and put my hand gently on her body where I could feel our baby kicking. There, I was sure, was his or her little foot or heel. I had felt it often by now and loved to touch it. Lisa put her hand on mine. We were a three-in-oneness now in great love and joy, a father, mother, and child mirroring as closely as we humans can the three-in-oneness of You, dear Father, Son and Holy Spirit. I reflected with awe that You gave us this moment with You and each other in a room and on a bed provided for us by my wife's mother who had once loathed me as her daughter's husband and wanted our child to be killed. *"Many, O LORD my God, are thy wonderful works which thou hast done, and thy thoughts which are to us-ward,"* Psalm 40:5. Then we drifted off to sleep, with our hands still joined lovingly above the child gently moving in the shelter of its mother's womb. I love to remember that holy and beautiful moment.

We were not allowed to rest there very long because Helen's voice called us to come downstairs for dinner. We had soup, sandwiches and some kind of dessert, saying little as we ate. Afterwards Mrs. Trent (I reminded myself to think of her as Freda) and Lisa went into the kitchen to do the dishes and visit a little with each other. Helen and Randy took me to the living room for a separate conversation of our own.

"We think you should know more about how Dad Trent passed away, James," Helen said. "Mom seemed to want to make her peace with you, but we will believe she really means it only if it lasts beyond tonight."

Randy nodded. "She might have an outbreak of fury against you again any time," he said, "because Dad Trent's death was connected with that vicious article about you in the paper a week or so ago. Freda is much too ready to believe anything she sees or hears in the news media, and that article was a total rehash of what the press published about you right after you became a Christian."

"What exactly happened with Dad Trent?" I asked. Helen and Randy looked at each other and then told me the story. It was not long, not complicated, and alas, completely according to the pattern between Freda and him which Lisa had described to me after our earlier visit. Freda had found the newspaper article about me and read it to Dad Trent. Contrary to his usual cowed silence, he had spoken up in my defense and the defense of biblical Christianity.

"Mom completely lost it," Helen said. "She screamed at him at the top of her voice. The neighbors next door heard bits and pieces of it and told us about it afterwards. She used all the cuss words and expletives for him and for you she could think of. She told him that if he became a religious fanatic like you, she didn't want him around the house any more. 'What use are you to me anyway?' she yelled, 'now that you are retired and just sit around the house all day like a bump on a log? The least you can do is shut up about that so-and-so and stop praying for him and that unwanted pregnancy he saddled our daughter with. Yes, I know you pray for them and I hate it! Either promise you'll stop it or leave right now!'"

"And Dad Trent got up and walked out the door," said Randy. "He had done that at other times when she was berating him and he couldn't take it any more. It was snowing heavily and a blizzard was on the way."

"He didn't come home that evening," Helen said. "The blizzard went on all night. Mom reported him missing to the police the next morning. They finally found him unconscious, frostbitten, and barely breathing somewhere far away from here late that afternoon. He was taken to the hospital and diagnosed with a stroke. He never woke up again and died that night. Mother has been inconsolable and crying almost constantly ever since. It was her fault that he went out and died such a horrible death, and she knew it."

We all remained silent for a while. I felt deeply sad that we had lost good Dad Trent and that we had lost him in this horrific way. At least Lisa and I had the memory of his love and goodness for us from the last time we had seen him. I was grateful that he had seen his daughter happy and blessed in her new marriage and her joyful expectation of her child. Unlike his poor wife, he had been able to share our joy, to establish a good relationship with me, calling me "son," and to look forward to being "Grandpa Trent." He and I had even promised to pray for each other, and he had kept his promise. This memory prompted me to ask Helen and Randy what they thought about Dad Trent's religion. "Would it be a Christian funeral?"

"Oh yes," Helen said, "actually our Uncle Charles, Dad's brother, will conduct it. Dad had left instructions for his funeral and this was one of them. Uncle Charles is a minister in a little denomination which split off from the United Reformed Church."

"You can set your mind at rest about his religion, James," Randy added. "He was brought up in the church like most everyone in his generation. He just didn't talk about it much, certainly not in front of Freda, who had become hostile to all things religious by the time I met her. But occasionally he would take me aside, talk of God and Christ, and tell me in that nice inoffensive way of his not to forget Him and to tell our children of Him."

"And I know he prayed for us and all our family," Helen said. "It's sweet of you to ask, but don't worry, James. I am sure our dad is in heaven now with God." I thanked them for this information and hoped it would provide comfort for Freda in the days to come.

"That won't happen soon," said Helen. "Right now she hates God for having taken Dad away from her. She told me so right after he died. I think in her heart she is now screaming at God and calling Him names just as she did with Dad and you."

"That's better than indifference," I said. "After the death of his beloved wife, the great Christian writer C. S. Lewis wrote a little book named *A Grief Observed*. That book is one long scream at God and calls Him names, like 'the cosmic sadist.' And God sat still for it."

You didn't get up and leave C. S. Lewis alone like Dad Trent did with Freda, Father, I thought; Your patience with us is immeasurably greater than our patience with each other. I also remembered how Dad Trent had asked me to pray that he might be patient. Those had been practically his last words to me. I had prayed that prayer for him later every time I thought of him and his blighted marriage. I saw that his patience had worn out one last time and that You in Your mercy had thereby delivered him from his sufferings through his death, even as You delivered C. S. Lewis's wife from her painful cancer through hers. Neither Dad Trent's prayers nor mine for his patience had been granted any more than C. S. Lewis's for his wife's healing, but You had given Dad Trent and Helen Joy Lewis something much better, their presence with You in glory. It was another fulfillment of Romans 8:28, *"All things work for good to them that love You, to them that are called according to Your purpose."*

Tears came to my eyes as I saw all this. At this very moment Freda and Lisa joined us. Lisa immediately saw my emotion and asked me what I was thinking about. I asked You in my heart whether I should share what You had just given me with the family, especially Freda, and You said, do. So I told it all to them, beginning with Dad Trent's so to speak underground Christian faith and omitting nothing.

There was a deep silence when I had finished. Freda was the first to speak afterwards; she thanked me with tears. It was our reconciliation and the start of a loving relationship between us. I believe, dear Father, that in that moment You began Your work of deliverance and salvation in her heart.

15
God's Love Includes God's Justice

I must now return to my mentoring role with Jonathan Wood. As could be expected, much of Jonathan's one on one directed readings course with me was really also mentoring in addition to our explicit weekly mentoring meetings. To my dismay even his conversion had not altogether extinguished his attraction to pantheism and universalism. For this reason I had assigned him several non-fiction works of C. S. Lewis in his directed readings. I hoped that this great Christian thinker's brilliant defense of the faith would anchor Jonathan's worldview more firmly in Your truth.

We began with Lewis's *Mere Christianity,* whose starting point is the fact that we all really know there is a standard of morality, a set of absolute ethical yeas and nays which we ought to obey. I explained to Jonathan that with pantheism there neither were nor could be any absolute ethical yeas and nays, because in pantheism *everything* is part of god or divine by definition, both what we call "good" and what we call "evil." The pantheist god is beyond good and evil. As C. S. Lewis states in Book II, Chapter 1 of *Mere Christianity,* pantheism was the philosophy of the great nineteenth century Prussian philosopher G. F. W. Hegel. I told Jonathan of Hegel's famous dictum, "What is, is right," which I had been fond of quoting to my students and to my religious or philosophical opponents in my atheist years.

"But not everything that is, is right," I said. "Surely you see that for yourself. Cheating on tests is not right. Cheating on one's spouse is not right. Abortion is not right. Seduction is not right." Jonathan got red in the face and bowed his head; too late I remembered how this example must hurt him. I said, "Sorry."

And he muttered, "No, no, you are right, of course."

I went on as quickly as I could, "For pantheist thinkers like Hegel, all these things and whatever else we call wrong is right because it is all part and parcel of creative or emergent evolution and its striving to express and complete itself."

"I think that's what Teilhard de Chardin believes, too," Jonathan said.

"Correct," I answered, "and Teilhard's thought was greatly influenced by the French philosopher Henri Bergson who wrote the world famous book *L'evolution creatrice* or *Creative Evolution* around the turn of the century. His philosophy was a spiritual version of Darwinism which teaches that chance alone is the ultimate cause of the small variations and the natural selection of the fittest by which evolution proceeded from non-life to life, from single celled organisms to the most complicated one, man, or 'from goo to you by way of the zoo' as some creationist Christians have called it." We both smiled at this humorous label. I went on, "Bergson critiqued Darwinism by saying that not sheer chance but rather a spiritual entity he called the '*elan vital*' or the 'Life Force' with its striving to fulfill its own purpose of self-realization is responsible for emergent evolution."

"Teilhard calls it 'the cosmic Christ,'" Jonathan murmured.

"Even that is foreshadowed by Lewis," I said, "in his great novel *Perelandra*, perhaps the greatest novel he wrote. I have wondered whether Lewis knew of Teilhard when he wrote that novel, first published in 1944, eleven years before Teilhard's death. At any rate Lewis anticipated Teilhard's version of what was behind or the essence of emergent evolution. Lewis's evil physicist Weston in *Perelandra* turns from atheist materialism to belief in emergent evolution where all is one and where mind or spirit, with its supposed unconscious, blind, inarticulate cosmic purpose, is present from the beginning. Weston actually speaks of it as 'the Holy Spirit.' That's not so different from Teilhard's 'cosmic Christ.'"

"But it's not the Christ of the Bible," Jonathan said. "That's one thing I know now for sure. Our Jesus Christ wouldn't change from almost nothing to everything over millions of years. '*He is the same yesterday, today and forever,*' Hebrews 13:8. He isn't identical with the universe. '*He is the Eternal Word, One with the Father, by Whom the world was created,*' John 1:1–3. His purpose is not unconscious, blind and inarticulate. On the contrary,' *the invisible things of him from the creation of the world are clearly seen, being understood by the things that are made, even His eternal power and Godhead; so that they are without excuse,*' Romans 1:20." He strongly emphasized the last sentence with total conviction. I almost clapped my hands in applause.

"That's right, Jonathan," I agreed, "so why is it that you sometimes still seem to find something good in pantheism?"

"Number One, I am not one hundred percent sure that evolution didn't take place," he answered. "Even C. S. Lewis sort of goes along with it in the last chapter of *Mere Christianity.*"

"He doesn't endorse it either, though," I countered. I thought that the part Jonathan referred to was the only flaw in that chapter, otherwise "pure gold" to me. I especially thrilled to its concluding sentences which so thoroughly bore out my own experience before and after my conversion. If we look for ourselves, Lewis wrote, we will find in the long run only loneliness, despair, futility, misery and decay. But if we look for Christ, he said, we will find Him, and with Him everlasting life and joy.

"Well, I am just not sure about it," he repeated. "Perhaps God used evolution somehow to bring about the world we see now. Perhaps the division between good and evil developed along with that process. That's something I heard from a teacher in my public high school. I know it isn't biblical, but I can't seem to get it out of my head."

"You need to study the many scientific evidences showing that evolution simply could not have happened," I said. "I have many helpful materials right here in my office, and there is a whole section on the study of origins in the university library. We have come a long way since 1961 when Dr. Henry Morris's book *The Genesis Flood* introduced biblical creation science to the public. We have nothing to fear from evolutionists. Besides, Scripture is quite clear about the fact that God did not create by evolution! He created by His Word. That part fell into place for me the very first night I read the Bible after my conversion. Just put that evolutionist teaching at your public high school out of your mind. I had to do it too."

Jonathan was satisfied, but still needed to discuss his second reason for being attracted by pantheism and universalism. "They seem, well, softer to me than Christianity," he mused, trying to put his speculation into words, "I think universalism portrays God as more merciful, more tolerant, more, well, easygoing than Christians do. I don't like the way C. S. Lewis speaks in *Mere Christianity* of the 'Life Force,' the god of pantheism. He says people like it because it won't interfere with them if they plan to do something bad, whereas the Christian God would. I like it because, well, it would not *judge* you or *punish* you *afterwards*."

"So what you object to," I clarified, "is the Christian God's judgment and punishment of evil deeds."

"Well—yes," Jonathan agreed after some reflection, "especially hell. Why must there be everlasting banishment from His presence in a prison of everlasting burning? It seems too harsh and cruel. And Lewis doesn't say a word about it in *Mere Christianity.*"

"He wrote a chapter called 'Hell' about it in his book *The Problem of Pain*," I said, "Read it if you like. I am not sure I agree with every statement in it. I disagree in particular that because God created man with free will, the ultimate loss of a single soul means the defeat of God's omnipotence."

"Explain that to me," Jonathan said.

I complied. "God (a) gave His Son Christ to die for us all, 1 Timothy 2:6," I said. "He wants all men to be saved, 1 Timothy 2:4, and many other Scriptures. But He does not want us to be saved by force but by our willing response, making possible our love for Him. Not love but hate, rebellion, or sullen submission is produced when people are forced to accept another's so-called love which is only the will to possess them! That is the conversion method of Islam, not Christianity."

"I know," Jonathan said very softly, "our God will not seduce or rape anyone."

I resumed, "Therefore by His omnipotence He (b) also made us with free will," I said. "Because of (a) and (b) combined we can say yes to Him as our Lord, be restored in His likeness and live with Him in His joy in heaven forever. Because of (b), and rejecting His will of (a), we can also say no to Him, prefer to be our own lords and masters, despise His offer of salvation based on Christ's sacrifice, refuse to be restored in His likeness and spend eternity without Him in hell, that is, apart from Him forever. But being apart from Him is utter misery, for He *Himself* is love, joy and peace."

"You know that from experience, don't you," Jonathan said softly.

"Yes, I do," I said, "and you do too. God did not force you to probe the abyss. His interference, if you want to call it that, was all on the other side—to rescue you from it and establish you in His joy and goodness if only you would let him."

"And those who won't let him?" he asked.

"They have what they want," I answered sadly. "I knew such a one not that long ago. He had sunk so low that he took pleasure in playing Christian music over and over again while imagining a man he hated being beaten to death with crowbars. He rejected God and committed suicide. I sometimes wonder whether he is imagining that scene now over and over again in hell."

Jonathan shuddered. I was thinking of Paul Reynolds, the financial supporter of the Bertrand Russell Institute who had hated me so much because I spoke to him of Your joy, Father, and I had been the man whose death he had imagined. Paul had rejected Your joy because he would not humble himself to pray to You for it, and chosen himself and his misery so abject that it drove him to suicide, and after that, hell.

"But that man's refusal did not defeat God's omnipotence," I said, "for God's omnipotence made it possible by the free will He gave him to choose his damnation. In *that* sense, and in that sense only, God willed it. And therefore His omnipotence was not defeated, although He has no pleasure over the death of a sinner, but would rather that he turned from his way and lived, Ezekiel 18:23. You must also consider," I added, "that our life today on earth is a sort of anteroom of hell because the good and the evil live together, and the evil often have power over the good. Not only justice but love demands that it will not always be like this. Think, Jonathan! If there were no separation between heaven and hell in the end as universalism demands, the saved and the damned, the good and the evil would *all* be unhappy, for neither would want to live forever with the other. As it is, the saved can finally look upon the face of our Father in heaven and rejoice with joy unspeakable in His eternal presence, and no one would ever seek again to take it from them."

I stopped, longing for that time *"as the hart panteth after the water brooks"* (Psalm 42:1). "And the damned would be relieved even in their misery, I suppose," I resumed, "by not ever having to look upon His face again as they had to at the judgment. They too would have their wish. C. S. Lewis said somewhere that hell is the last service God does for those for whom He can do nothing better."

Jonathan looked at me in agreement and gratitude. "You have convinced me completely, Dr. Barron," he said, "I hadn't thought this whole subject through. I see now that of course universalism would not make anyone happy, nor be more merciful in its 'tolerance' of evil than our God of the Bible. I will no longer 'probe the abyss' by doubting the righteousness of His judgment and punishment."

Pantheism, universalism, and to a degree emergent evolution were the last major theological-philosophical remnants of Jonathan's former unbelief we had had to overcome. Thank You so much, dear Father, for seeing us through it. It took much prayer and long hours of mentoring to provide for Jonathan the full certitude, joy and peace You had given me all at once at my conversion. But You know best how to deal with each one of us according to our individual uniqueness and need, and You know when a particular conflict is finally resolved.

16
Treasures of Darkness

You had given me the incomparable joy of seeing Jonathan come to You after praying for him and witnessing to him of You with all that was in me. I had dwelt with You the Consuming Fire and You had blessed me by setting his heart aflame as well. As I observed his walk with You afterwards, I could set my mind at rest over him as my truly born again son in the faith. When Dolly Hernandez began to counsel with me in January 1997, I thought much the same experience awaited me with her and looked forward to it.

But it was very different this time. I just said all that was in me had been involved in bringing Jonathan to You. It was not true, Father. Now I endured Your ripping me apart as it were to the deepest depth of my innermost self to lay bare what You had not compelled me to see before. I could bear it only because You, my good Shepherd with Your rod and staff to comfort me, were with me all through that valley of quite literally the shadow of death.

In the night before my first meeting with Dolly I awoke with a feeling of heavy sadness and impending great distress. I checked my luminous wrist watch and saw that it was only a quarter till four. I tried to go back to sleep, but sleep would not come. I lay still so as not to awake Lisa, peacefully breathing beside me. Finally I got up, dressed as quietly as I could and stole to the kitchen where I could turn on the light and read my Bible without disturbing her. It was now about five o'clock. It was pitch dark outside. Everything was completely still.

I opened my Bible. It fell open to Isaiah, Chapter 45, verse 3: *"I will give thee the treasures of darkness and hidden riches of secret places, that thou mayest know that I, the LORD, which call thee by thy name, am the God of Israel."* I knew You had first said this to King Cyrus centuries before Christ came to earth, but what did it mean for me, now? And You spoke to me gravely and as it were regretfully, like a physician who must use a razor-sharp scalpel in preparatory surgery and knows it will hurt, "Remember your daughter Ecstasy. Remember everything you can about her. Remember everything you did or did not do for her. Omit nothing. Look on it all and remember it well so you can truly help Dolly. I will be with you so you can bear it all to the end."

I sat there at that kitchen table in Fairfield under the untimely artificial light, my Bible in front of me, and saw in my mind the kitchen of the luxurious apartment I had shared with Nancy in the years when we were both on the faculty of Herbert Spencer University. I saw myself standing by the medicine cabinet in that other kitchen in the middle of the night, pouring some antacid medication into a teaspoon to relieve the pain of an ulcer attack. I heard the soft footsteps of one of my children. Then little Ecstasy appeared in the door, dressed in the cute pink flannel bunny pajamas which she loved, a little baby blanket tucked under her arm, her blonde hair untidy, her face serious and inquisitive as always, her eyes blinking a little as she anxiously looked at me. She must have been three or four years old then.

"Are you okay, Daddy?" she asked in her high little girl's voice. And I, God help me, said gruffly, "Yes, I am. Get back to bed!" She lingered; concern for me, as I now finally understood with a pang of shame and hurt, was written all over her face. "Get back to bed! Don't bother me!" I barked. She turned away dejectedly and disappeared. I heard the creaking of the floor as she went back to her bedroom.

Oh Father, I begged, please don't make me remember more scenes like this. But similar memories surfaced relentlessly one after another, each relatively insignificant by itself, all forming a sinister record of my self-absorbed rejection of my little girl's conscientious, timid, tender love for me. I had buried these memories deep in my heart after Ecstasy's botched abortion and death.

I had imposed the abortion on her over and against her desperate desire to give birth to her baby! I remembered the last weeks of her life. I saw her again clearly in my mind, the plump fourteen year old girl—eating had been her only pleasure, I now realized—in her unbecoming heavy sweaters and stirrup pants. I now admitted to You and myself that I had hated to be seen with her and to acknowledge her as my daughter because her appearance made me feel ashamed of her. And all that mattered to me then was that now she would shame me even more because she had gotten herself pregnant at thirteen.

Dear Father, I thought in despair, had there been no end to my vileness? It was out of my vileness that I disregarded her pleas to keep her baby and her furious outcries against Nancy and me. Her very last words, "I hate you! I wish you were dead!" which she screamed at us just before her anesthesia took hold rang again in my ears as though spoken right now in our kitchen in Fairfield. I put my hands over my ears to stifle those screams, but of course it did not help. The screams broke forth in my heart.

I also finally admitted that I, I alone, bore the responsibility and guilt for Ecstasy's death. Would not Nancy, who had wanted my children—children from me because she had loved me—have gone along with me if I had allowed Ecstasy's baby to be born? She would have lived, Father, and her baby would have lived. What would have been so unbearable about that? I might now have the joy of welcoming her and my grandchild by her as I had welcomed Luke and his family!

But then the abortion had killed her, not quickly but after a year in a coma on a ventilator. *That* memory did not surface now for the first time but had tormented me over and over again in the weeks and months immediately afterwards. I heard again the hissing of the ventilator. I saw again my daughter's corpselike body on the hospital bed, hooked up to various machines and nourished by a clear liquid feeding solution dripping into her bloodstream from above.

It was the fitting representation of my fatherhood to her. I had given her no hugs, no encouragement, no recognition, no personal interest and involvement in her life, not even acceptance of any affection she might feel for me—only artificial, mechanical maintenance of a father-daughter relationship that had never really existed and could be entirely turned off by the father because he had the power to do so. I had not kissed her very often in her life, and *never* while she lay comatose on her hospital bed during that last year.

For the first time in my life I now wondered whether I might have brought her out of her coma if I had shown her any sign of love, even just sitting down by her side and talking to her lovingly. I now remembered well documented stories of people in a coma who had been brought back to life and recovery even after years by the loving efforts of relatives or friends. In fact, pro-life people protesting Ecstasy's death by withdrawal of life support had told such stories at that time, but I had not paid attention. I had not *wanted* to pay attention.

I had not *wanted* to sit by her bed and speak to her lovingly! What I had craved instead was to stand in front of crowds of intellectuals like myself and speak to them arrogantly on infecting the common people we despised with our own death culture. I had not *wanted* to feel any obligation to try to bring my daughter back to life even by the slightest personal effort. When the costly machines to which she was hooked up failed to do that job, I signed the required authorization forms to have their use discontinued so other hands might turn off the switch or "pull the plug" and that the living corpse named Ecstasy Barron might finally "expire." And I remembered sighing with relief when it was over and done, and walking past the glum pro-life demonstrators at the hospital entrance with my head held high and my face set like a flint. And like Dr. Bernard Nathanson I had had no regrets whatever while doing all this, sharing "the mentality of the abortionist: another job well done, another demonstration of the moral neutrality of advanced technology in the hands of the amoral." The regrets, the waves of almost unbearable pain came only later, again and again, before and after my conversion, and now anew with undiminished fury.

Oh Father, why do You now give me all these "treasures of darkness" from the memories I suppressed because they hurt me so much? You need to remember them afresh, You said, because I am entrusting Dolly Hernandez to you. Her name is really "Dolores," which means "pains." She prefers to be called "Dolly," just as Ecstasy wanted to be called "Stacie" at the end. Dolly, like you yourself, doesn't want shame and pain but must go through it as Jesus did for the joy—My joy—set before Him (Hebrews 12:2). So My joy is set before you and her after you walk together through this present great trial.

Dolly sees you as her substitute father. You must see her as your substitute daughter. Be the sacrificial, loving father to her you never were to Ecstasy. Expect to be wounded by Dolly as loving fathers so often are by their children, and as I was by all mankind. I had to cut open your heart to restore to you the "treasures of darkness" you buried there. They are like a knife in your heart or a scourge on your back, but they are indispensable for your labor with Dolly Hernandez. You cannot show her My love through yours without drawing on them. Share them with her as I direct you. Your hurt will help heal her as all My children are healed by the scourging which fell on Christ (Isaiah 53:5). Be Christ to Dolly in His unfeigned, unconditional, unfailing love, as Sylvia was to you.

At this point the early dawn began to dispel the darkness outside and my dear wife joined me in the kitchen. I looked up at her and attempted to smile. She knew me well enough to recognize that I welcomed her presence and comfort, but without any questions or spoken words. She walked up to me and silently put her arms around me from behind so I could let my head lean back and rest on her breast. We stayed that way for a little while until I lifted my head and straightened my shoulders.

"All right now, James?" Lisa asked gently, her low, soft voice full of love.

"All right now, darling," I answered, "but pray for me. Dolly Hernandez will be here for counseling this afternoon. Please pray." Lisa nodded yes. I added with difficulty, "Pray God would show me moment by moment what to share—of my past—of what I did to Ecstasy. Pray I would know His presence with me all the time."

"That hard," Lisa said with pity. I thanked You that I did not have to explain further what I meant; she knew all my past and had made her peace with it long ago.

We had a light breakfast and turned to our scheduled duties. My classes at the university did not begin again until the second week of January, but my regular mentoring session with Jonathan was that morning. I intended to speak with him about his plans for his future relationship with Dolly so I might perhaps share them with her.

Jonathan was quite ready and willing to discuss with me what he had in mind. "I have thought it all out thoroughly," he said eagerly, "I have prayed about it, and I am sure this is what we should do. It's really quite simple as I see it. First, I must ask Dolly to forgive me for what I did. I will tell her that I have become a Christian and given up all my involvement in the occult. We can start over again with a clean slate. And after she forgives me I will ask her to marry me in our church right away."

"But does she believe as you do—as our church does?" I asked.

"She isn't a very strong Catholic, you know," he said, much too easily in my view, "that part will be all right. If we get married right away, only a little over two months will have gone by since, well, since we became pregnant, and all will be well."

He saw my questioning glance and added with total sincerity: "It really will, Dr. Barron! I'll be responsible to see to it that we will be a family and take good care of our child as we should, and other children God gives us. That's what I told my parents, too, and will tell it to Dolly's mother when I ask her to let me marry her. I am working a part-time job now and plan to get another one to support us." My heart went out to him at these words.

He ended slowly and reminiscently: "We were so much in love before. I haven't stopped loving Dolly, and I can't believe Dolly stopped loving me. What happened was horrible and it was all my fault, but we can't let it stand in the way of our happiness together! Please, Dr. Barron, prepare the way for me with Dolly. Tell her all I just told you. Pray she would be willing to meet with me and forgive me for what I did."

It seemed to me that Jonathan was much too optimistic in his assessment of the situation. My deep sadness and spiritual burden of the night before persisted. I told him I was seeing Dolly that afternoon, would tell her of his intentions, and attempt to persuade her to meet with him and forgive him.

17

Promoting the Death Culture

"Come with me," I said to Dolly Hernandez, "I want to show you something." We were sitting in the living room of my house the afternoon after Jonathan's mentoring session, and I had briefly shared his plans for the future with her. Her first reaction had been a noncommittal silence, followed by a decisive shake of her head.

"It would have to start with my meeting Jonathan," she said, "and I don't want to ever see him again after what he did to me." How do I change her mind, Father? I prayed. Shall I immediately resort to my "treasures of darkness" or begin with something more joyful and less ominous? You put the idea into my mind that I could show Dolly the room Lisa and I had prepared for our child in the first flush of our happiness over his or her conception. I got up and walked over to the room with Dolly right behind me.

I opened the door and had her come in. It was not a very large room, but it was cozy, happy and bright, just right for a little child to begin feeling at home in Your world, dear Father. The sun was streaming through the south window with its snowy white gauzy curtains. The wallpaper Lisa had chosen featured birds on flowery branches on a very light, almost white, beige background, "suitable for a boy or a girl," my experienced wife had said. We had painstakingly and lovingly put it up one happy Saturday in early October.

There was the baby bed, large enough to serve through our child's toddler stage, its firm mattress already covered with its fitted white sheet and a stack of baby blankets at its foot end. There was the dresser of wood painted a gleaming white, decorated with little decals of birds and flowers repeating the theme of the wallpaper. It held baby clothes, diapers, bathing and grooming supplies and any other odds and ends that might be needed. There were shelves for baby toys and even already books for very young children. There was a baby swing, a high chair, a regular chair, and a lovely old rocking chair Lisa had found in a secondhand furniture store.

"My wife and I thought we would like to sit here together sometimes," I explained, "she would use the rocking chair with little Lucinda or Jack and I the regular chair." (We had decided to name our child after my mother if a girl and after Lisa's father if a boy.)

"It's lovely," Dolly half whispered, "just lovely. You must have enjoyed getting it ready." She kept looking wistfully at everything.

"We did," I confirmed. "It was one of the greatest joys of our early life together. We used to go in here almost every evening to look at it all just before we went to bed. We still do it about once a week. We love to imagine what it will be like after our baby is born and home with us in this room."

"I'll tell you one thing, Dr. Barron," Dolly said with a little giggle. "Right at first you won't even use the baby bed at night, especially if Mrs. Barron is planning to nurse the baby."

"She is," I said, "but why would we not use the baby bed?"

"Because it would be too much of a hassle," Dolly said, "that's what my older married sister told me. You'll both be too tired to get up and get the baby from your room to this room and back again several times during the night. It will be much easier to just keep him right beside you in your own bed so he can nurse whenever he wants to right away. He won't need to cry, and you'll like it better that way too—to have your little baby right there next to you, all warm and cuddly."

She broke off. I knew she imagined her own baby like that, by her side. We walked back to the living room. After a brief silence I said gently, "Please reconsider, Dolly. Jonathan is now a Christian. He has broken off all ties with the occult. He loves you. He wants to marry you and be a good husband and father to you and your child. He is about to work two jobs to provide for you both."

I leaned forward and took her hands in mine. "Dolly!" I pleaded, "I showed you our baby's room to let you see how good it can be to be married and to prepare for your child. Why not at least give Jonathan a chance to meet you and beg you to forgive him?"

"He can beg as long as he wants," Dolly said sharply, pulling away her hands and sitting up straight and stiff in her chair. "That's easy for him and lets him off free! Melinda says—" She suddenly stopped, biting her lip.

"Who is Melinda?" I asked, sitting up straight in my turn. She is the death culture's advocate with Dolly, Your still small voice immediately told me. Be prepared to do battle, drawing on your "treasures of darkness."

"Melinda Johnson is a lady I know from Fairfield Business College," Dolly said both challengingly and defensively. "She is a job counselor by profession and took a class in office management with me. At the college's Christmas party I asked for her advice about what happened to me because she is a counselor, a woman, and it won't get back to my family through her." I thought it was understandable that Dolly had wanted to talk to the woman, but I was afraid that from now on Dolly might run whatever advice I gave her by Melinda Johnson and let her have the last word.

Dolly was obviously taken with her new confidante. "Melinda knows a lot more about life than I do," she said with naive awe. "You see, she is thirty-five years old, fifteen years older than I. She has been married and divorced, and she has had two abortions. She says if you do it early enough, there is nothing to it." Dolly looked at me almost defiantly and added, "When I told her how I got pregnant, she said I should get an abortion right away and be done with Jonathan for good. She said I must think of making a life of my own first of all."

The woman thinks exactly like I did at that age, I thought sadly. Please be with me and give me what to say to Dolly and how to say it, Father, I prayed. "Dolly," I asked, "what would your father have said about this advice?"

She looked at me, stricken. "He would have told me never to speak to Melinda again," she said. "He believed that abortion was a mortal sin. He said children were God's precious gifts to us."

"As you already know," I said. "I agree with him completely on abortion. Perhaps you can think of me a little as a sort of substitute father."

"That's right, Dr. Barron! I do think of you like that," Dolly eagerly interrupted. "Is that all right with you?" Her earlier near defiance reverted to her usual childlike, soft and gentle demeanor. How open she is in her malleable childlikeness to the suggestions and guidance of others, I thought sadly. It makes her very lovable and is doubtless one reason why Jonathan loves her so much, but it is also an open invitation to purveyors of evil like Melinda Johnson to try to seduce her away from You, Father.

"It is very much all right with me, Dolly," I said, "and I think of you as a sort of substitute daughter too, for my daughter Ecstasy. She died when she was fourteen, through my fault. I forced her to have an abortion. Her uterus was perforated, causing very heavy internal bleeding. She went into a coma and never came out of it. She was on life support for over a year till I finally had it discontinued."

"*O Dios mio, que barbaridad,*" murmured Dolly and looked at me with horror and compassion, "How awful! I am so sorry for you!"

"Don't be sorry for me," I said severely, "I was guilty of murder. I would never have done it if I had been a real father to her. It has taught me the hard way how to be like a real father to you now, with God's help. I will never counsel you to have an abortion, first because God forbids it in His Word, and also because of what I did to my daughter. I will not condone it if someone else recommends it to you. I promise you that if you decide on it, I will try to stop you in any way I can." I added penitently, "My poor little Ecstasy! She wanted so much to give birth to her baby. If I had only relented, she and the baby would be alive today." I must not speak of myself, I thought; I must focus strictly on Dolly and pry her loose from her death counselor.

"What else did Melinda tell you?" I asked. Dolly gave me a somewhat disjointed report of Melinda's opinions. Melinda had said that being a mere wife and mother, a stupid housewife, was a fate worse than death and anyhow outdated and despised among young modern women today. Marriage was nothing but slavery or boredom for a woman as it robbed her of her independence, professional advancement, and mental development. Having children aggravated all these terrible disadvantages and should be avoided at all costs. "And thanks to the militant feminists of the last generation and an open-minded Supreme Court we women now have complete reproductive freedom!" Melinda had proclaimed to a fascinated Dolly.

It was the typical women's liberation gospel I had once preached myself in many public speeches and articles. I thought with shame and horror that I had helped produce the Melinda Johnsons who were now promoting the death culture at the grass roots. Father, forgive me! I bear part of the blame for Dolly and millions of girls like her now killing their babies by abortion.

Melinda had also painted Dolly's promising future as an ambitious, hardworking, self-absorbed single professional woman in the brightest possible colors if only she concentrated on it. "You have graduated from high school," she had lectured her, "you belong to the most successful minority among young Hispanic women. Now you are going to business school, and after you get a good job you can save up enough money or get a minority scholarship or equal opportunity admission to a good college. All such chances to make something of yourself would be lost if you wind up as a single mother or marry that worthless man who knocked you up. You don't want to end up being a poor woman with a dead end job living in Fairfield's little Mexico like your mother, do you?"

Melinda had also described the methods of abortion, omitting what might go wrong. I reminded Dolly again of what had happened to Ecstasy, whose abortion had been done in the third month of pregnancy when it was supposed to be safest. She listened attentively and seemed to come around to my conviction. After a thoughtful silence she said haltingly, "You are so different from Melinda, Dr. Barron. She talks to me like she was making a motivational speech to a group. She studies me all the time from the outside as if I was a client in her counseling office. All she really wants is to get me to do what she wants me to and to think like she thinks. You talk to me like you really care and are hurt with me on the *inside*."

I nodded. "It is because Christ is in me loving you and hurting with you," I said, "I wish you could have Him in your heart too. Before I came to Him, I was exactly like Melinda Johnson. I only thought of myself and never hurt with anyone."

"Was it easier for you then?" Dolly asked in a whisper.

"Was it easier for me then?" I repeated. I could not answer right away. I had never asked myself that question. I saw that my whole witness to Dolly, even to everyone around me, hung upon the answer.

Oh Father, I prayed, You just cut open my heart last night so I would face my buried memories again. Your knife in my heart and the whiplash of the memories on my back hurt almost unbearably. I dare not tell anyone that it is easier for me to live with You now than it was before I knew You!

No, not "easier," You gently answered. Gethsemane, the mocking, the scourging, the cross on Calvary were not "easy" for Christ. He prayed to Me with tears to remove that cup from Him. But He also prayed that not His will but Mine be done, and My will was that *"though He were a Son, yet learned He obedience by the things which He suffered, and being made perfect, He became the author of eternal salvation unto all them that obey Him"* (Hebrews 5:8–9). No, it was not "easy"! But it was the prerequisite of being and becoming perfect in My sight even for Him My only begotten Son, and how much more for you, my sons and daughters by redemption and adoption! And remember, son, it was for the *joy* set before Him—My joy which I shared with you the moment after you received Me into your heart—that Jesus endured the cross, despising the shame (Hebrews 12:2). My joy is set before you and Dolly, too, whose father you are in this hour. Tell her!

I turned to Dolly. "It is not 'easier' for me now than then," I said, "but it is better, because I no longer suffer as a murderer, which I was, and which you would be if you aborted your baby. We no longer are meddlers or 'busybodies' in the affairs of others, like Melinda Johnson (1 Peter 4:15). Christ Himself had to learn obedience from the things which He suffered; how much more we! He did it for the joy, the Father's joy set before Him. His joy is for you and me as well. No, our new lives in Christ are not 'easier'! But even though we are crucified with Him, they are right and good, and even joyful with the deep, everlasting joy which is not of this world."

I then implored Dolly once more to let Jonathan ask for her forgiveness. "Christ forgave us our sins," I said. "We should forgive each other. The Lord's Prayer says, 'Forgive us our debts, even as we also have forgiven our debtors.' Please do it, Dolly. Ask God to help you do it."

"Don't you understand that I can't?" she cried out, "I still love him so much! If I see him again, I will fall all the way in love with him again. I want to but I am afraid of it too. He betrayed me before! I can't risk being betrayed again."

18

There Are No Accidents with God

From then on we who were closest to Jonathan and Dolly as well as Jonathan himself prayed desperately that their drama might yet have a good outcome, and above all that Dolly might not abort their child. We knew that "the serpent at Eden" had now gained immediate, powerful access to Dolly through Melinda Johnson. We entreated You that her influence might not stifle the inner voice of conscience in Dolly's heart. Jonathan, his parents, my son Luke and his family and especially my dear wife also prayed for me because I was the only one of us in regular contact with her.

Thank You, dear Father, that January went by and You had preserved Dolly from following Melinda's advice to abort the baby, which she kept imposing on Dolly much more often than I could counteract it at my weekly meetings with her. Melinda was now almost endlessly repeating the death culture's lie that the abortion would make everything all right.

"Your life will go on as though this whole nightmare had never happened to you," she would say to Dolly. "Look at me! I have had two abortions and they haven't harmed me a bit. On the contrary, they have ridded me of both the pregnancies." She never spoke of what had been gotten rid of as babies nor of the men who caused them. "And good riddance, I say! Who needs men anyway! Take them and drop them, I tell you." When Dolly repeated this motto to me at our last meeting in January, I could not help remembering how Neva had called my former contemptuous attitude towards the women I slept with "James loves them and leaves them." Again I saw with shame that Melinda Johnson and the old James Barron were as alike as two peas in a pod.

As I fought against Melinda's advice from the abyss, I was enabled by recent research to explode the death culture's soothing lie that once the abortion has been performed, the mother's life will go on just as it did before or better. Thanks to the faithful pro-life people who had investigated the harm abortion did to women, there was now much more information presenting the disastrous reality suppressed by the news media, the medical establishment, and government agencies. The book that especially helped me was *Lime 5* by Mark Crutcher (published by Life Dynamics, Inc., P. O. Box 2226, Denton, Texas 76202). By Your good providence it had just been published in 1996 so I could use it with Dolly and also in my spring semester ethics class. Its very first chapter, "Safe and Legal," described a multitude of abortions at all stages of pregnancy gone horribly awry. The book also described long term effects of abortion including ectopic pregnancy and subsequent sterility, breast cancer, and deep psychological harm due to the mothers' guilt feelings.

What can and often does happen in abortions is so horrible that at first I only read excerpts to Dolly. However, in February, the fourth month of her pregnancy, I asked her to read selected chapters herself when it became ominously apparent to me that she was still or perhaps even more than ever open to having an abortion due to Melinda Johnson's tireless persistence. Melinda did not scruple to tell Dolly that abortionists like Dr. Hellmann had much more compassion for girls like her than did opponents of abortion such as I. "Dr. Hellmann *does* something to help you deal with your problem," she said. "What is Dr. Barron doing for you except sitting there listening and talking?" And that was all, she said, we "anti-abortion" people, especially the judgmental Bible-believing Christians among us, did to help the poor women and girls caught with problem pregnancies!

I indignantly told Dolly the truth: *we,* not the pro-choice crowd, had pregnancy counseling services funded by voluntary contributions, not largely by tax monies like Planned Parenthood, and helping expectant mothers make a real choice between abortion and life for their children. *We,* not the pro-choice crowd, contributed money for the babies' delivery and aftercare, maternity and baby clothes, opened our homes for expectant mothers, and much else. I told Dolly that I had made sure she would receive all the help she needed for herself and the baby from the Fairfield and indeed also the Lonely Prairie and Battle Hill pro-life communities. *We,* not the pro-choice crowd, were the ones concerned about the proper sanitary maintenance of abortion clinics, which often operated in very unsanitary conditions and were less regulated and inspected by government agencies than veterinary clinics. *We* did all we could to research and publicize the risks of abortion so women considering it might at least make an *informed* choice. Abortion providers like Derek Hellmann only offered abortions and pocketed the not inconsiderable profits.

The "pro-choice" people's deepest rationale for their stand was that "choice" about abortion freed them from caring, really caring personally and individually not only for the child but also for the mother. I knew that because I had been one of their leaders and spokesmen for many years. In obedience to You, Father, I endured the pain and shame of sharing with Dolly how I, then vociferously "pro-choice," had shunned any personal involvement with Ecstasy all her life, but especially during her coma after her abortion. I told her how I had not *wanted* to sit by my daughter's bedside to speak to her lovingly and perhaps bring her out of her coma. I told her how I had signed with relief the authorization forms to have her life support machines switched off. I told her how I walked out of the hospital afterwards past the pro-life protesters with my head held high and my face hard. I told her that I had done it all with no regrets. I told her of Dr. Bernard Nathanson, the early leader of the "pro-choice" movement who had given it its name and had aborted thousands of babies, including his own child, without any compunction because he had shared "the mentality of the abortionist."

"How can we sanction the killing of our own children," I asked Dolly, "unless we secretly or blatantly put our own selves first? We cannot help not knowing that, and sooner or later the guilt of it will crush us." She nodded silently. She had kept her appointments with me and seemed willing to resist Melinda's death culture blandishments when she left, but I was not at peace about her nor did my sadness and premonition of impending catastrophe ever leave me all those weeks. However You, dear Father, gave me the sure knowledge that You were with me and never left me even for a moment.

You in Your mercy sent me my son Luke to help me. He came to our house unannounced the afternoon of the second Monday in February just after I returned from having brought Dolly back to the Fairfield Business College. Doubtless she would see Melinda Johnson soon afterwards and my efforts that day and perhaps throughout my relationship with Dolly would be undone. I was downcast and nearly hopeless about how it would all end. At least, I tried to comfort myself, Dolly is still carrying the baby. Her figure was beginning to show it.

And then I saw Luke's car parked in front of our home, and there he stood smiling to welcome me. "God put you on my mind all day today, Dad," he told me, "I felt I should come to see you as soon as I could. What excellent timing our Lord gave us! I just got here a couple of minutes ago. I can tell from your face something serious is burdening you. How can I help?"

"Oh Luke, I am so glad to see you," I said. "It's about Dolly Hernandez. I am afraid we are losing the battle for the life of her child." We went into the house, sat down, and I told him Jonathan and Dolly's whole story since Christmas. I had been able to share only bits and pieces with him when we had last met at the January "Order of Saint James" outreach in Battle Hill.

I dispassionately told him how You had cut open my heart to make me recall my buried painful memories of Ecstasy as the "treasures of darkness" I was to use with Dolly. It was a welcome relief to unburden myself before him. It also helped me see that by now I had used with Dolly every one of the hard memories You had made me face anew. I had omitted nothing, and I had used them as best I could at the times and in the manner You had laid on my heart. I realized that now there was nothing left for me except to pray that they might do the work in Dolly's heart for which You had purposed them.

Luke heard me out quietly with the calm, trust-inspiring compassion of the born and experienced Christian counselor. "It's really a wonderful story, Dad," he said at last, "of how our Lord has been using you all along, even through the experiences of your life before your conversion. They didn't just happen! There are no accidents with God. He made you exactly as you are. He knows the number of hairs on your head. He timed the moment of your conversion to the second. He saw you stand still at the door of that family reunion hall and directed little Sylvia to see you and cry out to you. And yes, He saw you before that when you did evil things and omitted doing what was right, and it is all working out now for good for them who love Him according to His purpose."

"Like my being with your birth mother and abandoning her and you," I said sadly.

"That, too," Luke acknowledged, "but also Lisa's overhearing you when you spoke of us to Jonathan Wood. God knew and prepared it all so I would be restored to you as your son, and so we would meet 'for such a time as this,' Esther 4:14. As He did for Queen Esther, He will now do for Dolly, and I believe for Jonathan, too. Our eternal God is from age to age the same. He does not change. There are no accidents with our all-knowing, all-powerful, just and faithful Father God!"

Luke looked at me with joy. "Dad, it is time for us to praise Him now," he said, "I believe He has sent me to you to tell you that soon—perhaps after a final trial, but soon—you will no longer have to grieve or be ashamed of anything you have done or not done in the past that might relate to this present trouble." After a moment he added even more joyfully, "It's a token of His good will for you to be fulfilled in His presence through all eternity. There you will no longer be ashamed of anything in your past! Be sure of it. *'They shall not be ashamed,' He says, 'that wait for me,'* Isaiah 49:23. It's beginning already here and now."

My heart thrilled to my son's message. I had no doubt it came from You. You had put me on his mind all day long so he would come all the way to Fairfield to give it to me. This reminded me again of how You had put Jonathan on my mind in New York the Saturday before that fateful Sunday after Halloween. But I had not called him as You asked me to. You had forgiven me, and Jonathan and his parents had too, but was not everything evil that had come to pass since then my fault?

"I am at the root of all this present trouble with Jonathan and Dolly," I said and told Luke what I had failed to do in obedience to You.

"If you haven't already, you ought to confess it to Dolly the next time you see her, and ask her to forgive you," he said, "but that is not the only thing you should share with her. As Solomon teaches us, *there is a time to every purpose under the heaven: a time to weep, and a time to laugh; a time to mourn, and a time to dance, Ecclesiastes 3:1, 4.*" Luke became utterly solemn. He put his hand on my arm as he continued, "Dad, you have been called to share your shame over your sinful past, but also your *joy*, God's joy He shared with you the moment after you received Him in your heart. Surely some elder in the faith has already told you that long ago."

"Yes," I said softly, "my beloved first mentor, Bernard Gottlieb. He told me that Brother Lawrence had rightly said that God often chooses those who had been the greatest sinners to receive His greatest grace, because this can reveal His goodness more dramatically, and that this was what He did with me—that, and sharing His joy with me when I returned to Him. He said that these were the two marks He set upon me, and that they were what He wanted me to share with others."

"Then do it," Luke said, "share your joy, our Heavenly Father's joy, with Dolly the next time you see her. Don't spend any more time battling the lies of the enemy by witnessing to her of your shame and hurt. You have done that now in full; God's time for you to weep and to mourn is ending. His time is coming for you soon to laugh and to dance. Tell Dolly of His joy. Use your favorite Scriptures as you do it. His Holy Spirit is stronger than the death culture's spirit from hell."

"Our glad Creator will have His good heart's desire fulfilled at last," I said. The words came from my earliest testimony to the men about to dismiss me from the Bertrand Russell Institute. They had brought one of them, my friend J. P. Knightley, to You, Father. Luke and I looked at each other in Your joy.

"Two more things," Luke said, "one, let us visit Dolly's mother together. Since Dolly's father was so strongly pro-life, her mother probably is too and might help us keep Dolly from an abortion. She surely knows by now that Dolly is pregnant—it's her fourth month. I understand Mrs. Hernandez was born in Mexico, and I can speak to her in her own native language. The other thing we need to do is get photos of Dolly to all the pro-life sidewalk counselors at the Hellmann Clinic. Melinda Johnson might persuade her to go ahead with the abortion and even drive her there. If necessary, we must try to stop her at the last moment from going in."

19
"It's Over and You Have Lost"

And now things proceeded with sudden, almost frightening speed. Just as You had urged Luke to reestablish me in Your original calling of sharing my shame over my evil past and also Your joy in my heart after receiving You, so You now urged me to bring that joy to Dolly.

Do it right away, You said, do not delay! The "serpent in Eden," as he did with Eve, is seducing Dolly by the temporary ease she can obtain by and for herself here and now. Show her the choice before her clearly between settling for the ease of this world or receiving Me, and with Me, My eternal joy, which is not of this world and incomparably greater and better.

The last line of my beloved Pascal Memorial shot into my mind: "Eternally joyful for one single day of renunciation on earth!" I saw that Your word to him in 1654 in Paris, France was the same as Your word to me in 1997 in Fairfield, America. Pascal, too, had deplored his earlier separation from You, confessing he had "run away from You, denied You, crucified You." But You the Consuming Fire—he called his vision of You "FIRE"—had burned away his rebellion and become his eternal joy.

With joy I prayed then and pray to You again now, recalling the words of the Pascal Memorial. How great and wonderful You are, ever living and never changing, dear and beloved Father, Son, and Holy Spirit, You Who speak to us as You spoke to Abraham, Isaac, and Jacob, You their and our feared and beloved God, *not* the God of philosophers and learned men! You the God of Jesus Christ, You Who gives us certitude, joy and peace, You Who gives us eternal life by letting us know You the only true God and Jesus Christ Whom You have sent—I love and praise You! For You I forget the whole world and find the renunciation of it total and sweet!

Thus strengthened, I called Dolly on the phone and asked her to meet with me as soon as possible. She was taken aback and almost refused because we had just met the day before but finally agreed to see me Wednesday, February 12, two days later. I began by asking her to forgive me for not calling Jonathan from New York back in November. Much like Jonathan she forgave me immediately, even telling me with her sweet gentle smile that she might have done the same in my situation. Also like Jonathan she felt my call would not have made any difference. "He would still have gone ahead with what he did," she said resignedly. "It just happened, or maybe it was fate."

"Dolly," I said, "it was neither chance nor fate. It was the outcome of our own free will obeying or opposing God's good will for us. I opposed God's good will by not warning Jonathan. Jonathan opposed God's good will by doing what he did. Thank you for forgiving me. I can't help but beg you again to forgive Jonathan as well."

"I can't risk it!" Dolly said, "I am not ready to risk it! Maybe I can later, when I don't love him any more."

At these words tears came into her eyes. "I can't imagine not loving him any more," she murmured piteously, "but I keep remembering what he did to me. It's a vicious circle! Forgiving him would put it all behind us, I know, but it would bring us together again. And I am back where I started—I am not ready to risk it!"

She looked past me as she added in a hard voice unlike her own, "Maybe I should do something that would *make* us stop loving each other. Melinda says abortion usually does that."

"For God's sake, Dolly," I said with fear, "please don't listen to her! I once did something much like this to end my own first love." I briefly told her the story of how I had broken off with little Karen Margrave on the first anniversary of our relationship. "At least I did not literally murder anyone then, as an abortion would," I said, "but I killed our love. It almost destroyed me. If I had not finally said yes to Karen's God, the real God Who is Love and Joy, I would have gone on loveless and joyless forever."

I came to the purpose of our meeting. "And that is what I really wanted to talk to you about so urgently," I said, "God loves us and wants to share His joy with us. His joy is so great that it blots out all grief, shame, and yes, fear in the end. He does not work by chance or fate! Nothing 'just happens' in His perfect providence! That is why He is not unreliable like chance or fate! And He is a Person! He loves us and walks and talks with us through our valleys of weeping and helps us make them places of springs. We can trust Him, love Him back and rejoice in Him even in the midst of suffering. He, His love and His great joy are incomparably better than any temporary ease, security or comfort here and now."

I had talked myself into enthusiasm about You, dear Father. It must have been showing on my face, for Dolly looked at me with a widening smile. I smiled back at her and went on: "That is why the Apostle Paul, who suffered greatly in God's service, could write us this message of joy: *'Rejoice in the Lord always: and again I say, Rejoice! Let your moderation be known unto all men. The Lord is at hand. Be careful for nothing; but in every thing by prayer and supplication with thanksgiving let your requests be made known unto God. And the peace of God, which passeth all understanding, shall keep your hearts and minds through Christ Jesus.'* That's in the Bible, in Philippians 4:4–7. Cast all your burden upon the Lord, Dolly! Live and rejoice in His joy!"

"It sounds so beautiful, Dr. Barron," Dolly said longingly, "it's almost too good to be true! I will think about it." We prayed together, and then she had to go. We agreed to meet again as usual the afternoon of the next Monday, February 24. All in all I was encouraged as we parted.

That same evening my son called me and told me of a telephone conversation he had just had with Mrs. Hernandez. He had tried to set up a time when he and I could both meet with her. He had introduced himself as my son and a long time Christian missionary in Mexico, of course speaking Spanish all the while. When he told her we wanted to visit with her about Dolly, she had burst out crying and then started talking to him at length.

She had known for some time that her daughter was pregnant, hoping that Dolly herself would bring up the matter. But that had not happened. "My daughter does not trust me," Mrs. Hernandez had said sadly, adding resentfully, "she trusts her new friend Melinda from her business college more than me, her own mother!" She did not like Melinda Johnson, whom she called a bad influence on her daughter.

Mrs. Hernandez was certain that Jonathan was the father of the baby and angry with him because he had stopped seeing Dolly. "They were so close before," Mrs. Hernandez said, "I would have liked it better if Dolores had dated a Latino young man, but Jonathan came from a good family and I hoped for the best, even though he had some bad friends."

And now that the pregnancy was starting to show, tongues began to wag in their neighborhood. "Why did Dolores have to bring this shame on us?" Mrs. Hernandez had asked Luke, "If my husband had still been with us, it would not have happened. He would have talked to Jonathan to do the right thing and marry her right away!"

Luke had then explained that Jonathan was willing to do that and wanted to meet with Dolly to ask her to forgive him for a wrong he had done to her, but that Dolly refused to see him. "The wrong was to get her pregnant," Mrs. Hernandez said sternly, and Luke had agreed. Then he told her that we were afraid Dolly was being talked into having an abortion by Melinda.

"An abortion! Never!" Mrs. Hernandez cried out. "It is a mortal sin! But I agree with you. That woman might just stop in front of our house early one morning, honk the horn of her car for Dolores to come out, like she does whenever she comes by, and take her to the abortion place in Battle Hill. Dolores trusts that woman more than me, her own mother, I tell you!"

In the end Mrs. Hernandez promised that she would immediately call Luke and me if she suspected that Melinda was carrying out this plan. She said she would also plead with Dolly to give birth to the baby, her grandchild. Luke and I felt the phone call had accomplished all we could hope for and thanked You for Mrs. Hernandez's help.

I informed Jonathan of all this. He immediately contacted all the area pro-life groups, told them that Melinda Johnson might bring Dolly to Hellmann's clinic for an abortion and asked that their sidewalk counselors do all they could to stop them. He had copies made of an ID type photo he had of Dolly for all the sidewalk counselors so they could recognize her. He took time off from both his jobs and all his classes on Thursday for driving to Lonely Prairie and Battle Hill to deliver the photos before Hellmann's clinic did business again on Friday, February 21. He also alerted our "Order of Saint James" members before our second outreach the upcoming Saturday. As I have described earlier, this was the first time all our students wore their "Little Brothers of Saint James" T-shirts and put an end to the "escorts from hell" taunting me as "Saint James."

Melinda Johnson and Dolly did not show up at Hellmann's clinic that Friday or Saturday. We all breathed a sigh of relief. Our baby—we had all begun to think of Jonathan and Dolly's baby as ours—had survived another week!

Near noon the following Monday morning right after my mentoring session with Jonathan my phone rang. A cool, arrogant female voice I had never heard before identified the caller as Melinda Johnson. "Dolores Hernandez will not be coming in for her counseling session with you this afternoon, Dr. Barron," she said imperiously, brooking no questions or comments, "and I would like to take her place." I said OK and she hung up immediately.

I asked my wife to be with us during my meeting with Melinda Johnson. I remembered from my years among enemies of the faith that they thought no trick too low to use against a prominent "failed atheist" like me. Being alone with me in my home might well be Melinda Johnson's plan to discredit me by falsely accusing me of sexual harassment.

Melinda Johnson arrived punctually. She was a svelte, well dressed woman of medium height. Her artificially bright blonde hair gleamed silvery white under the ceiling light of our living room. I could see why Dolly was impressed by her, but I also sensed the arrogance, hardness and love of power beneath the surface smoothness of this job counselor whose chosen profession was to evaluate, critique, and direct all who came to consult her. I also saw she had an eye for men and sought to arouse their lust.

To my disagreeable surprise she began our meeting by unashamedly looking me over from head to foot and telling me right in front of my wife that she thought me a very handsome man. "I can see why you don't let him out of your sight, Mrs. Barron," she told Lisa, "especially in your condition."

Thankfully Lisa has a great sense of humor and the gift of excellent repartees. "You are so right, Ms. Johnson," she smiled, "I feel so sorry for women who don't have a good and handsome husband and a baby on the way like I do." I barely stopped myself from laughing out loud as I saw Melinda's baffled expression and angry frown. Lisa and I winked at each other as we all took our seats around our living room table.

However, that was the meeting's last moment of relative lightness. "I'll come right to the point," Melinda said briskly. "We are all concerned about the fix Dolores has got herself into. She is a fine young lady and can have a good life if she can put this present obstacle totally behind her. Are we in agreement thus far, Dr. Barron?"

I nodded. "Good," Melinda said. "Now you seem to be working for a reconciliation between Dolores and Jonathan Wood. I think that's rather unrealistic in view of what happened between them."

"Not unrealistic," I said, "because forgiveness of a wrong done to us is the only way to put it truly behind us. My son, who is a family counselor, told me that lack of forgiveness on the part of his counselees causes them to store up more and more fury and bitterness in their hearts so they never heal of their hurts. I don't want that to happen to Dolly."

"Dolores," Melinda corrected and added with irritation, "what kind of a nickname is 'Dolly'? She isn't anybody's little doll to be played with! But let's get back to her problem. I assume your son is a *Christian* counselor, and so are you yourself, or trying to be one. You people always restrict the number of choices open to us in today's society! The choice open to Dolores is termination of the pregnancy. She should have had it done weeks ago, but you kept her from it. Who are you anyway to interfere? You are no relative of hers! You have no business telling her what's best for her! Let her make up her own mind!"

"I could say the same to you, Ms. Johnson," I countered, "the difference between us is that you presume to tell her what's best for her based only on your own fallible authority. I dare not advise Dolly based on such a flimsy ground. She came to me, trusting me as a sort of substitute father. I seek to help her based on the infallible authority of God and His Word, the Bible. It forbids abortion, and I will do all I can to stop Dolly from doing that to her child."

"It's me against God, then," Melinda said, "and it's the same for Dolores. You tried to bring her around to your God by telling her of His joy. His joy! But it didn't work. Now there is nothing more you can do to stop her from choosing, because she already has! That's why she wouldn't come to see you today. I will drive her to the Women's Drive-Through Clinic in Battle Hill this coming Saturday, March First, 1997, so she can have the procedure done, and not a moment too soon. It's over, Dr. Barron. You have lost."

And with her head held high and her face set like a flint Melinda Johnson said good-bye to us and walked out of our house.

20

"Claim the Victory"

All my life I have listened to classical music when troubled, tense, under great pressure or otherwise in special need of solace. You allowed me to keep this comfort after my conversion. After Lisa and my family gave me our piano for Christmas, I would also softly play and sing old Christian hymns at such times.

One of these times was the hour immediately following Melinda Johnson's visit. Utter emptiness was in my mind and heart as I went on softly touching the keys of the instrument. Slowly the story of the prophet Elijah fleeing from evil Queen Jezebel after his victory at Mount Carmel (1 Kings 19) came to me and formed a song set to simple music in a minor key. Here are the words:

(The prayer)
Take me home, let me go, Thee alone would I know!
Take me now, set me free From this life's vanity!
Zealously I have fought, Victory came to nought!
Ask no more, hear my cry: Grant me rest, let me die!
(Your answer)
I thy God am with thee! I have heard thy call!
I have blest thy labor! Thou shalt never fall.
Seven thousand others I have kept for Me
Who will not to idols bow their knee.
In my name and promise claim the victory!
Then in pow'r and glory reign with Me! Amen!

I jotted down the words and then I, who had never composed music in my life, drew the lines of the customary music score sheet on a blank sheet of paper and wrote the melody line and then the chords which accompanied it. It all took only about fifteen minutes. In astonishment, almost in awe, I played and sang the song as though it had always existed. And so it had! It had always existed with You, dear Father, to be given to me now when I, like Elijah, had thought myself defeated but was not because You had been with me all along.

An immense joy flooded my heart. "Lisa!" I called, but she did not hear me; I knew she must have withdrawn to her office so I could take refuge in the music unobserved. How well she understands me, I thought gratefully as I hastened to find her.

"It's not all over and we haven't lost," I called out to her as I opened the door to her office, "and you are the best wife in the whole world."

Lisa had been working at her computer and turned around to face me. "I am glad to hear you say that," she said, smiling, "now tell me why."

"Melinda Johnson," I exulted, "was cocky enough to tell us exactly when she plans to take Dolly to Hellmann's clinic. We have four days to do something about it! Talk to Dolly's mother, who is on our side, to make Dolly change her mind. Mobilize as many people as we can to keep vigil Saturday at Hellmann's entrance. Carry signs speaking directly to Dolly. Have our pregnancy help centers ready to assist her. And most important of all, get everyone we know in the churches and the pro-life groups to pray. Of course we ourselves—I, you, Jonathan, and if possible Luke and his family must be there at Hellmann's clinic on Saturday to pray and speak to Dolly if we can. Perhaps there is more we can do when the time comes. Oh no, it's not all over and we haven't lost!"

"You are right," Lisa said. She got up from her computer and walked over to me. "And why did you say I was the best wife in the whole world?" she asked.

"Only the best wife in the whole world," I answered, "understands that when her husband is down and out—as I was after that woman left—and shows it by wanting to be alone and play sad music, as I did—she should wait quietly and leave him to himself and God till he is better."

"I also understand," Lisa said, "that you feel ashamed to let me know when you are down and out. You don't talk about it, but I know anyway. You want to play sad music all by yourself. That's the sign. It's hard then to leave you alone and trust Him for you. Thank God it doesn't happen very often."

It was another deep and precious bond of the love between us, perhaps between all good wives and their husbands whom they must understand and comfort without spoken words.

We made all the preparations we had thought of. I was preoccupied and distracted as I taught my classes the rest of the week and told my students why. As a result they promised me they would pray for us, and for Melinda Johnson's plan to fail. All the "Little Brothers of Saint James" among them volunteered to come to Battle Hill to help us at the abortion clinic, aware that they might have to be there all day because Melinda Johnson might bring Dolly in at any time between 7:00 A.M. and 5:00 P.M. I was deeply encouraged and saw them all as among Your "seven thousand others who had not bowed their knee" to the idol of self-worship of our time.

On Saturday morning at about 5:30 we were already up and getting ready to drive to Hellmann's clinic when my telephone rang. In broken English Mrs. Hernandez told me "that woman" had just come by and picked up Dolly. She could hardly tell me the news because she was weeping. I knew she must have tried in vain to stop her daughter. I tried to comfort her, asked her to pray, and told her that we were on our way to stop the abortion with God's help. Oh Father, please comfort this dear mother! I prayed. Grant us victory also for her sake! I remembered the song you had given me and added, "I claim the victory in Your name and promise."

It takes about an hour and a half to drive from Fairfield to Battle Hill. Now we knew the confrontation would be almost as soon as the clinic opened. We must not be late! We must hurry!

At this early hour there usually was no traffic on the highway, but this time we found ourselves in a long caravan of cars driving in our direction as fast as the speed limit allowed. "My students! The 'seven thousand others'!" I exclaimed and laughed with joy. I explained to Lisa about the "seven thousand others" in Your answer to Elijah in 1 Kings 19 and also to me in the song You had given me.

After about half an hour car after car in our caravan passed a late model red car ahead of us. When we ourselves passed it, we saw that its driver was a woman with silvery white blonde hair. "Melinda!" Lisa and I exclaimed. We saw that we would arrive at Hellmann's before she did. However, we would need to park at a distance from the clinic, and that would shorten the time we had between our own arrival and hers. We must hurry as fast as we could! My sense of urgency was so strong that after we arrived and parked, I told Lisa that I would run to the clinic ahead of her so I myself would be there at all costs when Melinda and Dolly arrived. I stretched my hand towards her in good-bye and she grasped it with a smile. It was the last sign of our love for each other before what lay ahead of us.

The Hellmann Clinic is at the intersection of a busy thoroughfare and a narrow side street. Approaching cars must first slow down for the right hand turn into the side street, and then again for another right hand turn onto a one-lane driveway to the clinic's parking lot. We pro-life sidewalk counselors and demonstrators are legally allowed to stand on the sidewalk and to approach incoming cars across the strip of grass between it and the street. Of course we are prohibited by law to block the driveway.

The entire property is surrounded by a six-foot high chain link fence with a gate across the driveway. The "escorts from hell" unlock the gate, roll it open when business opens and shut it again after it closes. During business hours they stand inside the chain link fence to mock and curse us. The biggest and most aggressive ones cluster near the entrance, including the virtual giant we call "Tiny." When we have enough people we can surround the entire property. Thanks to our students this is how it was now.

I arrived at the entrance just as the "escorts" were about to open the gate. Our people were holding up their usual signs and also special posters saying, "Dolly, we love you," and "Dolly, please keep your baby." Right at the entrance stood Jonathan Wood, and with him Luke, Sarah, and my grandchildren. I took my place with them. Jonathan held up a big sign which read in huge letters "DOLLY, WILL YOU MARRY ME?" No one who drove in from the street could possibly miss it.

Three cars were waiting in line, Melinda's not among them. Lisa arrived and stood by my side. Luke led us in prayer. We tried to hand pro-life tracts to the waiting clients, but they would not accept them. The escorts opened the gate with a great clatter, and the first women about to undergo "the procedure" were brought in. A lull of several minutes followed, filled by the escorts' taunts and cuss words.

And then the red car for which we had braced ourselves drove slowly around the intersection and past the line of pro-lifers towards us. We could see the shiny blonde head of Melinda Johnson above the steering wheel, her face a study in hardness. Beside her Dolly sat staring straight ahead fixedly and unhappily. The car was slowly making its turn into the driveway.

Jonathan turned his sign so it fully faced the car. Dolly saw it and visibly shrank back in her seat. I stood right next to Jonathan and saw them look at each other. I felt the whole world was standing still for a heartbeat as her eyes widened and met his. She half turned towards him. Her face came alive with tender and irrepressible love.

Jonathan handed his sign to Luke. He stretched his arms out wide. "Come to me, Dolly!" he shouted. She turned fully to face him. Her lips moved. I thought she was saying yes.

The car had completed its turn onto the driveway. Only a few feet still separated it from me, the first of us by the gate. Once it entered the parking lot we could not intervene any more. The escorts from hell, with Tiny in the lead, were coming closer. The car inched ahead.

I had promised Dolly I would do all I could to stop her from having an abortion! I knew I broke the law but I also knew that "We ought to obey God rather than men" (Acts 5:29) and stepped forward into the car's path. I stood still in front of it as tall and straight as I could, my arms stretched out wide.

With a shuddering screech the car came to a halt inches from me. Dolly opened her door and slid out to the driveway. Jonathan rushed forward to hug her. I saw him lead her back safely to where my wife, Luke and his family stood ready to receive them.

Melinda Johnson looked at me with murder in her face. For a moment I thought she might run me over with her car. But she did not have to. Tiny and the escorts from hell had reached me now. I made no resistance as they tackled me and threw me roughly to the pavement. They showered me with curses as they began to kick me with their booted feet. Tiny repeatedly aimed at my ribs as his part in this outpour of fury. It hurt with every impact and soon with every breath I took. Finally he yanked me to my feet and punched me in the face as hard as he could with his big right fist. It felt as if he had broken my jaw. Blood trickled down my left cheek.

I heard the wailing of a police siren. Soon two policemen arrived on the scene. They arrested me because I had broken the law by stepping in front of Melinda's car. I was handcuffed, taken to police headquarters and booked. No one took any notice of what Tiny and his escorts had done to me. Since this was my first offense and my job and residence were in the state, my bail was set at "only" a thousand dollars. I was pushed into an empty holding cell without any bench or chairs. It stank. Its walls and floor were covered with vomit, excrement and vile graffiti. I could barely stand upright by now but shrank from sitting on the filthy floor or leaning against the reeking walls.

After about half an hour Lisa, Luke, and a number of my students and "Little Brothers of Saint James" came to police headquarters for me. They took up a collection among themselves and raised my bail then and there. When they first saw me after my release, an outcry went up from the whole group. Lisa and Luke told me later they had all feared from the way I looked that a long stay in the hospital lay ahead of me.

They took me to the nearest hospital emergency room. Thank You, Father, that the doctor found nothing worse had come from Tiny and the other escorts' assault on me than three cracked ribs, a spectacular black left eye and a deep blue-black bruise on my left cheek, plus many assorted other bruises all over my body. However, hospitalization was not required. My cracked ribs needed to be taped but had not punctured my lungs. Everything would hurt for a while but eventually heal. I was given a pain medication and released.

But what did it matter that my body would ache for weeks afterwards with every move and every step I took! For as my family and pro-life friends hastened to tell me, Jonathan and Dolly had reunited right there outside the Hellmann Clinic! Their baby was safe! They were going to get married! Even before they drove home to Fairfield in Jonathan's car they called both their parents, told them what had happened and received their consent. You had used me to bring about this blessed, happy ending.

You had honored my obedient claim to victory based on Your name and promise. I thank and praise You, dear faithful Father, that we *"are always delivered unto death for Jesus' sake, that the life also of Jesus may be made manifest in our mortal flesh"* and that *"our light affliction, which is but for a moment, worketh for us a far more exceeding and eternal weight of glory; while we look not at the things which are seen, but at the things which are not seen: for the things which are seen are temporal; but the things which are not seen are eternal"* (2 Corinthians 4:11, 17–18).

21

"Rejoice in My Joy"

For a while everyone who saw me and did not know how I had come by my black eye and big bruise on my cheek would ask me with horrified pity what had happened to me. I usually told them I had been roughed up by a bunch of thugs. It was true, short, and saved me from bringing Jonathan and Dolly's story into it. With brothers and sisters in the faith, however, as among my colleagues and my students at Fairfield University and the members of our church, I was more explicit.

Lisa wrote up an account of my "Last Stand at the Gates of Hell" for *News in Depth* and taped an interview with me for her weekly radio show. We asked each other with amusement what the mainline news media, always so ready to slander me, would do with this story and rightly guessed that they would kill it by silence. Gradually, as my body healed, my black eye returned to normal, and my facial bruise faded, the whole event began to recede to the back of our minds.

I received a long letter from Dolly and Jonathan. I read it with tears. Here it is:

"Dear Dr. Barron, our father in the faith,

We can never thank you enough for all you did for us. You brought us to Jesus Christ as our Lord and our Savior. You nursed us through our infancy in Him. You did it in part by not shunning the shame of confessing to us all the wrong you had done in the past so it might warn us not to walk that same path of evil. We can only guess how difficult that must have been for you. We want you to know we love and respect you all the more for it.

You did it in part by sharing your joy in the Lord. You said it was His joy He shared with you. We observed you and could not help believing you and longing to receive the joy you had too. We knew that we had to turn away from ourselves, ask His forgiveness for our sins standing between Him and us, surrender to Him, and open ourselves freely and totally to Him. How else could He open Himself freely to us, come to live in our hearts through His Holy Spirit, and give us His joy? So we did what was required, were reconciled to Him, and received His joy.

We understand that better now because we have done the same with each other. Unlike God, I (Jonathan) came to Dolly as a sinner so self-absorbed that I did not scruple to force my 'love' on her. As you know, it very nearly killed her love for me!

No wonder I (Dolly) was afraid to trust Jonathan ever again, and sometimes I hated him for what he had done. You, my dear 'substitute father,' never stopped begging me to forgive him. I knew I had to do that if I could ever freely love him again and be glad in loving him. You were the go-between, holding us together. Without you in our lives we would surely have lost each other. Thank you!

I (Jonathan) dare think what it was like with Dolly and me for God the Father with all us sinful people. He yearned to forgive us but couldn't unless His Son Jesus Christ died for our sins to make His forgiveness possible. His forgiveness was the key that would unlock the pouring out of His joy to us whom He created for His pleasure (Revelation 4:11). The pouring out of His joy to us is His pleasure! And Christ agreed so His Father could have His joy and pleasure! I think that was 'the joy set before Him' of Hebrews 12:2. Christ is the 'go-between' holding the Father and us together. You were like Christ, or Christ was in you, for Dolly and me.

You were like Christ to me (Dolly), dying a little for me every time you counseled me, and even ready to die for me and our baby physically when you stood there with your arms stretched out in front of Melinda's car at the clinic. I was afraid she might run over you and kill you. After seeing you there like this, and then on the ground being kicked, cursed and beaten for me and our baby, I forgave Jonathan and it is better between us now than it ever was.

By the way, Melinda Johnson is gone from my life now. She called me once after I left her behind at the clinic and berated me for my stupidity and ingratitude. I said I was sorry she felt that way, but that I was sure I had made the right choice.

We can now feel our baby move. We had an ultrasound picture made of him inside me. Yes, we are blessed with a little boy, and he is doing fine. He will be born in early July. We would not have him without you! His first name will be James, and we will tell him why when he is old enough to understand.

We plan to be married in Jonathan's and your church the Saturday before Palm Sunday, March 22, 1997. Please be there with us! We wish you could give Dolly away as the 'father of the bride,' but her mother's brother has insisted that he do that, so that is the arrangement.

Again, we thank you more than words can ever tell. Please continue to be in our lives even when we can't live close to each other any longer. As you know, I (Jonathan) am graduating from Fairfield University this spring. I have a teaching job lined up in New England in the fall with one of our Bible Wesleyan schools. Perhaps you can stop by and visit us when you next visit Mrs. Barron's family and your friends in New York.

God bless you always! In Jesus' love,
Jonathan and Dolly

My wife and I attended their wedding. It was performed by Pastor Benjamin Wood, Dr. Wood's brother, who had married Lisa and me. Pastor Wood used the same old traditional marriage rite for Jonathan and Dolly that he had used for us. Lisa and I often looked at each other and silently moved our lips in reaffirmation of our own marriage vows as Jonathan and Dolly pledged "to have and to hold each other as husband and wife from this day forward, for better for worse, for richer for poorer, in sickness and in health, to love and to cherish, till death us do part, according to God's holy ordinance." Mrs. Hernandez and I met face to face for the first time with tears and much love. Luke, Sarah and my grandchildren were with us, perhaps for the last time as they would return to Mexico in May.

A joyful reception followed in the church's parlor where Jonathan, Dolly and I had first met a short nine months ago. Many of the newlyweds' relatives and student friends attended, including most of the "Little Brothers of Saint James." However, some of them faithfully demonstrated at the Hellmann Clinic in their special T-shirts. They later jubilantly reported that three babies had been saved from abortion.

I began to demonstrate again myself at the Hellmann Clinic the third Saturday in April. Lisa came with me although it was uncomfortably close to the due date of the birth of our child. She said I must resume my pro-life witness as soon as I could, and that she would be by my side "even if I go into labor while we do this together." We stood amidst a veritable crowd of my "Little Brothers" who loudly cheered us when we arrived. I walked slowly by Lisa's side rather than running ahead of her. There was no need for special hurry this time, and my injured ribs still ached just enough for me to eschew running. I confess I was wickedly pleased to stand in my usual place where the escorts and especially Tiny could not help seeing that I had not quit the battle in spite of what they had done to me, and that my face and eye were now pretty well completely healed. They scowled and growled at me and I smiled back at them with a sunny smile. I did pray for them then but not with sadness as I usually do.

I will mention here that my "misdemeanor" in blocking the clinic driveway against Melinda's car came up months later in court. The judge sentenced me to pay a fine of five hundred dollars and to a jail sentence of six months, the latter replaced by probation. My fine was graciously paid by pro-life supporters in Battle Hill who had been present on the scene of the crime. "The real crime was committed by the escorts from hell and the entire abortion culture," they said aloud after my sentencing. The judge heard them and remained silent.

And now it was time for our child to be born. I brought Lisa to the hospital in time, and unlike with my other children I was present throughout the birth. Everything went very well. It was a solemn, joyful and unforgettable experience for me to see my daughter emerge into the world and hear her first cry. Our beautiful little Lucinda Elizabeth was born at ten o'clock the night of Thursday, April 24, 1997. We brought her home on April 26 and installed her in the room we had so happily prepared for her right after we knew she was on the way.

I report with a special salute to Dolly that indeed we did not use Lucinda's baby bed during the night for quite a while. Just as Dolly had predicted, we quickly tired of carrying her back and forth between her room and ours for feedings and other needs several times at night and instead had her cuddle between us in our own bed. We loved to feel her warm, soft little body near ours, and she obviously loved to feel us right next to her as she would stretch out her little hands even in her sleep to feel for us and be reassured. Breast feeding was also much easier that way for Lisa as she could attend without delay to Lucinda's slightest little sounds of hunger. We had a very happy little baby and bonded with her very quickly and completely. Let child-rearing experts shake their heads at what we did, but we would do it again!

Except when teaching my classes I often spelled Lisa taking care of Lucinda and doing household chores, cooking and grocery shopping. Our old friend Mrs. Van Houten's training of me in the latter three finally paid off. We took a lot more pictures than ever before, especially of our baby, and sent them east to Lisa's family, the Van Houtens, Bernard Gottlieb and J. P. and Brenda Knightley. We never got the same opinion from them about which of us Lucinda looked like. As we felt both of us looked all right, we were content to settle for our daughter's inheriting features from both of us. I did feel flattered when Freda Trent of all people told Lisa over the phone that she thought Lucinda looked a lot like me and that she was glad about it! It showed me Freda was accepting me more and more and perhaps even beginning to like me.

On July 6, Jonathan and Dolly's little boy was born healthy and well. They have named him James for me as they said they would, and like our Lucinda, he has inherited features from both his parents. He has Jonathan's tousled brown hair and what Dolly calls his "energetic mouth," but he also has Dolly's light brown skin and beautiful dark eyes. They will soon move to Burlington, Vermont, where John Dewey was born and grew up—the godless philosopher whom I tried to emulate in my godless days. Please bless them, dear Father, and let them bless others as they live out the faith in an area from which it is rapidly fading.

As I write this, dear Father, the summer of 1997 is slowly turning into fall. The first golden leaves are falling from the cottonwood trees here in my native Midwest I love so much. Soon the fall semester will start again. I will teach a new course I developed over the last few months on the refutation of the philosophy of self-love in its major historical forms, beginning with "the serpent in Eden." It is based on a statement by St. Augustine in *The City of God,* Book 14, Chapter 28: "Two cities have been formed by two loves: the earthly by the love of self, even to the contempt of God; the heavenly by the love of God, even to the contempt of self. The former, in a word, glories in itself, the latter in the Lord." On my way from the former to the latter "little Karen" shared St. Augustine's words "Thou hast made us for thyself, and our heart is restless till it rests in Thee" with me in the love of our youth. My heart rests in Thee now, Father, and once more St. Augustine sheds light upon my path. My own and mankind's experience through history confirm what he already understood and described so well sixteen hundred years ago. I discussed the course with Dr. Wood and he said all Christian schools of higher learning should teach one like it. I am certainly qualified to teach it by my background and conversion, both of which I will share with my students as You direct. I wish with all my heart that I could uproot every evil seed I planted in my past, dear Father! Please help me do so with all that is in me.

All that is in me, Father, includes the shame. Over and over I come back to it. On my fifty-sixth birthday July 14, I remembered once again, as year after year, my son Dylan's "Rousseau Academy Massacre." I pray once again that You would blot out my shame so I might be unreservedly grateful to You for my having been born and living before You. Will the good You let me do since my new birth ever outweigh the evil I did before it? Can little James Wood whose life I saved at Hellmann's clinic tip the balance against Dylan whose life I destroyed by my neglect, against the seven other lives he took, and against Ecstasy and her child whom I intentionally killed? Against Lisa's son whom I destroyed by my abhorrent book? Against Melinda Johnson whom I helped make a destroyer, and against all the people whom she destroys with my evil counsel of self-idolatry?

As so many times before, You now answer me and comfort me even as I write. "You have confessed your sins to me with tears so often before, son," You say, "and as so often before, My Word for you is right before you in Scripture, but you only read it with your eyes and do not eat, drink and digest it. Listen! You do not have to balance your bad deeds by your good deeds. It is impossible. The blood of Jesus Christ My Son cleanses you from all sin (1 John 1:7). The shame will strike you less and less often as you dread more and more your own hurt in hurting Me. In the end you will not need to be ashamed before Me any more at all; they shall not be ashamed that wait for Me! For you My son as for Me your Creator and Father to be and to be happy will be identical; in Me you will be your own happiness as I am mine. So be glad you were born on earth; be glad and rejoice that you were born again from above. Yea, son, live, and rejoice in My joy!"

Help me do this, dear Father and Jesus Christ. Without You I can do nothing. Do this in me, and all will be well with me forever. Amen.

The End

A Letter to Bernard Gottlieb

Dear Bernard, our dear mentor and friend,

We send you three manuscripts, the first, Part 1, by Karen Margrave MacPherson, the second and third, Parts 2 and 3, by James. Together they are a sort of spiritual biography of James before and after his conversion.

Part 1 was written by Karen at my request. Soon after I moved to Fairfield and married James I visited Swenson Books in Battle Hill in order to meet her. I persuaded her to write their story and her largely second hand description of his life from the time they broke up to his conversion thirty years later. I was impelled by my irrepressible newshound instinct! I had done what I thought was an exhaustive investigation of James' life before his conversion. However, I first heard of Karen only after he and I met. Despite James' public fame, no journalist had unearthed their story in public. It was the last remaining loose end in my investigation. I simply had to follow it!

James would not have liked what I did, so I never told him about it until now when we received Karen's manuscript and read it together for the first time. Her record contains misperceptions which only James himself with his personal knowledge of what really happened could correct, for example about his relationship with Nancy Berger.

Karen's record confirms the crucial responsibility, so abysmally neglected today, of parents, churches and Christian educators to establish Christian young people in the faith and a biblically grounded worldview so they can persevere in it under the world's attack especially in college and by the media. It confirms James' conviction that already for generations "traditional morality" or "Judeo-Christian values" have been like a tree inwardly ravaged by termites—the termites of individual selfishness—and ready to crumble into dust. The description of Karen's beautiful marriage, openness to the children God gives us, and the MacPherson family cohesion confirms James' and my joy in our own biblical Christian marriage "till death us do part," the only foundation, so widely and flagrantly despised today, for joyful family life and well raised children. Both Karen's and James' references to the Dorrie Fisher story show how much better unwanted pregnancies were handled by adoption before the 1960s in a still somewhat Christian culture than by the tens of millions of abortions in our death culture today. Karen praises man's exercising God-given dominion through manual labor in describing her father's gardening, as James praises and adopts the lifestyle of the Van Houtens. Material wealth ranks low all through Karen's account, as it does in James' reflections on "Sister Poverty" and in our adoption of John Wesley's maxim on income and spending. Again and again James stresses the crucial role of Christ-like forgiveness in our personal relations. You may find other Christian themes common to both "authors."

Most important, Karen in Part 1 and James after his conversion in Parts 2 and 3 do their utmost to convict and convert their loved ones (that is, everyone they meet) to know our Lord as the only true God, and Jesus Christ Whom He has sent (John 17:3), and in Him His certitude, His love and His everlasting joy. Pass these manuscripts on to others if you believe they might help them find Him.

In His love and everlasting joy always,
Lisa and James Barron

Contact Ellen Myers
ellenmyers1925@hotmail.com

or order more copies of this book at

TATE PUBLISHING, LLC

127 East Trade Center Terrace

Mustang, OK 73064

(888) 361 - 9473

Tate Publishing, LLC

www.tatepublishing.com

Lightning Source UK Ltd.
Milton Keynes UK
UKOW06f1029151216
290068UK00016B/605/P